AR
ANGRY ROBOT

MICHAEL NAYAK

SYMBIOTE

A NOVEL

ANGRY ROBOT
An imprint of Watkins Media Ltd

Unit 11, Shepperton House
89-93 Shepperton Road
London N1 3DF
UK

angryrobotbooks.com
twitter.com/angryrobotbooks
Just the two of us

An Angry Robot paperback original, 2025

Edited by Eleanor Teasdale, Andrew Hook and Robin Triggs
Cover by Karen Smith
Maps by antarcticglaciers.org, Antarctic Treaty system and Michael Nayak
Set in Meridien

ISBN 978 1 91599 842 2
Ebook ISBN 978 1 91599 843 9

Printed and bound in the United Kingdom by CPI Group (UK) Ltd, Croydon CR0 4YY.

9 8 7 6 5 4 3 2 1

Michael Nayak

SYMBIOTE

THE ICE PLAGUE WARS, BOOK I

For my mom and first cheerleader,
Kannama Nayak,
and
for S. K. Shamala, Shubha Kesavan, and Marina Therrien,
who helped me to grow wings and fly away.

May their tribe increase.

The Antarctic Treaty (1959):

Article I: Antarctica shall be used for peaceful purposes only. There shall be prohibited, inter alia, any measures of a military nature, such as the establishment of military bases and fortifications, the carrying out of military maneuvers, as well as the testing of any type of weapons. **[...]** The present treaty shall not prevent the use of military personnel or equipment for scientific research or for any other peaceful purposes.

Article III, §1(b): In order to promote international cooperation in scientific investigation in Antarctica, the Parties agree that scientific personnel shall be exchanged in Antarctica between expeditions and stations.

Article IV, §2(a): No acts or activities taking place while the present treaty is in force shall constitute a basis for asserting, supporting or denying a claim to territorial sovereignty in Antarctica, or create any rights of sovereignty in Antarctica.

Madrid Protocol (1991), Annex II, Article IV §1): No species of living organisms, flora or fauna, not native to the Antarctic Treaty area shall be introduced except in accordance with a permit. §9) The deliberate introduction of non-sterile soil into the Antarctic Treaty area is prohibited.

From the National Science Foundation's Antarctic Fact sheet (2013):

Through the United States Antarctic Program (USAP), the National Science Foundation (NSF) manages all U.S. scientific research and related logistics in Antarctica.

Astronomy and astrophysics are the primary scientific work carried out at Amundsen-Scott Research Station, South Pole. South Pole also is the site of long-term measurements of the relative proportions of gases that constitute the Earth's atmosphere.

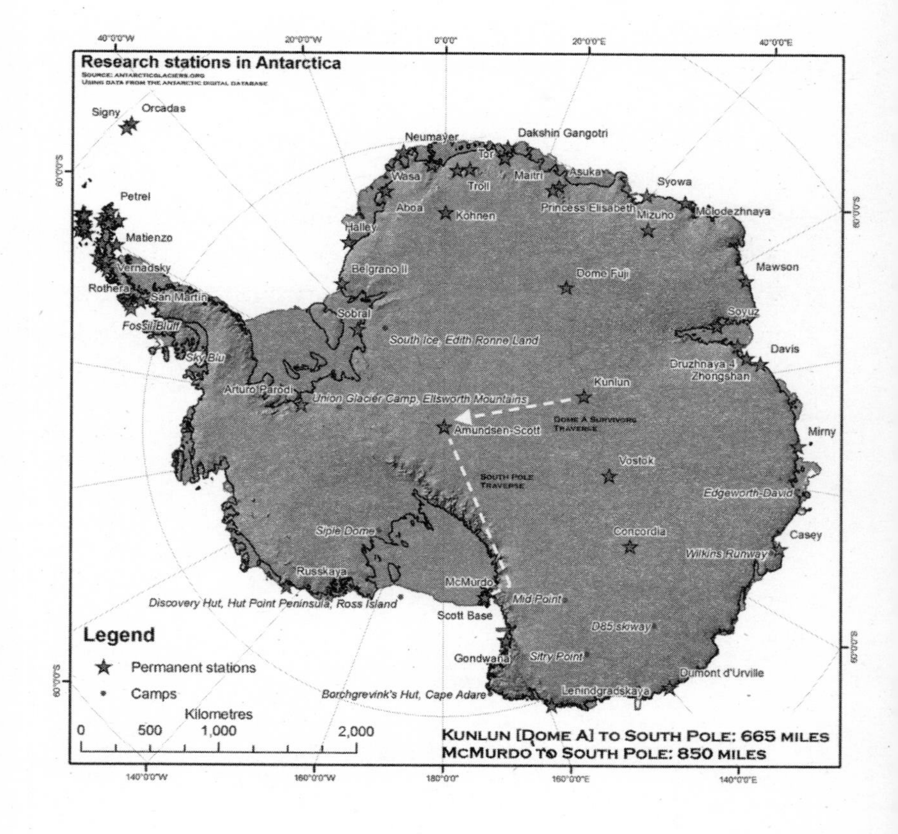

Research stations in Antarctica
Source: antarcticglaciers.org
Using data from the Antarctic digital database
40°0'0"W
20°0'0"W
0°0'0"
20°0'0"E
40°0'0"E
60°0'0"S
140°0'0"W
160°0'0"W
180°0'0"
160°0'0"E
140°0'0"E
Signy
Orcadas
Petrel
Matienzo
Vernadsky
Rothera
San Martin
Fossil Bluff
Sky Blu
Neumayer
Wasa
Aboa
Halley
Belgrano II
Sobral
Tor
Troll
Kohnen
Dakshin Gangotri
Maitri
Asuka
Princess Elisabeth
Syowa
Mizuho
Molodezhnaya
Dome Fuji
Mawson
Soyuz
Davis
Druzhnaya 4
Zhongshan
Kunlun
South Ice, Edith Ronne Land
Arturo Parodi
Union Glacier Camp, Ellsworth Mountains
Amundsen-Scott
Dome A Survivors Traverse
South Pole Traverse
Vostok
Mirny
Edgeworth-David
Concordia
Casey
Wilkins Runway
Siple Dome
Russkaya
McMurdo
Mid Point
Discovery Hut, Hut Point Peninsula, Ross Island
Scott Base
D85 skiway
Gondwana
Sitry Point
Dumont d'Urville
Borchgrevink's Hut, Cape Adare
Lenindgradskaya
Legend
Permanent stations
Camps
Kilometres
0
500
1,000
2,000
Kunlun [Dome A] to South Pole: 665 miles
McMurdo to South Pole: 850 miles

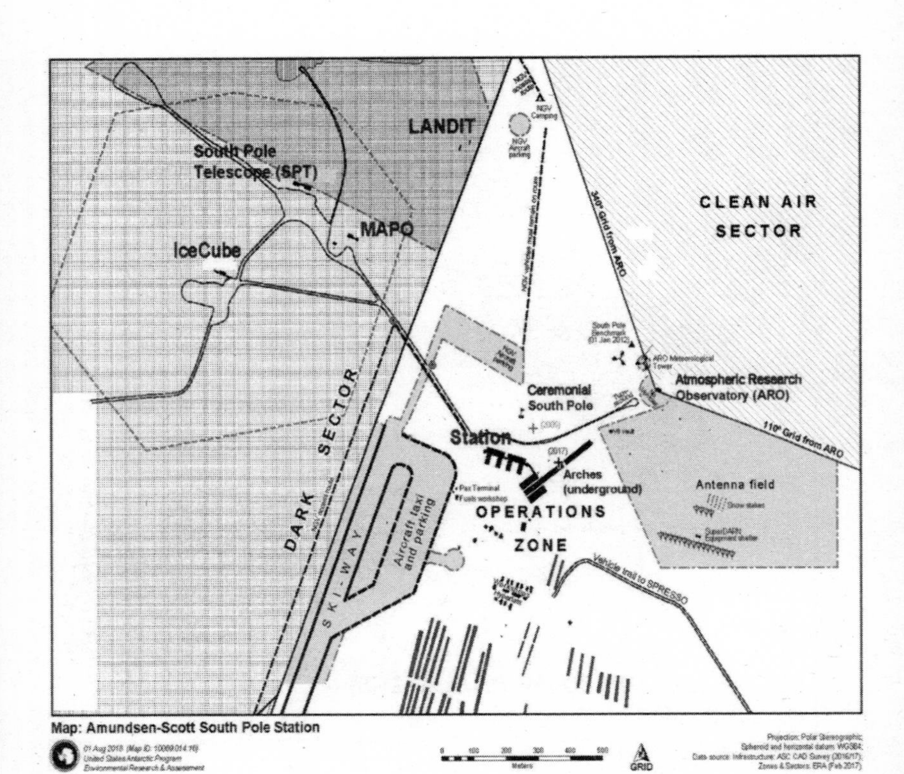
LANDIT
South Pole Telescope (SPT)
MAPO
IceCube
CLEAN AIR SECTOR
340° Grid from ARO
NGV Camping
NGV Aircraft parking
South Pole Benchmark (01 Jan 2012)
ARO Meteorological Tower
Atmospheric Research Observatory (ARO)
110° Grid from ARO
Ceremonial South Pole
(2006)
Station
(2017)
Arches (underground)
DARK SECTOR
OPERATIONS ZONE
Pax Terminal
Fuels workshop
Antenna field
Snow stakes
SuperDARN Equipment shelter
SKI-WAY
Aircraft taxi and parking
Vehicle trail to SPRESSO
Map: Amundsen-Scott South Pole Station
01 Aug 2018 (Map ID: 10069.014.16)
United States Antarctic Program
Environmental Research & Assessment
0
100
200
300
400
500
Meters
GRID
Projection: Polar Stereographic
Spheroid and horizontal datum: WGS84
Data source: Infrastructure: ASC CAD Survey (2016/17);
Zones & Sectors: ERA (Feb 2017)

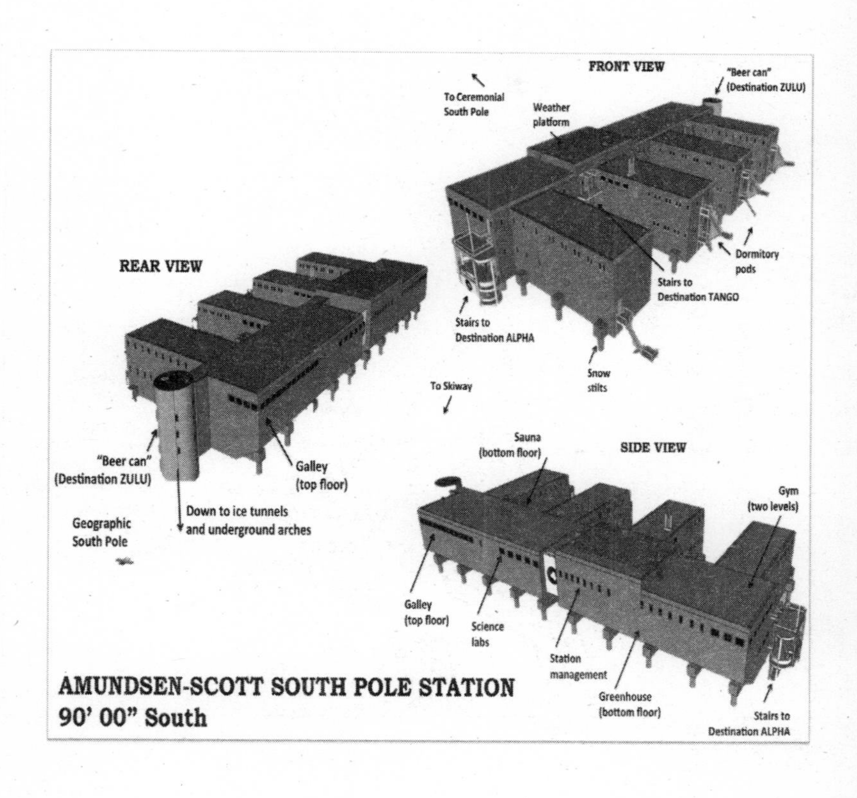
FRONT VIEW
"Beer can"
(Destination ZULU)
To Ceremonial
South Pole
Weather
platform
Dormitory
pods
Stairs to
Destination TANGO
REAR VIEW
Stairs to
Destination ALPHA
Snow
stilts
To Skiway
Sauna
(bottom floor)
SIDE VIEW
"Beer can"
(Destination ZULU)
Galley
(top floor)
Gym
(two levels)
Down to ice tunnels
and underground arches
Geographic
South Pole
Galley
(top floor)
Science
labs
Station
management
Greenhouse
(bottom floor)
Stairs to
Destination ALPHA
AMUNDSEN-SCOTT SOUTH POLE STATION
90' 00" South

AMUNDSEN-SCOTT SOUTH POLE STATION WINTER-OVER CREW, 2028

Total: 41 (29 support, 12 science staff; 31 male, 10 female)

Station Manager	Bill Gaudin
Deputy Station Manager	Andrea Rivey

SCIENCE TEAM

[Science Lead: Yanis Pohano]:

South Pole Telescope (SPT)	Yanis Pohano / Bethany Hamidani
Martin A. Pomerantz Observatory (MAPO)	Robert Booth / Khaled Zaidi
Atmospheric Research Observatory (ARO)	Jonah Mitchell / Ben Jacobs
Ice Cube Laboratory (ICL)	Kathryn Wagner / Greg Penny
South Pole Ice Core (SPICE)	Summer Kerce
Long-Duration Antarctic Night and Daytime Imaging Telescope (LANDIT)	Rajan Chariya
ASC Research Assistants	Mike McCafferty / Sheryl Whitney

ANTARCTIC SERVICES CONTRACT (ASC) SUPPORT TEAM

[Support lead: Andrea Rivey]:

Medical	Wei Jin (Physician)
	Jamie Carroll (Nurse Practitioner)
Dining	Lisa Kissinger (Head chef, Baker)
	Tommy TC Chapman (Breakfast, sous-chef)

	Daniel Baia (Line cook, Dishwasher)
Information Technology (IT)	Marty Horn (Lead, System Administrator)
	Kevin Eastburg (Computer Technician)
	José Ager (Satellite Communications)
Meteorology	Katie Caberto (Lead)
	Clint Gerencser (Meteorology Technician)
Cargo	Tim Fulton (Lead)
	Bret Okonkwo (Cargo carpenter)
	Siri Monthan (Heavy equipment operator)
	Bowman Moyer (Pipefitter)
Materials	Nathaniel Singh (Material specialist)
	Michele Reinert (Inventory specialist)
	Dave Atkins (Machinist)
Facilities	Luis Weeks (Lead)
	Joe Haskins (Maintenance engineer)
	Allen McKenzie (Waste specialist)
	Akinori Nakagawa (Electrician)
	Kenny Black (Power plant specialist)
	Jeremy Forystek (Electrician apprentice)
Carpentry	Keyon Geerts (Lead, foreman)
	Ryan Schnurbusch (Carpenter apprentice)
Plumbing	Spencer Kaur (Lead, foreman)
	Philip Cunningham (General plumber)

Prologue

There has never been a recorded case of murder anywhere on the Antarctic continent.

2028, the second year of the Pacific Rim War. A stalemate, the pundits and generals on both the Chinese and American sides say, but there is no forgiveness in war. Only patience until an advantage reveals itself.

February 22nd, 2028

In Christchurch, New Zealand, callsign Borak 27 lifts off from Runway 02. There are six people aboard the heavily modified Basler BT-67, but the manifest shows the aircraft as empty except for the two-pilot crew. Two hundred miles south of Invercargill, its transponder turns off. Borak 27 disappears from air traffic control scopes, headed due south.

June 13th, 2028

Two hundred yards from the geographic South Pole, Amundsen-Scott Station manager Bill Gaudin's lips are pressed tightly together, his face the color of dirty linen. During the Station's sliver of overhead satellite connectivity, downlinked at dial-up modem speeds, the latest image from Washington shows two Chinese snow-vehicles three-hundred miles away from their home base of Dome-A's Kunlun Station. Headed toward South Pole.

With eight days until the winter solstice, the final band of twilight fades from the horizon. The sun has set at the bottom of the world, where there is just one long day and one long night each year. The stars are out. The wan aurorae flicker intermittently across the sky like distant streamers. It will be completely dark for the next four months.

BOOK ONE
The First Two Deaths

JUNE 18TH – JUNE 21ST

I am not at ease, nor am I quiet;
I have no rest; but trouble comes.

Job 3:25-26

Chapter One

SOUTH POLE STATION, POPULATION: 41

June 18th, 91 miles from the South Pole

Rajan Chariya is startled to hear fear in Luis Weeks's voice. The harsh squelch of the radio bleeds everything out of the syllables except the words themselves, but he feels the terror lacing them as surely as he feels ice heavy on his eyelids. Ever since their first mile north and away from South Pole Station, to intercept the incoming Chinese traverse from Kunlun Station, he's been waiting for the guillotine to drop. Fearing it. A tense band around his chest that cuts deeper than the Antarctic wind.

Weeks's words begin spilling together. "Rajan-get-your-ass-over-here now now *now.*"

Rajan is already running, past the ring of flares enclosing the two hulking Chinese trucks, knees popping like firecrackers. That tense itch intensifies and runs with him.

It's Spencer he sees first, on his hands and knees in front of the second truck. Great gasping breaths plume beneath his hanging head. Akinori Nakagawa and Weeks stand on the ice by the truck's open door, dwarfed by its rugged snow-filled pontoon treads. Akinori's eyes keep skittering away, not looking at anything in particular. A galloping wave of dread threatens to close over Rajan because he knows that look; it's a look he hoped to never see again.

The vacant expression of someone slipping into shock.

Spencer Kaur looks up at Rajan Chariya, then the looming darkness beyond the truck door. "Don't… it's hell in there, man." His voice is a low, guttural moan.

A bright red flare squirts into the air, blooming over the three American Sno-Cats from Amundsen-Scott South Pole Station, squaring off against the two Chinese traverse trucks. The flares stain everything red, even the stars. The wind dies down. For a long moment, everything on the plateau is still.

Then the black of the night creeps back in, and with it Rajan feels gripped by a cold and unshakeable feeling of *two-ness*. A voice in his head, warmly familiar but coldly distant. A voice of headachy reflexes and fears of the unknown, ancestral and urgent and full of premonitory dread.

"You should take a look," Weeks interrupts Rajan's thoughts. His voice is brittle. "But be careful. That's a crime scene."

Rajan feels all their eyes on his skin. Like coiled cats in an apartment window, watching warily from behind a safe pane of glass.

The first murder in Antarctica and, somehow, he has become the decision maker.

A feeling of helplessness bubbles up within him. An urge to throw up his hands; explain that he is more at home at a scientific conference than in a military formation, that he's a first-timer to the ice and surely this is a job for someone with multiple seasons of experience. But he is also the only active-duty military member on the entire continent, because by treaty you can only come to Antarctica for scientific purposes. The rest of the world is at war, the Chinese have shown up inside a hundred miles of South Pole with a blood footprint, and he is the key that fits both locks.

He tries not to touch anything, not even the railing to pull himself up. Balancing carefully, he climbs the steps perched over the heavy caterpillar treads, then into the truck. The sullen glow from the flares dying into the ice become ghostly, fading before the deeper darkness inside.

His breath becomes an echo in his ears.

That's when the smell first hits him.

A ghastly rich stench; a sick-dead amalgam of blood and sweat and human decay. The dense, gut-wrenching way it *cloys* hints at what lies wrapped in the darkness of the cargo truck. That ancestral hunter voice in Rajan's head, the voice as familiar with being the predator as the prey, picks up steam. *Get out get out get out–*

He flicks on the flashlight. Its white beam lights up the body lying against the far wall.

He jerks back, like he's been punched. His mind makes the words *what the fuck*, but they won't go to his dry throat and just bounce between his ears. The light skitters up to the roof. Wide swaths of blood there, like a fist had been punching –

(*clawing*)

– at the roof.

Rajan's hand shakes, he can't make it stop, and the flashlight dips. The floor is slick with a thick layer of blood, smudged with bare footprints but growing more viscous as he traces it back, drawn like a ghastly magnet, and that's when he sees the guts of the Chinese man. His intestines and bloated stomach are split open, spilled out onto the floor, and the stink swells like a physical thing, a fist driving through Rajan's nose and into it. A glassy dead eye glares in the gory flare backlight like the eye of a goat in a slaughter yard. Meeting that eye, sharp shudders rack Rajan's body.

Half the man's skull is no more than pulpy blood clots smeared into the wall he is slumped against –

(*Get back GET OUT*)

– and still his killer hadn't stopped, because bone gleams at Rajan from head-sized dents in the wall of the truck.

His stomach does a jittery forward roll, and he stumbles back a step, grasping blindly for the door. Almost falling out of the truck as he slams it shut.

The wind rattles in his ears like all the dark things beneath the world gleefully free and glommed together. A hundred afterimages of the man's skull cracked *into* the wall whirl blackly before his eyes, knocking his thoughts into an uncertain sprawl. Rajan has seen bodies before. He has seen people shot. *I've been shot myself. But nothing…*

Nothing ever like this.

An endless river of snow kicks between his legs like fine baking flour, then flutters out of his flashlight beam and ceases to exist in the pitch Antarctic black. Rajan clutches his parka over his ribs, trying to hug himself warm, gasping the wind and cold in, but even outside, the sick-dead smell stays in his lungs.

"Holy shit," he says, at last.

"Spencer walked into that with no warning," Weeks says beside him. "Poor bastard."

Rajan looks over at Spencer and is immediately struck by the haggard pallor of the carpenter's face. The man is a sallow painting of himself, still on all fours, staring limply at his own icy vomit. Akinori wanders away, muttering to himself, words lost in the dark of the polar night.

"Who else has been in there?"

"Just Spencer, Akinori, and the two of us."

Rajan's temples jump and quiver. Like tiny fists beating

into the side of his face. "Nobody else enters this vehicle except Doc. No one."

His teeth chatter, he starts walking, and Weeks follows in his trail. It is bitterly cold, sixty-five degrees below zero, a physical wall that their lungs strain against with every breath. The dark emptiness of the Antarctic holds no light except from the indifferent stars; cloaks nothing except blowing snow to the horizon and beyond. It's hard not to think about how precipitously cold it is. How much it would hurt to die out here.

Rajan turns to look at the three Chinese scientists who had been in the traverse vehicles. They are all dressed in Antarctic-issue red parka jumpsuits with a thick black stripe sashing around the middle, huddled together, casting anxious glances his way. They know how it must look.

They've come from Kunlun Station on Dome Argus, known as Dome-A, an ice plateau sixteen thousand feet high. It's the coldest region in the world, with temperatures often below minus 100 degrees Fahrenheit. The Chinese have driven almost seven hundred miles toward them, the nearest humans on the ice continent, along a route that has never been attempted in the treachery of winter.

A thick feeling of tension creeps across Rajan like a metal guitar string being pulled too tight. He imagines deadly crevasses, invisible in the perpetual darkness. The ice, crackling mysteriously under the thick white quilt of the snow cover.

The safest place for them is huddled inside their Station, and yet here they are. Something has driven them out of Dome-A.

Something that outweighs the risk of a journey that could have killed them.

What if the rest of their Station looks like the back of their truck?

Rajan drifts to a stop in front of Bill Gaudin. The South Pole Station Manager stands with his arms crossed, facemask down, watching the truck with his permanent scowl. Gaudin's eyes, normally hazel green, have gone a slaty color, like a deep lake on a stormy day.

"Well?" he demands.

"There's no way a human being could do that much damage to himself. Definitely a murder. One of their crew." Rajan tries to shunt his brain out of the sludge that the stink has trapped his thoughts in. "Have we asked our visitors what happened?"

"Absolutely not," Gaudin says at once.

"*Why not*? They've got to know. They know."

"Because." Gaudin's hands snap to his hips. "If there was a death en route–"

"A murder," Rajan says flatly.

"– there's no jurisdiction. It's no man's country between the Stations."

No one has dedicated more time than Bill Gaudin to surfing the fickle waves of the Antarctic Treaty, and its geopolitical sensitivities, and Rajan can't keep a frustrated noise from bubbling out.

"Don't give me that attitude, Dr. Chariya," the manager says sourly. "We didn't spend two days punching trenches into the snow to stop them here out of goodwill. It's a time of war. We have to be careful how we get involved." His lip curls. "I would have thought you, of all people, would get that."

"I think we're involved either way now. If jurisdiction is an issue, let's get jurisdiction."

"What do you mean?"

"Cram them back in their vehicles and bring them to South Pole. It's an American station. The NSF's lawyers can figure out what to do next."

With the National Science Foundation in charge of all American research stations on the continent, Rajan can tell the idea of turning the diplomatic hassle into their problem appeals to Gaudin. "They'll need to be held separately," he muses. "Somewhere no one can talk to them and muddy the investigation."

"Except for the Doc, right?" Rajan interjects. "Doc Wei needs to determine time and cause of death?"

Gaudin is barely listening, stroking a mustache bushy with ice. "We'll isolate the vehicles by the berms," he says, referring to the collection of containers from previous seasons, obsolete or stored for returning summer scientists. It's called End-of-the-World for good reason. The Chinese vehicles would be covered in a layer of snow by week's end, indistinguishable from the other half-buried cargo.

"And them?" Rajan gestures at the three travelers but it feels jerky, like his arms are new to his body. "One of them is a killer. Maybe all of them."

"Shit, it's not like we have a jail. Hell, I can't even think of a door at Pole that locks."

Weeks steps up from just out of Gaudin's line of sight, where he's been lingering. "We could use ARO."

The Atmospheric Research Observatory sits on the edge of Pole's Clean Air Sector, half a kilometer northeast of the Station. Its isolation, designed for atmospheric purity to measure long-term trends of trace gases in the pristine South Pole air, could certainly be put to use to house unwelcome guests.

"They have a room that locks?"

Rajan nods. His lips feel cold and ashy. "ARO uses pressurized nitrogen to cryo-cool equipment. NSF Safety required them to secure the canisters so the whole building wouldn't turn into shrapnel. There's a reinforced room downstairs that locks from the outside."

"Then let's pack up and get the hell back to Pole."

Gaudin strides off, past the Chinese scientists. Rajan notices them shy away, cluster closer together. The knowledge drops into him with the cold certainty of a quarter slotting into a vending machine.

They're afraid.

Whatever they know, it scares the shit out of them.

He lifts his head to the Milky Way and lets a long shaky breath escape him. Sprawling above them in a corkscrew of cold light, the stars shine hard and bright, somehow closer at the bottom of the world. Gems he could pluck off the galaxy's dark skin and wear himself.

Leave them.

The intensity of the thought surprises him.

Drive back to Pole and let them run into those trenches and die out here.

In the same way the ancient instinct in Rajan's head knows the Chinese scientists are afraid, it knows that the thought of abandoning them has already crossed Gaudin's mind.

The NSF had been sending satellite imagery of the traverse from Dome-A limping across the ice toward them. Gaudin hadn't bothered to hide his fury that the NSF had wanted Rajan present at first contact. If he weren't here, perhaps Gaudin *would* have left them, even after their brutal trek halfway across the continent for help.

Kneecapped them, deflated their tires, and driven away.

You might be doing them and yourselves a favor, the voice in Rajan's head says quietly.

He looks at the three travelers, shying away from the burly station manager. He imagines what they've been through to get here, and something clicks in his throat as he swallows. *No way. I could never.*

But other doubts fill his head. Like the NSF insisting on his presence, even though he's a first-timer to the ice. Why would they do that? Had the Department of Defense been whispering in their ear?

And the NSF doesn't do satellite reconnaissance, Rajan knows that much. Some other three-letter organization is feeding them overhead imagery of the Chinese traverse's progress toward South Pole. How did they (whoever *they* were) pick up two tiny vehicles moving across the vast Antarctic wilderness?

Instead of asking Gaudin these things, he watches the Station manager walk away and tries not to think about what lies in the coffin on caterpillar-tracks behind him.

You'll be sorry, the hunter voice whispers quietly. *I can smell it. You'll be sorry.*

Chapter Two

TWO DAYS LATER

June 20th, 4:30 PM (New Zealand Standard Time)

Ben Jacobs stops what he's doing; looks over his shoulder. The television monitor across from the couch shows views from the four cameras mounted on each corner of the ARO building. The cameras are for monitoring macro-weather conditions, but one of them looks down the flag path to the Station, a quarter-mile away. There's no one on the path. Philip Cunningham rolls his eyes.

"Jonah's not coming, dude."

"Sorry, just habit. This is his place, really–"

"Dude."

Ben lowers his head between Philip's knees once more. Obliging, that's him all over. When he looks up, Philip has spread his arms across the back of the upstairs couch, looking up at the dusty ceiling tiles, a small smile touching his hard slash of a mouth.

Then his eyes slip closed, and he moans, and Ben is happy again.

Twenty minutes later, the windstorm has arrived. Philip stands at the window, naked, stretching luxuriously. The Station is close enough that Ben can usually see the satellite dishes on its roof, but all he sees now is a rising curtain of white. When the blowing snow grows into columns that blur the distinction between ground and velvet sky, ARO becomes invisible to the Station.

Out of sight and out of mind. It's a thought that never fails to make him uncomfortable.

Then again, the list of things that make Ben uncomfortable would fill a dictionary.

"Damn, it's nice out here," Philip says, idly fondling himself. "This whole palace to just you and Jonah. Y'all beakers have it good down here!"

"Every time you say *beaker*, I get the feeling it's not a compliment."

Philip brushes his long hair away from his angular face until it stands up in a shock wave.

"Look, I like ya," he says, and Ben's stomach tightens, already knowing he won't like whatever comes next. "Them other beakers can shine me a watery turd and choke it down with chopsticks." Philip's eyes, sunken deep in his face, glitter in their sockets like dark animals trapped in twin snares. "Like that bitch-Nazi Kathryn. Thinks she's better than me 'cuz of a coupla letters after her name. I'm fuckin' tired of it. Fuckin' tired of Antarctica, for that matter."

Philip is the second plumber, and Ben has run headlong into his inferiority complex all season. He'd never say it to his face, but it's probably why Philip hasn't been upgraded to foreman, even though he has two more seasons on the ice than his boss Spencer.

"It's been a pretty eventful season, though, right?" Ben hate-hate-*hates* how diffident he sounds, but once Phil starts spinning around his own axis like a furious little sun, it'll take most of the night for him to calm down. And this kind of storm-assured privacy doesn't come often.

Philip stops mid-gesture, staring at the oscilloscope across the room. He looks like a cartoon growing a thought bubble above his head. Ben tries not to giggle. Philip hates it when people laugh at him. Or around him, really, because it's impossible to convince him that they aren't laughing at him.

"Schnurbusch told me Gaudin is keeping them Commie beakers here. Is that true?"

"Um," Ben says, suddenly uncomfortable.

Without a further word, like a greyhound released from the gates, Philip bounds from the room.

Ben springs to his feet; struggles into his pants. His socked feet whisper quickly over the threadbare blue carpet, by the old laser tower and down the stairs, past plaques that hold the names of the two winter-overs that manage ARO every season.

I'm expendable. The plaques remind him of that every time he passes them. Jonah Mitchell's name appears on those plaques every other year, back to the building's construction in 1997, then every year for the last ten years. Jonah is the fountain of knowledge on how ARO works. His winter partner is usually, like Ben, a commissioned officer from the National Oceanic and Atmospheric Administration, the NOAA corps (*Science! Service! Stewardship! And that hidden fourth, solitude, forget it at your own peril*), but few of the officers return. The officers are expendable.

Another thought Ben is not comfortable with.

Downstairs, past the two office cubicles, instruments on long laboratory benches lurk like still gargoyles in the gloom. A little over a hundred years ago, Roald Amundsen and Robert Scott's push deep into the ice cap had been a direct function of how much their dogs and ponies could carry on sleds. Today, they might be cut off from the world during the dark winter, but thanks to the logistical magnitude of military airlift, now there are instruments, sofas, and a three-hundred-ton radio telescope at 90 South.

Ben turns on the yellow lights, revealing data recording servers, conference posters from NOAA researchers of years past, and the freezer door in the grid-east corner. He finds Philip crouching in front of it, studying the latch with an almost wild glee. The chrome of its sturdy lock leers at him like a carnival barker.

"Phil, no one's supposed to–"

Philip turns and it gives Ben a little start to see how bug-wide his eyes are. "Where's the key?"

"What?"

"Don't what *me*, Benny-boy." Philip strides up to him and Ben is suddenly reminded of a cop asking him to step out of the car. "I can't see Jonah playing jail den-mom, which means you have the key. I wanna see them."

"Well, not like this." Ben gestures to Philip's nakedness.

"They might be into it, never know." Philip grins, and there is something in that smile –

(*not something you know exactly what*)

(*unadulterated top-shelf crazy wrapped in human skin*)

– that makes him uneasy. Ben is grimly unsurprised to see that the plumber has a hard-on growing.

He keeps staring into Philip's gleaming eyes, willing himself not to chicken out and look away. At last, a hoarse laugh tumbles out of Philip's mouth. "Okay," he says. His tongue flicks out over his lips. "Okay, okay."

Ben itches the bridge of his nose as they return upstairs, and he watches Philip pull his clothes on. He tries to convince himself that he'll say no if that crazy light is still in Philip's eyes.

They walk downstairs and, as the lock falls away, a sudden and deep dread surges over him. A thousand generations of bad feelings, coming out of time to play the creeps up and down his spine. Ben's lizard brain is shouting, *loudly*, wants him to be anywhere else, the feeling so strong he finds himself fighting the urge to pick up his heels and just *run*. Out of there, out of the building, all the way back to the Station, windstorm be damned –

– but Philip is already pulling the door open.

The three Chinese winter-overs are sitting on the floor, clustered around open Meals-Ready-to-Eat bags. Without their jackets, they look emaciated and worn. "You fuckers speak English?" Philip demands, hands on his hips.

An old man gathers himself to his feet. He looks older than even old-man Jonah, with silvered hair and a wizened face. He speaks painstakingly, in a slow and respectful voice. "What is your name, sir?"

"Never mind my damn name." Philip's eyes draw down to ugly slits. "What the hell happened out at your Station?"

Ben gets the distinct impression the old man understands whom he is dealing with. "We have… emergency. Dr. Xiaofeng dead, in our truck. There is other… dead… Dome-A."

Xiaofeng. Ben says the name to himself so he remembers it for Gaudin later. A scientist, perhaps. Or maybe their medical doctor.

"Yeah? How many dead?"

The old man says something in Mandarin, then holds up ten fingers.

"Ten?"

He shows them two fingers.

"Two? Which is it? Oh, twelve!" Philip exclaims.

Ben's eyes widen with shock.

"You guys it for the Dome-A crew?"

"Please, slow."

He tosses his head impatiently. "Are y'all – the only – ones – alive?"

"We alive," comes the reply. "Only we. People... they sick. People little..." His eyes blink rapidly. Then the word comes to him, and it makes Ben's flesh crawl helplessly.

"They crazy. Very bad crazy when very bad cold."

Philip chuckles into his fist like a teenager stumbling across keys to his dad's convertible. "I know all about crazy in this fuckin' place, I tell you what."

"Phil." Ben's dominant voice surprises even him. He feels the need to treat the old Chinese man with some respect. He has survived the death of his crewmates, and a deadly traverse across a frozen continent, only to be trapped in the closest thing to an Antarctic jail cell. "That's enough."

"I'm just having a conversation, Benny-boy," Philip sings, hips throwing obscenely from side to side. He sounds –

(*say it Benny*)

– delighted.

"I said that's enough, dammit. Leave them alone."

Ben's fists clench by his side as Philip jumps forward instead. The plumber plucks the remainder of a sandwich away from one of the prisoners. He pops it in his mouth, jaws clicking, then wipes his hands deliberately all over the man's wind pants and jacket. Philip winks and lets out a booming laugh that reveals pieces of turkey in his teeth, then pats the man's cheek.

"Thanks for the great dinner conversation, fellas," he says, and just like that, he's out of the room, bounding up the stairs.

"I'm so sorry, he's... he's a fucking ass," Ben says, unpleasantly realizing how true it rings.

The silent cross of Antarctica is loneliness, a shadowy cloak growing over them like icy moss on stone from their very first moment on the plateau. Finding someone to be intimate with has been an unexpected salve, the most joyous balm scraping at that moss. And because of it, Ben knows he has fallen steadily deeper into craving Philip's companionship and touch across the winter. Ready and even eager to ignore most anything else about him.

Things like what was behind his eyes when toying with prisoners from a ravaged station.

Ben backs toward the doorway. "Listen, there's a windstorm that's picking up. Gale force squalls, triple digits below zero. It might get chilly in here, so I'll bring you a heater."

"Happy to arrival before storm," the old man says.

Ben nods. "I'll be back after it breaks."

The older man raises a hand. "Please, please wait." He has to think about each word. "It get very bad when it get very cold." He makes a gesture, like peeling the skin off his arms.

Ben takes another step back. Open palms. "Look, man, I don't–"

"Very bad!" The old man's hands are wringing. There's clearly more he wants to express. "Please, you *careful*."

"There are people who'll come talk to you." Words spill out of Ben's mouth as he backs away, light as snow snatched up by the wind. *Someone else's problem, someone else's fucking problem*. "Just don't eat all the food at once, okay?"

Ben slams the freezer door. His hands fumble at the lock, even as the muffled voices on the other side pick up, one ghastly chorus now. *Very bad. Very bad, very cold.* In that chorus, improbably, Ben finds a hard edge he can hang a hat on. The hell with being lonely –

(*for now just for now*)

– he'd rather ride out the storm alone.

Still… it'll be best to let Philip catch a few hours of sleep before starting a fight. Just so he doesn't hold a grudge.

It'll be a lonely winter if he decides to hold a grudge.

Chapter Three

Philip Cunningham stands in the cold, half-in and half-out of the open door of ARO. He has been standing there for several minutes, trying to decide whether to go back in and cuss Ben out some more.

Fuck it, he thinks. *I'm making like a tree and leafing. Damned if I'll stick around where I ain't wanted.*

He pulls the door of ARO shut behind him.

He tries to listen for the two clicks of the walk-in freezer style seals, which would keep the precious heat of the building in, but the wind is a roaring jet engine in his ears. He reaches behind his head for the fur-lined hood of his bulky red Antarctic parka. Issued by the NSF and affectionately known by the Polies as Big Red, the jackets are lined with fifteen pounds of sturdy insulation. *Fifteen sure sounds like a lot until ya realize it's a damn joke in temperatures this low, except…*

That's when Philip realizes that his face doesn't feel cold. Not really.

Matter of fact, it feels rather tingly with warmth.

He leaves the hood off and clumps down the metal stairs from the Dobson room on the second floor of ARO. He hops over the sheared banister to the snow, reaching out for the flag line. ARO stands on extendable stilt-like columns, but raising it would require a mechanical lift and crank that now sits beneath the snow. The lower floor is completely engulfed by the towering snowdrifts, windows showing nothing but packed whiteness.

By the time the bulk of ARO is swallowed into the snowy darkness behind Philip, he feels positively warm. A little hot, even, like he's sitting by a campfire. He's drifting, too, feet carrying him far enough that the path-marking flags are almost swallowed into the blowing snow. A stab of fear cuts through him when he notices how far he's strayed, but it's just born of habit. He feels fine.

Hell, he can feel his fingers pulsing hot, as if itching to be set free from his gloves.

The wind's dull roar has built into a screaming howl, an endless steam train slamming from nowhere to nowhere under the black sky. With every passing second he hears it more, but feels it less. He's not honestly sure how long it is until he gets his feet moving again. Then again, when the sky is just as dark as when he woke up, hands on a watch mean about as little as a compass needle this far south.

About as little as beaker mumblefuck bullshit on cosmic microwaves. Apparently that's a research topic at Pole. *Cosmic* microwaves, what even the shit does that mean?

Philip walks back to the flag-line, feet sinking through crunchy hills of ice. Snow spills over the top of his loosely laced boot, stings cold for a moment, then warmth flushes around his foot. "Fuckin' A," he says to the wind.

He clambers over the one-story tall snowbank on the lee side of the Station, half-walking, half-sliding down the icy footholds shoveled into it. The snow down his fleece feels good, so he lets himself slide the rest of the way like a wiper across a rainy windshield. Looking up at the massive pillars that keep the Station above the snow, he giggles to himself. Just lying there like a pup in the West Texas sun.

Some dormant survival instinct stirs him to his feet. He's almost drowsy with heat, cozy in the snow like a badger in its nest, but the Station will be warmer.

Much warmer, in fact.

Maybe too warm?

As Philip pulls himself up, his stomach starts to flip-flop. "Damn Chinaman gave me the scurvy with that sandwich," he hiccups to the wind. Even though it's been several hours since he ate it. "Makes sense. Fuckin' A you bet."

His gloved hands reach for the freezer handle on the double-latched door. He stumbles into the beer can, the vertical metal enclosure up the Station's west side, surrounding the outer stairway. Two levels above him are the Destination Zulu entrances. Five flights below are the ice tunnels connecting the Station to the subterranean arches for food, fuel and storage. The antechamber isn't climate controlled, but away from the wind, it's far warmer than the outside. Philip takes his gloves off and his hands flush deliciously with heat.

Like there's a fire, right under his skin, tingling its way up his arms.

He pushes through the Zulu doors – two sets of doors to seal the Station's heat in – and breaks into a painful sweat almost immediately. "Fuck, it's hot," he pants aloud.

(*fuckin' A*)

He lurches into the gear room on the right, letting his Big Red slump to the floor by Rajan's gear. A deep ache builds in his bones. He looks up blearily as he fumbles at his inner fleece, and sees Kathryn Wagner clipping her gloves neatly to her jacket. Her back is turned, but he recognizes the lurking mass of her wide shoulders. Her boots sit in a slush puddle.

"Wasn't bad out there, right?" Philip mumbles. "Kinda warm, really."

She turns toward the door, unwinding her scarf from her cold-reddened neck. Her hair hangs against her cheeks in matted strings, glowing with melting icicles. She doesn't reply.

"Hey, you hear me?" He can't remember when he slumped down to the bench beneath the jacket hooks. "It ain't that cold out!"

She clumps out of the room, not casting so much as a look in his direction. Fuckin'–

"– beaker bitch!" Philip yells.

His voice hangs in the air. He hears her stop outside and struggles to his feet like a kid swimming through a spider web. He stands there, swaying a little. *Come on. Go to the mat with me, I dare you. Come on.*

Then he hears her feet moving, heavy and deliberate, swinging away.

Philip sinks back to the bench, not sure if he's disappointed or relieved. He tugs his boots off and a painful prickle replaces the ring of warmth circling his foot. "She ain't no prize," he says aloud to the empty gear room. "Not with them hairy fuckin' arms."

He starts to shiver as he slides his snowpants off and coughs, tasting blood in the back of his throat. The haze growing around his head parts, a brief clear horizon in a bank of grey clouds, and like a slap in the face, he *remembers* how many times he wandered away from the flag line. He hadn't been trekking a straight line at all. Sure, he boomeranged back every so often, but he had really been walking off into the cold. A quiet scared voice in his head whispers that he's lucky, *damn* lucky, to be alive.

And yet, that doesn't feel true. *It was* warm *out there*.

So warm.

Philip leaves his gear in its untidy heap and half-stumbles, half-walks toward the bathroom, ping-ponging down the hallway. Past pictures of previous winter-over crews, framed for posterity under the aurorae, the cold a ghostlike fog misting the distance between lens and crewmember. They'll take their crew picture soon, when it drops below minus 100 F for the first time.

Frozen water is all around them, but it takes precious fuel to turn ice into liquid. Fuel powers everything from the lights to the telescopes to the Sno-Cats, so everyone at South Pole, summer or winter, is restricted to a two-minute shower just twice a week. Philip stands under the shower and turns the water on. It's ice-cold at first, which feels nice, but warms up quickly, steam filling the shower booth, and lance-like pains dig into his body like he's being stabbed with a very small knife hundreds of times. *Thousands* of times. It takes Philip completely by surprise. His knees buckle. He sags against the tile wall, cringing away from the steaming water, unable to even moan, until the shower times out after two minutes.

"*Ugggg*. Ug, that hurts." It's all he can summon. The thought jangles strangely and he realizes abruptly that he's been talking out loud. Maybe has been for a while? People will think he's babbling inanities, *like a senile fuckin' grandpa,* when in fact his thoughts have never been so clear. He's never called Kathryn a beaker bitch aloud, though he sure has thought it enough. *Hell, I reckon a discerning onlooker might even say I* finally *called her a beaker bitch aloud.*

"I don't feel bad," Philip addresses his grinning reflection in the bathroom mirror. Brushes some dark dust off his face. "She ain't no prize."

They'd started out friendly enough. Didn't everyone? Kathryn was German, and Philip grew up a bilingual military brat at Ramstein Air Force Base. Early in the season, when the evanescent summer season dickheads and LC-130 Hercules ski-planes were still flying between Pole and Mac Station, he'd chatted her up in German. She'd responded enthusiastically about her excitement to winter-over for the first time, with the IceCube Neutrino Observatory, and every vet knew ice rookies tended to mate up quick after the last plane left. Seeking solace the first time real loneliness came scratching into their minds. A guy had to lay the groundwork early if he didn't want to spend a long and dark winter being his own best friend in bed, and he'd felt good about his chances with Kathryn. Hell, she'd scare the cock right off some of them beaker boys, like skinny Yanis or that delicate-looking Khaled. A little more bullshitting in Mother Deutsch, some shots of Jack Danny, and she'd be all over him. So sure-honey-sure, things were real friendly.

Right up until Philip put his arm around her shoulder and his hand on her thigh, wearing a sunny confident smile on his face, and she told him she wasn't interested in male attention over the winter.

A guy got lonely at the Pole, but she was no prize. It slipped out of his mouth before he could catch it.

(*did it, did it really slip out, or did it maybe get kicked out*)

Fury entered Kathryn's doe-eyes, and she slapped him. Almost instinctively he reached out to grab her. Not intending to do anything, really, just show her he wasn't the kind of guy you went meat-handing right in the kisser; his damn nose was stinging like it was filling with blood, for fuck's sake. But she didn't just look strong, she *was* strong, and suddenly Philip was face down in the couch with his arm really fucking hurting as she twisted it behind him.

And that had been that. Ben came around a little later and sure-honey-sure, Philip didn't mind a little fun for the boss between the legs, *got an equal opportunity pecker that takes every opportunity,* but he hadn't forgotten the way that beaker bitch manhandled him. And then refused to speak to him, for months, not even bothering to pretend, so the whole damn Station then knew something went awry between them. *I've heard the beakers laughing. Fuckin'* know *what that's about, don't I?*

Exhaustion worms under his skin and behind his eyeballs. He thinks about eating dinner, and his stomach turns. The hot tingles are back with a vengeance, and he feels queasy all the way down to his toes. He limps toward his bed.

Philip can't tell how long he has been talking to himself in the dark.

Across enough time, everyone's odds of surviving the night drip down to nil, but Philip reckons his odds have reached zero-point-zero because he can't possibly keep breathing when he's this hot. Fever is all he can remember. He lies spread-eagled across the mattress with springs like knives, face and neck pressed against the cool window. His days-old tattoo itches, but really it's his whole body. Everything, *everything* feels too hot. His eyeballs are burning up in their sockets, and he has a hard-on he can't put away. Every few minutes he grabs it and tries to masturbate, but within a few seconds his cock feels like dry kindling about to catch fire and he lets go with a sick little whimper. Goes back to pressing against the window.

Boiling. Slowly boiling.

I'm boiling.

A muffled bang on the thin cork of his bedroom wall makes Philip sit up abruptly.

"Shut the fuck up, bro!" Nate Singh yells from next door.

Has he been talking aloud again? His tongue laps against the dry sides of his mouth like sand on parchment, fingers hooking into claws. "You shut the fuck up!" he screams back.

He collapses back to his pillow, wriggling to press his belly button into the coolness of the window. He doesn't know when he starts speaking out loud again. *I'm in an oven. I'm the frog in the pot and I'm slowly boiling.*

At last Philip gets himself up and out of bed, swaying like a flag in the wind. The cloud of heat around him seems to thicken. He makes himself keep moving, arms outstretched like he's on a tightrope, until he stands on the second floor in front of the clinic. It's unlit, but the phone mounted to the wall has pager numbers for both Dr. Wei Jin and Nurse Practitioner Jamie Carroll.

Boiling. Slowly boiling.

He makes a call.

Jamie Carroll appears less than a minute later. She's usually exquisitely made-up; this is the first time Philip is seeing the lines in her round face, the zit on her chin, the tangles of oily dyed hair standing up in every direction. She hustles him into the clinic, flicking on the lights. "On the exam table," she points, shaking out a pair of blue latex gloves. "What's wrong?"

"I'm burning up."

(*boiling*)

His tongue hangs out, lumpy and swollen and filling his mouth. "I've got a fever so hot, I'm just… boiling up."

"All right, open wide." She pushes a thermometer under his tongue, then places her stethoscope on his chest. He can hear his own heart galloping a mile a minute. "It's okay," she murmurs softly, her Brooklyn accent dropping away for a moment. She shifts the stethoscope to his back. "Just breathe. Nice and calm now."

The thermometer beeps. Philip looks at her like a dog at its master on a sweltering hot day, begging to be let inside.

"Is it bad? Feels like a helluva fever."

Jamie frowns. "You're cold, Phil." She shakes the thermometer, then lays her bare wrist on his forehead. "Yeah, you feel like an icicle. It might be an infection."

"Fuckin' A."

She frowns at his tone, and her hands go to her wide hips. "Do you know what might be responsible? Come on now."

Philip hesitates, then unbuttons his shirt. The plastic-wrapped tattoo is high on his left shoulder, just a few days old, bleeding lightly from all the itching he's been doing. A tattoo of the Pole acquired at the Pole, a four-point compass with all directions pointing north, is a secret rite of passage for veterans of multiple seasons; a more exclusive club than even the 300 Club. Jamie swears under her breath.

"Is this Dave Atkins's handiwork?" she demands.

"Uh, I'd rather not say, if that's okay."

"Dave makes his ink out of heavy metals. Not exactly the safest thing to be mixing into your bloodstream." Her tone adds, *you idiot man-child*.

She peels the plastic off gently, then uses a pipette to take a sample of blood from the tiny welts bubbling to the surface. She prepares a microscopic slide with a deftness that suggests practice, and peers at it through the scope.

"Well, it doesn't *look* like blood poisoning," Jamie says at last. "And I don't see any sepsis on you. Let's get this bandaged up right. Sure you don't have any chills?"

"Totally the opposite. Feels like it's fuckin' summer in Vegas. Can't you feel it?"

"You feel cold to me, but hot flashes might be your body's reaction to a minor infection. Antibiotics should flush it out."

"I'm havin' trouble sleeping, I'm feelin' so bad."

"I'm prescribing some pills that'll knock you right out. It'll pack a wallop for the next forty-eight hours, so no operating machinery, okay? Call in sick with Spencer in the morning."

"But it ain't... it's hot, like, everywhere. My *hair* feels hot."

"Take the meds, okay?" She snaps her gloves off and tries to catch a yawn. "One pill now, one when you wake up. Come see me if you still feel hot tomorrow afternoon."

And just like that, it's over. Philip stands outside the clinic for several minutes after she returns to bed, jittery and slicked with sweat. He knows the antibiotics will kick in soon, but it's just *so* fucking hot in the meantime.

Fucking *boiling*.

"I need some *air*," he says aloud, and it sounds right.

Philip pads downstairs and pushes through the double doors at Destination Tango, the grid-north entrance to the Station. The blast of frigid air on the deck knifes into his chest, takes his breath away. The thought of how nuts it is to be outdoors at the South Pole in nothing but his shirt and pajama pants flits across his mind, but just then, like a switch flicked to off, the stifling heat surrounding him begins to relax...

(*oh God yes PLEASE Jesus*)

...then fade.

Like he has been a chew toy between a dog's canines, just dropped to the carpet.

Philip lets out a breath shaky with relief; lets himself breathe, deeply in, deeply out. He is relieved to find his thoughts inside his head again.

The aurorae are out, gamboling faintly just above the horizon. Even after multiple winters down south, their mysterious light is still bewitching. Philip inches forward to follow them with his eyes, reaching for the railing – ah, *fuck*. Too late, he feels his bare hand start to freeze to it. He pulls back, ripping the skin on his palm open. Pain flares, brightly, but quickly goes numb.

In the distance, the snow clears around the red beacon atop ARO. His hard-on isn't a roiling oven coil in his pants anymore, and he feels quite pleasantly erect in the cool of the night. *Maybe I oughta head back there; make it up with Ben.*

Then his eyes move over the snow toward the Dark Sector. A sullen red glow winks on the horizon.

That way lies the IceCube Neutrino Observatory. Kathryn's beaker palace.

Most of the Station will be huddled indoors until the cold snap breaks, three long days from now. His heart falls quiet, fluttering. Almost pausing.

"What the hell are you doing, Phil?"

The muffled shout catches him by surprise. He whirls like a panther on the prowl to face Rob Booth, recognizable only by the Velcro nametag on his Big Red. He's covered up from head to toe in ski mask, goggles, and cold weather gear.

"Are you trying to die of frostbite? It's ninety below zero!"

"Fuck off, beaker." The words roll off his tongue, smooth in their contempt.

Philip regrets it, almost immediately. Rob is one half of the telescope team for MAPO, and yes, a beaker, but the hardy old geezer doesn't isolate himself from the support crew. He's one of the true Polies, the ones who *get* how it works when you're alone together this far down the ass of nowhere. But with that German cunt on Philip's mind, it slips out before he can zip up the thought.

Rob turns away without a word.

Philip stares after him for a long time, a lonely figure following the flag line west toward the Dark Sector, swallowed quickly by the curtain of blowing snow. The Dark Sector is where all the light-sensitive telescopes are – the Martin A. Pomerantz Observatory, or MAPO, the South Pole Telescope, Rajan Chariya's Long-Duration Antarctic Night and Daytime Imaging Telescope, or LANDIT–

And IceCube.

"Just a little scare." The sound of his voice is the sound of his thoughts, inseparable. "Little old-fashioned brown-pants scare."

He doesn't want Big Red, but he does want the radio inside it, so he goes back inside. The coolness fades quickly, and by the time he has struggled into his boots and windpants, he's back to feeling like he's inside an oven. He clomps outside, following the path Rob had taken fifteen minutes ago. He stays with the flag line this time, each step sure. His brisk stride gets his heart beating, and by the time Philip is halfway to the Dark Sector, there's a heat wave inside his clothes. He unzips his fleece, then removes it altogether and ties it around his waist. The breeze tickles his nipples inside his T-shirt.

Then his vision blinks black.

The snow cuts out.

He strips his gloves off and rubs his eyes as he walks. Still black. He rubs them savagely again, and as they clear, he sees the dark bulk of MAPO to his right. Everything looks tinged with crimson, as if a vat of gore has been splashed across the continent. On the left, another quarter-mile down a flagged path, is the looming four-story structure of ICL, the IceCube Laboratory.

His teeth are bared, spit frozen in the corners of his mouth. His gloves fall to the snow. He keeps walking.

Restricting access to a building in a place where the temperature drops into triple-digit negatives isn't just a bad idea; it's a life-threatening one. ICL isn't locked. Its heaters are cranked up, blasting torrid waves into his face. The first thing Philip does is turn off the central heat.

The second isn't hard to figure out. *I might be just the fuckin' plumber, but it ain't rocket science. Beakers care about data.* Just one node offline in the server room, and Kathryn will come running. Sure-honey-sure, she talks a big mumblefuck about taus and muons and electron energies, but she's just a computer plumber with a PhD.

Like him, her job is to keep the system online and flushing.

As he walks back down the stairs, catching the draft from the open door and letting its delicious coolness soothe him, he realizes *they* will get paged. Each of the telescopes, except Rajan's, has two winter-overs. The page will go out to Kathryn *and* Greg Penny. They trade on-duty times like Ben and Jonah at ARO. One of them will be on duty tonight.

Philip sits down, drained, head hanging loosely between his knees like a broken doll. He waits for the motion-activated lights to die out. "Hope it ain't Penny," he says to the carpet. Ice shakes out of his hair and melts slowly on it. "But it don't really matter."

A dull hammer starts beating at his temples, and he blinks away black.

"Long as it's a beaker," he mumbles, and the lights go out.

11:35 PM

Philip sees the shape emerge from the snow-stained darkness, walking up the hill toward ICL. It wears the same standard-issue Big Red jacket, black windpants and ski mask as everyone else, but he recognizes the way Kathryn walks as clearly as if he were seeing her cold-reddened face.

He giggles with glee, like an excited kid about to go on his first scavenger hunt. He pulls his ski mask up from around his neck and puts his fleece back on to cover his new tattoo. The heat barely grumbles. It's just a ready *thrum,* pulsing in time with his heartbeat.

His tongue, running over his lips, feels like a thawing popsicle just out of the freezer.

"Just a little scare," Philip Cunningham whispers to the darkness.

Chapter Four

A hard stripe in him. That's what Keyon Geerts remembers most about Helena. High-school girlfriend, not the first to see his cock but the first to agree to go down on it, she's always uncomfortably fresh in his memory, though it has been twenty years since he has laid eyes on her. There's a hard stripe in you, Keyon. Her face sad and a little scared as she said it. Something that's like biting into a dinner plate.

It was true that he could just... forget to care about people's feelings. The hard stripe *enjoyed* the tears and the hurt. It tickled him with congratulations because he'd caught the infection early and built up immunity to all that untidy emotion.

Keyon can think of no finer place to be than the darkness of the South Pole. The Station is the perfect microcosm of human angst. Isolated from the world, so many sweet flavors of anguish linger in the hallways. People fall silent for weeks at a time. Relationships start with a hot flame and die into ash with the same snap. Hardened veterans who think they understand loneliness find a new depth to drown in. But Keyon?

Keyon is a dry rock in the surf. Free to reach out with a casual word of malice or a pointed question, then step back and watch the puppets dance. He can incept a flesh-eating thought, like a sly invasive seed, and watch it germinate in the pressure-cooker of the claustrophobic halls. Months of condensed isolation in which to keep his face pressed against the fishbowl, watching the silly creatures flutter about. Mouths opening and closing vacantly, banging into walls they didn't know he'd built.

God left some part of you out when He made you in your bitch mother's belly, Helena had said at the end.

For a time, Keyon had doubted he was even capable of affection for another human being, but that was before Katie Caberto. They'd met his fourth winter on the ice, the season he'd worked the winter-over crew into a deep split, two opposing factions like the Red Sea, a near-mutiny; a wildly successful year. He'd had his eye on Siri, a deceptively innocent-looking first-timer ripe for the puppet strings, but then he'd met Katie.

The first woman he'd ever met as insatiable as he was in the bedroom.

Katie was too nice, down in her core, but nobody was perfect.

As the years went on, though, the hard-stripe voice and its sly suggestions reemerged. Wasn't she almost *too* grateful for his attention? Always the bridesmaid loving from the shadows, never the bride in the spotlight? Seven winters in, he's played every storyline before. Perhaps it's time to give the fish called Katie a starring role in this season's fishbowl…

Except there's an unexpected road bump.

After nine months a year in isolation with her for the last four years, something suspiciously like affection for her has grown over him.

An aching of fondness at the little things. Like her

ridiculously tiny big toe, her cold-reddened nose, or her face splitting into the waif-like smile he liked –

(*loved? no definitely not*)

– so much. And she could be such a tigress when they were intimate –

(*intimate what is this a Hallmark movie? fucked, when we fucked dammit*)

– together. Certainly an affection he could cast aside, there's never been an emotion he *couldn't* cast aside... but then again, there's always Rajan. Ever the man with his finger on the pulse, Keyon knows there's something brewing between Rajan and Summer, and Summer is with Tim. All the trimmings of a classic South Pole triangle.

Except the rookies are too easy to marionette on his strings, oblivious to the currents seething around them. He is an artist of chaos, and the South Pole love triangle is painting by numbers. Which brings the hard-stripe voice's magnifying lens back onto Katie.

His dilemma ends with a glorious bang when the Chinese traverse shows up.

He maneuvers himself onto the crew to meet them on the ice, content at first just to get away from the confines of the Station. But when he sees Rajan's face turn ashy-brown after stumbling out of the Dome-A truck, a breathy gasping excitement takes hold of him. The dull look in Spencer's eyes after going inside gives him a hard-on that won't quit.

At End-of-the-World, as Doc Wei examines the body, Keyon can barely stop himself from jumping up after the doc and thrusting his head into the truck. He wants (*needs*) to know what is inside it.

To see it and smell it for himself, and then paint his *Guernica* of chaos.

The final South Pole hard-stripe masterpiece.

That afternoon, before the windstorm, Keyon slips out to the End-of-the-World.

He takes the winding stairs down from Destination Zulu, dropping into the ice tunnels. Through the food arch, the cargo storage arch, then the winding staircase up to the frozen hatch. The banister is layered with fine patterns of condensed ice, hung like crystal taken painstakingly off a chandelier.

The hard-stripe voice cackles in his head as he lights up an acetylene flame torch.

When enough ice has sloughed off, Keyon braces his strong shoulder against the hatch and pushes. Heaped snow spills onto his head and into the hood of his Big Red, and he climbs up into the minus 65 F night.

Over his shoulder, all he can see of the hulking Station is the winking red light of Katie's weather beacons. He turns toward End-of-the-World. The wind is picking up, and he periodically grasps for the line between the route flags like a raft in a surging ocean. It's cold now, but his reward will be three days of storm isolation. A brewing pot of doubt ripe for his brand of spice.

He knows exactly where the Chinese truck is in the dark junkyard. It crouches in the darkness, a black engine of doom, ice thick on its windshield.

The body is still inside; the back door left cracked per Doc Wei's orders, to allow the corpse to remain cool and not decompose.

Despite the insistent cold, he is hard.

He can almost smell it.

Chapter Five

Kathryn tosses her Big Red and mitts over a chair sloppily pulled into the middle of the dark lab. Snow shakes out over the steps as she stomps up toward the server room on the second floor of IceCube.

The motion-activated light flickers gently. She scans the five towers of floor-to-ceiling servers. Green lights blink steadily in all of them except one.

"*Ätzend,* Penny," she sighs, and plugs a loose power cable back into its socket.

She pulls the keyboard out from the server rack and types two commands into the prompt. Numbers flash onto the screen. *Node 4, server 24, booting, 3%.*

Kathryn yawns, and something moves behind her. She whips around, sharply.

Server lights blink placidly.

She pushes the keyboard back into the rack and yawns again, deeply. Thermoregulatory yawning is the body's way of responding to the brutal cold of the walk over. The building is chilly, and silent without the constant background rumble of the heater. Why is the heater off?

She crosses out of the server room, through the office to the outer walkway, and then suddenly stops.

It feels like she's being watched.

She looks left, then right down the walkway. No one. Just

her, in a freezing building eight hundred miles from human habitation. The five-thousand odd neutrino detectors, buried kilometers beneath the surface, need the massive polar ice sheet to produce a sufficient energy density of reflected particles, but the isolation of the whole enterprise never fails to grab her attention.

The motion light blinks out. She stands quietly, hands on the railing, looking down into the center of IceCube. Taking a moment to enjoy the serenity–

The lights flicker on.

Her head jerks around as a weight like a ramming truck slams into her from behind.

Philip can almost *taste* her shock.

His mouth fixes open in a silent laugh behind his mask. His cold hand squeezes her breast from behind, the other covering her nose and mouth.

Her hips bump back against him – more like a shove – and he stumbles a little.

Before he can recover she braces against the railing and now she *hammers* into him, knocking him backward. His hand pulls vainly at her nose and lip, then he stumbles to a crashing stop against the half-open office door.

For the second time that season, Philip Cunningham is caught by surprise at how strong she is.

He springs forward, pushing off the door.

His body is an arrow.

His purpose is single-minded.

Her fist jabs out toward him and Philip is suddenly staring up at the ceiling tiles, head throbbing with sharp pain. A long streamer of snotty blood bridges his face and the floor.

He touches his mask and his pale hand comes away spotty.

"The fuck," he pants in disbelief.

"Philip," Kathryn snarls. Her German accent is thick and heavy. "I knew I smelled crazy."

He rips off the mask, hair tumbling loose. His breath whistles unpleasantly through his nose. "It's going to be more than a little scare now, bitch."

She doesn't look frightened. On the contrary, her eyes glitter dangerously.

His lips thin with anger, drawn down over teeth stained with blood.

She puts her hands up in a boxing stance. "Come on then, big man."

Philip lets out a roar and charges, head down. All out. Fuckin' slam her, take her over the railing, sort out what's left after–

Her arms come up, she shifts and heaves, and the ceiling and the floor change places on him. Philip feels himself falling, a sudden wind springing through his hair, then his face crunches into the side of a table. It folds under his weight and his body follows, driving the breath out of him like a collapsing tire.

The heat of the building ebbs away from his body.

His eyes flutter open. Reluctantly. She's standing on the walkway, an entire story above him, upside down to him. It's difficult to feel anything. He's splayed across the floor like a broken toy, arms stiffly at his sides.

And then she spits.

He sees her saliva streak lazily over the railing, like an elongated raindrop, then it lands wet on his cheek. Her scornful laugh burns in his ears.

"Big man wants to do some groping, huh?" Her voice is

guttural, taunting. "What happened, big man? Not as big as you thought?"

The thick port wine of fury buzzes in Philip's head like an angry hive.

His vision blinks black.

His neck pops like a noisy zipper, body rotating under it. He thrusts himself *up*, sailing straight off the floor in an impossible arc. His face is fixed in a rictus grin as her face swims closer, closer, until he can see the flecks of shock in her eyes, then he vaults over the railing –

(*though we could go through it if we wanted*)

– and smashes into her with a hot strength that surges like a pump.

She crashes through the glass into the office in front of the server room. She scrambles up remarkably quickly, but Philip's skin feels hot like the sun, and this time he knows, he fuckin' *knows* what to do with that heat. He yanks her off her feet. Her arm swims up, fingers hooked into claws thrusting at his eyes, but she is molasses and he is motherfuckin' LIGHTNING.

He sweeps her arm aside easily. His fist is a swinging hammer, and her mouth explodes into a bloody mess. She whines as if she's been burned. His next punch pulls her clean off her feet and backward through the flimsy wooden door. Her head cracks against the first server bank.

He tastes a drop of her blood on his lips.

"Beaker bitch," Philip pants, and runs. *Right at her, I'm gonna melt her into the servers she loves so much–*

He sees her weave.

(*shit wait shit*)

He swings, too late, and his fist collides with the metal server rack.

Philip's fingers fold backward like they're made of paper. His bones splinter like potato chips. A whimper of agony escapes him. Kathryn springs past him on her hands and knees, then pushes herself to her feet.

Already running.

He stumbles out onto the walkway in time to see her clatter down the steps, the weight of her white bunny boots making her clumsy. She reaches wildly for the banister and manages to half-skate, half-fall to the first floor. Her hand reaches out, snatching up her Big Red jacket, then she runs into the cold, down the large hill of snow lifting IceCube out of the surrounding drifts.

Philip watches Kathryn race fast through the deep snow, arms out as she tries not to fall. He can hear the breath wheezing through her in quick, punctured gasps.

She runs, runs… then looks over her shoulder. Sweat stands out on her face in deadly round beads.

He meets her gaze.

As he runs right at her.

He's an angry dog turned full-on wolf, eyes black holes in his face fixed on her. A wrecking-ball, wrapped in nothing but a bloodstained shirt, bearing down–

He slams into her from behind, throws her forward so hard that snow closes over her ears, then it tumbles across her face as he wrenches her over. His fist falls; her mouth gouts blood in a red arc. She gives out a rattling moan, and as he straightens into a crouch above her she coughs a tooth up onto her cheek.

Philip's mangled bare fingers reach for her throat. He can see her fear, painted brightly across her face. His grin feels like a scimitar, shining in the night. No time to think.

No need to think.

"You're no prize," he pants.

Her fists feebly claw at his face, but his cold hands are fastened on like ice bonded to her skin. His fingers disappear into her neck.

Time blurs into a warm mist.

When he tries to stand, his hands have sunk so deep into her throat that he has to peel them away, like fingers trapped underneath a decal. Both his bare wrists are slimed with blood.

His breath is a hot file rasping in and out of his throat.

There's a white light in his head, like a cataract over one eye, and it's drawing closer.

Whispering to him.

Kathryn's staring eyeball looks up at him, shot with red and unseeing.

Philip spits, slowly.

Watches it splatter and freeze on her skin like an obscene crystal earring.

She had almost made it to MAPO. It's less than two hundred yards away, though it wouldn't have offered her much refuge. There are no lights on, not even a beacon.

Philip reaches down and seizes Kathryn by the hair. Her body unfolds like a pretzel, working its way out of her unzipped jacket, carving a bloodstained canal in the snow behind him. He sets his eyes on the unlit MAPO building. Unlike its affluent cousin IceCube, sitting on top of a well-groomed hill, MAPO is almost sunken into the snow. Like ARO, its drift snowbanks are almost as tall as its roof, getting steeper with every passing day and windstorm.

He hauls Kathryn up the snowbank, driven by a hot strength not entirely his own, until he can look down into the bowl-like depression that hints at the stilts holding MAPO up. His shirt hangs open now, exposing his bare chest to the icy wind. A laugh bubbles up in his throat, leaving him giddy. "Feeling good!" he roars hoarsely. That song by the Ramones, was it *Blitzkrieg Bop*? Sure blitzkrieged the hell out of this beaker bitch's bop.

Philip hefts her up.

Hey-ho, let's-go!

He tosses her carelessly over his head.

Feelin-good, fuckin-A!

She sails into the abyss like a Raggedy Ann doll. Her body hits the snow, tumbles, and rolls into the shadows beneath the building. Philip keeps laughing as he pulls away his torn shirt. He feels invincible. *Fuckin' unstoppable, baby, this train don't ever stop.*

The wind tosses the shirt up amid the snowflakes, then whips it into the darkness.

He turns his head to the dark flickering sky and howls with unending mirth, a mirth that is also not entirely his own.

From the darkened window of MAPO, Rob Booth stares down at Philip Cunningham, face white with fear. It has finally happened.

After years of near-madness, someone has finally snapped on the ice.

Abruptly, Philip looks up toward him.

The spit in Rob's mouth dries up, and he ducks to the floor, but he knows he's too late.

Chapter Six

SOUTH POLE STATION POPULATION: 40 (PRISONERS: 3; DECEASED: 1)

June 21st, 2028. 12:30 AM

"It's been months and this is the first time I've seen you pissed off," Jonah Mitchell remarks.

Rajan begins pacing again. Back and forth, back and forth, in the small outer room of the greenhouse. He's supposed to be drinking wine, unwinding, but instead he's back to beating his head against a wall that won't budge.

"Look, I get it, we can't have everyone playing detective," Rajan says, by way of reply. "But it's not gonna compromise one damn thing if Doc Wei asks the Dome-A people a few reasonable questions. Like *what the hell happened in the back of that truck*. Or at their Station."

"So what did Gaudin say?"

Humidity spills over the climate-controlled greenhouse room in damp waves, a reminder of how dry the Antarctic desert is. Jonah sits on a futon, his back to the foggy window looking out on the hallway. The room is bathed in the sterile yellow light of a dozen sunlamps. Rows of plants sit behind a set of three double-paned glass doors. The plants are hydroponic, to comply with Antarctic Treaty rules prohibiting non-native soil; their greenery an almost visceral contrast to the unending white outside. People at

Pole have just three escapes from their environment: the gym, the greenhouse, or the bottom of a liquor bottle, and Rajan's favorite is the greenhouse. The feel of humidity on his skin, and the visual aesthetic of flourishing flora, are reminders of a world beyond the desolate emptiness.

"He wants the US Marshal present for *any* interactions with the Chinese."

"The Marshal at Mac Station?" Mac, or McMurdo Station, is nearly a thousand miles away, at the southern tip of Ross Island. "The one who can't reach us until November?"

"The very same." Rajan laughs, unsteadily, pulling his hair through his fingers. It's been months since he had a haircut, and at this point it's just an untamed fro of tightly knotted curls. "Fucking Gaudin, man."

"I could tell you some stories."

"Like how he's drunk at breakfast every day? Like how he's sleeping with Andrea, when she's his deputy?"

"Just the cherry on the shit cake. Five years ago, Gaudin got his foot in the door at ASC management thanks to a recommendation from his mentor. A guy named Paolo Rivey."

"As… in… Andrea Rivey?" It shouldn't surprise Rajan, but it does. "He's having an affair with his mentor's *wife*?"

Jonah's reply is just a deep sigh.

Rajan stares into his cup, thoughts far away. When he looks up, he finds Jonah watching him with a careful expression.

"Are you worried?"

"About what?"

Jonah's sunken dark eyes find his. "This war coming to Antarctica."

Hell yeah, he thinks, but tries to sound pleasantly bemused. "I'm just a scientist, man."

"A *military* scientist," Jonah presses.

Rajan shifts, uncomfortably. "All I know is that wars are won by advantage. We're a speck in an ice desert. What possible advantage could anyone gain down here?"

Jonah nods, but now Rajan's mouth twists with barely-contained irritation. "But that's *exactly* why I wanted someone to talk to the fellas from Dome-A. With the full story, we could reassure anyone worried about Chinese visitors at an American station... you've been doing this a while, Jonah. What the hell is Gaudin playing at?"

It's an understatement; this is Jonah's twenty-third season at Pole. Only Rob Booth has more ice time, ever, and at this point it's just an endurance contest between the two OAEs, or Old Antarctic Explorers, to see who'll walk away first.

"There have been compromised investigations before. Our traveler from Dome-A isn't the first dead body at Pole under suspicious circumstances."

"I thought there had never been a murder in Antarctica before," Rajan says with a frown.

"The Station doc ruled Rodney Marks' death a suicide, so you're not wrong."

A small smile flickers onto Rajan's face. "You know where all the bodies are buried, don't you?"

"Bodies and Stations, my young friend." Jonah returns his smile. "You heard that name?"

"Rodney Marks? I don't think so."

"An Australian wintering at Pole in the 2000 season. This was at the old dome Station, now sunk beneath the drifts. They called it a suicide, but it seems damn odd that he'd go to the clinic three times complaining of worsening stomachaches and not tell them that he'd poisoned himself with methanol."

"Whoa. Suspicious indeed."

"And we'll never get to the bottom of it because the manager basically made no effort to preserve any evidence. People threw away his belongings. They cleaned up his work area. His girlfriend lived in his room for the rest of the season. They made a coffin and buried him in the ice, for Pete's sake, only to dig him back up for the autopsy. When Christchurch police tried to investigate, no one who wintered with Marks would talk to them."

"What?"

"Myself included, I'm ashamed to say."

"I don't understand." Rajan sits up.

"What if I told you the word went around that saying critical things about the program–"

"Like what?"

"Drunken fights in the snow. Substance abuse of various flavors. The lack of meds to treat mid-season depression... *whatever*. If I told you airing that dirty laundry might get you banned from returning to Pole again, would you say that's credible?"

"Hell yeah. It's a total mafia system for the loggies. Only people whom management likes get invited back."

"Oh, it's even more of a mafia on the scientist side. Why do you think ARO is almost buried in the drifts?" Jonah sounds tired. "NOAA won't pay to lift it. They think it's NSF's job to maintain the buildings, and they're not wrong. But everyone scratches NSF's back because, by congressional mandate, they control access to this continent. And what does NSF fear more than anything?"

"Bad press," Rajan replies at once. "Anything that gives the pro-war, anti-science hawks in Congress another talking point."

"And a Chinese scientist murdered at *not* our station, by

someone who was *not* one of us, can only create bad press…"

"If *we* fuck something up." An ugly confused laugh jars out of him. "So there's a guy in that truck with his *head smashed in*… and we're just going to pretend like nothing happened."

"That's how the political winds blow. It's Marshal Pabon's problem now."

They lapse into silence, deflated; stare into their red solo cups. South Pole Station doesn't have a bar, just a store run by Michele Reinert, the crew's inventory specialist. The store is only open for four hours twice a month because, this deep into the season, the only thing anyone's buying is strictly rationed alcohol.

"I'm not saying this wine is terrible…"

Rajan can't help but chuckle at that.

"But next season, you oughta snap up the good stuff from the store early. Even fermented vinegar will fetch a price in Angry August and Stabby September."

More of a morbid prediction than a reality, no real stabbings had been reported in September. But on 9 October 2018, at Russia's Bellingshausen Station, engineer Sergey Savitsky stabbed welder Oleg Beloguzov in the heart with a kitchen knife, the first attempted murder on the Antarctic continent. Apparently a long-running hostility boiled over when Oleg took to spoiling the endings of books that Sergey was reading to pass the time.

"You know, I've been cold for so long that my life in Hawaii may be nothing more than a dream I once had–" Rajan breaks off sharply. "Did you hear something?"

The crackle of the radio carries over the rumble of the humidifier. "– right."

He checks his radio, clipped to his belt. "It's not mine."

Jonah rummages inside his fleece. A crackle, then a voice

that's barely audible above the static, hushed and garbled. Whispering right into the transmitter.

"Jonah... is Rob." Crackle. "– was right."

"Say again, unreadable."

When Robert Booth speaks next his voice is very clear. "If something happens to me. If something happens to me, it was Philip Cunningham." His voice drops back to the static-filled whisper. "Do... copy?"

Jonah goes utterly still. Only his mouth moves. "Rob, what's going on?"

A long pause.

"He's not on the main channel," Jonah says tensely.

"Because Philip has a radio too." Rajan speaks faster as Jonah's channel begins sparking static again. "Find out where he is."

"He killed Kathryn. Philip ki... Kathryn. I saw... it. I saw him do it."

Cold shock stabs through Rajan, nailing him to the floor. That same shock seeps into Jonah's lined face, like water trickling into sand. "Tell me where you are, Rob."

"I'm... MAPO," Rob whispers back. "Don't know... he is."

"Stay on my channel," Jonah says. "I've got Rajan with me and we're coming to get you. Keep your radio volume down."

Rajan is already pulling his jacket on.

"Be careful... please," Rob whispers. "He's dangerous. He strangled... right out... the snow. *I think he saw me.*"

They run upstairs, boots falling heavy on the metal steps. Jonah trails Rajan through the berthing doors of his dorm wing. A series of blue doors open off the hallway. Most are colorfully adorned, but the second-to-last door has just a piece of duct tape with DR. RAJAN CHARIYA written in black marker on it.

The small room is monastic. A twin bunk bed on risers, cranked almost to the ceiling. Below it, a small standard issue desk and almirah for clothes. No pictures, no cards. A single narrow window is blacked out with cardboard for sleeping. The floor is scattered with piles of stray electrical equipment and unwashed clothes.

Rajan snatches two heat guns out of charging cradles on the table. He uses them to thaw telescope hardware if he's swapping parts; they are each the size of a small hair dryer, with a lithium-ion battery pack at their base.

"Switch is on the side," he says rapidly. The copper taste of danger has transformed his persona and voice into a tense, military-drilled command mode. "Heats up to four-hundred degrees in four seconds. Jam it into his face, if it comes to that, and pull the trigger. We can apologize later."

"Got it."

Rajan's mind is whirling. "We need a backup, and I think we can trust Siri."

Jonah nods.

All the winter-overs that regularly travel more than a quarter-mile away from the Station have a personal radio channel, including heavy-lift vehicle operator Siri Monthan. Rajan has grown close with Siri over the last few months. Even harbored a small crush on her, which he'd then tried to crush *out* of existence when the gossip network told him she'd taken up with Khaled... who was Rob Booth's MAPO counterpart. There aren't many degrees of separation between South Pole residents.

He keys in her personal channel number from memory.

Lucky number thirteen. "Siri, Siri, this is Rajan. If you can hear this, meet me in the gear room, it's urgent. Repeat, it's urgent."

In the gear room, Jonah steps into his boots and windpants with the quick ease of long practice. "Look down there," he says.

Rajan glances at the untidy pile of clothes by his feet, which includes a Big Red jacket, and stops short. Stares at the name on the Velcro tag.

"This is Philip's."

"Yeah."

"There's no way he walked to ICL without a jacket. *There's no way.*"

It's an understatement. Given the conditions outside, it will take less than a minute to get frostbite and lose a limb. A jacket isn't just mandatory; it's a thin shield against certain death.

Jonah's reply is interrupted by a shadow across the door. Rajan looks up to see Summer Kerce.

Meeting her eyes, an odd mix of excitement and longing washes over him. *Through* him. Dark chestnut hair tumbles halfway down her back in damp wavy curls. Her bare shoulders are the color of coffee framed against the creamy whiteness of her filmy camisole. Just looking at the small upward tilt of her eyes, and the set of her bloodless lips, is enough to make Rajan brightly aware of how lonely he is. A causal link hard to explain and harder to shake.

Siri was a crush, a familiar feeling, a light and almost playful tickle, but Summer is a *want,* a persistent urge so deep it's almost primal, loaded with a longing intensity he could never have imagined before coming to the Pole. He doesn't know how much is her, and how much is them being trapped here together, but it doesn't matter. Not practically. She makes him think of a time when men would bash each other bloody with clubs for the right to mate with a woman.

Makes him long for a club, and that scares Rajan more than he's willing to admit.

Summer is the winter-over scientist for SPICE, the South Pole Ice Core. Over the daylight season, the SPICE team had drilled over a mile beneath the Pole, collecting ice core samples to study the geology and climate of the ancient Earth. Summer is a post-doc biologist at Princeton, searching for traces of ancient extremophile bacteria within the primordial ice. Over the winter, she's also carving out and cataloging smaller samples in the Cryo Lab for transport off-continent.

She gives him a little smile. "I saw lights in here and thought I'd see who was crazy enough to head out into the storm." Her voice is soft and husky.

"Just got to go, ah–" Rajan glances at Jonah; the older scientist gives the smallest shake of the head. "Check something out at my telescope, before the cold sets in."

One of her legs scratches behind the other. "Be careful. It's dangerous out there."

"You're more right than you know." He grabs his inner and outer gloves off their hook; shoves them into the pocket of Big Red. "Siri will get us if we run into trouble. Hey, Siri?"

Summer turns to see a small blonde with short spiky hair and petite pixie-like features. "Not your iPhone," she says, still panting from running over.

"Well, I'm worried about you," Summer says, turning back to him. "It looks brutal outside."

Jonah makes an impatient noise and he says, hurriedly, "Sorry, Summer. We've got to–"

"I'll get out of your hair." She takes a step backward. Gives him another wide smile. "Stay warm!"

He forces himself not to watch her leave by keeping his eyes focused on Siri. "I need a favor," he tells her. "And I need you to not ask me any questions."

Curiosity is written all over her lightly freckled face, but to his relief, she keeps it to herself and just nods, bright green eyes serious.

"Jonah and I are headed to MAPO. If you don't hear from either of us every fifteen minutes, *every fifteen minutes,* you wake Gaudin and you get everyone out there, okay?"

"I can do that."

"We'll be going there off the flagged path."

Now Siri looks worried.

"Jonah has a GPS unit," Rajan adds.

"GPS units can fail," she replies. "Most electronics aren't designed for how cold it is here."

He gives her a smile. Appreciating her worry. She doesn't return it.

"Look. The Dark Sector is laid out like hands on a clock," he says. "IceCube at nine o'clock from the Station. MAPO and South Pole Telescope at ten o'clock, and I'm at eleven. That way we all get our segments of the sky without interfering with each other. Nothing in the eight o'clock direction past the skiway. Jupiter rises in the east at about four o'clock from the Station and travels west in an ellipse. Then it heads back east. It doesn't drop below the horizon during the winter, so I'll always be able to find it, and reference from there. I'm hoping I won't need to, but that's how we'd find our way to one of the other buildings if we had to. Fair enough?"

She nods, reluctantly. "Okay. And you'll tell me why this is necessary later?"

"And I'll tell you why later, yes."

Jonah pushes his way through the double-latched door to Destination Zulu, and Rajan follows him out into the storm.

Rajan sinks into the ungroomed snow up to his calf, then heaves forward again. The ground elevation of eleven-thousand feet at South Pole normally leaves him winded, but the gale force winds buffeting the dark world outside has taken that to another level. The storm hurls itself at them in a violent scream. The very air inside his lungs seems to be freezing; his thin breath tears through his throat like a dagger.

Every two minutes they break into a shuffling run. Jonah sets a steady pace, headlamp dancing over his portable GPS receiver. They are moving off-route, trusting the GPS to guide them to MAPO. If Philip has killed Kathryn, they don't want to run into him along the flagged trail.

They'd rather surprise Philip, instead of the other way around.

Rajan sees Jonah duck his head under his arm and does the same. It's easier to draw a breath there without fighting the wind. One foot in front of the other, the weather the whipped cream of torture on his misery cake. It had been over two-hundred degrees warmer, but the run to MAPO reminds him, oddly, of his deployment to Syria.

Head down with purpose, moving into danger.

"Philip and Kathryn have had some kind of disagreement for a while," he manages when the older man slows to a walk. The wind rips the words out of his mouth and flings them north, but he talks anyway, because if he can't stop dwelling on how much everything hurts, he won't be able to keep up when they must run again. He was in Hawaii before this, for God's sake. Working at a telescope on top of a mountain with slopes so green they took on a verdant glimmer on a sunny day. Jonah's old, but he's acclimatized. He has the home-field advantage.

"If I had to fit a curve to the data, I'd say he asked and she said no. I recognize the vibe," Jonah replies.

They struggle into a faster pace. The snow answers them, reins them back, blows off the ground into their eyes. The drifts grow deeper, every step a struggle against his burning legs. His windpants are sugared to the waist. Snow fills up his world with white blankness. His eyelashes freeze together, heavy with ice. For a while, his consciousness narrows to a pencil beam, just the back of Jonah's red jacket and the starlit sky.

Uphill, more uphill, braving the wind, until they reach the crest.

"I think we always knew this day would come," Jonah says. Quietly, almost to himself.

"We?"

"The OAEs. Those of us with multiple seasons here. You ever hear of Deadwood?"

"Mining town in the frontier West?"

"Illegal mining town, actually. It was on Sioux land, so there was no law or government." He wheezes unsteadily under his armpit. "South Pole is the modern-day Deadwood. Wild and harsh and isolated… and, politically, it belongs to everyone and no one. It was only a matter of time until something boiled over, Deadwood style. There have been some close calls, but…"

"Oh, I know. I was right there when Yanis shwacked Dave with a plate."

"A love triangle is a recurring Pole soap opera." Rajan gets the sudden feeling Jonah is eyeing him underneath his mask and goggles.

The wind beats on them heavily as they head downhill. Rajan's lungs are tight as a band in his chest. "You mean Summer, don't you?"

Jonah shrugs vaguely.

"I haven't slept with Summer. She's with Tim Fulton."

Jonah's head moves in his direction. "I haven't chased a woman down here since you were in middle school, but even an old fart like me can tell there's something there."

Rajan draws a deep breath that is painful for more reasons than just the weather. His voice comes out queerly flat. "Summer had her chance."

As if by unspoken agreement, they pick up into a run.

October of last year; firefighting training in Denver. A mandatory box to check for every winter-over, but for Summer and Rajan, who had been training partners for two weeks, it became the site of a brightly simmering attraction. Things spilled over while bar-hopping on their last day together in Denver. They hadn't been able to take their hands off each other. If she hadn't been drunk by the time they made it to his room, there would have been a lot more than that. Summer had fallen asleep in his bed, and Rajan had an early flight back home to Maui, so he left her a note by the bedside. Why not, right? They would have all winter together.

Looking forward to picking up where we left off at Pole.

Summer deployed for her fourth season on the ice shortly after the Denver training, since SPICE could only drill in the daylight warmth. Rajan's telescope ended up delayed at customs in New Zealand, and he didn't arrive until early December.

Jonah and Rajan slow to a walk. "That way," the old man pants. "I saw IceCube's beacon for a second."

Rajan squints, but can barely see his hand in front of his face. He fumbles into his jacket and pulls out his radio. The battery is already down to 60% with the cold. "Siri, you copy?"

"Loud and clear."

"Re-hack the clock." A deep breath rattles with a sunken sound, churning shallowly in his throat. "Fifteen more minutes."

"Can I ask you something?" Jonah asks. "Just to keep my mind off what may be ahead."

"That's not the worst idea."

"What happened with Summer?"

With someone else, Rajan would have deflected the question. But if anyone can understand the overlap between raw loneliness and suppressed desire in Antarctica, it's Jonah. "We had a little thing at firefighting school," he says. Shaky white puffs of vapor stream from his dry lips. "But by the time I showed up here, she was already with Tim."

It sounds so trite to sum it up that way. Rajan thinks of her brown hair spread across his pillow in Denver. Her toes sticking out from under the sheets. The sun falling gently across her high cheekbones and generous lips. He should have stayed, should have missed that flight and been there when she woke up, except how hard would the hammer of finding out she was with Tim have hit him then?

It's been hard enough shaking her off his mind when it had been just a few kisses.

"They were together on the ice last summer," Jonah says.

It's painful to even think about replying. He's heard the rumors. He wants to run, just to snatch this conversation up and throw it into the wind, but his legs are heavy logs, his toes limp stubs of ice inside his bulbous bunny boots. He barely has enough gas in the tank to keep lifting his feet.

"If I had to guess, it was an ice thing," Jonah continued. "One of the most momentous relationships of my life was with a woman who was with me in Antarctica, and with her husband and two kids back home. She called me her ice husband. It took me a long time to realize that meant *not real.*"

It's one of the first times Jonah has volunteered something personal about himself. He's spent nine months out of every year for the last decade isolated from the world; Rajan doesn't need to be told that relationship hadn't ended well.

"This won't bring you any closure, but at least you'll know," Jonah continues. "Tim wasn't going to come back, but he signed up when he heard she would be wintering. They probably just fell into what they left off with last season."

The implication is clear. Tim Fulton had been just an ice thing for Summer; last year's news. Maybe she'd wanted to move on, but it had meant more to Tim. "She wouldn't have fallen into anything she didn't want to fall into," Rajan says, more roughly than he intends. Because the wistful smiles and long looks only remind him that she deliberately chose someone else. That he would always be a season late and a dollar short.

"And how would you start that conversation with someone you'll see every day for the next year?" Jonah asks.

Sometimes this place can really be a long thin dagger in the gut.

"It's done now."

"If I had to guess again," Jonah sighs, "it's just getting

started. But thanks for letting me distract myself from… darker thoughts."

They start running again, cutting grid-east now. The concept of a grid for direction is unique to South Pole, from where any and every direction points only north. The wind moves the snow in curtains that whip back and forth, and Rajan can barely tell which way is sky, and which is ground. The journey feels like it will never end. They'll just keep walking, then running, then walking again, until the wind blows hard enough to topple them into the snow and bury them.

Then the bulk of MAPO appears, the dish-shaped baffle surrounding the telescope emerging like a ghost from the shadows. "There's no beacon." His breath comes in ragged gasps, voice wheezy and nasal. "Shouldn't there be a beacon?"

"Rob's auroral time lapses are famous." Jonah puts his hands on his waist, taking a deep puffy breath. "The beacon light spoils the shot, so he might have been setting up for a photo."

The snow curtain shifts, and Rajan sees something move in the distance. A hunched figure that looks like a man on foot, moving at a loping gallop. Too fast for the conditions.

Instinctively, he drops to his knees in the snow. The primeval voice is back and pulsing, pushing exhaustion out of his mind like a cold broom. His arms unconsciously go to his knees, as if he holds a rifle between them. For just a moment, the blowing snow is blowing sand, the heat of the Syrian sun is beating down on the back of his neck, and Lieutenant Rajan Chariya is listening for footsteps, thumb hovering over the safety of an M-16 carbine.

Instead of a trigger, he presses the transmit button on his radio, then releases it. If Rob can't talk, he can blip his transmitter to acknowledge them.

"Jonah, is that you?" Rob's voice, clear. Almost no static. Close by.

"It is," Jonah replies into his radio. "Where's Philip?"

"I just saw him." Even over the radio Robert sounds disbelieving. "He's heading back to IceCube."

"We'll head there. If we don't check back in within a half-hour, get to Station and tell Gaudin what you saw." He puts the radio down, then places it to his lips again. "Stay off the flagged routes."

"Be careful. Please."

Fear trickles into the hollows of Rajan's body, colder than the air, stiffening his muscles. Dulling his senses. There's something out here in the snow with them. Something wild.

It's time to put his head into the lion's mouth and see how heavy the bite is.

Chapter Seven

Jonah and Rajan circle IceCube, far enough from the windows to stay hidden behind the blowing snow. They climb the drifts behind the building to the rear entrance. Rajan reaches into his jacket and unstraps his heat gun. It fits comfortably into his gloved grip. He pulls the trigger briefly, and the tip smokes in the cold air.

Jonah crouches below the porthole set in the door. He raises his goggles onto his forehead, pulls his mask down to his chin, then takes hold of the handle. Looks at Rajan.

Rajan freezes for a moment that unspools sluggishly. He was raised with religion, has been a faithful Christian for most of his life, but he hasn't prayed in years. Hasn't been able to face God since what he had done in Syria.

Please, Jesus. This building is the valley of the shadow of death, I can feel it.

Rajan holds up three fingers.

Please God… please watch my back.

Jonah waits one beat, two, then pulls the door open. Rajan bursts in, crouched low, heat gun stiff-armed in front of him.

He finds himself in a long office, with cube dividers that don't reach to the ceiling. The sensor on the motion-detected light switch blinks but doesn't trigger. His feet roll silently across the carpet, head on a swivel.

It has been years since he's held a gun, but the tactical

movements are all too familiar. Clear the corners. Clear across. Clear the room. He comes to rest at a metal walkway, waits a beat, then surges to the left. More offices, another quiet left–

Broken glass on the floor.

He's looking toward the building's central shaft, which extends up to the starlit ceiling dome. Above him, railings on metal walkways lead into more shadowy offices. He stands like a statue, heat gun close to his body.

In the silence, he can hear humming. Tuneless humming.

Hey-ho lets-go. Hey-ho lets-go…

Small step forward. Out from under the walkway into the open central area, eyes trying to pierce the darkness. He sees a splintered table, partially hidden behind a potted plant. Caved in. Like someone has smashed through it.

Another step, quietly.

A drop of water falls on his head, and he whirls–

Rajan's head swivels up to see Philip staring down at him from the walkway.

Philip's long hair stands off his skull in wild shocks. Dripping with the gleam of melting ice, like he has just been outside, except the plumber is wearing nothing but windpants, shoulder straps pooled at his hips. An open wound on his shoulder has frozen into a stiff caking. His tongue hangs out from between his teeth. White and sharp and gleaming, like the teeth of a fox.

"Hey buddy," Rajan says.

"Hey buddy," Philip says mechanically.

Rajan starts to walk sideways, toward the stairs, to go up to him. Philip doesn't move, but his face suddenly grows menacing. His tongue rolls into his mouth and his lips pull off his teeth, incisors bared in a snarl.

Rajan stops.

Careful. Careful now.

He stays absolutely still.

That's the face of a hunting dog with its tail pointing. Once he gets moving all he'll want is to rip your fucking throat out.

"We got a call saying Kathryn didn't check back in." His voice echoes uncomfortably and he can't help thinking about how far they are from anything resembling law enforcement. "She was on her way here. Have you seen her?"

Philip spreads his arms wide. "Nope," he says gleefully. "Not a sight of her."

The movement causes the motion-detector to trigger the light above him. Philip's chest is bare, skin a corpse-like bluish tinge, the wiry muscle in his arms strung out like he has been weightlifting. His forehead is white as a camera flash, and Rajan sees the madness in his eyes. Clear as the full moon in the night sky, like a sailor drunk on salt water.

Years before, crouched behind a wall in Syria listening for footsteps, Rajan came to learn the pointed crawly feeling of his next move meaning the difference between life or death. It was the backyard of a friendly farmer's house, but someone had seen them, and the only question was whether to wait to be found or come out shooting and hope surprise carried the day. A life-or-death choice.

The first time he felt that primordial hunter voice awaken in his brain and quietly speak.

That voice tells him this is one of those life-or-death moments.

"Guess that's that." He breaks the silence uneasily. "We'll see you back at the Station?"

No reply from Philip. He looks behind him at the smashed

table. Jonah is across the room, almost invisible in the shadows underneath a walkway, watching them. Rajan steps back, toward the front door and Jonah. Philip's eyes follow his, shining with an angry little glitter.

He takes another step back, suppressing the urge to run.

Philip doesn't move.

Another silent step, then another. Jonah reaches the front door of IceCube, opens it in one smooth movement, and they walk out and pull it closed behind them.

The two men step backward, hearts pounding in their ears.

The door stays closed.

At last, they turn their backs, walking briskly down the snow-hill in the direction of MAPO. All too aware they are in full sight of every east-facing window at IceCube.

(*The hunting dog bounds up from behind*)

Rajan's head whips around –

– no one. The windows of IceCube are doused in shadow.

He stands bug-eyed in the dark for a long minute, hairs along the nape of his neck turning into uneasy hackles beneath his balaclava. He can imagine Philip lurking by a window, tongue lolling, humming and trying to decide whether to chase them down.

Jonah clicks his headlamp on. "Footprints here."

The line of holes dotting the snow is immediately visible. The drifts are deep; anyone heading this way would have sunk in almost to their knees. A slow chill crawls up Rajan's spine.

He has a feeling they are following Kathryn Wagner's last steps.

A little over three-quarters of the way to MAPO, the

footprints jumble together, creating a snow angel in the windswept plain. Beyond that, drag marks carve a channel through the snow.

Rajan gets down on hands and knees. The snow shifts loosely, exposing a cavity.

He has managed to squash down his fear thus far, but it suddenly blazes up like a glowing ember finding air. "I need light down here."

Jonah sets his heat gun down in the snow, then crouches and points his flashlight.

There is frozen blood in the ice.

A lot of blood.

The drag marks lead into the shadow of MAPO's wooden telescope baffle, up the side of a drift, until they are staring into the dark bowl-like void beneath the building.

"Fuck," Jonah says tensely.

They look behind them, flashlights shining into the snowy darkness, but they are alone. Hearing nothing but the wind.

"Siri, fifteen more minutes," Rajan says into his radio.

The snow bottoms out two stories underneath MAPO. On two sides, the drifts reach up higher than the building. Claustrophobia caresses him with a silky hand, then takes a choke-firm grip. The darkness is thick with abandon. The wind riding up the side of the drift is muffled, like they are hearing it through a spacesuit.

"Rajan." Jonah's voice is flat.

Kathryn lies face up in the snow. Her open eyes stare dully at them, skin bleached by the harsh flashlight. Blood is frozen around her smashed nose and down the sides of her face. A red tendril snakes up toward her open eye, pooling beneath her lower eyelid.

Rajan bends down, and her face moves.

He lets out a hoarse shout and leaps backward, falling into the snow and scrambling to his knees. "Did you *see that*?"

Jonah has taken a half-step back out of reflex; he aims the light at her face again. Rajan inches closer. Just enough to see her open eyes, and the clots of flash-frozen blood stained against her blue skin–

The face moves again. *Shifts,* like an upper layer has broken loose and is writhing on top of her nose and mouth. A thousand transparent worms–

Shifting toward him.

Rajan scrambles at his jacket, for his radio. "Siri," he says urgently. "Siri, get–"

(*IT'S HERE*)

A chill seizes him. The words dry up in his throat.

He turns –

(*the hunting dog bounds up from behind*)

– and Philip Cunningham stands there, so close he could be Rajan's shadow.

His lips are drawn all the way off his gums. Drool hangs in frozen icicles from his mouth. His eyes are wide and blank.

He has no shirt on.

Philip's strong hands grab Rajan by the throat.

Chapter Eight

Rajan is dying.

He's lying in the dirt, staring into the blinding sun. Bright rings of rainbow colors surround it like an aura. Harsh glaring light lays a burning strip across his face. Slowly, other senses begin seeping in.

The sounds of bullets smashing through glass and driving through plaster.

The smell of cordite.

I was shooting at the Jeep and a flash and then–

Then I got shot.

The thought triggers a pain reaction and suddenly his chest is on fire. He looks down, expecting to see a bloody hole, but there's only the dented plate of his body armor, the back-plate digging painfully into his skin. His gun lies at his side and he reaches for it.

He blinks, and there's nothing in his hand. The sun is Philip's manic eye, blazing down from above him. Black comets shoot around his field of vision, then his skull is pushed down into the snow, breaking through it, cold spilling over his face.

Again. Snow into his nose.

Crouched over him, Philip pulls his head up by his neck, massive hands crushing his throat, drawing him closer like a sadistic child wanting to see the wings separate from the fly. There's something hypnotic about his demented staring eyes. A merciless inertia creeps into Rajan's limp body.

His head flickers and buzzes as he flounders, lost in grey tones of semi-consciousness–

Rajan shakes away his thick outer glove.

(*Fight kick claw do something DO SOMETHING*)

He jabs his stiff pointer finger, still encased in an inner glove, right into Philip's eye.

He keeps his finger rigid as it punches through the filmy sponginess of his cornea.

Philip howls, and Jonah throws himself onto Philip's back.

Rajan keeps pushing until it feels like his thinly gloved knuckle is buried in Philip's eye socket.

Philip rears, pulling away, yanking Rajan's finger with him as he rises from a crouch to his knees with a wild scream. Jonah flies off him like a cape in the wind. The madman fumbles at his eyeball, making incomprehensible sounds, but it hangs out of his socket now, blood leaking thickly down his face. Philip's good eye stares at the blood pooling into his cupped fingers, then he turns the full venom of his misshapen gaze onto Rajan.

He screams, hands extending into claws.

He *dives* at Rajan.

Philip's hands scrabble for his throat, eyeball sliding and quivering against his face like a frenzied yo-yo. This time the grip is vice-like, immediate, and Rajan's vision goes black. His tongue pokes into the cold, gasping for air that isn't there.

A dull ringing –

(*ringing like a bell the hunting dog got my bell rung*)

– and the grip on his throat relaxes. He looks up, dazed,

in time to see Rob Booth give a shrill scream and smash a snow shovel the size of two dinner plates roundly into Philip's head.

A sick flat sound, like a palm slapping water.

Philip keels over. His hanging eye is frozen to the side of his face, nose bent almost into his cheekbone, but *he is still moving*. He drags himself on his elbows, pushing with his legs like a water-soaked insect. Good eye intent on Rajan.

The hunting dog, single-minded.

Rajan struggles backward, hands swiping frantically in the snow. He fumbles his goggles off with his sleeve and clambers to his knees. Reaches behind him.

Jams his heat gun into the icy flesh of Philip's neck.

Philip lets out a scream, long and keening–

(*It hurts it hurts it hurts IT HURTS*!)

Something dark shifts on Philip's face. A black river spills down his eye socket into his nose. His mouth is a dark throbbing cavern.

He lurches back up to his knees.

Rob's shovel whistles through the air before it finds its mark, knocking him flat. Philip grunts gutturally, like an animal, and Rob hits him again with a panicked scream. Again. The shovel keeps coming down, a wet sound beating into the air.

Over and over and over, until the old man can't heft the shovel anymore.

Blood glimmers darkly on the snow.

Rajan and Jonah sit slumped on either side of the body. They stare at each other in still, stunned silence. Rob sags to his knees, and his scream dwindles to a wordless blubber.

Lying in bed under a scratchy woolen blanket, Rajan often

sees blue sparks of static electricity arcing in the high-altitude dry air when he moves his legs too quickly. Sometimes the air itself seems to lie heavy with charged particles. Philip is finally still, and very dead, but there's a different heaviness in the air now. A sense that they have entered the shadow of some dark great onrushing thing.

He has seen it, half-naked and grinning under MAPO, and now the high iron of terror sings in his veins.

Because it'll be months until this night of deaths at the South Pole is over.

Chapter Nine

SOUTH POLE STATION POPULATION: 39 (PRISONERS: 3; DECEASED: 2)

June 21st, 1:40 AM

Rajan.

Rajan.

Rajan.

He looks around stupidly, then at his hand, which is squawking at him. His radio. "Rajan, last call, man. *Should I get Gaudin*?"

"No," he rasps. He's slumped on the floor inside MAPO, ice melting in a pool around him. His throat can barely form words. He brings the radio up and tries again. "No need."

"Are you okay?" Siri says. "Your last transmission cut off."

Rajan thinks back to the impossible image of Philip's icy chest glimmering above him, grasping hands pressing the breath out of him. An image right out of the milky night venom of fantasy. Is he okay?

He doesn't know if he'll ever be okay.

After some amount of time, enough that the ice on his boots has sloughed off, Rajan struggles to his feet and into the machinist's shop deeper in the building. The world is a reddish fog of slow-motion agony. He finds some water and splashes it down his throat, but he can taste slick blood and it's too painful to swallow. He lets the water dribble out of his mouth.

He walks back, weak and shaky. Rob and Jonah have dragged themselves to their feet by the stairs. Jonah looks like he might grey out with shock at any moment. "What the hell," he manages.

"Yeah."

"Kathryn is *dead*. He killed her."

Rob lets out a breath that snags on the start of a sob. "And I killed him."

"He had no shirt on," Rajan says. He coughs and tries again. His voice is a strangled whisper. "It's not a close walk from IceCube to MAPO."

"I saw him earlier," Rob says from between his hands. "At the Station. He was outdoors with no fleece, no jacket."

"It's negative ninety out. Maybe a hundred. *He should be dead."*

The three men look at each other. The queasy yellow stench of fear passes between them.

Rajan's hunter voice growls in his ear, so close it could have been a person standing behind him.

Get moving before the fear stabs you and you bleed all your courage out.

His words sound alien to him, as if pushed out of a slowly swelling blimp. "Let's get a better look at what we're dealing with."

The flickering lights of their torches pass over massive streaks of blood. Philip's body gives off an obscene steam as it cools rapidly, the cold reaching in through the gap where his throat and jaw had once been.

Just a few feet away is Kathryn's body, face up, eyes open. Rajan's flashlight picks out a dent in the drift hill, then skid marks.

"It looks like he threw her from here," Rob shouts down from the top of the snowbank. "I can see where she impacted."

"She's a stout German girl," Jonah replies, bewildered.

Rajan touches his throat uncomfortably. "Trust me, he was strong." He looks up at Rob. Knowing he'd be dead if the old man hadn't seen them from MAPO and come out to save them.

Rob picks his way down the snowbank toward him, away from where Kathryn had slid to her resting place. "This is… this is beyond nuts," Jonah mutters.

"Actually, I've seen a similar scene recently," Rajan realizes suddenly.

He turns to Jonah and Rob, feeling sick to his stomach. "In the truck from Dome-A. If I had to guess… those Chinese scientists did something very similar to their traveling companion."

Remembering the vicious dents in the ceiling of the Chinese truck, he looks back at Philip and feels a chill.

"Maybe for a similar reason," Rajan says.

He unclips his radio. "Siri," he croaks. "I need you to get on the PA system. Wake the Station up. Wake everyone up."

BOOK TWO
The Ice and Fire Baths

JUNE 21ST

This is an evil, in all that happens under the sun,
that the same fate comes to everyone.
The hearts of all are full of evil;
madness is in their hearts while they live,
and after that they go to the dead.

Ecclesiastes 9:3

EXCERPT from:

In the Wake of War: A First-hand Account of Humanity's Deadliest Struggle

Winner of the Pulitzer Prize for Explanatory Reporting (posthumously awarded)
Assembled from the diaries of Mariana Egan, War Correspondent, *Chicago Tribune*

As presented at the Fifth Global Conference for Armament Limitation, Geneva, 2043 AD.

[Excerpt begins]

The city of Nanjing was new overlaying old, a film of almost cheerful industrial grime laid over dusty imperial tombs. World travelers knew of Beijing and Shanghai and even the gaudy Guangzhou, but Nanjing was still an enigma to most. Even to me, though I'd been there a month. It was 2019, just another beat for a world-weary reporter, until I found myself in the city's beating heart on a Friday afternoon, just past a thickly congested roundabout, and the alarms began wailing.

I'd seen the speakers everywhere - in every plaza and park, atop every building - but it meant no more to me than the ubiquitous security cameras. Just another way to remind you Communist China was always watching. The siren didn't last long. Just ten seconds. But after it went off, everything stopped.

Everything.

Cars drifted to a halt in the street. People stopped walking. The constant noise and fracas of the metropolis dwindled to a murmur. Everyone immobile, as if listening to something I couldn't hear.

Today, this wouldn't surprise anyone. But in pre-war China, the heyday of America-driven 2019, it was shocking to see a bustling city of seven million people stop in its tracks and *listen*.

Exactly a minute, then the sirens went off again for ten seconds, and the city of Nanjing sprang back to life like a switch had been flipped. Cars honked, eyes went back to phones, street vendors picked up their raucous cries. For a moment, I wondered if I'd imagined the whole thing.

Mei explained it to me; sweet Mei Lingling, who would have her own role to play in what followed. She was a Professor of Glaciology, but she'd also grown up in Nanjing. Could read her city like she could read crevasses on an Antarctic floe. The sirens went off every Friday, right at noon. Ten seconds on, a minute off, ten seconds on.

Nanjing was once a historical seat of power, capital of Imperial China, but that ended the last time those sirens sounded for real. 1937, when Japanese invaders poured down the eastern coast of China, invading Beijing, Shanghai, then Nanjing. Over eighty years ago, but the Rape of Nanjing lives on in the DNA of this country.

Every Friday the siren blew and children stopped playing. Teenagers looked away from their phones. Eyes went distant. If the sirens sounded at any other time, on any other day, it meant foreign boots had landed on Chinese soil. It was time to leave the city, go into the woods lining the banks of the Qinhuai River, and kill anyone who looked like a foreigner.

Watching a city of seven million go silent, remembering an invasion almost a century old, struck me as incredible, but quickly thereafter, chilling. They were remembering, but also, they were training.

It would be four years until those sirens would blow, piercing every ear for an hour straight when American bombers surged across the Yellow Sea, but I think that moment in the plaza was when I first wondered if we might lose the war with China.

Chapter Ten

SOUTH POLE STATION POPULATION: 39 (PRISONERS: 3; DECEASED: 2)

June 21st, 3:00 AM

The galley of South Pole Station sits at the end of the long hallway on the second floor. Standing behind the buffet line, the flags of the Ceremonial South Pole would normally be visible directly ahead through the tall windows. But ever since the two-week long sunset, cardboard cutouts have been up over the windows, to minimize ambient light into the aurora cameras atop the station. They make the darkness more pervasive, the galley dull and claustrophobic. As people trickle in, Rajan starts taking down the cardboard, letting the meager starlight and view of the outside world spill in. The wind is howling now, raising a white curtain almost to his eye level, four stories above the snow.

Even months in, most of the science crew lump themselves together at their usual table in the galley's center. Bethany Hamidani and Yanis Pohano sit practically hip-to-hip. In the corner, Robert Booth's usual table, where he sits by himself or with Jonah, is empty. And Siri stands by the small hot bar carved into the corner of the galley while Gaudin and Andrea take turns accosting her.

It had been her voice on the public address system, rousing them from their slumber for an emergency all-call.

Even from across the long room, their body language isn't hard to read. Siri listens to them berate her, demanding answers, wordlessly. Her eyes flick toward Rajan as he walks up behind them.

Rajan has met his share of people like Gaudin in the military. The kind who ride their subordinates with a mean saddle but lick up to those higher on the food chain like eager-to-please puppies. The kind who listen to nothing but the echo of their own voices unless someone else holds the whip to shut them up.

Gaudin and Andrea follow Siri's gaze and turn toward him, and he knows he can leave the Station Manager no room for input or course correction.

"Both of you. Take a seat," Rajan says. No sign of hoarseness or hesitation. "We'll get started in a moment."

The military taught him the *command voice* as an officer cadet in boot camp. It comes from the gut, omits soft syllables, and demands attention. But it isn't just the voice that gets a soldier's attention. It's the officer's whole bearing. The fear in Rajan's throat has numbed him but it has also stripped a layer off his personality. One closer to the hard stony center. It has made him less of a scientist, and more of a soldier.

A soldier who expects to be obeyed.

Rajan takes a step forward, so close he can smell the sour odor of whisky on Gaudin's heavy breath. "I said. *Sit. Down,*" he says, very slowly and deliberately. In that moment, he's ready to punch the larger man in the throat to get his compliance. If it comes to that. He's ready for it to come to that.

Gaudin stiffens. He sees it in Rajan's face. He takes a step back.

Rajan turns away as if that flinch has decided who is in

charge. He walks over to Siri, keeping his back to the galley and Gaudin.

"Wow," Siri murmurs. "I would've bought popcorn if I'd known the show would be this spicy."

Rajan shrugs, almost angrily. "Hopefully four years from now someone isn't telling the story of the first-timer asshole who thought he could run the place better than the manager."

"Not from the stars do I my judgment pluck. And yet methinks I have astronomy."

Her words startle him out of the fight-or-flight response pounding through his veins. "Did you… just… quote Shakespeare at me?"

"Don't look so surprised, mister man. Shakespearean sonnets are an integral part of an English lit major's repertoire."

"And how are they with rent money?"

"Not so integral, sadly, which is why I drive a bulldozer in Antarctica now."

Rob and Jonah walk in, past the dish pit. Rob looks white and distraught, and Rajan reaches out to squeeze his shoulder. He recognizes the glazed look in the old man's eye all too well. Self-defense, they'd told him after Syria, but that was just a legal word that absolved him of nothing.

He's a killer, something Rajan will never stop carrying with him, and he hadn't known the man he'd killed the way Rob had.

Hadn't trained with, eaten with and laughed with him.

He has the sudden feeling that Rob will never come back to Pole. For much the same reason that Rajan himself hasn't been back to church.

"Let's do this," Jonah mutters.

Heads turn as Rob, Jonah, and Rajan walk to the front of the room. People begin falling silent. Rajan pulls out a small table, drags it to the window. He takes his time, until every eye is on him, then climbs onto the table.

There are unspoken rules for a freshman winter-over at Pole. The best way to get along is to find a more experienced Polie (in Rajan's case, Jonah), follow their general lead, pitch in to help with the communal grunt work whenever possible, and otherwise keep your head down. Standing up on this table, feeling absurdly visible, Rajan feels himself shed the passive scientist persona he has adopted and embrace the officer within. Speeches about death do not come naturally to his scientist self, but his military self knows all about it.

Knows the only way out is forward.

On the radio clipped to his belt, he depresses the transmit switch on the common channel. His throat feels thick, but when he speaks, it's in the command voice from his diaphragm, and it carries clearly.

"For those not in the Station, I'm broadcasting this via radio as well. As of this moment, Rob and Jonah are the only others that know this, but everyone needs to hear the whole story right from the source."

Nothing moves, it seems, not even the wind outside.

"Kathryn Wagner is dead. She was murdered."

Instant bedlam.

The galley erupts with exclamations and noise. "Lucky" Greg Penny, Kathryn's IceCube partner, struggles to process what he's hearing, face crumpling and squeezing. In front of Rajan, Gaudin's eyes bulge and he springs to his feet. Rajan holds up his hand for silence, but the idea of one of them being murdered at the South Pole is catching like wildfire before a careless smoker. Suddenly he finds himself wishing that someone else could be up here. He looks down, almost pleadingly, at the two veteran Polies beside him.

Siri lets out a shrill wolf whistle from the back of the room.

"Shut the fuck up!" she bellows.

Like a butcher's cleaver dropping, the noise in the room quells.

"Listen to what he has to say!" she shouts into the pregnant pause.

A sullen eddy of whispers ripples, then stills. Rob and Jonah step forward, on either side of him. Both men look up at him and nod, gravely. A look that says: we're in this together.

"Rob saw who did it," Rajan says into the silence.

Ben sits very, very still on the couch in the ARO building, a quarter-mile away from where Rajan is speaking. His hair falls in a lank wave across his forehead. His fingers are numb over the radio clutched in his hand.

Kathryn is dead.

And suddenly Ben can't breathe, drowning in the awful feeling that he knows who–

(*no oh God oh God no not–*)

The radio sparks, shattering the room.

"Rob saw who did it," Rajan says. "He saw Philip Cunningham kill Kathryn."

Kathryn is dead.

And Philip killed her.

Ben slaps himself across the face, so hard a fleck of spit flies out of his mouth.

Siri whistles, twice and shrilly, before the shouts of *where is he* and *have you seen Philip* pick up. The galley quiets down almost immediately. Gaudin's face works in an uneasy contortion of anger and disbelief; he sinks into his seat. Andrea's hand creeps toward his, then stills on her leg.

"Philip killed Kathryn at IceCube, then dragged her body and tossed it under MAPO. I think he hoped the storm drifts over the next few days would cover her up. It might have worked if Rob hadn't been at MAPO recording with his aurora cameras."

The small scientist adjusts his glasses, hand running nervously over his baldpate. "I redirected one of the cameras over to him," Rob says softly.

A low mutter runs through the galley like a brisk breeze.

"The image quality isn't great because it's dark. But when it's cleaned up it'll show him throwing her down the drifts."

Rajan's voice is a dry bolt. "Jonah and I went out to IceCube. Philip had no reason to be there, especially in the middle of a storm, but that's where we found him. He denied seeing Kathryn. It was clear he was lying, so we went to MAPO, where we found her body. Philip followed us there and attacked us underneath the building." As he speaks, he unwinds the thick black scarf around his neck.

A shocked murmur courses through the crowd as he peels it away. Between sunken finger marks, his neck has swollen up like lumpy inner tubes. His brown Indian skin is a mottled black and purple, bulging thickly as if a callous child has pumped too much air into it.

"There's more."

The thought keeps slipping up through the basement of Ben's mind like a glacial arrowhead, skewering him repeatedly. Killed her. He had killed her.

Sure, Philip grumbled about Kathryn. But kill her?

(*unadulterated*)

Then try to hide her body in the storm?

(*unadulterated top-shelf crazy wrapped in human skin*)

"There's reason to believe Philip *lured* Kathryn out there by taking down one of the IceCube servers, knowing she would have to respond. And if not for Rob, Philip would have killed me too," Rajan is saying.

Philip Cunningham, so angry at the world. Ben aches for him because he's *also* angry, at the hand that has dealt him cards from a dead deck his whole life. He, too, is tired of searching for the eyes that hide behind the flames and never let him see. Except he's weak where Philip was strong. Cries where Philip would have raged.

The radio squelches quietly, a lance reaching out from a quarter-mile away to spear Ben through the heart with deadly accuracy.

"We killed him in self-defense. Philip Cunningham is also dead."

Suddenly, Ben is crying, crushed by a weight he can't begin to describe–

Except *God*, he wants to rage! He wants to be furious with loss, instead of crushed by it; he wants to beat his fists on his chest and put them through walls and roar like a wounded bear. He should feel sad for Kathryn, or worried about the crew's morale for the winter, but all Ben wants in that moment is Philip back.

A warm body above him to convince him that he can't, can't *possibly*, be as alone as he thinks he is in the world.

Uneasy murmurs and strangled gasps rumble through

the galley, like high-voltage cables sparking. Several eyes have taken on a glazed, starey look.

"Philip had issues with Kathryn, and everyone in this room knows why." Rajan's voice comes to his own ears from down a yawning canyon. "She was a beaker, and he was a loggie. We all heard his comments. They were harsh, they were divisive, and every one of us chose to say nothing. And here we are, thirty-nine crew members instead of the forty-one we should be. We saw the first ever murder in Antarctica, with the Chinese traverse, and now we've seen the first at South Pole. That's why I'm up here."

He scans the faces of his crewmates, willing them to *listen* to his next words. "This is going to make headlines around the world. People will wonder if it's safe to send others down here to be cut off from civilization. For all of us, and the Polies who come after us, *we have to come together* and put the petty bullshit behind us. So please. Please think about how *you* can wipe the slate clean."

His command voice fades into a hoarse shout, but he needs to get out one last thing, because this is all the Polies will talk about. At the next SATCOM pass, people will email their friends back home about this. Some like-hungry asshole will post it on social media, then it'll be in the news, and then there'll be no stopping it.

"The satellite will be up next in about twelve hours, at which time we'll notify the NSF about what happened. Out of respect for Kathryn and Philip's families, please, please, don't share what you just heard with anyone on the mainland until the NSF notifies their next-of-kin."

His voice is almost gone.

"It's what you'd want us to do for you."

The moment Rajan steps down from the table, the spell

is broken, and the galley morphs into a crowded railway station. He is swarmed by clamoring people, questions, and shouted demands for details. His brain is spongy raw hamburger now, and all he wants is to curl up in a ball and try to make sense of what he saw under MAPO. That bare chest, shiny with ice. That black river pouring out of a mangled eye. Rajan shakes his head, over and over, voice only a cracking whisper now.

"You know everything I know," he croaks. "We need to focus on what happens next."

Gaudin pushes his way over, Andrea drifting in his wake. His eyes are shiny marbles sparkling with anger. The smell of whisky is stronger, like his rage is boiling the alcohol out through his pores.

"I want to see the three of you in my office *right now.*"

Gaudin doesn't wait for the door of the Station Manager's office to close behind Rob and Jonah to begin shouting. "Did my Station turn into a sitcom stage while I was asleep? You bring something like this to me *first*. You don't go around starting your own reality show for the whole Station to watch!"

He looks inflamed. The rolls of fat bursting out of his collar throb with righteous indignation. The pouty vacuous expression on Andrea Rivey's face rearranges itself into an unctuous glare. She moves over to Gaudin's side, arms crossed, and offers him a thin, hard, coy smile that dances in the corner of her mouth. Witnessing their mating dance, Rajan just feels tired. *I almost died under a telescope in Antarctica. The half-naked man who strangled me wasn't fazed by the heart-stopping cold. And my station manager is worried about a* scene*?*

He starts to reply but all he can manage is an inaudible whisper. He can feel himself shutting down, wiped dry by the adrenalin and emotional exhaustion of the last few hours.

Then, from behind him, a voice.

"Let me interrupt this little piece of theater," Jonah Mitchell steps forward. "What Rajan is too polite to say is that you are a fucking drunk, Bill. And your deputy's only qualification is riding your tiny dick. The two of you barely keep up when things are normal, and this Station is now in crisis mode."

Gaudin starts to splutter, and Jonah slams his fist into his desk. "Shall we go to your room and count empty alcohol bottles? Should I ask Michele how deep into next month's booze rations we already are?" Jonah's normally placid face burns with fury. "Deny it. I *dare* you to deny it, so I can have the pleasure of proving it."

Andrea opens her mouth, and Jonah directs a withering look of contempt in her direction. "I can't even tell you how uninterested I am in anything you have to say."

Her eyes streak with shock.

"Now if we're done huffing and puffing, let me answer the question you didn't ask, Gaudin," Jonah says. "Rob and I talked Rajan into getting up there. This is an unprecedented moment at Pole. We needed someone to try and unify people, and that isn't Rob or me. But it's also sure not a drunk, or the town adulterer."

Rob clears his throat, and Jonah's mouth snaps closed with a click of his teeth. A woman like Andrea had broken Jonah's heart, Rajan realizes. Someone with a family on the mainland, who took Jonah as an ice husband to salve her loneliness with, but shook him off like snow from her boots afterward. And passions at the Pole could scald like the sun through a magnifying lens.

If what Jonah felt was anything like what I feel when I look at Summer with Tim Fulton…

Rajan knows he wouldn't just dislike Andrea. He would *hate* her.

Rob speaks quietly. "Jonah and I don't want another Rodney Marks situation, and I don't think you do either, Gaudin. So. Before you storm out, we actually do need you to make some leadership decisions because, except for one hour of satellite internet every day, we're on our own."

His soft words are the final pin deflating Gaudin's balloon of righteous rage. The silence in the office is deafening, finally making Rajan's strained whisper audible.

"The NSF needs to hear what happened from management. From you, Gaudin," he says. "Rob will include his aurora footage for them to clean up and give to the FBI. The three of us will sign statements with *all* the relevant background. The derogatory comments Philip made about beakers. The atmosphere of scientists antagonistic to loggies, and vice versa, that's existed here for years." He leans forward. "The satellite comes overhead in twelve hours, and our statements will be transmitted without any change. No cover-ups. No politics."

The big man shrinks away, eyes fixed on the purple and black marks around his neck.

"The next question is what to do with the bodies under MAPO."

Gaudin's eyes flick between them. A pulse beats in his meaty forehead. His shoulders are hunched as if from a blow, but all Rajan sees is a bully whose platform has been yanked. Andrea is doing her best not to look at anyone, hand twisting around her ring finger. A finger that hasn't worn its wedding band in months.

"Bring them back to Station," Gaudin mumbles. "Put them in the ice tunnels."

"Maybe somewhere working people won't stumble across them," Rob suggests gently. "There's a utility room at MAPO that opens to the outside. That keeps the bodies remote, but cold enough that they won't decompose. Doc Wei did something similar with the Chinese corpse."

"I'll tell you right now, NSF will want drug tests," Gaudin says.

"Fair enough," Rob says in his calm voice. Rajan suddenly wonders if he has kids or grandkids, back in the world. "We'll send a Sno-Cat out for the bodies. They come back for Doc to examine, then get returned to MAPO for the season. That okay with you?"

"I don't know, it must be, you seem to be making all the decisions around here," he snaps. "Can I leave now, or do you have more shit to sling at my walls?"

Without waiting for a response, Gaudin barges by them and storms out of his own office. Andrea scuttles after him.

Jonah lets out a long breath. "I've been waiting a decade to say that to his face," he says, looking disgusted. "It only took two people dying to get up the nerve."

Ben sits rigidly on the couch, feeling the burn of his own hand fade slowly, thoughts cascading and spiraling. Trouble runs across his face like the shadow of a storm cloud spreading across a field. Sooner or later, someone will find out about his relationship with Philip. He doesn't know how it'll happen, but someone always does at Pole. Rajan is right; this will be a sensational story. And he's trapped in the middle of it.

This awful forlorn winter won't end when he gets off the C-17 aircraft in Christchurch.

There will be questions, interviews, investigations. Recriminations and reports to his superiors. A life of failure laid out by the press for the world to see and mock. Running away from his leering father and zealot mother – only to wash out of the US Navy for smoking weed. (A global force for good, the commercials said, but it had turned into a global tour of illicit substances.) Forced to return home to Idaho, desperate for company, sneaking a high-school ex-boyfriend into his bedroom – only to endure the pray-the-gay-away conversion therapy his mother forced him into. Then the police report from his attempted suicide. Then being the boyfriend of the first murderer at the South Pole.

More slights dealt from the dead deck. More rocks waiting to be kicked over.

The thought of his high-school ex brings a bitter crescent of a smile as he remembers getting high and trading blowjobs in the parking lot of *Hobby Lobby*. Their little fuck-you to the store's politics, and the state's possession laws.

And speaking of possession…

There's weed at the Station. Ben knows it like he knows sky is up and cold is here. Oh sure, the treaty says you can't have soil to grow, but it's just another possession law, and he's not the only one who'd thumb a nose at it. Ben had recognized the red rims in the eyes of souz-chef Tommy Chapman, known as TC, after the last Pole karaoke night. He'd looked like that during his Navy days.

Ben stands, shakily. The Station is lost in the distance now, leaving him even more alone. Always on the outside looking in, even at the bottom of the world. But getting high will wipe that despair away. Boil his feelings down to an emotional frame that fits, even temporarily. Something other than this Romeo and Romeo tragedy to occupy his thoughts.

Maybe he can just call TC up.

Feel him out.

But South Pole is all on one phone system, which routes back to a Denver exchange. The NSF owns the exchange, and two people have just died. Surely they'll look at the call logs. *It's what I'd do, and I was dumb enough to get kicked out of the Navy.*

Ben's hand pauses on the phone's keypad. He doesn't even remember picking it up.

Maybe a quick scouting trip back to Station?

He looks out at the snow with a sense of longing. Thinking of the chill of the polar air makes him oddly happy. It will feel nice out there. A little drafty, but pleasant.

But it will have to wait until morning, because he can't meet anyone's eyes. No way. Not with the unbridled feelings galloping through him.

Ben buries his head in his lap and cries some more, then pulls himself into the fetal position under a blanket on the couch. Eventually, he drifts into a fitful sleep.

And dreams a very strange dream.

He's with Philip, except Philip is glowing. He radiates warmth like a stove, heat tightening his skin and making it look shiny. Almost see-through. They are walking toward the Dark Sector together, but Philip doesn't have a shirt on. Ben looks down–

– and neither does he. The wind feels light and pleasant on his skin. The cold crunch of the ice between his bare toes is mildly ticklish, but when he looks behind him, his skin is peeling away on the ice. A trail of bloody footprints stretches to the horizon, back toward the Station.

Ben looks to Philip, worried, but Philip strides on, a confident smile on his face. His eyes glow in the polar dark like a lynx and, before them, MAPO looms out of the shadows. They are running now, fast and light like the wind, and out of the snow, Kathryn emerges. Her terrified eyes peer behind her like two frightened mice trapped against the far wall of their cages. She screams and *they* jump, because they are one now, Ben is Philip and Philip is he; they fall on her, reach for her throat, strangle the struggle out of her. Her blue eyes turn into dull cloudy marbles, and they have never NEVER felt so HAPPY, so FREEEEEEE–

Ben bangs awake in the dark grave of the early morning with a scream.

His mouth is dry but he's dripping with sweat, like he can still feel Philip's dream warmth.

"Oh God," he moans. "God, what the hell was that?"

(*you were right there*)

(*we were right there*)

Chapter Eleven

Doc Wei is getting high on his own medication.

It starts with a soft itch in the Station doctor's throat, an itch exactly the size of a Percocet tablet. Stick that Perc under his tongue and things would start to feel *allll right.* Ignore that urge, though, and his lips get parched. The insides of his cheeks grow cold. A slow, sucking hunger turns him into a sweaty mess. All of it goes away the second he splits that sampler open. Two pills in it, pop 'em like candy, yum and yum again, and the edge melts off everything. Yum-yum.

Obtain medical advice before taking this medication, the label says. Past a certain point in the season, the pills won't get used by their expiry date, and his medical advice to himself is to waste not, want not. He justifies it the same way every time he cracks a sampler pack: *I'll just kick it when I get home.* It would be easy, because at home he had responsibilities, and *that,* oh that is the sharp edge that tickles beneath the bone.

With no hope of a medical evacuation, the position of winter doc at Pole demands an exquisitely knowledgeable emergency surgeon, versatile enough to diagnose and treat even without the full complement of medical equipment. Doc Wei is knowledgeable and versatile. He'd known about the isolation and the darkness. Cliquey people, bitter cold? All easy.

The *fucking boredom,* though? Another story. Another story entirely.

He's on crew to combat an extreme medical emergency at a moment's notice, but the reality is bumps, bruises and the occasional case of vanilla frostbite. The only time the Stanford-Harvard surgeon picked up his scalpel this season was to extract a piece of chipped dinner plate from the scalp of Dave Atkins. He's a medical insurance policy, a *breathtakingly* long way down from the excitement of running the top emergency trauma room in the country.

For the first month, Wei showed up to the clinic every day, but there was nothing to do. *Nothing.* He prescribed high-altitude acclimation medication, then everyone acclimated and didn't need pills anymore. He started doing routine medical checkups, but Pole had given him a nurse who could prescribe, and when Jamie Carroll began to bristle at him taking over things in her job description, the boredom became thick and insurmountable. His sharp mind was a hungry hamster, wheel spinning madly in search of something to bite into, growing more frantic the less it produced.

An edge that started to drive him mad.

The yum-yums let his brain stop spinning so frantically. One minute it's after lunch, floating on a Perc-cloud puzzling about Morgellons disease or hypsarrhythmia, then he blinks and it's 8 PM, hey-hey-hey, time to grab dinner and head to bed. Sleep fourteen hours, wake up, glimpse the heavy boulder of depression rolling downhill, and pop two to keep the edge nice and fuzzy. Rinse-repeat.

He'll shrug it off back in the world, obviously.

Obviously.

The yum-yums give him weird dreams, so Doc Wei

awakens unsettled when Siri's voice comes across the PA system at 3 AM. He thinks about not dragging himself out of bed, but waking up will be an opportunity to finally examine the blood and skin samples taken two days ago at End-of-the-World from the deceased Chinese scientist. He'd been planning to do it right after he'd collected them, but time has a way of floating away on the Perc. And it's not like there's a raging rush, right? No Marshal at the Station; no one breaking down his door with investigative urgency. Boredom is the problem, but it's also the solution.

The shock of hearing that two more people are dead jolts Doc Wei to his very core; an unpleasantly clear look at how much crud has calcified on top of his razor-sharp surgeon instinct. A man dead in a truck driven halfway across a frozen continent, and *it has barely nudged his curiosity*. Wei flees to the clinic right after, aflame with guilt, and even he can't ignore the way he beelines right for the medicine cabinet.

One quick yum-yum, then right to work, an early start on the day examining the dead man's samples.

Well, okay, two, because it wouldn't do to just leave the solo boy lying around for Jamie to find. It's fine. It's all fine. Plenty of time to kick it when he gets home.

By four AM, Wei has run the basic panels on the blood sample. No drugs, no alcohol. He scratches vigorously at his elbow as he preps a sample slide. He's been feeling itchy lately, with occasional tingles in his extremities.

Is it finally time to dial back the P-candy? Medical advice says… still a long winter ahead.

He puts his eye to the microscope, then sits back just as quickly.

He rubs his tired eyes, trying to blink away the fuzziness

in his brain. The clinic seems suddenly stuffier and hotter. He looks back at the microscope.

The sample is crawling with something black.

He enhances the magnification and amends his thought. Not crawling, but twitching. Whatever covers this skin is moving very, very barely. Almost imperceptibly.

Slowly, painstakingly, with the speed of a first-year medical student, Wei makes up another slide from the first of two samples he'd taken from the body in the Dome-A truck. He uses a different microscope; the clinic has three. He takes a deep breath, feeling thin air burn at the base of his lungs. The altitude of Pole is 9,300 feet, but since barometric pressure decreases with distance from the equator, it feels like 11,000 feet. The equivalent of being constantly hypoxic.

And, can't forget, sky-high.

The microscopic image resolves into thousands of black-tinged microbial structures. With another unpleasant shock, he realizes they are mostly transparent. The black he'd noted earlier is just a tinted speck dotting each cell, making them hard to see.

He zooms out.

The transparency covers every millimeter of skin on the slide.

Not thousands. *Millions* of microbes.

He places his finger on the slide to shift it, and his body turns into a statue.

In the microscope, underneath the white of his latex glove, he sees dark and familiar specks.

Carefully, hands shaking a little, Wei takes a skin culture from his own hand. Classic sample cross-contamination, that's all. Time for bed, and no wake-up yum-yums tomorrow. Doctor's orders.

But when Wei places his own skin under the microscope, he sees the same microbes.

There aren't as many. Even at highest magnification, they aren't all over the skin but in tight clusters, like a spotty infection that hasn't festered yet.

He looks back at the Dome-A sample, seething with microbes like bees swarming a hive.

Wei feels blank, swimming through a sleepy grey confusion. He thinks back to the truck. He'd been fairly sober, mostly thanks to the cold at End-of-the-World. He had taken two samples, then gotten the hell out of that macabre truck. He'd collected the first sample correctly, for sure. The second… well…

He doesn't remember the second.

Wei realizes he needs to address the real issue.

He rummages around the medical fridge until he finds the bottle of ipecac syrup. The clinic stocks it as an emetic, mandated ever since the methanol poisoning case of Rodney Marks. He administers himself an uncomfortably full dose.

Within minutes, his stomach begins lurching. He walks to the sink in as dignified a manner as he can summon, and throws up until his stomach muscles cramp. Most of the Perc has probably entered his bloodstream, so Wei isn't sure how much is placebo effect, but his head feels clearer. He pops a mint candy, carefully washes all signs of vomit away, then pages Jamie.

When she enters, he's sitting calmly on a patient table, teeth crunching into a third mint. "Hope I didn't disturb any fun with Daniel," he cracks.

Careful, doc, you've never really been all that personal with Jamie. Dial it back.

Daniel Baia is the dishwasher and line cook. For the first few months, Jamie made noises about how cute he was. Recently that has dried up, either due to Wei's lack of response or, more likely, because she has confirmed he thinks the same about her, too.

Jamie doesn't reply; despite her made-up face, she looks tired, and her eyes are red-rimmed and unhappy. "You okay, Jamie?"

"Just... Lisa and Michele are organizing a vigil for Kathryn and Philip tomorrow, and that sort of threw me for a loop. I mean, on the one hand, they are – were – both our crewmates. But..."

"But he killed her."

She nods desolately, rambling now. "We're the closest thing to shrinks these people have, and there are going to be a lot of mixed feelings. Pressure from the mainland once they find out. Oh God, *media*." She hesitates. "Philip came to see me before he went to IceCube."

"Philip? Really?"

"Paged me around 10:30 PM. I gave him some antibios." Her hands move around her ample frame aimlessly, and it turns into a shudder. "Kathryn must have been on his mind when he sat where you're sitting."

"Speaking of which." Wei knows he sounds callous, but now that she doesn't know he's high, he's eager to nip the small talk in the bud and press forward. The sentiment is the most like himself he's felt all season.

Her face rearranges itself. "Right."

"I need a second-check. There are two skin samples over there. I've analyzed the first but haven't touched the second. Take your time and be as careful as you can."

He watches her work. She is methodical and precise, even

though it's 4:30 in the morning. He feels briefly envious of her prowess.

"Now take a skin culture from me, being careful not to cross-contaminate."

She disinfects his left arm, then uses a small blade to expertly skim off an epidermal sample. She gives him a running commentary as she swaps slides. A microbial growth of some kind, thousands of cells in small, isolated clusters. Then the Dome-A sample: millions of the same cells, covering every inch of skin.

"That's what I saw. So either somehow I contaminated both skin samples when I took them, or..."

His voice drops away, because for *the first time* he's asking himself what the hell the microbes are. Right as his nurse is asking him the same thing.

Fantastic, he thinks, even as he says, "I haven't figured that one out yet."

"This digital microscope has a Bluetooth readout," she says. "Give me a second to dig my cell phone out of my suitcase, then you can do the doctor thing and second-guess me."

Ever since Wei landed at Pole he has felt like something was missing and, as she walks away, he realizes what it is. No one has a cell phone in their hand. People eating alone in the galley aren't on their smartphones pretending to be busy. People walk the hallways, but their heads aren't bent away from eye contact with the world around them.

There's no Wi-Fi at the bottom of the planet. Nothing for a smartphone to connect to, except perhaps a microscope.

When Jamie returns, she ratchets the microscope lens up as high as it will go from the base. He rolls up his sleeve and places his arm under the microscope. She turns her head away from him, looking at her phone.

"Whoa."

"What?"

She doesn't reply.

"*What*?"

She lifts the screen to where he can see it.

It's like a forest has taken over. Clusters of black-tinged, transparent microbes up and down his entire arm. He puts his other arm under the lens. The image changes but shows him effectively the same thing.

He stands back, reeling a little. "Get a sample from my chest and legs."

Jamie works quickly, catching his worry now. The results are the same. Tens of thousands of invisible microbes cover most of his body.

"The relative density suggests the source is the first sample, and I'm a secondary contamination," he says tightly. His surgeon brain is back, a welcome visitor, the frizziness from the Perc chased away by adrenalin. "Check yourself next. Maybe the microbes transfer by touch."

"You rubbed your chest all over someone? Doc, I had no idea you were so frisky."

"They likely spread from a point of original contact." He ignores her thin witticism.

She pulls her gloves off and places her fingers under the microscope. "Maybe it's like that kids' movie gag," she says, still trying to sound light. "It's the lens that's stained." Then she blinks, and her tone changes.

"I see a few microbes. None where my gloves were, but on my left wrist." She reaches for a pencil and pulls the gloves gingerly toward the microscope.

"Contact with me while you were collecting my skin sample? *Shit*."

"The gloves have microbes on them too. Tight clusters, dark, just a few," Jamie says. "Dozens, not hundreds, per cluster."

"Okay. Okay, we need to test a transfer hypothesis. Get a sample from somewhere we had no skin-on-skin contact. Be careful about contaminating yourself."

She nods, her face checkered with lines of worry. She strips off her shirt, then dons a pair of tall gloves that come up to her elbows. She carefully takes a skin sample from her ribs, right below her bra. She places it under the microscope and peers at it, rotating the magnification knob.

"Anything?" he says tightly.

She turns, face betraying her relief. "Nothing. It's clean." She stares at her wrists. "What the heck is it?"

"I don't know," Wei struggles to keep his head clear. "Usually at 1000x microbes are alive, moving…" A moment later, he says, "They're *dormant.*"

He can tell that word scares her. "It's on me now, whatever it is."

"If it's dormant, it's probably not multiplying."

"I don't know, it covered you up pretty fast. Where did the source sample come from?"

He stares at her.

"Tell me!"

"From the Chinese traverse," he says unwillingly.

"From the people who are *alive*? Or dead?" she demands.

"Dead. But taking samples from the survivors is an excellent idea." The rusted wheels in his brain are slowly churning now. "So, anyone who had contact with that truck, or that body, or with any of the Dome-A folks, could have this microbe on their skin."

Jamie nods. "We need to know what happens when this organism stops being dormant."

Chapter Twelve

You can't have a vigil without a body, so here they are. Siri parks the heavy-lift vehicle by the snow drift piling up against MAPO, and Akinori, Spencer, and Kenny Black disappear under the building.

It takes them almost forty minutes in the bitter cold to photograph and heave Kathryn's body up the steep drift, by which time she's ready with the industrial plastic laid out on the snow. Spencer and Kenny lay Kathryn in its center and wrap her up so she can be lifted into the large scooper, mounted on a long articulating arm in front of the cab.

But they are acting a little strange, Siri thinks.

Twitchy. Scratchy.

"Fuck me," Spencer says suddenly. "When did it get so hot around here?"

So *hot?*

He claws at his Big Red, like it's strangling him. Siri flinches away, alarmed. Spencer wrestles with his jacket, harder, stepping right into Kathryn's body, then he pulls Big Red over his head like a slip, taking his fleece with it. As if he can't be bothered with the zipper.

Siri stares at him, unable to believe what she's seeing. The wind catches Spencer's long-sleeved thermal undershirt, pulling it up to reveal his white flesh, and *his skin is crawling with a writhing sea of black.*

Kenny jumps on Spencer, trying to push his jacket back on. They wrestle around in the snow, and Siri looks down. Her heart begins to knock against her ribcage.

Kathryn's face is moving.

Coming free.

Her face is a mask of thousands of crawling translucent worms. It ripples up off the body, a grotesque inverted mirror reaching toward Siri.

That's when Akinori emerges from the dark underbelly of MAPO.

Shirt off.

Bare torso exposed to the wind and the cold.

He *howls* at the stars, like a monster out of a dream.

Then he lowers his head and charges at Siri.

Chapter Thirteen

SOUTH POLE STATION POPULATION: 39 (PRISONERS: 3; DECEASED: 2)

Siri clambers into the running Sno-Cat and slams the door right as Akinori throws himself on it.

Kenny has lost interest in restraining Spencer and is on the snow, jackknifing violently as he claws at his own jacket. Whatever is happening to him is happening fast. But Spencer hasn't forgotten him. As Siri watches through the windshield, he places his booted foot almost tenderly against Kenny's neck, then reaches down, seizes Kenny's arm and pulls up violently.

Blood splashes across her headlights.

Siri screams. Her fear bulges, a runaway elephant filling up her chest, crowding her breath out of it.

Her door rattles and her head snaps to the side.

Akinori.

Every muscle in his neck, and every vein in Akinori's bald head, pulses with blood. His eye sockets are dripping black holes. His lips are coated with swirling transparent residue, peeled back to reveal his teeth.

He lets out another howl and smashes his head through the Sno-Cat's window.

He looks up, blood streaming from a slashed eye, nose cut to ribbons. His skin glitters with flecks of glass embedded in it. A grin springs up, huge and obscene in the night.

Siri's fright wells up from a place just above her ribcage. She inspects it, like it's something outside her body. Then she drops on her side, lifts up her foot, and kicks him right in the teeth.

Akinori falls soundlessly from the vehicle.

She fumbles for the gear knob, trying to force the rumbling Sno-Cat into reverse, but then he vaults back up –

Seemingly straight off the snow.

Half his body cresting cleanly through the window.

Blood from his bald head lands in her lap. He writhes like a mad animal, arms by his side.

Trying to worm into the cab.

Looking at her with flat and unsmiling eyes ringed with black.

She can't stop screaming, but she's also moving, reaching over him. She yanks the seatbelt out and winds it rapidly around his neck. It's all she has. Once and twice. Akinori jerks, his right hand in a claw. It flops up from his side and gouges her face. She shrinks back against the passenger door as he wriggles furiously forward, jet-black eyes now leaking with dark tendrils and fixed on her. She can feel a burning crazy heat radiating from him. His bare torso gleams with a sheet of ice.

Her hands fumble behind her. Trapped.

The seatbelt arrests Akinori in place, inches from her.

She finds the door latch and pulls.

She falls backward immediately, hits her head on the compacted snow so hard her world goes black. She fights against it, knowing instinctively she won't wake up again.

She lunges away, stumbling to her feet, dizzy. She falls, picks herself up, and looks back in time to see Akinori's bloody head hanging out of the open door, tongue lolling hungrily.

A hand like driftwood stretches toward her.

His howl rises to a fishwife shriek, and Siri sets her face into the wind. The snow is blinding but if she can't see, neither can Akinori. She runs for her life, faster, faster, until she can't see him or the Sno-Cat or MAPO anymore.

Then the ground swims, up like a lurching bowl, and she blacks out before she cracks into it.

Siri is a Minnesota farmer, born and raised. She knows when the cold is just a weighty mind-monkey she must throw off her back, and when it means real, real danger. This is the second one.

She knows it even before she lifts her head and sees the frozen patch of blood she has been lying in.

The cold has burned out banks of her memory. Whole sections seem reduced to scorched server cabinets, little more than unplugged wires and blackened relays inside. A warm patch on her head twinges deeply when she touches it. She suddenly realizes she has no ski mask on. No goggles around her neck. She pulls her balaclava over her face, scrunching her eyes up against the blowing snow.

No buildings loom, not even in the distance.

No flag lines.

Just snow in all directions, wind tugging hard at her jacket and freezing all sensation from her cheeks.

Dark fear seizes her.

Siri holds it carefully. *Hold that scare in both hands,* Momma would say, *and it can't grow too big to squash.* She pats herself down. She still has her Big Red; that's life now. But no radio inside it, only the lanyard it had once been attached to.

She shivers violently as memories tumble around her brain like clothes in a washing machine. Kathryn. Philip. The black river oozing out of Akinori's flat dark eyes. Her cheek throbs like an aching wound. The heat in her cheek, where he hit her, feels like it is *spreading*.

She looks around, feeling her eyes grow. Beginning to shiver helplessly.

(*Rajan*)

(*Rajan and the stars*)

Antarctica is a desert; it hardly ever snows from the sky. The snow in her face is being kicked up from the ice sheet in long, curling ropes whipping together; it's a no-moon night but the dark sky is still visible. She stays on her knees, scanning the sky. Rajan is at the Pole to study Jupiter with his telescope. What else had he said?

"The Dark Sector is laid out like hands on a clock," Rajan's voice speaks in Siri's head.

She sees it then, a bright unblinking star, and her heart leaps. Jupiter points west at this time of night. And she's lost somewhere in the Dark Sector, which is grid-west of the Station.

The right side of her jaw begins to pulse. It's getting more and more difficult to catch her breath in the thin air. She must hurry or die… but picking the wrong direction will also kill her.

The wind blows east to west at Pole, Rajan is grumbling in her head. *So of course, the tallest drifts to dig through to get to LANDIT are right up my damn steps–*

(*LANDIT?*)

(*His telescope*)

(*East to west it means something*)

Siri turns, slowly, on her hands and knees. The wind is loud... louder... then directly in her ear. Her left ear.

The wind blows east to west at Pole. Come on, Siri, you're almost there.

She had run into the wind. That means she is east of MAPO now; had been headed toward the clean air sector. Nothing in her path except cold and inevitable death.

To find the Station, she needs to cut south.

She looks up at Jupiter. Jupiter in the west. If she keeps Jupiter over her right shoulder, and the wind between her forehead and left ear, she'll be angling south to southwest.

In theory.

She struggles up and up, to her feet. When the options are to walk, or lie down and die in the snow, it's as good a direction as any.

Chapter Fourteen

7:10 AM

At first, the smell of soil and the feel of humidity in the greenhouse are overwhelming. Like eating nothing but bread and dry cheese for months and then being thrust directly into his mummy's Indian kitchen, brimming with spices. But the warmth and humidity are different, and in Antarctica, different is refreshing. Rajan finds the hydroponic plants soothing. He likes the feel of the leaves between his fingers. It relaxes him. Lets him think.

He feels dog-tired, and he hasn't slept in too long, but he needs to think.

Kathryn and Philip. The odd love triangle of Yanis, Dave, and Bethany. Tim, Summer, and him. Siri, Khaled, and him. Richard Mason, not on the ice with them, a lifetime ago and continents away. The three Chinese refugees, now prisoners at ARO with Ben. Bill Gaudin glaring down at them all, stinking of whisky. All ingredients in the boiling pot of the Station, and underneath, brewing, the fright of a situation threatening to burst over them like a storm cloud lurking on the horizon. The anxiety of realizing how isolated they are from help. The inescapable feeling that they are trapped, backs to a cliff, being edged implacably toward the edge; a chess game they didn't know they were playing, but are losing.

Ice-cold hands curling implacably around his throat.

Rajan looks up from his reverie to see Summer looking at him and he jumps back in surprise. “Holy shit!”

“Sorry! I called your name when I came in, but you were zonked!”

He is immediately struck by how pretty she is. Her hair is up, two dark curled tendrils falling on either side of her angular face. Jeans and a patterned tank top seem to flaunt the tight allure of her body, though he's probably thinking that only because jeans have become a rarity in the last few months. Most Polies have taken to wearing sweatpants or an underlayer of thermals, sometimes for unfortunate weeks at a time; something to pull snowgear on top of, or sleep in.

“I was woolgathering far, far away.” Rajan rubs his neck and chuckles. “What's up?”

“Just wanted to tell you that… I thought you handled the whole thing this morning really well.” Her smile is rich and inviting. “The bit about coming together, especially. It hit home for a lot of us. You're good with people. Leading them, I mean.”

Rajan's mind registers the compliment but he's distracted, trying to pick up the thread of his earlier thoughts. He has the distinct feeling he'd noticed something important –

(*one of these is not like the other*)

– but it's slipping away.

Summer hesitates, like she wants to say more, then takes a step back.

“Anyway,” she says, shy now. “Just wanted to tell you that.”

“Well, wait, hang on.”

She stops, tucking one wisp of hair behind her ear. She

looks at him with a speculation that makes him tingle, and Rajan struggles to arrange his thoughts coherently. A corner of his mind is busy resenting how he feels like a clumsy teenager sweet-talking a girl for the first time. "Were you close with Kathryn?"

"No more than you," she says. "She was tight with Greg Penny–"

"The other IceCuber, sure."

"And Rob, too. They spoke German with each other all the time."

So it had been a one-two punch for the old man. This deep into the winter, a Polie friend could feel closer than anyone in the world; a much-needed crutch to lean on when loneliness bared its fangs. Rajan reminds himself to talk to Rob soon.

He voices one of the dark thoughts circling his mind. "I just can't believe Philip killed her. Stalked and killed her. It sounds so… fucking evil, because what was he going to do after that? Play innocent for four months while we worried about a killer in our midst?"

"This is a strange place, Rajan," she says quietly. Something funny hitches in her voice. "I've been coming here four years and every year it seems like… like I learn something new I don't like about myself."

"Anything so far this year?"

The caves of her eyes are like cell doors slamming shut.

"Shit, I'm sorry, that was an awful question."

Her luminous eyes search his. "Have you found anything like that?"

"I'm sure I will."

He looks up in time to see Tim Fulton through the greenhouse window, running down the hall, a panicked look on his face. He doesn't even notice Summer, which gets a bad feeling ticking in Rajan's throat. "I should see what's going on. Maybe the crew is back with the bodies."

He starts moving, then hesitates. "Thank you, Summer. It was sweet of you to find me and tell me that."

Rajan pulls the door open. He gets only a few steps after Tim before Summer yells behind him. "*Hey*. I'm coming with you."

He stops short in the hallway. "Could I stop you if I wanted?"

Her face crinkles agreeably, but he gets the feeling that her eyes are suddenly watchful. "So you *do* remember me."

"Is anything wrong?" Luis Weeks asks as he rolls up his sleeve.

"Nothing at all," Jamie says, very casually. "Need a scrape from you. Actually, why don't you do it?" She smiles brightly. "Just a little flake of skin."

She prepares the slide with his sample, careful to use fresh long gloves. Doc Wei walks over to her. She shifts ever so slightly away from him as she talks.

"He's *crawling,*" she whispers.

"Weeks went inside the Dome-A truck! So whatever this fuzz is…"

"Yeah. Comes from that truck. You didn't screw up the protocol."

"And it spreads by touch."

"Doc!"

Wei whips around.

Behind him, Tim Fulton looks wild. "Doc, there's been another death."

"*What*?" Weeks rises from the exam table, shock on his face.

"An hour after Rajan's all-call–" Tim looks at his watch. "Three hours ago. A Sno-Cat with four people went to the Dark Sector to bring back the bodies. They haven't made it back. I called Yanis to find–"

The door pushes open, and Rajan and Summer spill in.

"That news moved fast even by Pole standards," Jamie remarks from the corner.

"Tim, who was in the Sno-Cat?" Wei asks.

"Siri, she's my best snow operator."

"Siri!" Rajan exclaims. Behind him, Summer's face tightens.

"And Spencer, since he was Philip's boss." Tim continues. "Akinori is a hobbyist photographer, so he was going to document the scene. And Kenny Black."

"So what happened?"

"They stopped answering their radios two hours ago. Yanis was at South Pole Telescope, so I asked him to head over to MAPO. He found their Sno-Cat, but it's empty. And he found Kenny in the snow." Tim's eyes are haunted. "He was beaten to death."

"Explain that." Wei scratches his arms, agitated.

"Yanis said his arm had been ripped *clean off*."

"Where are the others?" Weeks interjects. "Spencer, Siri, Akinori?"

"I've been calling their channels. They've disappeared."

"They're *all* missing?"

"We need to find them!"

"Doc, you need to go take a look at Kenny's body."

"Everyone shut up and let me think," Wei snaps.

He takes a deep breath. Here it is. The moment when he steps up.

(*I'm not ready*)

Out of nowhere, a strange phrase comes to mind –

(*fuckin-A not ready, you bet*)

– then he bats it away. "Jamie, go tell Gaudin and Andrea."

He opens his mouth to issue the next order–

And nothing comes out.

He's out of ideas. Spent. They'd sent four people to get two bodies, and now there's one more body and three missing. Does he send more people out when the last mission has gone badly wrong?

Well? *Does* he?

His brain comes up double-zero. House number, everybody loses.

Wei looks up, eyes empty and helpless, and Rajan steps smoothly in.

"There'll be time to examine the bodies later," Rajan says. He'd looked punched in the gut hearing Siri's name among the missing, but there's no sign of that now. "We have to make the living our focus. The fewer people who know about this, the less people can panic, so I'm looking at the search party right here. Weeks, take Tim and warm up a Sno-Cat. Summer, you help me pack the survival gear. Jamie, tell Gaudin what's happening, but only after we've left. It's 7:20 AM now. How soon can we be ready to push?"

"Top of the hour," Tim says.

"Doc, you should get some sleep." Rajan's voice is scratchy but firm. "We'll need you soon."

Chapter Fifteen

The clinic empties as quickly as it had filled up. Wei Jin feels an immense sense of relief and, just as quickly, a full and *crawling* sense of frustration. He's been making life or death decisions for longer than Rajan has been alive, and yet he'd been unable to make a simple decision the freaking kid soldier had made *in an instant.* Was he slowing down? Or…

Wei stops in his tracks. Jamie, who has started to walk out after Rajan, looks back at him.

Or is Rajan so calm in the face of repeated death –

(*he's military and here he is when the Chinese show up*)

– because he's been *expecting* this to happen?

"You okay, Wei?" Jamie asks.

Wei shudders, suddenly scared.

"Spencer," he says at last. "Spencer went inside the Chinese truck. So did Akinori."

"Okay?"

"And now another person is dead in a brutal fashion. Something requiring raw strength, like heave-tossing Kathryn under MAPO. Like the dead guy who almost punched a hole in the truck roof."

"Wait. You're seeing a connection between the microbes and these deaths?"

"I don't, that's the fucking thing." He lets out a gnashing

sound of frustration. "Weeks proved that the Dome-A truck is the source of microbes. So anyone else who went into that truck, like I did, probably has them on their skin too. But Philip wasn't part of the group that went out to meet the Chinese. I can't draw a line between Dome-A and Philip… which means there's something I'm missing."

After she leaves, Wei tries to take several deep, calming breaths. He's still a doctor, dammit. Still better than most of the quacks running up their retirement accounts in private practice. He just needs to get back to the basics.

He starts with the slides they've collected so far – from him, the Dome-A dead man, Jamie, and Weeks. He unscrews the base plate from the battery-powered analog microscope and hefts it with one hand, now able to place it directly over his arm. He spends several minutes scrutinizing the cellular structure of the tiny microbes clustering sluggishly on his skin, referencing *Schaechter's Mechanisms of Microbial Disease* periodically. He walks by the Percocet cabinet and realizes it's the third time he's done that. In a movie, this would be the montage of him pulling his shit together and having his Eureka moment but, in real life, there's only an agonizingly slow march to Fort Nothing-at-all.

He pushes his way out of the clinic, away from the silky caress of medical temptation. He is dog-tired, but there's something nagging at him. Wei Jin, Chief of Emergency Medicine at Johns Hopkins, wouldn't have rested until he'd figured it out, so neither would his pale junkie ghost.

In the galley the breakfast buffet isn't open yet, but TC and Daniel are hard at work. Jamie's boy-toy Daniel is in his late twenties, conventionally handsome despite his precipitously thinning hair. TC's thick lips are drawn back to reveal snaggleteeth; the Australian's resting expression vacillates between weighing whether to punch his tray of eggs or bear-hug it.

Wei drifts across the galley and pours himself a cup of coffee. It feels like being a first-year resident again. Too tired to think, but no time to sleep before his next shift. Back then he'd sit in the hospital cafeteria, letting people drift around him, managing to find a moment of Zen before another marathon in the ER. He'd surface to find that his bright brain had somehow organized his thoughts as he'd been zoned out, new insights ready for the taking.

So he sits at a small table by himself, and lets his mind drift with the steam seeping out of his coffee cup. Past the frustration of who he had been, who he is now, and the contrast between the two. Past the darkness outside, and the people lost within it. Drifting to the thing that's really important – those microbes, some black, some transparent but still *so many of them*. Dormant.

Waiting.

Waiting for what?

That is the question that really needs to be answered.

Most surgeons his age are prescribing each other Viagra and trying to spend their way out of their social caverns. New Corvettes, new breasts on their influencer girlfriends, new boats and houses. Wei has never been married, lives a five-minute walk from work, and hates parallel parking. Professional drive, not personal, has always been his guiding star, which is why serving as the over-qualified Band-Aid applier at Pole has hit him like a kick in the solar plexus. For all their sakes, he needs to remember his way back to his old self again.

Because his medical instinct, dull as it may be, is telling

him that the string of recent deaths is the *start* of something, not the end.

And as that mysterious something is starting–

A no-shit military officer just happens to be on the crew?

And what does that mean for what comes next?

As he scratches his neck and sips his coffee, another whisper steals into the Zen of his wandering mind.

This whisper does not date back to med school.

It's whiny, unctuous, needy. Nagging, when it's been too long between pills. Urging, *why not two* every time he breaks open a sampler and vows to take only one. Wei keeps snapping out of his medical reverie as his mind boomerangs back in the direction of his supply cabinet.

He takes a gulp of coffee, and it's cold. Frustrated, he jerks upright from his seat.

From a little further away, Jonah looks toward him. "You here to watch the show too?"

Wei realizes the cardboard has been taken down from the galley windows. Stepping forward, he sees the white billow of smoke from the vertical exhaust of a Sno-Cat at the edge of the arches. Its headlights look woeful against the formidable black stove of the polar night.

"Someone's headed off to the Dark Sector."

"Yeah," Doc Wei says, distractedly. He needs more time to put the pieces together before the ice-cold bodies show up. Before he's put on the spot again. He starts to walk away –

(*back to the yum-yums, a quick one-two, one for me and one for you*)

– then stops.

(*just to calm the nerves, hey-hey-hey*)

"Jonah, you've been to ARO recently, right?"

"Normally my answer would be yes, but Ben asked to handle things during the storm."

"Those scientists from Dome-A are out there."

A look of distaste crosses Jonah's face. "And when this season is over, I'm going to have some words with NOAA about Gaudin turning my building into a prison."

Wei's foot is twitching with impatience. "Can I see you in Medical for a moment?"

"What about?"

"One of the, ah, prisoners, as you called them, never got a coronavirus shot," he says breezily. "Just checking if people who have had contact with them are showing any symptoms."

"I haven't been in contact with them at all."

"A negative hypothesis is still useful. Would you mind?"

Doc Wei fusses about Jonah, fresh gloves on to prevent any spread, taking his temperature, looking down his throat, measuring his blood pressure and a host of other equally useless things. His mind is working now, *really fucking working*. He feels like the smartest man alive, and tries not to drown in the shame that washes over him. Is this what it has been like to be him *his whole life*?

"Well, looks like you're fine," he says brightly. "Last box to check is a light sensitivity test. I'll deprive you of light for one minute, then see how your pupils react. Put this on, please."

Wei's gloved hands extend a long cloth napkin that will double as a blindfold. He keeps his patient smile centered as Jonah's eyes scour him inquiringly.

Then Jonah ties it around his eyes, knotting it in the back.

Wei races across the lab and unplugs the analog microscope from its charger. Jonah's hands are on his thighs as he sits upright on the table. Wei points the microscope at them, then places his eye against the viewer.

Nothing at 100x. He scans across Jonah's hands.

There they are.

A small cluster of microbes, huddling together as if for warmth. They are darker, the black flecks more noticeable. He feels the tickle of a hypothesis.

Wei looks up, and Jonah's flat eyes are watching him steadily.

The loosely-tied blindfold has slipped down his nose, sitting around his lower eyelids.

Wei grins uneasily, feeling like a new resident embarrassed by the local hypochondriac. "Light sensitivity for the coronavirus was a bit much, then."

"Every third person around this Station has a PhD," Jonah says evenly. "If you have to lie, you might want to make that lie an above-average one."

"I'm sorry about the subterfuge," Wei says, with difficult dignity. "I don't want anyone to worry about a wild theory."

"But?"

Words coated with fentanyl dribble out of his mouth. "Have you had any direct physical contact – a handshake, a hug, anything – with Spencer Kaur?"

"No."

"You're sure?"

Jonah's face wrinkles with amiable humor. "Doc, I can count on my fingers the number of people I even bother to talk to. I'm sure."

"Luis Weeks?"

Jonah thinks for a while before answering. "No."

"Akinori Nakagawa."

"No."

"Rajan."

"We've hung out. But no physical contact."

There's only one other person, then, who could have had first-hand exposure to the Dome-A truck. Because the truck hadn't driven itself. Its drivers were resident at ARO, with–

"Ben."

He answers immediately. "Yes. Two days ago, during our handover at ARO. Just before the windstorm came in. We shook hands."

Wei's eyes sharpen. "Ben and Philip Cunningham. Was there a connection there?"

Jonah's eyes narrow. "Tell me why you need to know."

Wei sees, immediately, that it would be pointless to argue with him. "Okay. Let me show you something."

He talks the NOAA scientist through using the magnification knob as he points the microscope at his own skin. "It's a microbial... well, normally I'd call it an infestation, except it's not really doing anything. I could flake it off, piece by piece, if I wanted to. It doesn't burrow, and it's not engaged in mitosis. But I'm positive that its source is the Dome-A truck."

He takes Jonah through his reasoning chain. Weeks is crawling with millions of the microbes, so is he, and so was the dead Chinese scientist in the truck. Jamie has them from incidental contact with him. Jonah has them, in low concentration, probably from similar contact with Ben... and Ben likely has them from the Dome-A scientists being imprisoned at ARO.

"The sheer number of organisms on Weeks and myself indicate that they multiply fast, but I haven't been able to determine under what conditions. It could be something environmental in the truck, maybe radiation? But the resulting reaction might be more insidious."

Jonah looks up, his face impassive.

It's helping Doc Wei to lay his thoughts out aloud. "There have been three deaths on the ice in a short span of time – all violent. The Chinese scientist in that truck either bashed his own head in, or somebody did it for him. Philip beat Kathryn to death. And just an hour ago, I found out Kenny Black was beaten to death too." Jonah's arms hump up in gooseflesh. "I don't have the full story, but Spencer and Akinori were there, and they both went into the Dome-A truck. A series of violent deaths since that truck arrived, and maybe not coincidentally, that truck also brought a microbial infection with it. It spreads by touch and seems to have an exponential capacity for growth." Hearing it out loud, Doc Wei realizes that he's very worried indeed.

"And Philip?"

"Philip doesn't fit that pattern. He didn't go out to meet the Chinese traverse. He hasn't had contact with the Dome-A truck or people, unless..."

"Unless there's a connection between him and Ben. That's why you're asking."

"Yes."

"Thank you, Doctor. Yes, there was a connection. I'm fairly certain they were lovers."

"Ben is gay?" Wei exclaims.

"I believe so."

"He should have disclosed that to me."

"So you can write it down in a file?" Jonah shakes his head. "I think Ben volunteered for storm duty at ARO so he could have a little honeymoon with Philip. If Ben is crawling with microbes, as you describe, then Philip must have been too."

So all three violent deaths could be linked to microbial exposure from the Dome-A truck or crew. Wei feels his skin go cold.

Because he has the microbes on him too, as thick as anyone.

A bright question flares in his mind and begins racing around like a jockey on a horseracing track.

Do the microbes have a gestation period? A time-based activation?

Is he on a clock that ran out for Philip, Spencer and Akinori?

Jonah stands. "Thanks for telling me about the missing people."

"Hang on." Fear twists beneath his calm outer demeanor. "Do you know Rajan's private channel number?"

"Fifty-one," he replies. "Like Area 51."

That joke hits a little too close to home.

The doctor remains still for a long time after Jonah leaves. Hefting the radio up and down in his hand. Then he presses the transmit button.

"Rajan, this is Doc Wei on Channel 51."

The sound of loud static. "Rajan here." His voice is fuzzy and indistinct; he's far away.

"I need you to bring the bodies back so I can examine them. Kathryn, Philip, Kenny."

"Doc, there are three people lost out here. In this claustrophobic darkness. Even with cold weather gear, they don't have long." His voice is even, but Wei hears the strain underlining every syllable. "I can't break off the search for the living to bring back the dead."

Panic creeps up on Wei with its nightrobe open and gathers him into its depths. *They're probably dead already,* he wants to scream, *but I'm alive, and I may be next*!

Somehow, he manages to keep his voice level. "But your Sno-Cats won't run forever in the cold. When you come back to warm them up before heading back out, bring a body with you. Any one."

"Fair enough," Rajan says.

"I need to examine it away from the main Station. Bring it to the fuel arches. I'll have Keyon Geerts clear a spot."

Chapter Sixteen

There's something trying to get Siri's attention.

(*dying death please*)

She fights her eyes to half-mast with a pronounced effort. Her eyelids are gummed together by half-melted ice. Her arm drags across the floor –

(*carpet it's carpet*)

– and she pushes up to a sitting position.

Her body explodes into the cramps of dead circulation. Blood pumps through her veins, making her limbs jerk. The pain is a good sign; she hasn't suffered nerve damage.

Siri is thirsty; thirsty like she has never been in her life. Her throat is a dry well layered in sandpaper. She reaches down to a large finger of ice stuck to her boot, pulls it off. She lets out a groan of satisfaction as it turns slushy on her snowburned lips, which is when she realizes that her face hurts.

Really hurts.

She had kept her balaclava up, her face in the hood of her jacket. She's still in Big Red and her snowpants. This doesn't feel like frostbite–

(*worm. Worming into the Sno-Cat*)

(*seatbelt around his neck wrap it up tight tighter TIGHTER*)

It comes back to her in a hot rush. Akinori's hand, frozen in a meat claw, gouging her. A strange heat where he'd gotten her, like a glowing sun on her face, even though she can see her breath pluming.

She catches sight of the industrial-size heater across the single-room building. Her cramping legs cry out, but she sets her lips in a firm line and pulls herself across the carpet to it. Slams the power switch with the heel of her hand. The coils in the heater begin to click and hiss.

The slash in her cheek lights up with a bright lancing pain that makes her flinch away –

(*dying death no no*)

– but her head is ringing like a bell now. A soft moan bubbles past her lips, a sound like the whistle of a kettle on a hot burner. It's time to lie down, and this time she can let herself do it.

When Siri reawakens, the ice on her jacket has melted into slush. The cut on her face is no longer pulsing. Still, the room keeps spinning for several long moments. The snowdrifts outside have permanently darkened the windows against the winking starlight, and a single bulb flickers with tentative light from the greasy gasoline generator.

This is LANDIT.

She totters forward on wooden legs to the worn desk and begins pulling at drawers.

The last drawer is locked. She wrenches it open with a grunt. Inside lies a high-frequency radio set, with a hand-held microphone. She can call for help.

It hits her then, with all the force of a raised sledgehammer, and she bursts into tears. How narrowly she has escaped the cold with her life. LANDIT is nothing more than a corrugated metal container on stilts on the empty plain. Even after the blowing snow cleared enough to see the rotating telescope dome atop the half-buried container, and its beckoning red beacon, Siri remembers doubting if she could stay upright long enough to make it there.

She holds the radio mike with both hands, like a prayer, sobbing between deep shuddering breaths. Siri wasn't raised with religion, but in that moment, she feels touched by a power beyond the world of her senses. She should have died out there, but for some reason beyond her understanding, she has been spared.

She dials up Channel 51 and presses the button, tasting her own tears on the mike. She had been the one to jokingly assign that channel to Rajan at the start of the season.

"Rajan, do you copy?"

He responds immediately, like he has been waiting for her to call. *"Siri."*

"Hey, man," she says weakly, and feels tears collect in her eyes. "Hey, it's been a day."

The door to the LANDIT enclosure bursts open and Rajan fills the entrance. The cold from the door makes Siri's cheek light up, but before she can consider it further she is swallowed up in a bear hug. She laughs into his chest and feels the sudden lurch of tears again. It feels really good to be hugged, and she clutches onto him, eyes bright.

"I was fucking worried about you," he says.

She looks up at him, fondly aware of how comical they look side-by-side. He is a broad-shouldered Indian man, darkly handsome, with a big sloping head capped by icy curly hair, and she is a pixie-small Scandinavian at four feet and ten inches tall. He grins down at her and –

(*don't do it*)

– ruffles her short spiky blond hair affectionately. He knows she hates that, and she laughs weakly.

"Dude, I was worried about me too. I think your astronomy lesson saved my life."

Tim closes the door behind Summer and squeezes around Rajan to hug her. Summer stands behind him, face inscrutable as ever.

Tim sounds like he's also close to crying. "We thought we'd lost you."

Siri feels a sudden fondness for her boss. Hell, for *everyone* at the South Pole; even Summer, whom she has had a fair number of unfavorable thoughts about. *We're dysfunctional as all hell, but we're family.*

"Where are Akinori and Spencer?" Tim asks.

Siri feels her face tighten. "Last I saw of Akinori, he was trying to kill me."

"Uh..." Rajan's eyes are heavy, two cold flints knifing out of wintry ground. "Was he..."

He makes a gesture with his jacket, like it has fallen off his shoulders.

Her eyes widen. "Yeah, he didn't even have a shirt on. And Spencer was trying to take his clothes off." She snaps up. "Spencer killed Kenny. He... he..."

"We found him. We found his body at MAPO." Rajan nods quickly.

"What the hell is going on?" she whispers.

"I wish I freaking knew. But judging by this–" He gestures at the sullen purple marks on his own throat– "We're both lucky to be alive."

Siri touches her cheek. "*Spencer took off his boots.* Right there on the ice. I've never seen anything like it."

Summer lets out a long, dry breath. "There's only one way the body responds to that kind of exposure."

Tim and Siri both nod soberly.

"You didn't find any sign of them?"

Tim shakes his head. "The wind is up to fifty knots now. If Spencer and Akinori keeled over, they're at the bottom of a new snow dune somewhere between here and the South Pole." He looks at Rajan, as if for approval. "It would take a coordinated grid search effort to find them."

Rajan nods.

Siri can see that he understands.

When he speaks, his voice is as tuneless as the ringing of a cracked tower bell. "Let's grab a body for Doc and head back. Gaudin can decide whether we should keep searching."

Except there's no way Gaudin will approve that. He'll make noises about the darkness, the storm, the risk. He'll want to wait for daylight. There'll be a different Station Manager in the summer, and recovering the bodies in four-foot drifts will be their problem.

And Rajan knows that.

By passing the buck to Gaudin, he has effectively decided they won't be searching anymore.

Somehow, he has become the lynchpin people turn to for tough decisions. For better or worse, Rajan is their Captain now.

And their winter crew has dwindled from forty-one to thirty-six.

They drive away from LANDIT, following flag lines to MAPO. They pull up beside the other Sno-Cat; its engine is silent and will probably never start again. Siri sees, with a little shudder, that the passenger door still gapes open.

If she looks inside, she knows she'll see blood on the seatbelt.

Rajan looks back at her. "Are you okay?" His voice is very gentle.

There's a high atonal dinging in her ears. "I'm fine."

"We need to pick up a body for Doc," he says. "Just one."

Siri sits very still. "Take Kathryn. She's already wrapped up for transport. They… before they…"

"Yeah."

"Be careful, okay?" she says. "I don't know what's going on, but –"

"It's okay. If she's wrapped, the scoop on the Sno-Cat will do all the work."

Tim looks over. "Should we get Philip too?"

"He killed her," Summer says bluntly. "He can stay down there a little longer."

Chapter Seventeen

SOUTH POLE STATION POPULATION: 36 (PRISONERS: 3; DECEASED: 5)

Is he a psychopath?

Keyon Geerts has wondered this often, with no particular emotion about the question. When you spend your days thinking about how to troll and manipulate the people in close proximity to you, for no other reason than that their angst entertains you, you *should* ask yourself some hard questions. Is he a psychopath?

No, Keyon has decided. He just… doesn't care about the things most people care about.

More of a sociopath, if anything. And what's wrong with that? The word's ugly connotations aside, feelings are terrible. They torture you. Pop up when least desired and roil your every waking moment. He's been through his fair share of childhood trauma – perhaps a few people's share of childhood trauma – and he has no desire to feel that leaky and vulnerable again.

Keyon suspects that a large number of people would choose to be like him, if they could. The life of a sociopath is pretty calm, all things considered. There's not much camaraderie or caring, but there isn't much crying or anxiety, either.

And planning the season's chaos is just… fun. He's like a kid assembling a dollhouse without instructions, trying pieces forward and sideways before deciding where they slot in best.

You're a clot waiting to turn into an aneurysm, Keyon, his ex-fiancé had said to him on her way out of his life. You're a splinter of bone on the hunt for a soft organ to puncture.

In the meantime, though, there's never a shortage of work.

The word comes down through Weeks that an area in front of the arches needs to be cleared of snow, per Doc Wei. Keyon thinks about asking why, then decides he doesn't care. He's been fuzzy lately, losing time, his mind a boomerang in a dark cave ever since he'd walked out to End-of-the-World to look at –

(*and touch don't forget you touched him he was cold like marble*)

– the dead Chinese visitor from Dome-A.

Is he a sociopath? His mind drifts back to that question. He hadn't been horrified by the mangled body. The hard stripe voice had been silent in contemplating wonder, but interested. Fascinated, even.

He snaps himself back to reality. *Come on, Keyon, focus.* Things are evolving rapidly. People are *dead*. His *Guernica* of chaos will paint itself if he doesn't get his mind right, and quickly.

Keyon Geerts climbs into the cab of the last Sno-Cat at nine in the morning, six hours after Rajan's all-call about Philip and Kathryn's death. He works within the warm cab for a half-hour, using the scooper to bulldoze away snow piled up against the entrance to the sub-surface arches. He feels itchy below his ski mask but ignores it, mind busy with figuring out new angles on his game. Rajan and Summer will be his targets, he's decided, with an arc to draw Siri and

Khaled in. He's already planted the unsigned solstice card in Summer's lab that will kick it all off. Not particularly elegant or clever as a first move, but the deepest graves start with tiny scoops of dirt.

He emerges from the warmed cab once the job is done, shovel in hand, to knock snow loose from between the teeth of the scooper. The fuel arches swing between five degrees below and five above freezing. If he doesn't clear the scooper, best case, the snow will freeze into blocks that will need to be ice-picked out. Worst case, it'll melt to water, then freeze on the floor and take him out next time. The hard-stripe knows this well. He had once spread snow around Corey Biesen's Sno-Cat, then melted it with a heat gun. Watching that asshole break his hip had been a highlight of last winter.

Almost as soon as he steps outside, Keyon begins to feel different.

Less cold, for one.

A gentle, almost suffusing warmth spreads deliciously down his arms, then up his neck. He pulls off his ski mask as he works. He could whistle. It's actually warm enough out to whistle.

Less than a minute later, he gets back into the Sno-Cat, and turns the heat up to the maximum out of habit. Almost immediately a shocking pain shoots across his body, stabbing him in all the places that were just warm.

(*but it'll feel good outside try it try it please*)

He feels tingly for a long time, even after returning to the warmth of his room. Katie calls, but he lets the phone in his room ring. Suddenly, he doesn't feel so well.

* * *

Ben swims up out of sleep with a headache and a hard painful sweat all over his body. The ceiling seems closer to his head. The walls pulse with their proximity. He knows what his shrink would say – Ben, you're fixating – *but you're not here, doc, so you can't help me.*

A sudden furious anger sweeps through him. Screw it. He has to help himself. If they find out and fire him, so be it.

He picks up the phone.

TC's smooth Australian voice comes down the line. "Benjamin."

"I'm sorry to call you at work."

"Nah mate, brekky is out and it's self-serve. Talk to me."

"Listen, ah, I… I can't sleep. I'm having trouble sleeping. I heard you might know someone who can help with that?"

Ben cringes as the line falls silent. He has no choice but to wait. No choice but to twitch, either. Itching his scalp, then his chest, then his legs. *God, I need a hit. It's just the only thing that makes any kind of sense right now.*

TC's voice sounds careful and guarded. "I'm the guy."

"You are? Hey, awesome. Can I… can I get some, ah, can I get a small supply, maybe?"

TC lapses into silence again and Ben's knuckles turn white on the phone handset. Please, he almost says aloud. He needs something, *anything*, to take his mind away from the prison of this reality.

"This for you or someone else?"

The flood of relief is so large it turns his knees into water. "Just me. Just me, I promise."

"I could work something out, mate. But we should talk terms in person."

Ben looks up at the clock. “Uh, I’m supposed to be manning ARO for the next day or two, but I could come over.”

“Probably best if we did it out there?”

“Ah. Makes sense. Great, great. Thanks so much.”

“It’s not easy to come by.”

“Totally,” he says hurriedly. “A premium on the rare stuff is to be expected.”

A sunny smile enters TC’s voice. “Then I’ll pop over, end of my shift. Should be done soon. You got implements, then?”

Ben can’t help it; he’s grinning, slack-jawed, like a kid on a sugar rush. “I’ve used an apple before.”

“Ha, good luck with freshies, mate. Dave, though.”

“Atkins? The machinist?”

“He fashioned something I can bring. It’s not easy to come by either.”

“I’m good for both.”

10:20 AM

“Okay,” Wei says. “Moment of truth.”

He pressurizes the Hazmat suit.

Oxygen blows past his face and clears his facemask. He checks his leak valves. “My suit integrity looks good.”

Jamie grumbles under her breath as she tries to force her bunny boot into the steel-toed overboots. The plastic crinkles around her like a potato chip bag. The Pole is equipped with two sets of Level B Hazmat gear in case of a chemical fire. Fully encapsulating chem-suits, replete with two-way communications, chemically resistant gloves, and oxygen tanks for isolated air and positive pressure.

"Let's get moving before I melt in here." Jamie's voice is clipped and metallic in the suit's internal speakers.

South Pole Station is two long hallways stacked on top of each other and four dormitory wings thrusting out of one side, all sitting on a massive set of stilts. Down the winding stairs from Destination Zulu, at the bottom of the beer can, they drop into tunnels carved beneath the ice shelf like long legs under the body of a spider.

They flit between pools of light from generator-powered bulbs hung every few yards. Jagged blocky teeth in the walls and ceiling mark where the ice has been hand-cut with old-fashioned chainsaws. Pipes carrying water, fuel and sewage run by their knees. In the ambient temperature of minus 50 degrees, the oppressive heat inside the chem-suit begins dropping off, and Wei finds himself glad for Big Red underneath.

Several "shrines" are carved into the ice walls; shelf-like cutouts left behind by each winter crew to commemorate their season. Most are filled with inside jokes but others are more obvious, like the frozen can of peaches marked by a placard: "We ate everything… but not this."

They weave through the food arch, where five years of frozen cans and meats are stored at minus 30 degrees on towering pallets reaching up to the cavernous ceiling. If you're eating something less than three years old at Pole, the joke goes, you were probably lied to. The darkened cargo storage arch is next, then the gigantic subterranean warehouse splits toward the vehicles in the fuel arch and the massive fuel bladders. The ice tunnel dead-ends in a dimly-lit spiral metal staircase up to a frozen hatch, with its ornamental-looking ice chandelier.

Wei's eyes fix upward. The ice crystals have frozen there,

but in an ugly splotch. Someone has been through this hatch, and recently.

To make matters worse, his mouth is dry in an all-too-familiar way.

The radio squawks. Rajan. “Doc, we’re here.”

They huff their way through the porthole up into the winter darkness and wait in the small area that Keyon cleared earlier. The Sno-Cat trundles toward them, headlights shining blearily.

“What’s with the haz suits?” He can hear the surprise in Rajan’s voice.

“Just a precaution. Don’t read too much into it.”

The Sno-Cat’s scoop lowers slowly, but Kathryn’s body still hits the ice with a teeth-gritting flat thump. “Give me some light, but I need room,” Wei says.

The Sno-Cat rumbles backward to a stop twenty meters away. Its headlights illuminate the wrapped body and, even through the plastic layers, Wei can see Kathryn’s eyes, half-lidded and staring at him almost accusingly.

He swallows.

“Cut away the plastic, but try not to touch the body,” he tells Jamie.

Wei opens his medical case on the snow. He powers up a heat gun and warms the microscope, then Jamie reaches out for it. She looks back and Kathryn’s face shifts.

Jamie screams. The microscope thuds dully into the snow.

“Did you see that?” she shrieks.

“What? See what?”

“Her face moved!”

Wei looks at the body. For a moment the aurora australis glow darkly in Kathryn’s open pupils, like a cat’s eyes. He starts to reply, then freezes. Kathryn's face *slides,* like a reflection in a lake, sideways toward him.

"I see it," he says tightly. He reaches a finger out toward the body. Closer…

He waits.

Closer again…

A transparent layer lurches up toward his finger like an angry pimple, and Wei snatches his hand back like it's been burned.

"Put the microscope above her cheek. *Don't touch her."*

Jamie extends both arms, holding the microscope stiffly, body craned back as far as she can get. Wei gets down into a squat, and pitches slowly forward until his faceshield rests against the microscope. He rotates the magnification knob and her skin jumps into focus.

Kathryn is *crawling* with microbes.

Every inch of her skin is covered with completely transparent microbes. So many, in fact, that they have congealed into one continuous layer, *writhing* with movement.

"There's… billions of them," he pants, slack-jawed. "They're active. They're moving!" His face presses against the microscope and Jamie grunts, using all her strength to hold it up and away from Kathryn's skin. "I can actually *see* them multiplying!"

The cell division rate is faster than anything Wei has ever seen. The growth is beyond exponential. The writhing motion is layers of microbes sliding against one another, *rotating*. The layers on top, closer to the environment, are sliding down, deeper, closer to Kathryn's face.

To their *nutrient* source, he realizes with a slow horror.

The cold air is a catalyst, speeding up the mitosis. The

newly born cells need food, so they burrow into themselves, like a knife cutting through old skin–

His vision starts to blur.

Wei lifts his head from the microscope and Jamie lets out a limp sigh of relief. His head bobs inside his Hazmat suit like a balloon inside a kid's tent. Everything looks sliding and unclear, like he's underwater.

"What is it?" Jamie asks.

"My mask freezing up, I think."

"I'll give it some heat."

She places the microscope in his medical case and turns the heat gun on. Aims it in his direction.

The faceshield of the suit instantly turns black.

Wei jumps backward, arms flailing. "What the fuck!" Jamie exclaims.

As soon as he gets some distance from her, the black begins to swim, then fade. It hits him like a hammer.

The blackness in the microbes is heat-triggered.

Like a scar.

"Jamie, get the microscope!" he barks. "Look at my faceshield in it!"

She scrambles to get it. He holds his arm out, shining a flashlight on his own face, dimly aware of how ludicrous they must look to the people in the Sno-Cat.

"Holy shit, doc," Jamie pants. "There are *so many* on you. Your suit is covered in them."

"It's okay." It's okay, right? "Uh, I'm positively pressurized. They can't get inside."

Nevertheless, his heart is galloping. Sweat collects at his temples. "They're incredibly active… that's what was happening when Kathryn's face moved. They literally multiplied upward, trying to reach a new source of food.

It's… it's like…" His hands flounder in the air. "Imagine being born, and then immediately giving birth yourself, and hoisting your baby up on your shoulders… *repeated thousands of times over*. Given their microscopic size… bridging that distance would be like traveling up from here to the Space Station."

His faceshield is transparent again, occasionally swimming. He's seeing through the microbes.

Wei presses the transmit button on his waist, turning to the parked Sno-Cat. "I need to see Philip. It's urgent and could answer some questions about what happened to Akinori and Spencer. Can you drive us over?"

"Gonna be a tight fit with those suits."

On their intercom, Jamie: "We can't ride in the cab. Not with these microbes as active as they are."

Wei goes out over the radio. "We're running a no-touch protocol. Can we ride in the scoop?"

Siri comes on. "You can, but it'll be a cold ride."

"We're not exposed to the wind, and our air is internally circulated. Shouldn't be too bad."

The Sno-Cat rumbles forward. "I'd like to drop Siri off here, doc," Rajan says. "She was out in the cold for a while, she needs to rest."

The yum-yum whisper in Wei's brain has been chased away by the urgency of the situation. Akinori and Spencer had been outside for tens of minutes. At the growth rates he's seeing, they would have been overtaken. He has no idea how long Siri has been outside, but it has been a while.

If the organisms really are cold-activated, any dormant microbes on Siri could explode in number, even in the short walk from the Sno-Cat to the Station.

He needs to know more before putting her at risk.

"She's safest if she sticks with us for now."

The Sno-Cat's scooper arm levers down, until it's almost touching the ground. Jamie climbs in, awkwardly, shuffling forward until her back is flattened against the curve of the snow scoop. Wei clambers up next, knees popping painfully. It lifts, and they slide forward, stomachs pancaking over half the windshield like gigantic white bug splats.

Inside, Summer says, "This is one of the weirder things I've seen in Antarctica."

With a lurch that smacks them against the windshield hard enough to click their teeth together, the Sno-Cat turns, away from the splashing lights of the Station. Wei looks over his shoulder at Kathryn's body. The edges of the plastic flap up over her face, then back to the snow. Nausea tilts his stomach, and he squeezes his eyes shut.

Inside his suit, the temperature drops another degree.

The dream tatters and unravels, a rancid aftertaste of some forgotten meal.

This time Ben sees Rajan in his reverie, stumbling backward. Sees the fear burning across his face like a cloth-wrapped torch in a gothic cellar. Philip wraps his (*their*) hands around Rajan's neck, and then it's just Ben, enjoying the raw feel of choking the breath out of him.

(*they might be into it*)

(*very bad crazy when very bad cold*)

Ben wakes up to find he's still laughing a little.

Though he'd turned the heat off hours ago, and it's cold enough to see his breath, sweat still pours off his body in sticky waves. His leg vibrates against the coffee table. It builds into a frenzied knock until he can't stand it anymore, and he springs across the room to find TC's bag of hydroponically-grown marijuana.

Ten times the going cost on the mainland, but he had paid it gratefully.

Ben flicks the lighter, takes a deep hit, holds it in his lungs for as long as he can.

The trembling in his leg slows, then stops.

The walls relax and sag away from him. His head clears, and without thinking, he exhales smoke that curls lazily up toward the ceiling.

Oh shit.

Smoking indoors! If Jonah gets so much as a whiff of marijuana, Ben will find himself on the plane of shame with the other misbehaved or undesired winter-overs, facing a NOAA inquiry board on the other end. He rushes next door into the Dobson observation room. It occupies the corner of ARO's second floor, with tall windows on adjacent walls for ozone measurements, and a door that opens to the second-floor landing. Ben throws the door open, and cruelly cold air sweeps in at once. His icy breath thickens.

Weirdly, the hot painful tingling subsides… like a fading campfire.

He stands in the doorway for a long minute, enjoying how refreshing it feels. Like standing on the beach in Diego Garcia, really. All that's missing is water between his toes.

One more hit. Then we'll be able –

(*we?*)

– to think clearly.

Ben flexes his fingers. They're stiff, which is odd, because he doesn't feel cold.

In fact, the longer he stands there, the better he feels.

Chapter Eighteen

11:10 AM

Siri hadn't lied; it's a long and cold ride to MAPO in the scooper of the Sno-Cat. Wei begins to see his own breath inside his faceshield and tries desperately not to think about what might soon begin multiplying on his skin.

Positive pressure or not, the microbes are already inside the suit with him.

Tim pulls up by the dead Sno-Cat for the third time that day. He lowers the scooper as delicately as he can, but Wei and Jamie still half-fall out.

"Don't leave the warmth of the cab under any circumstances," Wei says over the radio. "We'll make this quick."

(*you better believe it*)

He wades awkwardly down the drift, followed by Jamie. The flashlight barely cuts through the darkness under MAPO and he almost steps into the body. The thick frozen splashes of blood are frozen over and sprinkled with white snowflakes, but the gruesome manner of Philip's death is still immediately evident.

Wei realizes he doesn't need the microscope.

Something transparent is sliding across Philip's features in a thick gluey gel.

Sloping away.

Then closer.

Like ocean tides lapping up the beach and sullenly withdrawing.

Wei stares at this cycle in revulsion. Something reaches off the body's face – a cold, transparent, eager death mask with the distorted features of Philip Cunningham – collapses, churns, then rears back up toward him. Jamie utters a desolate little laugh that slithers up and down his spine uncomfortably.

"Interpolating backward from Kathryn's rate of growth," he says, "Philip definitely had microbial company on his skin when he went homicidal."

A light dusting of blown snow covers Philip's chest. Wei brushes it away. His gloved hand comes away with a cataract of heaving microbes.

Jamie sucks in her breath uneasily. "He was half-naked, man, what the *fuck*."

Philip's bare chest is blue, nipples like purple-black bruises. A fine layer of frost covers his skin. Here, too, the transparent layer is thick and moving, a rubbery gel spreading over his chest. A bootprint is imprinted onto the snow by his side, where Philip's fingers have been crushed under the surface. Wei pulls his hand out of the snow and sets it on top of his chest. Almost immediately, the throbbing gel seeps toward it.

"Interesting," he murmurs.

"What?"

"See this? These microbes respond to *levels* of cold. His hand was buried in the snow, and now that's where the action is. The snow offered enough insulation that the microbes couldn't reach their full growth rate. They must have an extremely cold activation temperature."

All of a sudden, he becomes aware of two things.

It's cold inside his suit.

And he's starting to feel a hot tingling itch. In fact, he's been itchy for a *while*.

"I don't have much time left," he says, an apprehensive flicker in his eyes. The temperature in his suit is dropping, but he's starting to feel like he's slowly being pushed into an oven. "Heat gun, Jamie."

He lifts the microscope and angles it at Philip's hand, trying to catch the edge of the advancing gelatinous mucus oozing greedily down his wrist. Tens of millions of microbes on this arm alone. Enough that he can *see* them flowing downhill.

"Blast it," he says. Sweat trickles down his face. "Right above this edge."

The air shimmers in front of her heat gun. Almost immediately, the edge of the microbes turns black, curling at the edges like paper in a fire. The advance stops, then backs up, swelling at Philip's forearm as if trying to find an equilibrium spot. The blackness grows quickly, a Sharpie-like line emerging and thickening on Philip's wrist.

"Less heat now."

Jamie backs the gun away. The blackness fades quickly, like it had on his faceshield. In less than a minute, the edge is translucent again, but he can detect a black tinge to individual microbes through the microscope. That's what his microbes look like, he thinks. Inside his suit.

"Now scorch them."

Jamie holds the gun right above Philip's wrist. The splotch of deep black grows thicker and tighter, radiating outward in evil ripples that match the heat output of the gun. The microbes scald to a crisp as far up as Philip's left elbow. On his chest, the black edges retreat away from his left side, leaving the skin bare and exposed to the cold. He can see Philip's ribs, and a tide-like movement under the skin.

They're down there, *eating* him. Sucking him dry like a juicebox.

"Leave it there. One more whole minute."

They wait. Jamie on her knees by the corpse, Wei trying to breathe evenly and not think about how cold –

(*and then hot*)

– he feels inside his suit. His heart beats loudly in his ears. He presses his radio and describes his own symptoms.

"Do any of you feel hot anywhere? Or a tingling. Like after your leg falls asleep."

Jamie looks up at him. Her eyes are too wide. "That's what Philip reported when he came into the clinic."

Siri comes on the radio. "I do. Only my face though. My cheek."

"Do you know if... did anything..."

"Akinori," she says flatly.

Jamie withdraws the heat gun, and Wei places the microscope just above the blackened edges of the microbial advance. He can immediately tell the organisms are dead. Shriveled up, solidly black all the way through like charcoal, with no movement even at the highest magnification level.

He pans up to the expanding black circles. Up by Philip's elbow, the microbes look dormant, like those on his own skin. Tinged black from exposure to heat, but not dead.

Dormant.

He stands. "Time to get the hell out of here."

The sauna at South Pole was only used on special occasions, such as the Pole's 300 challenge, which created members to one of the most exclusive clubs in the world.

New applicants to the '300 Club', and previous members re-attempting the feat, met in the sauna when it dropped below minus 100 F outside. They would warm the sauna up to an almost unbearable 200 F, then strip every article of clothing off except for boots, and race out the back door of the Station for *the run*. To be a member of the 300 Club, you had to make it one-hundred yards to the Ceremonial South Pole and circle it while naked, crossing every line of longitude on the globe. Then back to the three-hundred-degree swing of the sauna, and plenty of alcohol to commemorate running "around the world", naked and unafraid.

This time, however, the use of the sauna is grimmer. Life and death, even.

Wei leads the way around the Station, to the ladder up the outside to the door of the sauna. "Come on, quickly! Everyone goes," he says, firmly. "Everyone. Hurry!"

Wei and Jamie, Summer and Tim, Siri and Rajan. The six of them squeeze into the antechamber of the sauna. Siri starts moaning as soon as the door to the cold closes behind them. She clutches her face, nails piercing her skin in half-moons, and twists back toward the exit.

"Stop her!" Wei barks. Summer barely catches her before she reaches the door handle. "Does anyone know how to start this thing?"

"I do." Tim leaps across to the outer room, flicking on the dark red sauna lights. "How high?"

"Hot as it goes. Two hundred degrees." Wei is starting to feel scorched himself. In fact, he actively *does not want* the heat to go any higher. 200 F doesn't just sound like torture. It sounds like –

(*dying*)

– death. That same pain is etched into Siri's face.

As the heaters kick on, Wei understands what it would be like to be nailed into his own coffin and then shot like a bullet right into the sun. "Everyone strip," he pants. "Your clothes probably have more microbes on them than you do."

They look at each other awkwardly. Hesitating.

"Fucking get on with it!" Wei roars. His brain is frying sunny side up right behind his eyes, breathlessly writhing at the idea of *more* heat. "Jamie, *get this damn thing off me.*"

She reaches for the zipper on his suit. Rajan wrestles himself out of Big Red. Siri's fingers dig, like claws, into her bleeding cheek, then she lunges against Summer for the door.

"Tim, help her!" Jamie points. "Get her clothes off!"

Siri's eyes are capital O's of pain as they drag her to the floor. Her fingers scratch at the floor. Two fingernails peel back like wet decals.

Wei screams as Jamie tugs his mask off, and the last of the icy air inside spills out. The heat of the sauna encloses him like a rubber mask. "I can't breathe," he gasps. "I need..."

He pushes across the sauna. Dragging Jamie with him, ignoring her warning shouts.

He needs to go outside.

Just for a second.

He's going to die in here if he can't–

Rajan barrels into him. Wei stumbles to a knee and Rajan grabs him from behind. "Go, Jamie," he grates. "Get the suit off."

Summer looks over her shoulder at Wei, who is almost to the door, then doubles her efforts to pull Siri's windpants off. For a few moments the reddened room is filled with the grim sounds of exertion. The pile of clothes in the corner grows. Summer pins Siri down to the dry planks while Tim hurriedly strips, then they change positions.

"I'm sorry," Tim whispers to Siri as she bucks under him, naked and focused on nothing but the door. "I'm sorry I'm sorry I'm sorry–"

Rajan and Jamie pull Wei up and seat him on a warm bench that's rapidly growing hot. He clutches himself, nails digging into his skin. "It hurts." His eyes look haunted. "They're hurting me."

Jamie sits before him and picks up his hands in hers. "It's a survival response. Be strong, Wei. You can *do* this."

He nods, sweat sloughing off his brow. His head throbs like a tender tomato too full of quickly expanding blood. She releases him and he trembles on the bench, but doesn't move for the door. She hurriedly unzips her sweaty overboots, stepping out of the Hazmat suit.

Wei looks up at Rajan, who is already naked. He sees a scarred dimple in his chest, like something firm was once shoved into his skin. He knows the look of an impact scar from a body armor plate. A pretty close-range shot, from the looks of it.

"Save the suits," Wei's teeth grind together like nails on a chalkboard. "Stretch them out, let them warm. We might need them."

"Let's do the same with Big Reds," Rajan suggests.

The temperature gauge flicks above +100 F, and suddenly, both Siri and Wei scream, a base scream that drills into everyone's ears like thin silver nails. It goes on and on, climbing and echoing and vibrating in their skulls.

Siri's face turns black.

Darkness spills outward from the slash on her cheek, scalding tears flowing with it.

Wei's hand reaches out, grasping, and Siri puts her hand in his.

His arms morph into black, like an invisible blowtorch crisping him.

The other four back away from them. Siri and Wei are still screaming. Blood sparks on Wei's hand as Siri's nails dig into him. The blackness coils upward on Wei's arms, across his chest and down his back.

Then, like a switch turned off, the screaming stops. They sit, gasping, legs thrumming on the wooden floor in a constant vibrating beat.

Jamie looks down to see her wrists turning dark in pulsing bands. Summer's neck and left shoulder pick up spots, like freckles painting themselves onto her naked skin. Rajan sinks to his knees silently, the finger imprints on his neck turning the same deep black as Wei's arms. He gasps for breath, eyes large white shocks in his face.

The heat keeps rising.

At 150 degrees, the black layer begins peeling away, falling to the floor in dusty clumps. Rajan lets out a limp sigh as breathing becomes easier. Spit shines like chrome on his bared teeth and jaw. Siri and Doc Wei still clutch each other's hands, and the blonde in Siri's hair begins to show through.

Wei opens his eyes.

"Fuck," he whispers, "that." His face is puffy and tear-streaked.

Rajan raises himself slowly to a bench. His fingers massage his throat. The needle flicks up and stays at 200 degrees, and now the darkness is actively falling away, like gently blowing black snow.

They stare at each other, naked and panting.

Rajan whispers hoarsely, "What… the fucking hell… was that?"

It is just after noon on the winter solstice. The answer to his question, however, lies almost four months in the past.

Chapter Nineteen

February 22nd, 2028

At 0220 local time, callsign Borak 27 lifted off from Runway 02 in Christchurch, New Zealand. There were six people aboard, but the official manifest only showed two pilots onboard the Basler airplane. Two hundred miles south of Invercargill, its transponder turned off.

Eight hours later, Borak 27 overflew McMurdo Station on the coast of Antarctica.

At 77 degrees South, the sun was a fading red and orange glow barely lighting the horizon. South Pole had closed down nine days ago for the isolated winter. The last LC-130 ski plane had departed the continent, headed stateside for a retrofit, then bound for the Pacific theater and combat. But the Mac airfields had one more crew to refuel before they were done for the summer.

The Basler set down at Williams Airfield, two compacted snow runways seven miles away from Mac Station. Unlike Pole, where the skiway was within visual range of the Station, "Willy" was far from prying eyes. Despite that, the shades on every window were pulled down. Only one pilot stepped out of the plane to direct the Mactown fuelies. Two hours later the Basler was airborne, flying deeper into the continent.

In the back, Dr. Richard Mason's stomach was a roiling pot of snakes. If he could deliver results with this operation, he would become known as the kind of man who found unorthodox solutions to get things done – a patriot in the very best American tradition. It was more than just a useful reputation.

It was a seat at a very select table of wartime decision-makers.

Because, even though it was easy to forget this far from civilization, the world was at war.

Thirty minutes out from the scheduled drop time over Dome-A, Mason walked up the narrow aisle to the cockpit. The pilot was an experienced civilian Antarctic operator, but the co-pilot was an Air Force test pilot and C-17 Special Operations Low Level graduate with special-access security clearances. SOLL pilots executed high-risk, high-precision airdrop operations around the world, and had supported clandestine drops over enemy territory for decades. Mason tapped him on the shoulder and made a phone call hand-gesture.

The co-pilot dialed up an encrypted UHF frequency reserved for military use. The signal bounced off a CIA operations facility in the southern hemisphere to headquarters in Langley. In the HAVE VIKING mission room, someone would be checking video surveillance feed from the sixteen cameras at the Dome-A Kunlun Station. The Basler carried four hours of extra fuel if they needed to linger until the crew was asleep.

They didn't want anyone awake and looking up at the sunlit sky.

The response came back in minutes. "Condition green confirmed."

"Cleared to ingress," Mason said, and went back to his seat.

The two burly loadmasters behind him began to inspect the cargo. The unmarked airdrop container was on rails by the tail door. Trigger the door, the rails, and the container would be off and sailing down under GPS-guided parachute to its destination. Half a mile downrange of the main Dome-A Station, but just a few hundred yards from the glaciology and ice core outpost on the northern edge of the Chinese site.

Mason peered through his binoculars, eyes huge and lambent, trying to catch the Dome Argus station beneath him as they set up on their first north to south run. Hope, awe, and dread brimmed in his eyes. The Station was so tiny, a literal black speck in an ocean of white, tracks of summer snow-movers marking butterfly shapes in the ice around it. The co-pilot was flying now. Mason listened to him on the intercom as he reported winds at altitude so the airdrop loadmasters could adjust their predictions, then he executed a practice jump run. Mason was pushed out of his seat, belly straining against the seatbelt as the Basler dived down from 27,000 feet. The airdrop specialists counted down to release at 18,000 feet mean sea level, just 2,000 feet above the high terrain.

Then they climbed back up. No more practice. It was time.

Mason was the only one aboard who knew that all fifteen people on the ice below might not survive the winter. The thought didn't trouble him much. Science wasn't always clean or considerate of life.

In fact, evolution set out to kill everything.

Only those who adapted survived.

He kept his binoculars trained on the site as they spiral-dived toward it. The unmarked cargo had three small explosive charges. The first would consume the parachute. The second would propel the containment sphere fifty yards downrange and destroy the cargo container. The third charge was so tiny it would barely take off a fingernail, triggered by a double-thermocouple. Once it got colder than minus 75 degrees, a small vial of acid would get crushed, and the containment sphere would begin beeping loudly for attention. The acid would start gently burning through a copper diaphragm, calibrated to the micro-inch. It would burn through in twenty-four hours, triggering the second thermocouple and the tiny explosive charge that would fracture the sphere along pre-drilled facets.

Nature would take its course from there.

The loadmasters counted down to release, and a smile appeared on Mason's face, as radiant as the summer sun burning off ground fog. His stomach unclenched and, suddenly, he felt good.

Chapter Twenty

SOUTH POLE STATION POPULATION: 36 (PRISONERS: 3; DECEASED: 5)

June 21st, 12:10 PM

Keyon Geerts steps into the beer can.

The damn heat flashes are acting up and a dose of winter cool seems like all that can calm them down. He isn't stupid enough to go all the way outdoors, though his mind keeps returning to that thought. He steps inside as soon as the tingling dies away, but his body lights up again almost immediately, more painfully, as if begging him –

(*dying no please*)

– to stay outside a little longer.

Just a little longer.

1:20 PM

Ben Jacobs bangs awake from another awful dream, except this one is just a terrible unending scream pulling his head apart; like millions of dying jackals baying all at once. Furious tears slip out of his eyes. Ben sits up–

– and hears movement on the stairs.

If this is Jonah, I'm done, done and fucking cooked.

Ben fumbles for the bag of jolly green TC had sold him, to hide it.

It's empty.

(*already*?)

A shadow comes up the stairs and down the landing. He tenses up.

The shadow resolves into TC, and every muscle in Ben's body weakens with relief. He tries to laugh, but all that comes out is a bubble of spit.

The big chef looks frozen. Ice lines his hood, frozen into his eyelashes and the zipper of his jacket. With a grateful sigh, he sets down the large cooler he's carrying. It's food for the Dome-A prisoners, out of sight but not out of the Station's mind. Not yet.

"Mate, you look like you need a sickie–"

Then his nostrils flare, like a bull seeing red.

"Have you been smoking inside the building?"

Ben nods vacantly. Reality has sunk down a long hole over the last few hours, a feverish blur of itching, trembling, and frantic tokes to get it to stop. He feels gritty and scratchy, like he's coming off a multi-day acid trip, his brain not fully reassembled.

TC's scream snaps him into reality.

"What the fuck is wrong with you?"

The cook advances into the room. "It fucking stinks of pot in here, you daft dag! I've been gone three hours!" The amiable snaggle-toothed smile is gone from TC's face. In place of the genial Aussie is a towering man so angry that ice shakes free of him with every furious word. "Three hours, and this place has turned into a stoner den!"

"It's okay!" Ben puts his arms out, placating. Obliging, always obliging. His voice is spring water burbling over smooth rocks. "The weed's all gone–"

"Fuck me dead, this sofa. It's *a cloth sofa,* you bloody idiot!"

He leaps over to the sofa, fists knotting up in the cushion, then he thrusts his nose into it and flings it across the room. "You don't think Jonah will notice how his couch smells?" He advances on Ben. "You don't think NSF is going to ask how marijuana ended up in fucking Antarctica? Because it sure didn't come through Kiwi agricultural inspection, *did it*?"

Like a cold bucket of water in the face, Ben sees the room from TC's point of view. A week's supply of pot in just a few hours, *it's all gone*. It's a wonder he can arrange two coherent thoughts in sequence. TC's fists are knotting up at his sides, moving in a menacing way Ben recognizes all too well. It was the way his father had moved when he'd come into Ben's room, breath sour with whisky. Soon enough, he'd be swinging those fists.

Then he'd be unbuckling his belt.

Ben shrinks away from him, into the Dobson room, until the cold draft from the cracked door tickles the back of his neck. TC is still roaring. "I should have known better than to sell to a bloody beaker addict. Couldn't stop yourself, *could you*?"

Ben stops moving.

His head cocks to the side. Someone else is talking. And he is…

He's very interested in what they have to say.

TC stops, taken aback. "Hey, dickhead," he demands roughly. "You got something to say for yourself?"

Ben shivers from head to toe. Like he's shaking cat hair off. He takes a deliberate step back.

He reaches behind him.

He throws the door all the way open.

Cold air rushes in, the door barely blocking the fury of

the storm winds. Snow piled up against it blows past his feet. TC flinches away. "The hell are you doing?"

Ben catches sight of his reflection, in the shiny metal of an aneroid barometer. Something frightening has happened to his face. It has become very still, and slate hard. His eyes are open, rolled up to distended straining whites, like a mare left outside in a thunderstorm.

"I need more," Ben whispers. His voice comes from the bottom of a deep well.

"What?"

"The weed is all gone. I need more."

TC takes an uneasy step backward. His fists have unclenched.

Ben gives the cook his most winning smile, and his lips freeze in the bared position. "I need more, man."

TC backs out of the Dobson room like a stray dog that's getting nervous. "There's three days of food in that cooler for the Chinese guys. You and this wanking place can have each other."

He turns away, back toward the stairwell.

Ben leaps across the Dobson room onto him.

He throws the big cook off his feet, into the computer table at the far end of the room. The monitor tips over with a screeching crash, yanking the keyboard with it. Ben has never been in a fight, has shrunk away from conflict all his life, but now he advances on TC.

He blinks away black.

"It burns," he says, tongue thick in his throat. Wide grin frozen onto his face. "It burns so badly you can't imagine the pain."

"Fuck this shit," TC says, and springs up from the floor. His big body is behind his fist, and he plants it firmly into the side of Ben's face.

Ben feels his teeth crunch, pushed together like a swinging chain-link fence. Warm blood explodes into his mouth, two teeth fly out from between his lips, but his face doesn't move an inch. He doesn't have to let it. He *won't* let it. TC's fist keeps advancing, his fingers bending now, crumpling backward up to his wrist. The cook withdraws his fist, whimpering, hand hanging limply like a wet dishrag.

"I could show you the pain." Ben's breath whistles through the vacant spots in his teeth. He decides –

(*we decide*)

– he will show him.

He surges forward, body-slamming TC against the wall, and *feels them move*, a wave of heat pushing off his body and over TC's. His hand grasps the cook's throat –

(*you take that you're no prize beaker bitch*)

– in a vice-grip. "I need more," he breathes into the cook's neck. "It makes the pain –"

(*transition*)

"– easier."

TC whimpers. "I can't."

Ben tastes flecks of teeth on his tongue. His hand tightens. TC grasps it, tugging desperately. Ben might be smaller, but his grip is absolute.

"It's a small growth, man," TC wheezes. "I'm soil restricted! Please!"

Ben lets out a roar of frustration; hurls TC off his feet across the room. His head cracks on the hard edge of the sofa. The cook pushes himself to his feet, belly-flopping over the coffee table, then lumbers into a run, toward the stairs, without a backward glance.

Running for his life.

Ben starts pulsing with heat again, but this heat feels good. Feels *righteous.*

(*We're finally ready*)

(*Ben what are you doing Ben*)

A deep bubbling laugh comes from somewhere deep within him. From us.

(*Go fucking get him*)

We run. Full-bore, fast like lightning –

(*fuckin' A*)

– past the Dobson machine, through the open door into the glorious cold. Ben's foot finds the edge of the railing and we leap off the top level of ARO, straight down to the ice. The snow is warm like beach sand in the fall. The cool wind howls, and we shriek back at it with fierce joy.

We turn Ben so we can watch TC run, his red jacket a bloody stain on the dark horizon.

We unzip Ben's fleece jacket.

Fold it up carefully; lay it where we can find the hated thing again.

We place Ben's hands in the small of his back, like a runner before a sprint, and he grimaces pleasurably as his spine cracks. We set his feet in the snow, crouched at the ready block.

"We're coming for you," we whisper.

(*beaker bitch*)

We burst into a run.

Chapter Twenty-One

The demands of his stomach force Keyon Geerts out of bed just after two in the afternoon. He experiences an almost physical *revulsion* to the idea but he stumbles into the bathroom, turns the shower onto its hottest setting and thrusts himself underneath its steaming spray. It takes all his willpower not to scream with pain. He ignores the water restrictions and punches the tap button again. Gasping hot fire. He hits the button again and throws up over his bare toes. One more time, and when the water dries up, he feels better.

Much better, in fact.

He walks into the galley, arms swinging slowly. He feels like he's been blacked out for a while; the worst bender of his life. He picks up a plate, and falls into line behind Clint Gerencser, the junior meteorologist and Katie's backup.

Katie slides up and squeezes his arm companionably. "Hey, stranger. Doing okay?"

"Better now. What were you and Jonah gossiping about over yonder?"

Her face clouds over. "Just those poor souls from Dome-A. After all they've been through, we haven't even let them come over here and sleep in a real bed." She grimaces, then her usual big smile appears. "I have fresh coffee! My second-to-last package. Saved you some."

"You're a lifesaver."

He watches her head across the galley. She turns and waves cheerily at him, his shoulder twitches with heat–

(*both of yuh I hope yuh fall and break yer neck*)

– and a loud voice full of incoherent rage slams him like his ears have been boxed.

(*SHOW THE WORLD no fear, boy, and it gonna bend like a twizzler. WHY ARE YOU SO WEAK*)

Keyon's plate drops from his hands and he clamps his hands over his ears–

(*This world's all about weakness and showing it got-damn none. Shit boy you think I'm a looker? No matta I still walk up like I'mma fuck her in the ass and guess what, nuttin more out of her dumb cunt mouth than go slow please daddy when I bend her over*)

The plate smashes on the floor, and the voice clanging in his head changes, becomes whiny–

(*I wanna be strong like yuh daddy I want her so bad it hurts when I jack off but I can't*)

"Hey man," Clint says in his drawling voice. "Yuh doin' all right?"

(*I hate yuh both pair of cunts both of yuh cunts*)

Keyon stares at him and he *knows*, just knows that the voices in his head belong to Clint Gerencser and Clint's cunt rapist of a dad. They echo in his mind like stones flung into a well, dripping with an unmistakable sense of malevolence.

(*twenty-five to life in Beaumont Federal Penitentiary*)

(*hope yuh get TRAPPED under a wooden beam and can't breathe before yuh DIE*)

Clint smiles at him. "Keyon?"

(*Then I'll get Katie she'll wish she paid attention to me then, nuttin more out of her dumb cunt mouth than go slow please daddy when I*)

Keyon springs at him.

The big carpenter's fists knot up in Clint's shirt, and he throws Clint to the floor. The smaller man gasps like a punctured balloon, but his eyes spark and Keyon can *hear* the bright raw hatred in them, pounding like a bongo drum.

(*HOPE YUH DIE BLACK BASTARD I HOPE YUH DIE*)

"I'm not going to die anytime soon." Keyon's smile widens emptily. "But you might."

He sees the little man's eyes widen. "Yer' crazy," Clint shrills in a high voice.

Footsteps rush toward them. In a moment it'll be over. "You so much as think about Katie again, boy," he hisses, "and you gonna *learn* how crazy I can get."

Then arms are pulling him up, yanking them apart. He lets himself be dragged off Clint. "I'm all right," he says calmly. "Just needed to have a word, I'm all right."

"Plum fuckin' crazy!" Clint blubbers histrionically across the galley. "I just asked him if he was okay!"

Keyon untangles himself; ignores the eyes of the galley, staring at him like crows perched on a telephone wire. He sits down across from Katie, whose watery blue eyes are large with shock.

"Don't turn your back on Clint," Keyon says emphatically. "He is not a good hombre."

(*he's no prize*)

"Are you feeling all right?" Katie asks urgently. "This isn't you."

With the shock of a slap, Keyon realizes *it isn't him at all.*

He's the instigator. The manipulator. He pulls *other* people off each other. He is never *ever* the pig in the mud getting dirty!

That's when he realizes that his tingles are back.

He feels hot, flushed, and most of all, angry. He wants to

snatch up his fork and sprint across the galley and watch Clint's eyes go wide as he punctures his weaselly throat with it. Even as he's thinking what a terrible idea that would be, his legs are tensing up, like he's a second away from launching across the room.

"I don't, actually." He draws a shaky breath. "I don't feel… right."

Katie stands. "Let's go see Doc, Key."

"I've already missed most of the workday."

"I'll tell Weeks you're at medical. You go there right now."

He rises reluctantly. A smile flickers onto his face. "You worried about me?"

She shakes her head, rueful. "I'm always worried about you."

"I could get used to that."

"Go on now," she says, but she's smiling, too.

That's when the alarms break into life across South Pole Station.

Chapter Twenty-Two

June 21st, 1:00 PM
Two hours prior to the alarms

For the sauna six – Siri and Rajan, Summer and Tim, Wei and Jamie – seeing each other naked in the sauna was not as humiliating as the day would get. Because even after sweating until Tim Fulton is lobster red and Summer's handprints brightly dimple the skin on her thighs, they still have to be sure it's worked.

Doc Wei pulls the temperature down to 90 degrees Fahrenheit, and Jamie brings a microscope into the sauna. Wei has Siri lie down on the wooden planks, and the others turn away to give her some modicum of privacy. Jamie holds her hand. "He can't get it up, anyway," she jokes.

"It's all right," Siri intones.

"If I never see you again after this winter, Jamie–" Wei grumbles, eye pressed to the scope.

"You'll miss me. Just wait."

Wei scours every inch of Siri's flesh with the microscope. It's slow and painstaking work, and she takes it with as much equanimity as she can summon. At the end of the inspection, the only place Wei finds the microbes is in her hair. They've fallen away from her skin everywhere else, but her hair follicles are thick with microbial growths, and it's hard to verify if the sauna treatment has killed them all, or if some are still dormant.

"Shave her head," Jamie says. "Hell, we should *all* shave our heads."

"What on Earth for?"

"Wait, what?"

"Shave my *whole* head? *Hell* to the no," Summer objects most strenuously of all.

"But it's not over once we walk out of here," Jamie pleads. "There could be a microbial parasite on any person and any surface out there. *It passes by touch.* The only way we can make sure anyone is clean is to see every inch of you."

"I really don't think–" Summer begins.

"We're doing it," Siri says quietly. Her eyes are red, and the gash in her cheek has turned an ugly purple. "I'll have to go out there, probably many times, to prep the runway so all of us can go home. I want it as easy as possible for Doc to make sure I'm clean, because God help me, I never want to go through what I just experienced ever again."

Reluctant nods; Summer crosses her arms and glowers, but she's done objecting. Jamie leaves the sauna and returns with a razor. One by one, the six submit to having their heads shaven. Wei examines them from shiny head to reddened toe, and once Jamie has done the same to him, proclaims himself satisfied.

The two medical professionals stay behind to inspect the Hazmat suits. Summer, Siri, Tim, and Rajan cluster in the cooler outer area, wrapped in sauna towels and rubbing their nubbin-smooth heads awkwardly. Summer catches a glimpse of her reflection and pulls a face. "Jeez, I look like a boy."

"Not with those tits, you don't. Me, on the other hand…"

Siri says. Suddenly overcome by the absurdity of the situation, they burst into hysterical laughter.

"What a day," Tim says weakly. "Time for a stiff drink. You guys with me?"

"I'll take the fucking bottle, boss," Siri says immediately, to more laughs.

"I've been on the go for twenty-four hours without sleep," Rajan says. "I need to crash."

"Yeah. I'm going to do the same," Summer says. She meets his eyes, and Rajan wonders, suddenly, if she has been waiting to hear his answer.

Wei emerges from the sauna then. "Summer, can I get you to come to the clinic with me? I'd like to get your biologist opinion on some microbe slides I've put together."

Summer takes another look through the microscope. "This is absolutely fascinating."

"What can you tell me about the biology of these microbes?" Wei asks.

"Not much without gene sequence analysis. It's definitely a dormant extremophile, and based on the cellular structure, well, I can't be sure–"

"Summer, this isn't a peer-reviewed journal article," Wei says. "Give me your first impressions."

She sits back. "I'd say this microbe, or at least this *type* of microbe, is indigenous to Antarctica."

Wei's eyebrows climb. "That is... not what I was expecting to hear."

"This is kind of how I ended up in Antarctica, actually," she says. "I'm lost when it comes to microwave backgrounds and astro-seismology, because molecular biology is my field. But when I was in grad school in Massachusetts–"

"You can just say Harvard," Wei interrupts. "Take it from someone who went to the little school by the river. No one actually cares in the real world."

She glares at him, then continues icily. "At *Harvard,* four years ago, a paleoclimate team reached out to my department asking if someone could fly out to Antarctica and give them an opinion on some weird organisms they'd found while on a drill. My advisor had always wanted to go to Antarctica, and he thought I needed some field experience, so we ended up on a bumpy Twin Otter out to Lake Byrd. Do you know where that is?"

Wei shakes his head. "Not a fishing hole in Michigan?"

"It's an underground lake, deep under the ice, on the East Antarctic Ice Sheet. I'm talking *deep.*" Summer sits forward, excitement in her eyes. "Four-and-a-half kilometers below the ice, they'd found extremophile microbes that I couldn't identify as belonging to *any* known microbial genus. It was such an exciting find that I ended up switching my whole research to it. It's why I'm still dealing with Antarctic ice cores."

"Is there a non-academic reason it was so exciting?" Wei asks.

"Hell yes!" she says emphatically. "Every life form on Earth evolved to take advantage of a range of constants, but none of those constants were present here. Despite total darkness and extreme cold and high pressure, deep under the ice, life still *found a way.*" Her eyes are shining. "The microbes Harvard found had evolved into unique gene sequences. Their metabolic processes were totally different. Jonny and I – Dr. Jon Kim, my advisor at Harvard

– never fully determined the nutrient source for these microbes, but Lake Byrd is connected to this massive subglacial ice-lake system that runs underneath most of the continent. We theorized that the microbes could remain dormant for extremely long periods of time, maybe even centuries, and had evolved to *bring themselves online* when the lake currents drifted them into the way of a new nutrient source." She gestures toward the microscope. "These cellular structures look fundamentally similar to what I saw at Lake Byrd."

Wei tries to keep the suspicion out of his voice. "How the hell do these microbes go from an Antarctic lake four kilometers down, to up here?"

She laughs. "The Chinese were coring at Dome-A."

"What?"

"Like SPICE, like me! Dome Argus is one of the driest places on Earth, and it sits on top of a massive primordial mountain range, so it's a great spot to drill a core for paleoclimate research. I heard they did a summer drill, so their winter-overs were probably analyzing the samples. Maybe they didn't do a very good job with containment?"

"Well. That's not as, ah, malign as I was thinking." Of late, his musings have taken him to wondering about Rajan's presence at the Pole. Suspecting some sort of God-awful military experiment gone wrong.

But Summer's eyes are intense now. "I couldn't disagree more. These organisms live in some of the harshest conditions on our planet. They are *highly* versatile at adapting to a microclimate based on external stimuli, and they're practically alien when you compare their gene sequences to anything in the world today. They come from a time when humans didn't even exist. This is their Christopher

Columbus moment. They've just found a new microclimate, and a new species to use as a nutrient source. I'd be very worried about where their adaptive abilities go next."

Chapter Twenty-Three

Rajan slips off his shirt and collapses into bed. He's asleep within two minutes.

A deep, shuddering sigh escapes him as his mind walks back over the force around his neck in the sauna, clinging to him like a boa constrictor. He'd *felt* it cry, somehow. It had been like killing something alive.

His heavy eyes close, and he slips into sketchy dreams, full of shapes more sensed than seen. He's back in the flare-red glow in the Dome-A truck –

Breathing its foul stench, trying not to touch anything–

But this time the Syrian man's eyes float in the darkness.

The man he'd killed years ago stares up at him, tongue lolling, then his face stretches in the confident grin of two friends who share a secret.

Hey Rajan, his grin speaks. *Life down there at Pole sure is a hoot, huh?*

Blood wells up around the man's tongue.

His laugh continues to widen, blood spilling through the words and out of his mouth and over Rajan.

Suddenly drenching the floor of the Dome-A truck.

Just another desert, my friend. Desert, dessert. Say, listen. I'm about to eat you like a filet.

Rajan feels himself start to slip. He struggles, frantically, but collapses to his knees, then down he goes, splashing into the blood, gasping for breath but not finding any. His body washes against the wall, even as the grinning voice closes–

I'm going to slurp the marrow out of your bones and MUNCH on your SKIN like GUM–

A soft knock on the door.

His eyes open, and Summer steps into his room.

Rajan flies upright like he's been stuck with a cattle prod. The dream slides off in shiny fragments, littering the floor of his mind like a broken wine glass not yet swept up.

"Summer, what… hi, what are you doing here?"

She has changed into a soft grey knitted top, flannel pants, and a cute grey beanie that hides her bare scalp. Her eyes fasten onto his, and Rajan knows he could drown in them.

Perhaps he needs to start swimming right now.

"All these people dying… looking at these microbes with Doc…" she murmurs. "It kicked my brain out of whatever funk it's been in all season. And I've been thinking…"

"Thinking about what?"

She takes a step forward, then another. So close that he can see the gold flecks in her endless sapphire eyes. So close he can touch her just by leaning forward.

"Thinking about what, Summer?"

"I want you," she says, simply. "I want to go back to where we were in Denver. I thought about coming to you when I saw the solstice card in my lab, but after–"

"Card, what card?"

"–after people started dying… I mean, this infestation might still kill us. And I couldn't bear it if I didn't try to make us happen."

Rajan feels many things in that moment, but most of it

is loathing. Because he will say the words… but he knows how this will end. How he *wants* it to end.

So he says the words.

"Summer, you're with Tim."

She sighs, beautiful and lost and alone. "That was an ice thing left over from last year. I've just been too weak to end it. Or scared. But this winter was always meant to be you and me."

She looks up at him. "I'm not scared anymore. Are you?"

If he really means it, he'll tell her to go to Tim and break up with him first. He'll tell her to leave his room, right now.

But he doesn't really want her to leave.

She leans up toward him.

Now. Now, you fool. Stop her.

Instead, he kisses her.

Her lips are soft and pliable, and he falls into them like a boulder into a lake.

The warmth of her tongue surges into his mouth and he seizes her the way he's dreamed about doing; pulls her hips to his hips, his mouth to her mouth. He has *never* felt desire this strong; didn't know he was capable of this much bare want.

She clutches his neck, pressing against him, then she takes his hand from her waist and gently slides it up her side, until it rests against the swell of her full breast. He can feel her heart, skidding beneath his palm at a breakneck pace.

Then she takes his hand lower.

He pulls his fingers away. Ends the kiss, gently but firmly. "Summer…" In that moment, though his heart is pounding frantically enough for dark spots to dance before his eyes, he really means it.

She steps back and pulls her fleece over her head. Nothing more than a bra underneath.

"Summer..." he says, and this time he doesn't mean it at all.

She reaches behind her, keeping her eyes on him. Pauses. He doesn't say anything, and her bra comes off.

"Tell me you don't want me."

"I do want you. But that's – Summer, that's not the point."

"It's the only point," she says.

He feels a dull flare of anger. "You're too used to Antarctica. You think you can get whatever and whoever you want."

She doesn't reply. Doesn't take the bait. She bends her head, her soft cheek brushing his nipples. She kisses the scar on his chest. She lowers herself to her knees, then slowly reaches up to place her hands on his belt.

"Then stop me," she whispers. She unzips his pants. He wonders, suddenly, if he's still dreaming. If the Syrian man is about to emerge; flow in under the door on a river of blood.

Her eyes never leave his. "Stop me right now."

He doesn't. She brings her mouth to him, he groans–

– and the alarm blares. A klaxon, three times, an abrupt, urgent sound.

An automated voice Rajan has never heard before comes over the speakers.

Fire alert – in the – food arch.

Chapter Twenty-Four

"Shit!" Summer jumps to her feet. "I'm on fire team!"

Fire alert – in the – food arch.

"Go," he says, but she's already snatching up her shirt.

Filled with industrial chemicals and fuels of all volatilities, the labs and arches at South Pole make the Station one big kindling ready for the match. In past seasons, a dedicated fire technician has been part of the crew. It's why Nomex pants stand at the base of each crewmember's fire locker, coiled and ready to jump into. Hoses are prepped, helmets facing the right way, oxygen tanks filled. Every winter resident, scientist or loggie, is a trained firefighter, the crew split into two teams so that a group can be on call at all times. Once every two weeks, the whole Station holds practice fire drills, and even jaded veteran Polies take them seriously.

Fire is life and death at the bottom of the world.

Summer runs out of the door, accelerating to an all-out sprint. Rajan drifts into the hallway in her wake. He flattens against the wall as Yanis runs by, intent on his locker. Rajan looks up at the red fire lights strobing across the hallway, and a primal fear washes out the disjointed patchwork quilt of his thoughts.

A second later his radio squeals and a voice screams across the common channel.

It's TC! He's gone fucking nuts!

Then the sound of screaming–

– and the radio goes dead.

June 21st, 2:35 PM

Part of fire team A has already assembled near Destination Alpha, the "front" entrance of the Station facing east. Rajan sees the rest of the team clattering down the steps at mid-hallway, fully kitted up. Then a mighty yell comes down the hallway, so loud it drowns out the klaxoning alarms.

"NOOOOOOOOO!"

(*Fire alert – in the – food arch*)

Doc Wei races down the hallway, white lab coat flying. Jamie is right behind him, screaming like she's possessed, a fire axe clutched in both hands.

Rajan breaks into a loping run after them.

Wei throws himself ahead of the fire team, against the Destination Alpha doors, arms stretched wide. "You can't leave!" he shouts.

"What the hell?" Dave Atkins demands. "Get out of the way, Doc!"

Jamie dives behind Wei and shoves her axe through the handles of the door. Confused yells fill the air. Wei waves back the fire teams clustered by the entrance; Jamie holds onto the axe with all her strength as Kevin Eastburg from IT tries to wrestle her out of the way. Somehow Wei catches sight of Rajan, right as the fire team begins milling around in the other direction.

"Rajan!" he screams with that mighty roar. "Get the other door!"

There's a time to ask questions, and a time to snap to and follow orders. Rajan reverses and takes off running immediately, down the hallway, back toward Destination Zulu.

Like a stampeding herd, most of the fire team rumbles after him.

Rajan spins in his tracks and throws an elbow through the glass case mounted on the wall. He rips a fire axe out, and jerks the handle sideways like a mop, just in time to catch Yanis between the legs. The tall scientist trips spectacularly, cracking his fire helmet against the wall.

Rajan leaps back two, then three steps. His Antarctic Program cap falls off, exposing his bald head. "Get back!" he shouts. "Head back to Doc. GET BACK!"

The herd pauses. He fixes a fierce look on his face, wielding the axe in wide, dangerous swings.

"BACK UP!" His voice cracks painfully.

Jamie's voice squeals across their radios. "Everyone, do not go outside. I repeat, *stay inside the Station! This is a medical emergency!"*

"Stay inside!" Rajan takes up the shout. "Stay inside!"

"Stay inside!" Summer jumps to the front of the retreating group of firefighters in her fire gear, also waving them back. "We need to stay inside!"

Her helmet falls off, and the lights bounce off her bald head. "Listen to Doc!" she yells, and finally, there's silence, except for the klaxoning fire alarm. Eyes turn back to Destination Alpha.

"ALL OF YOU! I know there's a fire, but there's an infection on your skins that will *kill you* if you go outside!" Wei shouts. "The only people safe to fight this fire are those who have been treated. Those with shaved heads!"

An uneasy, restless murmur sweeps through the crowd, breaking the inertia. Suddenly people are moving out of the way, no longer a mob lurking threateningly. Summer and Rajan push forward to stand beside Wei and Jamie. The four of them are noticeably bald.

Rajan turns to Weeks. "Give me your fire gear."

Weeks stares.

Summer steps up beside him. "Right now, Weeks!" Her words are a drill-sergeant shout in his face.

"Okay," Weeks mutters. "Okay, okay."

As he shucks out of his gear, Summer gets on her radio. "Tim and Siri, Tim and Siri, get your fire gear on and meet us at Alpha! Everyone else in the Station – do not leave!"

Rajan looks up. "We need heat guns! As many as we can get."

"The science lab!" Bethany Hamidani shouts from the back of the crowd. She takes off running.

"Everyone else into the lower gym," Wei says.

Siri pounds down the stairs, wrestling herself into her fire jacket. "How many people in the arches?" she asks.

"Six, maybe eight." Tim is right behind her, helmet askew on his head. Rajan looks away from him.

Bethany runs up, a heat gun in each hand. "Who needs them?"

"I'll take one," Rajan says.

"I'll take the other," Siri says grimly.

"Okay, on me, let's move!"

A few Polies linger in the hallway after they leave, muttering. Looking at each other for clarification. Drifting toward the lower gym, but not entering it.

"Fuck this shit, man," Dave Atkins says. "There's a fire, and we should be out there."

No one moves, but no one stops him either. Dave barges past Wei and Jamie, and pulls on the door.

It doesn't budge.

On the other side of the thick metal doors, Rajan's fire axe rattles between the handles.

Jamie steps up and places the heft of her axe against Dave's neck. She pushes just enough for him to feel the weight of her grip behind it.

Her eyes fix him to the spot. "No one's going to be a dumb cow and start a fucking panic," she says, loudly and clearly. "Get your ass in the gym, Atkins."

"Oh God," Tim Fulton says in a breaking, childish voice.

They are outside, in the dark cold, facing the aboveground entrance to the arches.

A pyre of flame gushes out of the food arch.

It shoots through the ventilator shafts into the frigid air.

In the middle of the entrance, naked, backlit by the fire and bare chest glistening black, the big cook TC holds a man bodily up above his head like a Russian weightlifter. The fire has fused his lips shut, his eyelids are frayed flaps, but as they run up, the four of them can see the hot and militant joy in his face.

It fills them with the paralyzed but frantic horror that chickens feel for the weasel.

TC hurls the man like a soccer ball.

The man flies almost halfway to them and slams into the ice, butt-first. A blur of red, then the jacket begins to twitch. Carpenter apprentice Ryan Schnurbusch struggles with his fleece, trying to tear it off.

When Rajan looks up, TC is gone.

They enter the arch entrance, sloping underground, the snow giving way to cold concrete.

Inside the food arch, dark clouds of acrid smoke belch toward them. Fire-training muscle memory kicks in; they strap masks and regulators to their faces, buddy-opening each other's oxygen tanks. Tim opens up his hose at the first hint of flames, water gushing out toward a crisped fuel can that sits at the center of the blaze, popping madly in the heat.

"Rajan, look out!"

He whirls as Jeremy Forystek, the junior electrician, emerges out of the smoke.

His shirt is gone.

Black crispy microbes dance all over his skin.

He charges silently at them, fists frozen into claws, mouth open in a malicious rictus.

Rajan twists the release valve on his hose. It's all he can think to do. High-pressure water blasts Jeremy right in the chest; he's struck down to his hands and knees like a pin knocked by a bowling ball. Blood sparks at his knees, then, suddenly, he stops moving.

Resisting the water pressure.

The water pounds at his skin but he doesn't budge. Thin blood runs furiously into the water.

Somehow, he gets to his feet.

Arms spread, he pushes forward into the water hose lashing him. Eyes unblinking and boring into Rajan's.

Summer steps up beside him and opens her hose, catching him low by the knees. Jeremy is knocked off his feet, falling forward. His arms don't move to break his fall, and his jaw snaps downward into the concrete. His eyes roll in their sockets, and he flops over.

I think he's dead.

Summer advances into the smoke.

More small fires burn around strewn kerosene cans with cloth poking out of their lips, but the main fire quickly becomes visible: a shooting column of flame that has blown a massive hole through the ceiling and six feet of ice above it. Wind and snow tumble down through the crushed roof. Somewhere in the distance, Rajan hears screaming. He recognizes the sound.

Microbes, dying in the heat.

They aim their hoses at the base of the fire. The heat is a roiling wave. Rajan's thoughts are jagged, incoherent. Are they fighting one danger only to release another? Are the fires to fight the microbes or allow them to spread? Smoke billows thick in the air –

– and out of it, three of their winter-over crew emerge at a run.

Naked, bodies covered with jagged black microbe fire rings, faces frozen into grins.

They jump on Summer and Tim, knocking them to the ground. Tim pushes Allen McKenzie off, trying to get to his feet, but Bret Okonkwo knocks him back down, trying to straddle him, claws scrabbling for his throat. Tim's cry catches in mid-sentence as his breath shuts down, then Siri jabs her heat gun into the back of Okonkwo's neck.

He screams, body spasming like he has been electrocuted. Siri keeps pushing with the heat gun, also screaming aloud, panic on panic, until the gun melts through his skin into the soft tissue at the base of his skull.

He goes silent.

Allen McKenzie jumps away from Summer, hitting Siri in a broad tackle. Her head hits the concrete with a flat nasty thud. She moans, clutching her skull, heat gun skittering away.

That moan breaks Rajan's inertia and he whips his hose around, seating it against his hip, and blasts Siri's attacker. The water engulfs both of them. She coughs, trying to block the flow, but Allen grins and sets his stance. Pushing into the spray.

"Come at me, fuckwit," Rajan says through his teeth.

Siri kicks frantically backwards, sliding away from the gush of the hose. Finds her heat gun. She scrabbles around and thrusts it into Allen's foot.

He falls onto his side, clutching his leg. Rajan doesn't hesitate. He closes the distance.

Keeps the hose blasting right into his face.

Allen spasms as he chokes.

For a moment his eyes are clear of dark residue. There's only confusion in them, as if he's coming out of a trance. Uncertain of where he is, and why he's being put to death.

A grassfire of pain lights in Rajan's heart, but his face stays grim.

The hose doesn't move.

Allen's legs jerk spastically, then his ribcage stops in mid-heave. His chest settles under the spray, slowly, like the weight of a truck squatting down on four flat tires.

Water flows out of his staring eyes and nose, and Rajan feels a part of him die inside.

Tim steps up to the fire, hose sweeping across the base of the flames. Rajan blinks, and Summer is by his side. The fire is dying out a little. Tears ooze out of his overbright eyes, stained with soot. He turns and adds his hose to theirs.

A woman rushes by them, no shirt on, her bra stained black with greasy smoke. Rajan tenses, but Lisa Kissinger keeps running, past them and up the ramp. The grandmother of four shouts with hoarse glee as she enters the cold, and then she's gone.

Eight crewmembers are no longer with them after the fire.

Lisa Kissinger, baker and dining lead.

Tommy "TC" Chapman, breakfast cook and sous-chef.

Bret Okonkwo, cargo carpenter.

Nathaniel Singh, materials specialist.

Ryan Schnurbusch, carpenter apprentice.

Allen McKenzie, waste specialist.

Jeremy Forystek, electrician apprentice.

Bowman Moyer, pipefitter.

Rajan would later wonder why TC had chosen to start a fire, the last thing he would have expected thermophobic life forms to do.

The unthinkable explanation is that TC started the fire to lure half the Station outside in the form of a fire team. In the cold, the microbes resting dormant on their skin would come alive and begin to eat into their hosts.

That explanation would suggest an intelligent life form capable of aggregate thought.

Capable, perhaps, of hunting its prey.

EXCERPT from:

In the Wake of War: A First-hand Account of Humanity's Deadliest Struggle

Assembled from the diaries of Mariana Egan

[Excerpt begins]

Every journalist covering national security in the modern era understands cybersecurity like a semi-pro. There's a thin line between using the First Amendment to expose government malfeasance, and publishing secrets that benefit the enemy.

During a time of war, that thin line gets so bony it can almost disappear.

Every article I publish lists my public encryption key, which lets anyone upload files to me on six different encrypted messaging services. I have two dozen ways a source can get me their private key, depending on the level of paranoia I feel. The Tribune has a dozen staff members who once drew paychecks from the NSA working data protection. I'd seen top-secret data, sensitive compartmented intelligence… and I'd never seen anything like this document.

I know it's a time of war. I've seen cell-phone videos of what the Chinese Army is doing to partisans sabotaging their occupation of Taipei. But mutations? Level A Hazmat gear? People begging for evacuation?

And then there were the rumors. People on social media who said they couldn't reach their friends at the South Pole even after weeks, though the NSF blamed a freak solar storm for an interruption in SATCOM. The dark web rumors about deaths at a Chinese Station in Antarctica. The increase in black-hat traffic targeting people making those posts.

And my friend, sweet Mei Lingling from Nanjing, who had gone down to winter-over at Dome-A and hadn't been heard from in months.

After what happened with General Rason, I knew I wouldn't be trusted in the halls of the Pentagon ever again. It was as good a time as any to chase this story back to its location of origin.

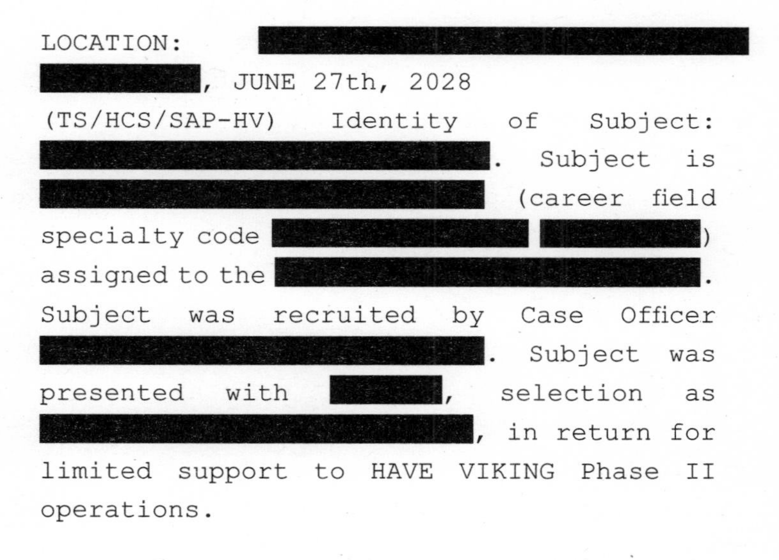

TRANSCRIPT OF ENCRYPTED COMMUNICATION

LOCATION: ████████████████

█████, JUNE 27th, 2028

(TS/HCS/SAP-HV) Identity of Subject: ██████████████. Subject is ██████████████ (career field specialty code ████████ █████) assigned to the █████████████. Subject was recruited by Case Officer ██████████████. Subject was presented with ████, selection as ██████████████, in return for limited support to HAVE VIKING Phase II operations.

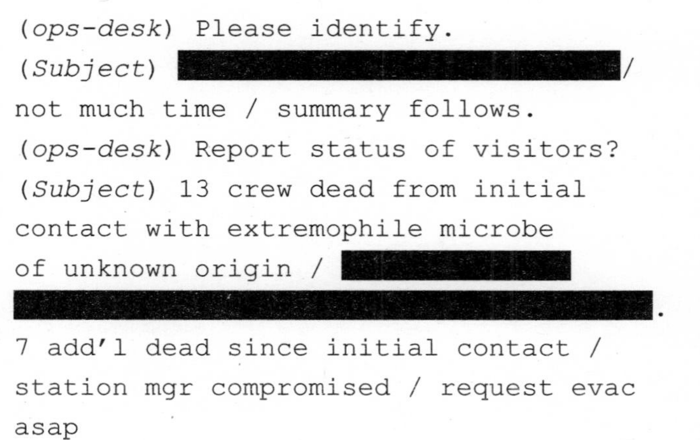

(*ops-desk*) Please identify.
(*Subject*) ██████████████/
not much time / summary follows.
(*ops-desk*) Report status of visitors?
(*Subject*) 13 crew dead from initial contact with extremophile microbe of unknown origin / ███████
████████████████████.
7 add’l dead since initial contact / station mgr compromised / request evac asap

(*ops-desk*) Say nature of mutation?
(*ops-desk*) Symptoms?
(Subject) Confirm medical evac as soon as wx permits.
(*ops-desk*) More information needed. Do you have a report with details?
(*Subject*) You're not fucking listening.
(*ops-desk*) Evac confirmed asap wx.
(*ops-desk*) Say nature of microbe mutation, upload report?
(*Subject*) Fuck you. Details available on evac so better hope we make it. Persons touching down must have Level A Hazmat gear. Aircraft must have USAF Transport Isolation System or equiv.
(*ops-desk*) Can you say symptoms, possible mitigation?
(*Subject*) Consider all survivors infected until tested negative.

Chapter Twenty-Five

LANGLEY, VIRGINIA

June 20th, 10:30 PM

(June 21st, 4:30 PM, New Zealand Standard Time)

"Dr. Mason? The satellite is live in three minutes."

Richard Mason hates being distracted. But, more importantly, he's scared and he doesn't want anyone to see it in his eyes.

He grunts in response, keeping his face fixed on the three computer screens on his desk. The screen with the yellow TOP SECRET//SAP-HV/TK banner is subdivided into sixteen video screens. As his eyes flick between the screens, fright stabs into him again.

All sixteen screens are still. Nothing moves, except the wind sweeping through the half-open door on Screen 8. The snowdrift piled against it mounts just a little higher every day. The pant leg on the man lying face down in an archipelago of dark blood icicles tugs just a little farther up. But, as always, Mason's eyes come back to Screen 12, where Mei Lingling lays with her head in the sink. It seems undignified, somehow, for that to be how somebody from the CAA – the ludicrously-named Chinese Antarctic Administration of the State Antarctic Research Committee – will find her.

She had been a renowned glaciologist once; a full Professor at Nanjing University.

Career on the rise but hit a terminal trough over a sink.

On the center of the dining table behind Mei is an unmarked clear containment sphere, fractured along several facets like a peeled flower. The screens are soundless, but he knows it's beeping softly and insistently.

Casualties had always been in the projections. The violence and *scale* of the microbial outgrowth once in its native environment, however, had been entirely unexpected.

Screen 2, a man tumbled at the foot of his bed, a kitchen knife buried in his back.

Screen 6, a scientist with no shirt on, sprawled wide in the snow like a scarecrow blown over in the night.

Screen 15, a heap of ice that no longer resembles a human corpse.

Nothing moves.

Except that's only true in the visible wavelengths. In the ultraviolet, every single dead body is positively *squirming* with activity. The former glaciologist over the sink has moved two inches since dying five weeks ago. The level of virulent, almost hostile growth has blown the fancy DARPA models right out of the window.

So far out that just thinking about it makes the fear tickle in his throat again.

Mason stands. After the satellite pass it'll be time to go home, but Screen 12 will stay with him, behind his eyes. Especially when he looks at his wife.

Tingzhi Mason looks a little like Mei Lingling.

He wakes up regularly now, dreaming of the mother of his child draped over their sink at home. Eyes fixed open in recrimination.

The CIA scientist strides out of his office to the vault at the end of the bland grey hallway. Above the door, an

LED screen scrolls with text: TOP SECRET // SAP ACCESS REQUIRED. Mason presses his badge against the reader and keys in an eight-digit pin.

He hardens his face. His eyes go blank.

He enters.

The satellite control center is dark. The large screens against the far wall have not yet lit up with live imagery.

"Mason." CIA Deputy Director for Operations Bill Stone emerges smoothly from the shadows.

As DDO, Stone holds the national authority to be the single focal point for execution of US clandestine operations. Not just for the CIA, as in the old days, but for all seventeen organizations in the US intelligence community. Stone's job is to handle the dirty work, but that isn't the only reason people call him Evil Bill behind his back. The man is a ghostly gargoyle, age written into every line in his scarred face.

"Sir."

"HAVE VIKING is turning into a cluster fuck."

"There's still useful data to be gathered." Mason's voice emerges cool and collected. He is a professional. He has won medals. He has weathered fuckups before. Mitigating a fuck-up more frequently makes a career at CIA than running a squeaky-clean op start-to-finish.

"We wired Dome-A for data," Stone hisses in his ear. "And I had no American deaths to explain to Director Navarro. You want to tell me how you plan to extract useful data from a Station where you have no eyes and no spectral analysis?"

"Someone will survive." Mason keeps his eyes straight ahead. The screens begin flickering. "Enough to compare the Dome-A spread to the South Pole spread and determine any anomalies."

"Since they missed their last comm pass, I'm curious what this confidence is rooted in."

The large screens dissolve into a vast expanse of snow. Dancing aurorae hover over the edge of the planet, visible from space. A speck of a Station in the middle of it all, at the South Pole of the planet. The satellite image zooms in.

The scorch marks on the snow by the food arch are immediately evident. The sensor angle doesn't let them see the extent of the damage but there is clearly a hole into which massive amounts of ice and snow have fallen. The satellite view skitters, then tracks over the snow.

Outside the food arch a naked body is dusted over with snow, a picture eerily like the one from Dome-A. Another lies on a plastic sheet, pixelated face staring upward.

"It's spreading," Stone whispers. Mason feels his breath tickle his neck. He doesn't reply.

He's scared again, but not of Bill Stone.

The only video feeds they have access to at Pole begin blinking in. Reels of digital video from the cameras on every corner of ARO are downlinked for later analysis. The video begins to get fuzzy as the satellite travels over the horizon from its target.

"Dr. Jon Kim. You remember him, right?"

"Right," Mason is careful to let no dislike trickle into his voice. "Program Manager at DARPA Biological Technologies Office. Former Harvard professor."

"He just sent me a rather interesting presentation," Stone says. "He remains convinced that our little extremophiles will undergo a forced evolution once they are brought out of a closed ecosystem."

"He's as wrong now as he was before. We saw no such evolution at Dome-A."

"Ah, but he says the takeover at Dome-A was too quick. Didn't necessitate a forced response because the microbes overcame every nutrient source in a matter of days. South Pole is a bigger station. More population diversity. More time needed to overwhelm it."

"Jonny Kim would nuke a nursery to study what radiation did to baby carcasses," Mason says evenly. "I wouldn't put much stock in his overkill theories."

"But should the microbes evolve to tolerate a less extreme environment, you underestimate how interesting I would find that," Stone replies. "So interesting that I'd give the gold star to whoever brought me that data. I'd hate to think my best scientist wasn't up to the job."

Mason's face doesn't change, but he doesn't go home after the satellite pass, either. He spends the next two hours on the phone with Antarctic Logistics, LLC, negotiating another Basler aircraft flight as soon as the weather would allow.

This time down to South Pole.

He falls asleep in his office and dreams of his wife lying dead over the sink.

Chapter Twenty-Six

SOUTH POLE STATION POPULATION: 28 (PRISONERS: 3; DECEASED: 13)

June 21st, 4:40 PM

"Okay, pressurizing up to three positive–"

"Nope, stop, I'm leaking. The seals are fucking shot from the sauna."

Wei and Jamie look up jerkily as the door to the South Pole clinic slams open. Station manager Bill Gaudin's eyes are furious, his face a congested purple. Andrea trails behind him. As always, her expression mirrors his.

"Where the fuck have you two been–" he rasps.

Wei looks at Jamie, and she slips backward. Brushes past Andrea.

She quietly snicks the lock of the door to the clinic shut.

"– we're in the middle of a fire emergency!" Gaudin says loudly. "Get your butts to the gym and get to work!"

Wei picks up a long scalpel. It rests easily in the gloved grip of his Hazmat suit.

Gaudin's eyes are drawn to its shiny tip, which now points at his gut.

A deadly silence falls over the clinic.

Wei's voice is eerily calm, but his eyes are hazy steel. "If you don't calm down right now, I'm going to sedate you for everyone's safety. Do you understand?"

"What the fuck?" Gaudin's wrinkled mouth opens and closes.

"Tell me you understand."

"I heard. I don't understand."

"That's good enough. Maybe it's just that time in the season when we're all a little frustrated, but the first symptom of the infection going around is rage. So you'd better show me some self-control, because if you raise your voice one – more – time – you will awaken handcuffed to your bed and confined to quarters on medical orders until sunrise."

The soft jabs with the knife arrest Gaudin's attention.

"Jamie?"

The nurse steps forward, herding Andrea back toward Gaudin with her larger size. "Both of you strip down. Everything comes off."

"What?" Andrea's hands cross over her breasts protectively. "Hell no!"

"Or I sedate you. Those are the options."

"Doc, there are firefighters out there who need your help," Gaudin says, careful to keep his voice low. "Your friends."

"I'm focusing on an issue that could kill *all* of us, not just a few. That's my medical judgment, and Jamie agrees with me. Now. Clothes off so I can examine you."

"Fuck that," Andrea says forcefully. Loudly. "You can't make me."

Wei is exasperated. "If you're concerned about me seeing you naked, Jamie will–"

Andrea breaks into a run. She lunges away from Jamie, sidestepping around her.

Jamie moves quickly, despite her Hazmat suit. As Andrea

blazes by, she reaches out and stabs her in the neck with a needle. It looks *painful.*

Andrea reaches the door.

She grasps the knob.

Her other hand reaches up to touch the needle embedded in her skin, plunger all the way down. She looks back at Jamie. Her lips start to form the word *bitch,* then her muscles just quit, and she slides heavily down to the tile.

Jamie reaches across to a medical cart and picks up another syringe. Bites the cap off and spits it out.

Looks at Gaudin.

Gaudin begins taking his clothes off.

"Will you at least tell me why the hell I'm doing this?"

"As soon as I've cleared you. That's a promise."

Wei takes fifteen solid minutes with his microscope, inspecting Gaudin's skin, before he looks up. "He should be clean."

"You didn't check his hair."

"I don't think–"

"Fuck thinking," Jamie snaps. "Fuck embarrassment. People are dying. I'm done worrying about fragile egos."

She pulls open a drawer and withdraws an electric razor.

"Whoa! What the fuck?" Gaudin's voice rises to its normal bellicose roar.

Jamie speaks through thinned lips. "I've seen three dead bodies today and there are more to come. Just fucking try me, buddy."

Jamie shaves his head, none too gently, and Wei can tell the hard young nurse has no love for him. She leaves nothing behind but a row of razor-burn pimples and the clear lines of a widow's peak. Gaudin glances at the shaggy locks of greying hair littering the floor. The corners of his mouth droop, and Wei feels fleetingly bad for him. It's been a rough winter for everyone.

"I'm clean, whatever that means," Gaudin says once he's done with the microscope. "So please. Pretty please, with candied sugar on top. Tell me what the fuck just happened."

Wei looks over his shoulder. "Jamie, get Andrea behind the curtain. Make sure she's awake before you start stripping her, please." Jamie rolls her eyes and Wei sighs, clouding the inside of his facemask. "Bill. Would you help me get this suit off?"

He sags onto a stool, brow damp with perspiration. He feels rundown. Like he's been sprinting for miles without stopping to consider his body's opinion on it. Behind the curtain, a razor starts buzzing. Despite himself, Wei has to chuckle. He'd told her not to undress Andrea… but he'd said nothing about shaving her head.

It takes a while for Wei to outline what he knows, starting with the people who entered the Dome-A truck and picked up the microbes first. "The microbes kill their host, so they're parasites," he finishes wearily. "They wait on your skin until you end up in the cold, then they multiply, and you become a danger to yourself and the rest of us. That's what just happened in the arches."

Except the microbes don't just wait.

Somehow, they actively encourage their hosts to go into the cold.

He'd felt those thoughts. So naggingly persuasive.

"And… we all have it? Well, I didn't. Right?"

"That's right. It passes by touch. Spencer was the first one exposed, and he's dead. Akinori went in that truck, and he's dead too."

Movement sparks behind the curtain. Andrea's voice, groggy and confused. Then Jamie, in firm tones triumphant with Brooklyn inflection.

"Rajan was in there," Gaudin glowers. "Weeks went in too!"

"They're not the only ones to be worried about now. *Anyone* who has been in close physical contact with them since are in danger. We need to address the problem, not the symptom."

A shrill braying wail erupts behind the curtain. *"You bitch you took my hair*!"

Wei keeps his eyes on Gaudin. "Starting at the top, with you and Andrea, Jamie and I intend to scan everybody. If you see someone without a shaved head, we haven't examined them. That makes them a danger to this Station's residents."

"And what about those who are infected? You know how to cure them?"

("Bitch, you fucking bitch, I'm gonna fuck you *up!"*)

"Uh-huh. Bake the microbes to death with 200 degrees of heat in the sauna."

The curtain draws back behind him. "She clean too?" Wei says over his shoulder.

"No."

"What?" He turns.

Jamie shakes her head grimly. "Based on the spread, I'd say recent close contact with someone who had first-hand exposure."

Wei coughs. "Uh, interesting. Do you think–"

Gaudin's face darkens. *"Weeks,"* he hisses.

For a big man, he moves fast; so fast Wei doesn't react in time to stop him. He bolts past Jamie and rips the curtain aside.

"You bitch!" Gaudin shrieks.

Andrea's eyes widen and she drops her hands from her slick head. Tears have put black hollows under her eyes and cut pale channels through her makeup. A mastectomy scar runs up one side of her chest.

"Billy–"

"You're with that rat motherfucker Weeks? Behind my back?"

"Gaudin," Jamie says.

He stabs a shaking finger at Andrea. "I got you this job. I went to bat for you, you ungrateful cunt!"

Wei stands up, and the room echoes with his booming voice. "BILL!"

Gaudin turns, accusing finger still stretched out at Andrea.

"Can't you see this is not the time?" the doctor shouts. "People are *dying*! And more deaths are certain unless you pull your head out of your ass and prioritize. DO YOU HEAR ME?"

Silence falls. A long silence, in which Wei glares thunderously at the Station manager, and Gaudin slowly deflates. Andrea shrivels up into a ball. Her fish-belly white legs, sown with puffy varicose veins, are drawn up against her chest. Both hands cover her hairless head. She looks haggard and half-crazy. Maybe it's the harsh white light, or their newly bald heads, but both Bill and Andrea seem smaller.

"I need you to get everyone into the lower gym. We shave them all, check them all, and put them all in the sauna. Even those with shaved heads, even us, in case of reinfection," Wei says. "Then we bring our Dome-A visitors over, and we do the same to them. All of that, and only that, is the priority right now. Can you help, or not?"

Gaudin swallows painfully.

"Yeah." He looks back at Jamie and Andrea. "Yeah, but this isn't over."

5:00 PM

Bill Gaudin makes the announcement over the public address system. Every crewmember in the Station (which is everyone except Ben Jacobs and the Chinese prisoners) is to report immediately to the lower gym. Most of them are there already.

The gym spans both floors of the Station. The lower gym is on the ground level, next to Destination Alpha, and is mostly a basketball court. This is where monthly karaoke, the 90 South volleyball league, and other social events are held. Overlooking it through a wide pane of glass, accessible only from the second floor, is a small upper gym; a workout room with treadmills, weights, and a narrow view of the ice outside.

Downstairs, confused voices stain the air. Rajan flits between people, trying to answer questions where he can. The trunklines for the internet run through the ice tunnels and the connection has been severed after the fires. Four people are confirmed dead. Four more, including TC, are missing. Summer wanders in, limping, her face and yellow fire-resistant pants discolored with smoke. She folds to her knees like a stick puppet under the basketball net, breathes deeply into an oxygen mask, and coughs soot into her fist. Rajan sees her staring dully at the spots of blood on his fire jacket. His words wash over her like a fall breeze.

She's killed someone too, for the first time. He recognizes the look.

More and more of them are getting blood on their hands.

Wei picks up the phone hanging on the wall of the upper gym, punches in the code for the PA system, and his voice booms out over the basketball court.

"Good evening, Polies. This is Doc Wei. I'm up here."

The eyes of the crew below turn up to the window. A surprised murmur runs through the crowd as they see the Hazmat suits. The seals are ruined from exposure to the extreme heat of the sauna, but Jamie and Wei aren't wearing them for functionality.

They need everyone to play ball. This is for effect.

"By now you've all been witness to some pretty strange things. Rage attacks, people taking their shirts off at eighty below, the first murder in Antarctica... and then several more. Every one of us has lost someone dear to us."

Murmurs. Nods.

"There are two important things you should all know. First, you may all be infected with a dangerous parasite that is responsible for all these deaths. If you have this parasite on you, and you go into the cold – that includes the beer can and the ice tunnels – you will almost certainly die. But the second thing is just as important: we know how to kill it."

Even through the glass, he can tell there's perfect silence in the gym below.

"Look around and you'll notice that some of your fellow Polies have had their heads shaved. With one exception, these people are parasite-free. We'll have you come up here, two by two. Jamie and I will examine you for this infestation, answer all your questions, and take samples so we can study this organism and protect future Polies. It will take time, so please be patient with us, but I promise you that by midnight, this Station will be parasite-free."

He looks down at the crowd. "Now. Who wants their free haircut first?"

10:05 PM

No winter season lacks for memorably awkward moments, karaoke in the lower gym being just one example. But twenty-seven people crammed into the eight-person sauna, newly bald and naked except for a single towel wrapped around each of them, would forever be the new standard.

The temperature needle stands at eighty degrees. Some people sit, some stand; they are all shiny with sweat. Someone giggles, a high and nervous cackle that dries up the second Doc Wei enters with Jamie.

Wei has his Hazmat suit on, but Jamie wears just a towel around her pale body. She carries her fire axe in both hands. There are two entrances to the sauna; a front door opening into a corridor of the Station and a back door usually used only for 300 Club events, opening onto a ladder that goes down the back of the Station toward the Ceremonial South Pole. Jamie takes up a position by the back door, and her face looks carved from stone.

"By tonight, I hope this nightmare will be behind us all." Wei looks around. "You should know that the microbes have a survival response. When the temperature rises high enough, they will fight back. You will want to run out of that door into the cold so the pain will stop. It sounds crazy, right? People running naked into the cold; that never happens at Pole."

A few half-hearted murmurs trickle out of 300 Club members.

"But that's why we're *all* here, infected and un-infected alike. If you're clean, you will save someone's life in the next fifteen minutes. If you see someone having an adverse response, understand they are not themselves. Do whatever you must to restrain them. Jamie's not here to fight anyone trying to leave through the back door over there. She's here to make sure that if you leave, you don't get back in."

The murmurs dry up. Wei steps out without a further word.

He places a fire axe through the handles of the front door.

Then he turns the temperature up as far as it will go.

Keyon Geerts immediately feels the effects of the heat. Katie watches him anxiously. Andrea slumps in a corner, chewing her nails, bald head slick with pearls of sweat. She lets out an occasional silent spasm. From across the sauna, Gaudin's eyes crawl venomously over her, then Weeks, who sits on the floor, arms wrapped around his knees, large gold-rimmed glasses steamed up. He looks very different without his long grey ponytail and beard. Rajan looks across the small sauna at Summer, who sits uncomfortably next to Tim. His arm is around her.

Keyon cracks first. He rocks back and forth, muttering to himself, then abruptly springs to his feet. "Oh Lord Jesus, it hurts."

"Tim, get over there," Jamie directs. "Stay calm, everyone. There'll be more."

Weeks is next. His head lashes from side to side. There's foam on his lips. He doesn't cry out, just bolts determinedly at Jamie and the door. She swings the handle of the axe, cracking him firmly in the side of the head, and Rajan jumps on top of him.

Weeks fights him, furiously and silently, and it takes four people to restrain him, by which time half the sauna is stirring restlessly, like a basket full of mewling hungry cats.

Suddenly it seems like there are too many of *them*. Enough to overwhelm the healthy and barrel out into the cold.

Patches of skin turn black. Then the screaming begins.

Wei stands at the door, drawn face showing his age, watching the bizarre scene play out. Weeks and Andrea spasm on the floor. Gaudin stands on a bench, shying away from Michele, who gasps in painful little yelps. Towels go flying as the healthy attempt to restrain their infected friends. And the hellish screaming goes on and on and on, a hailstorm of painful copper spikes sinking deeper into everyone's head.

Until, finally, it is over.

Weeks stops screaming first. The blackness swallowing his whole body begins to curl up and flake away, withering to the floor. Keyon falls silent next, then Andrea. Katie is still sobbing, splayed and naked on the floor of the sauna, black dust spilling away from her. Jonah sits on a wooden bench, cradling blackened fingers like a bouquet of burnt flowers. Dave Atkins and Yanis Pohano, who have spent the season locked in a bitter rivalry over Bethany Hamidani, are a unified front for perhaps the first time ever, restraining research assistant Sheryl Whitney. The steel din subsides into smaller moans and cries as the microbes release their death-grip on their hosts.

At last, only steaming silence.

"The 300 Club has really gone downhill," someone mutters. No one laughs.

The winter crew sits on the floor, or slumped on the wooden slats, trying not to look at each other. Most of them are naked now, hot phantoms sticky with sweat, a pile of sooty towels lumped in the corner. They wait, stricken or scared or both, then someone starts to clap.

Another person joins in.

Then another.

The claps come faster, more vigorous, until they sweep the room in a quickly building manic frenzy. Small puffs of black dust rise from the wooden slats.

Slowly, silence falls over the sauna. A victorious silence.

"Great job, everyone." Rajan breathes into it almost reverently. "*We made it.*"

The coils of the sauna tick quietly. One by one, the Polies straighten, gather themselves. Grin ruefully, breathe shaky sighs of relief. Weeks goes to cover himself up, then draws his hand back from the sooty dark towel in revulsion. Jamie releases her death grip on the axe.

"Thank God," she says, at last. "The nightmare is over."

Later, as he sits in the sauna alone, sweating, Wei is swept with the sudden certainty that those words will soon rise and spit wetly in their faces, like a mocking monsoon wind.

By midnight the Station is a silent graveyard. The Polies barricade and lock every entrance to the Station from the inside, including the back door to the sauna, so the missing infected crewmembers can't get in. Jonah gathers a few volunteers to help Daniel Baia consolidate what food there is inside into the galley; no one will be taking a cold trip through the ice tunnels to what remains of the food arch. Weeks turns the Station's temperature up to a balmy eighty-two degrees. Khaled goes by Siri's room, hoping their near-death experience has changed her mind about breaking up, only to find that the opposite is true. Her concussion is making her head spin, and she tells him in no uncertain terms that the next time he comes by hoping to get lucky, that luck will be to the tune of a Vans sneaker size five between his legs. Doc Wei fights the good fight, loses, pops one Perc, a second immediately after it, and falls fast asleep. Gaudin sits rigid on the bed in his room, hard springs knifing into his fleshy thighs. He stares into the distance, drinking straight out of a whisky bottle. None of his thoughts are pleasant, or even particularly sane.

The lights glow over empty hallways. No one notices the soft pushing on the doors.

First Destination Alpha, then Tango, then up the beer can to Zulu.

The back entrance to the sauna, then the external fire exits to each of the dorm wings rattle, but don't give.

Eventually the common radio channel squeals with static.

"Is anyone there? The station's all locked up, would someone let me in?"

Ben Jacobs stands in the beer can.

Chapter Twenty-Seven

Ben Jacobs stands in the beer can, dressed in Big Red, looking cold and confused. A small group of Polies at Destination Zulu stare at him through the porthole windows, an egg-carton of eyes filled with dismay and simmering hostility.

"Hang tight, Ben." Jonah's voice on the radio is that of an age-rusted tape squeaking in the cassette player. "We need Doc to get here."

It takes Jamie a while to revive Wei from his drugged sleep. His eyes look panicky and bloodshot when he finally awakes. "Come on," she says, her voice gentle. "We might have some trouble."

Wei feels the tension in the hairless crowd as he walks up to Destination Zulu. The Polies are as restless as unfed tigers in a zoo cage. Pacing, back and forth, almost hungrily. For the first time he isn't afraid of the microbe but of the humans he's locked in a two-story tin box with. They look ready to tear Ben apart with their bare hands.

Wei holds up the numbers 45 with his fingers, then makes a dialing gesture. Ben fiddles with his radio.

"Doc? Can you hear me?"

"Ben, why aren't you sheltering in place?"

"Uh, maybe in all the craziness they got forgotten… but our Chinese friends are out of food! TC was supposed to bring supplies, but he never made it. There was a lot going on over the radio, and then it all went silent, so I thought I'd better come over."

"That was not smart."

"But I'm fine!" Ben beams. He's speaking with a bit of a lisp. "A little cold standing here, but fine."

The doctor stares through the porthole at him. He'd assumed Philip had gotten the microbe from Ben, but it could have been directly from the Chinese scientists. And if Ben really is clear, he'll be safer in the Station with everyone else.

"What the heck is going on, anyway?"

"I'll explain soon. For now, I can't let you in unless you agree to have your head shaved and be examined for a microbe infection."

"Jeez, doc, my hair? Really?"

"Do you see a single head with hair on it on this side of the door?"

Ben squints through the porthole, then sighs and spreads his arms. "Whatever, I guess."

Wei looks over his shoulder and issues curt orders. The group of onlookers organizes into two rows, like a defensive line about to receive a kickoff. Jamie hefts her axe, then Wei unchains the door.

"Come in and kneel down right here," Wei says.

For five long seconds, Ben doesn't move. He stares at them, one by one.

As if trying to calculate something.

Jamie's fingers tighten on her axe.

Then he says, in a friendly voice, "Sure thing."

Ben steps inside the warm station. He shrugs off his jacket, unzips his fleece, and goes to his knees beside Jamie. She stays rooted to the spot for a long moment, staring at him. Wei shifts uneasily, then she hands her axe to Keyon and pulls on tall gloves.

Wei observes Ben carefully as she shaves his head. His skin is reddened, probably from the cold walk over, but he doesn't seem itchy or otherwise bothered by the elevated temperature in the Station. The doctor pulls out his microscope. The skull is one of the first places where the microbial infestation is noticeable, and he combs over Ben's head closely.

At last, he stands back. "He's clear so far, but let's move the cordon to medical, just in case he turns aggressive in there."

"I'm aggressive for a sandwich right now, that's about it," Ben says cheerfully. Oddly spaced caverns flash in his mouth.

"And what about the others at ARO?" Johan asks. The word *prisoners* hangs in the air, unsaid.

"One crisis at a time," Wei replies.

Wei spends forty-five minutes going over Ben on the observation table in the clinic. Finally, he straightens and looks at Jamie with relief. "He's clear," he says.

"Except for his dental," Jamie cracks. "Jeez, Ben, I hope the other guy looks worse."

"Just being clumsy," Ben replies, even as Wei says, "Jamie, for Pete's sake."

"What?" she shrugs. "Should we put him in the sauna, just in case?"

"We could," Wei shrugs. "He's clean, though."

"I mean, so what if –"

"Whoa, hey there," Ben throws his hands up. "Look, I can be okay with being shaven, and stripped, and even stared at for minutes on end, but I gotta draw the line somewhere."

"And your line is the sauna?" Jamie raises an eyebrow.

"Hey, when you get full-body heat rashes, you come talk to me." Ben winces, as if just thinking about it causes him pain. "There's a reason I'm not in the 300 Club, and it ain't the cold."

"It's fine, Jamie." The doctor sounds weary; ready to return to bed, and his drugged sleep. "Welcome back, Ben."

"Thanks, doc," Ben grins, revealing reddened gums and several missing teeth. "We're happy to be on the inside."

BOOK THREE
Quarantine

JUNE 22ND – JUNE 26TH

The light of righteousness did not shine on us,
and the sun did not rise upon us.
We took our fill of the paths of lawlessness and destruction,
and we journeyed through trackless deserts.

Wisdom 5:6-7

EXCERPT from:

In the Wake of War: A First-hand Account of Humanity's Deadliest Struggle,

Assembled from the diaries of Mariana Egan

[Excerpt begins]

When the first bombs dropped over Beijing in October 2027, I was embedded with the Wolf Pack, the 8th Fighter Wing out of Kunsan Air Base in South Korea. I remember the elation in the war room when satellite imagery reported a direct hit to Zhongnanhai. Of course, the seat of the Chinese communist party, their White House, had long been deserted, but that didn't matter.

The building was 700 years old, priceless history burning within its walls, but that didn't matter either. A visceral bullet had been fired into the heart of China's expansionist ambitions.

The truth is, the Americans won the war too quickly.

Since the Vietnam War, America had built an arsenal like no other. A generation of warriors sharpened their teeth on the permissive theaters of the Middle East. They made war, studied the results, then applied improvements - all while the war still raged. Fifteen years in the deserts of Iraq and mountains of Afghanistan taught everyone from flag-officers to grim young element leaders how to fight with increasing lethality. Gather intel from nothing. Make real-time decisions. Use artificial intelligence to achieve stunning precision and defeat deception tactics. Train and hunt beside allied nations. China was no push-over adversary, of course. In three years of warfare, the Allied Army would never get beyond the razor-wire and thin foothold of a flimsy forward operating base. But the Chinese military had not been to war like America had.

They had saber-rattled, run drills, spent billions on armaments and a blue-water Navy, but their Admirals and Generals had not weathered Day One of a real war. America's warmakers had combat experience and the certain knowledge that their population would not tolerate a long battle. America moved quickly and their opponents crumbled quickly.

Too quickly.

Many books will be written about the Taiwan straits, the islands created out of nothing but dredged-up sand and cement poured on coral, and the first Chinese surge from those islands on the eve of the US recognizing Taiwan as an independent country. Many others will analyze America's decision not to meet the Chinese where they were ready, in Taipei, but to take the fight to their borders. The precision strikes of Halloween, when the US Air Force decapitated the North Korean regime almost single-handedly, will occupy its rightful place in the annals of military history beside Dunkirk and Normandy. The North Koreans got just one ICBM launch away, and it fell into the seas just east of Tokyo, a quick and savage end to two generations of nuclear ambitions. Overnight, China had a two-front war. As troops from seven NATO countries poured north across the 38th parallel, their Navy was stretched too thin, their Air Force was safe only over mainland China, the streets of Taiwan were a haven of guerilla warfare, and the only thing on their side was half-a-million cannon fodder soldiers amassing at the Tripoint border with Russia and North Korea.

America could have stopped there. Should have stopped there. But like a tigress on the hunt, a finely-tuned war machine doesn't consider stopping when its prey is on the run. Bombs dropped on Beijing; civilian pundits in distant safe harbor made gleeful projections for how the Allies would carve up China once Xi's Communists had been sent packing. And that Russia could not abide.

Like the Americans, the Russians had a war machine with real experience. Fostered in Syria and Libya; pruned by their disastrous campaign in Ukraine. It didn't have the surgeon-like American precision, but neither did it need such a thing. All Russia needed was an excuse to step in, and two foreign armies on its doorstep was just that.

An excuse to get involved.

Chapter Twenty-Eight

South Pole Station is silent.

The view from any window is a depressing shadowy whiteout, and the cardboard cutouts are back up in the galley. Thirteen people are dead. Most of their bodies won't be recovered. Everyone is numb.

Tim Fulton is especially numb.

It has been twenty-four hours since Tim's first time in the sauna, watching Wei and Siri almost die. Fourteen hours since the second time, watching the bugs attack everyone else.

Eight hours since Summer told him she no longer wanted to be with him.

It had been just an ice thing last year, she had said.

He shouldn't have come this year, she had said.

And the cruelest blow of all saved for last.

"I'm going to be with someone else, Tim. I'm so sorry to do this now... but if there's one thing the last twenty-four hours has shown me, it's that life is short. I have to chase my own happiness."

Tim sits on the floor of his room. Her words swell to take up all the air, strangling him as surely as the microbes had.

I have to chase my own happiness.

An irrational thought zooms boldly across his mind like a meteor –

(*Am I right? Fuckin' A*)

– and his chest closes up with tears he cannot cry.

I have to chase my own happiness.

She had never been happy. Meanwhile, he had been as deliriously happy as a prospector discovering a strain of gold deeper than anything in the territories. Of course he'd tried to come back and stake a claim.

But he was just somebody to pass the time with.

A bit player. The credits had rolled, and he hadn't noticed.

Tim doesn't leave his dark room until dinner time. In the galley, before he even reaches for a plate, guilt blooms across Yanis and Bethany's faces as they turn to look at him.

With a crashing feeling, he realizes they're talking about him. His breakup with Summer is making the rounds.

Thirteen people fucking dead, and his breakup is making the rounds.

Tim leaves the galley. Tries not to run on the way back to his room. He stands in the dark with his forehead against his door, and her words come back to beat him (*I have*) over the head (*to chase*) and stab him in the side (*my own happiness*).

Tim has never been lucky with women. His high-school girlfriend Shubhangi broke up with him right before prom. There was no other man; she went alone. She just didn't want to go with him. In college there was June, who stopped returning Tim's calls one day and, for the next two years, walked determinedly past him on campus like she'd never known him. At his first job it took months to get up the courage to ask Gail out only for her to say I'm sorry, I don't think of you that way. Then Benji in marketing dumped Gail, dumped her hard, and she changed her answer. They had a nice time for a while, but something about him just wasn't enough. Gail boomeranged back to Benji.

I have to chase my own happiness. I'm going to be with someone else.

Benji and Gail broke up again, but Gail didn't come back to him.

Tim wonders if what Yanis and Bethany had *really* been whispering about was Summer's new beau.

It would be Rajan the scientist, of course.

Rajan, Mister Man in Charge.

Rajan, just another fucking Benji.

With Kamala, Tim had found color in his monochromatic existence for the first time. Things weren't perfect; she had a hard edge she impaled him on when she felt vindictive, which was often. Toward the end, he'd harbored a suspicion that she was cheating on him. Another Benji, lurking somewhere in the wings. But weirdly, he hadn't cared.

Lying in his cold bed at South Pole, Tim re-examines this thought and decides that yes, it's true. He hadn't cared. He'd been happy, and the reason was simple: Sam. Their child, their beautiful baby. Sam was his life, the color in his day. Sam's gurgling laugh blunted the sharp point of Kamala's bite. And when Sam was taken away, all Tim wanted was to flee, as far away from the world as he could get.

The South Pole was pretty far from the world.

When happiness found him there, with Summer, Tim should have suspected a farce. But even after the incredible loss he'd suffered, he dared to believe in love again, and so the familiar sledgehammer returned. Benji, back for what was his. No more color in his life, and nowhere on the planet far enough to escape from that.

The tears break through the dam then. For Summer, for his child, for his life of failure. For the heartbreaks that have been the cement between each achingly small brick of joy.

It leaves him raw, bruised, and beaten, even more than the microbe had.

Tim's alarm goes off with a shrill spike the next morning, and he listens to it peal and thinks about how nice it might be to kill himself.

There's no work to go to. No one is leaving the station. No matter how many invisible microbes are glommed onto their faces or crotches as they sleep or fuck, they will be safe inside the warm Station. Someday there will be a job to go to, but today the Pole crew is living in quaran-times.

The public address system scratches into life. "This is Comms with a reminder from Station management. No one is to leave the Station. The beer can and the observation decks are off limits. There will be only two meals served due to food rationing. Please join everyone for a memorial for our thirteen lost tomorrow, in the galley, ten AM."

Tim doesn't leave his room at all that day. Doesn't leave his bed. He eats a protein bar but is not even hungry enough to finish it. He tries to go back to sleep.

Outside, the windstorm begins to die down.

The following morning the memorial drives Tim out of his room. He slips into the galley twenty minutes after it has begun and stands against the back wall, looking between the heads of the winter crew. At the front of the room, Weeks leads them through a fumbling prayer, then Michele Reinert's warbling voice rises, alone, singing words that Tim recognizes. *O Christ, whose voice the waters heard, and hushed their raging at Thy word / Who walked on the foaming deep, and calm amid its rage did sleep / O hear us when we cry to thee, for those in peril on the sea.*

The hymn for those lost to the infinite depths of the ocean strikes a raw chord in him, briefly dimming Tim's sense of detachment. Looks of shock sit on every face in the galley. Even the sworn atheists in the crowd have their heads bowed. The large galley looks empty. People cluster in smaller groups, but every clique has someone missing.

"We've lost one out of three people we started this winter season with. Thirteen families on the mainland who will never be whole again," Andrea says. The deputy manager's voice is reedy, scared. She looks like a shell of herself, hands wringing openly, this unexpected moment of leadership dwarfing her. Tim looks around for Gaudin but doesn't see him. Doesn't see Ben either.

He does see Summer, though, looking beautiful and lost, and the sudden urge to put his arms around her makes him feel dizzy and helpless.

Andrea's voice quivers as she tries to find her footing in the spotlight. "All the rest of us still here can do is hold onto each other, as tightly as we can, and make it to sunrise together."

"What about next season?" Rob Booth, Antarctic veteran of two decades, asks quietly. "Will there even be a next season?"

No one knows how to respond. Many of the Polies are repeat crewmembers. They have left families and creature comforts behind, time and again, to be the flimsy arms holding up humanity's flag at the bottom of the world. Losing the Pole is personal – just as personal as losing a crewmate.

It suddenly hurts to be here, choked by loss of all kinds. Tim takes a small step back, then another.

"Oh Lord," Tim hears Jamie mutter softly to Daniel. "I

wonder if this is how it felt to be at Dome-A Station a few weeks ago."

"Not much of a silver lining, but at least we're not prisoners at someone else's Station."

Tim fades into the corridor, then back to his room.

This time, Ager and Kevin Eastburg are the only people in the galley, quietly arguing over layers of network diagrams spread across the bench tables. Tim scurries past them, feeling their eyes on his back, hoping they won't say anything to him.

Normally, the leftovers fridge would be filled with plastic-wrapped trays holding the remains of the previous day's buffet. But with no access to the food arch, and rationing, it's empty except for two lonely plastic containers. Back in his room, Tim eats cold fried peas and week-old clumpy hash-browns with his fingers. He tries to check email, but the SATCOM is down. The cables from the satellite dishes run through the ice tunnels, which is probably what Ager and Kevin had been arguing about.

He is truly all alone.

A soft knock sounds on his door.

Tim sits still and quiet. Barely breathing. His lights are off. He's terrified that it's Summer, come to do a pity check-up. Or worse, Rajan, come to have a man-to-man talk, see if he can be *cool* with it or if it's going to be a *problem*.

He wonders how quickly he can bleed out if he slashes his wrists right now.

The knock comes quietly again.

"Tim, it's Jonah."

He lets out a long breath. If anyone at Pole is least likely to make a social call for platitudes, it's the introverted misanthrope Jonah. "I'm coming."

Tim turns on the light. Wipes his face dry. Starts to look for a comb, then remembers he doesn't have hair anymore.

At the door, Jonah bears no expression on his face. "I thought I'd come by and fill you in on what's going on," he says evenly. He makes no mention of Summer, though he must know, and for that Tim is truly, sheepishly grateful.

"Medical has been scanning public use areas for microbes. They've found… a few. Dormant, but we've all probably picked up a few more bugs from random surfaces."

Tim flinches.

"Doc thinks it won't be bad. A couple of pinpricks in the sauna. Expect Andrea to sign you up for a Pole-wide rotating sauna schedule. That'll be the new norm."

"And SATCOM is down, right?"

"Yeah. A simple fix, but no one's chomping at the bit to go into the tunnels to repair it. We've got fuel for two weeks, but only enough food for a week, so maybe then."

Tim sighs. "At least we've got a week. Maybe they can repair the Hazmat suits."

"Yeah." Jonah grimaces. "That works out fine for everyone here at Station."

"Uh-huh?" Then it hits him, and he feels like a complete asshole. "Oh God. The Dome-A visitors."

"Prisoners, more like. They're locked up… and they've been without food for two, maybe three days now. I don't subscribe to the *they brought it here, they can reap the consequences* talk going around. And yet…" Jonah looks at his hands. "Yet I'm not volunteering to walk across the snow with food when it's minus 100 degrees out and I *know* the parasites are active at that temperature. Neither is anyone else."

Tim hears himself speak from very far away. "I'll do it."

"Oh no," Jonah says immediately. "No, I wasn't suggesting–"

"You weren't. I was."

"Somebody's going to end up with the short straw to go into the cold for food. It doesn't have to be you. It could be anyone."

"But you said it. That's a week from now."

Tim is thankful Jonah can't hear how dark his thoughts are. He's freefalling, and the only way he could possibly feel worse would be to *protect* that shitty existence while someone else starves to death a quarter-mile away.

"I won't even have to expose myself to a hundred below if I take a Sno-Cat."

"Except between the Sno-Cat and ARO. And it's negative fifty in the tunnels on your way to the fuel arch. Doc thinks that's not the most active temperature for the microbes, but that's a theory based on a single observation."

Jonah looks incredibly uncomfortable, as if he's responsible for imprinting the idea onto Tim's brain. The truth is so much simpler. *I'm going to kill myself, one way or the other. It might as well be* for *something, instead of to* avoid *something.*

Tim says, "I'll do it."

Chapter Twenty-Nine

The whole Station is lined up along the first floor, watching Tim clomp down the hallway in his snow-boots and Big Red, skin still sweaty from his sauna bath. He looks straight ahead to Doc Wei, waiting by Destination Zulu. He passes Rajan, who looks somberly after him, then Summer, who looks horrified, her fingers stuffed in her mouth. Like she has something she wants to say, except, she's already said what she really means, hasn't she?

It won't be too bad if the bugs do get me, he thinks. *Let her wrestle with the real cost of her happiness.*

Andrea steps in front of Tim; there's no sign of Gaudin again. Or Ben. "Are you sure you want to do this?" she says. "The Chinese brought the bugs here. We don't owe them anything."

"That's not the way I want to think." His voice carries in the quiet hallway. "I don't think it's how any of us should think."

Tim turns over his shoulder and allows himself one very small moment to bask in everyone's eyes on him. "Those three Chinese scientists may not have started the season with us, but they're at Pole now. That makes them Polies too."

It isn't quite Lincoln-level oratory, but it'll do.

Wei clips a black case to a duffel bag of food. Inside, Tim

knows, are two microscopes, one digital and one analog, and four microbe samples in a climate-controlled cooler. He nods somberly at Wei as he picks it up. He feels like one of the Mercury astronauts, carrying a case with his breathing oxygen. On his way to his spaceship, where death might await.

Tim feels his lips, then his legs, start to tremble, but he clenches his jaw and faces forward. Wei pulls the door open, and he steps into the beer can.

Chapter Thirty

June 24th, 1:00 PM

Through the porthole of Destination Zulu, Tim can see the worried faces of the crew. He hangs there for a moment, trying to pick out Summer's face to fix in his memory one last time. But he doesn't see her, and it doesn't matter, because until the day he dies –

(*could be today bucko*)

– he will remember her as she was when she told him she was moving on. Smooth, beautiful, and marble-cold, every atom pre-arranged and immovable.

Tim turns his back on the Station.

His boots clatter loudly on the rungs. His breath flows heavier as the metal of the Station gives way to the ice of the Antarctic.

A radio squawks at his waist. Tim is carrying two radios. Ager has fixed the transmit button on one radio to be permanently on, so they can hear him breathe. Know he's alive even if he's not talking; mine his death for data if needed. Doc Wei's voice comes through a different channel on the other radio.

"How're you doing, Tim?"

How is he doing? *I'm wishing I'd been raised with God in my life. At least then I could feel some hope for a better existence after this one.*

How is he *doing*? The lights are out in the subterranean levels, his headlamp the only illumination, and the darkness is stripping away the dull blanket swaddling his emotions, dwarfing him in a sadness so immense he can't even begin to explain it. *Isolation is a constant companion in Antarctica, but mine feels like the black tunnel ahead. The little light I carry has no hope against the endless darkness. That's how I'm doing.*

He has to say something, though. "Been a while since I've been out here. Feels good."

Well, lookie here, kids. Looks like today's contestant Timmy is an honest-to-God prodigy at this martyr shit.

Tim forges deeper into the tunnel, breath puffing in faintly lit clouds. He wants Summer to hear his last breaths. If he must die, he wants it to be this way.

Halfway down the tunnel, Tim sets the medical case into the ice wall, beside the Buzz Aldrin shrine. This cutout in the wall dates to the 2016 summer season, when the second man on the moon visited the South Pole. Part of a tourist trip on a private airplane, the former astronaut had fallen ill immediately after flying in. Altitude sickness deteriorated to fluid in his lungs, and the Pole doc had recommended an immediate evacuation. The Polies created a shrine memorializing either the novelty or inanity of his presence; only that season's crew knew which. Inside a glass box is a tissue Buzz supposedly left behind in the clinic.

Monogrammed by the Pole machinist, a plaque: "Stay back! Space germs."

If you only knew how infectious the Pole can be, Buzz.

Apparently Buzz had also tweeted, from Antarctica, a picture of a pyramid-shaped mountain, captioning it: "We are all in danger. It is evil itself." Tim has no idea if that's true or an urban myth, but standing in a tunnel everyone else is too afraid to venture into, it sure feels true.

Tim uses tongs within the cooler to pull out two microscope slides and sets them in the ice shelf. He warms up the analog microscope with the heat gun, then slips the first slide under its lens.

"This is the sample from Kathryn's body, at… it's minus 46 now. Wow, uh, it's covered. There's black-tinged stuff everywhere."

"Is it moving? Do you see any cellular division?" Wei's voice is tinny through the second radio.

Tim squints. Wei has talked him through a series of slides collected from previously infected Polies, so he knows roughly what he's looking for. "Uh… it's pretty still. No multiplication."

He follows the same process with the second sample; this one from Wei's previously infected skin after the sauna treatment. "Nothing here," he reports. "No microbes, no growth."

"Check again. Be very thorough. Check all the magnifications."

Tim spends ten minutes staring at every inch of the second sample, shifting his legs to keep the cold away. "I got nothing, Doc."

"Awesome," Wei says warmly. "The ice tunnels may be warm enough to be safe. That's great news. Great."

Tim laughs emptily. It hangs in the derelict air of the tunnel, a cold and unhappy sound.

He plods deeper into the pitch black. The tunnel loops around the food arch and emerges into the warmer, faintly-lit fuel arch. The smell of smoke is stronger here. He disconnects the Sno-Cat from its trickle charger and rolls up the two corrugated doors separating the arch from the ramp to the outside. Cold air rushes in, and he flees back to the warmth of the Sno-Cat, suddenly afraid.

The cold is something to fear now. A catalyst that favors the enemy.

Tim trundles the Sno-Cat up the ramp, then past the Station. The stilted ARO is just visible against the horizon, red beacon flashing, and he drives slowly and carefully toward it.

"What's the temperature outside?" Wei.

"Minus 88. Parasite heaven." Tim doesn't give himself time to think. "Time to find out if your sauna therapy really works, Doc."

He leaves the engine running.

Jerks open the door, grabs the duffel bag, and runs for the door of ARO.

Runs like his life depends on it.

The thermostat is off and he hears the wind booming somewhere. He cranks the heat up, then races upstairs, past plaques of previous winter-over staff. The main room smells rank, like a college kid's dorm room. *If this weren't Antarctica, I might think it smells like stale weed.* The Dobson room door is inexplicably open. Quickly, heart racing, Tim closes it. "You raised in a barn, Ben?" he mutters aloud.

"What? What's going on?" Wei asks.

"Ben just didn't pull a door fully closed when he left. No big deal."

Cutting off the wind means he can now feel the heater

pumping warm air into the room. Downstairs, he strips off his clothes so he can see every inch of his own skin, plugs the digital microscope into the wall, and uses the screen of Jamie's cell phone to examine himself closely. His hands, legs, crotch.

"Far as I can tell, I'm still clear," he declares.

"How do you feel?" Wei asks. "Angry, tired?"

"A little tired, but just from running in here. I think I'm fine."

"Okay. Set up the other two samples."

Tim opens the door to the outside. Cold wind sweeps in, chilling him to the core. He's less scared of it now that he knows he's bug-free, but that's no reason to dawdle. He places the second pair of microbe slides outside on the metal landing, ten feet apart, then slams the door.

Once he catches his breath, he walks down to the locked nitrogen room on the first floor. He hesitates, then bangs his gloved fist on the door.

"Hello in there! Can you hear me?"

A mill of voices grows quickly behind the door. Only one speaks in English. "Yes!" he hears. "Please open, please!"

Then another word that sends guilt lancing through him. "Hungry!"

"I have food, okay? Lots of food! But you have deadly microbes on you, so I need you to step back."

"Please, open door! *Open door*!" He hears a thud, like someone throwing themselves against the metal door. The voices get more frantic. Another thud.

"Listen!" Tim shouts desperately. "I'm the only one who will come out here. *Listen*! So if you touch me, and I get sick, there's no more food. Do you understand? Step back from the door!"

One voice rises above the others, speaking hoarsely in

another language. The clamor falls until only that voice remains, then it switches to English. "We step back, sir," the voice says.

Tim hesitates. They would be justified not to trust him; to force their way out the second he unlocks the door. If he comes into contact with them… if they take his Sno-Cat…

Well, he'd come here to die, hadn't he?

Best get on with it.

Tim unlocks the door.

A gust of warmer air washes over him, then peters out. It's below freezing inside the cell, but still warmer than the rest of ARO; a single heater glows against the far wall where three stick-thin men stand. On the back of the wave of warmth wafts another smell, like feces left to thicken in the sun.

Tim hefts the large case filled with food into the room. "If you ration this, it's enough to last you for two weeks. By that time we'll be running out of food ourselves back at the Station. So either we'll figure something out, or we'll starve together."

The oldest man speaks, and he realizes this is who had calmed the other two. "Thank you for food," he says in slow English.

"Do you… know about the microbes? The parasites on your skin?"

The man spreads his arms, conveying confusion. Tim explains slowly, the best he can, what Wei has learned about the microbes. "We think they came with you from Dome-A. Are you familiar with these?"

Tim opens the medical case and slides a skin biopsy kit across the floor toward them. The three men take turns poring it over, and the third one replies rapidly in Mandarin. The old man translates. "For skin. Skin graft?"

"Skin sample, yes. Our doctor is trying to figure out when it might be safe to expose ourselves to the cold. If we could get samples from you, it might confirm a few things."

The men talk among themselves. "We help. But in here is not good. Very..." The old man makes a gesture for small, but Tim understands. He means imprisoned. Cut off. Not in charge of his own destiny, unable to tell if he will live or die.

"Please. You can let... outside?"

"No!" Tim exclaims. "The outside is very dangerous if the microbes are on your skin."

The old man points at him. "Outside."

"Tim, Gaudin is going to flip his shit," Wei says over the radio. "They could leave ARO at any time. Bring their microbes to the Station and reinfect all of us."

"They almost starved to death locked in here," Tim flares up. "I won't be responsible for letting that happen again." He looks at the old man, who seems to have followed the conversation. "It's *very* important that you stay inside this building. Do you understand? If you leave... you'll become like your friend in the truck."

The old man says, somberly, "Angry."

Tim nods. "Angry. Stay here, keep the heat on, and you'll be safe." He stands back from the door. "Please, be careful not to touch me. But come on, get out of there."

The other two refugees look up, hope coloring their faces. The old man smiles for the first time, revealing a gap in his front teeth. It stirs something in Tim's memory. "What is your name, sir?"

It's a sorry smile, but he manages one anyway. "Tim. My name is Tim."

The man puts his hand on his chest. "Jiang Cheng." He points at the man on his right, pulling out the skin biopsy kit.

"Qu Tanzhou." Then at the man on his left. "Liu Nengye."

"Nice to meet you all. I'm so sorry for how you've been treated."

"Bad time," the old man says. "Bad time for all."

"You lost people, yes?"

Jiang nods and shows two sets of six fingers. "Dome-A."

"We've lost thirteen," Tim says, heavily. "We think the microbes are responsible for the violent behavior. But we know how to kill them."

Jiang speaks rapidly in his language, and the others' heads swivel up immediately.

"Extreme heat, and lots of it. We used the sauna, back at our Station, to get them off our skins. Once it warms up a little, we can bring you across and get you in there. But until then you'll have to sit tight."

"Sit tight," Jiang repeats, then grins. "We have sit tight some time now." He struggles to find words for something, then throws up his hands and lets out a stream of foreign syllables.

"Tim, look at their samples, then pack them up," Wei says. "I'm going to get Khaled. He spent a summer doing field work in Xi'an. I think it's high time we found out what happened at their station."

The nightmare at Dome-A started insidiously.

Jiang speaks slowly, and Khaled Zaidi translates over the radio for Tim to hear.

The Chinese crew of fourteen men and one woman had been on the ice since the start of the summer, acclimating to the 16,000-foot altitude. There were two teams of scientists. The first were astronomers – like South Pole, the high altitudes, perpetual night, and katabatic atmosphere at Dome-A created ideal conditions. The second were glaciologists. The plateau lay over the sub-glacial Gamburtsev Mountains, the ice below their feet over three miles deep. Over the summer, with a larger team, they drilled down over a mile, extracting a unique ice core sample with a climatological and atmospheric gas record over a million years old. Like SPICE, the extracted core was too large to fly off Antarctica, so they had turned the drill site into a remote lab a quarter-mile away from the main Station.

The ice core lab was where the trouble first began.

It was little more than LANDIT; a remote container on stilts, set on top of a hole that had once extended a mile down. The three winter glaciologists usually headed out to their site on Tuesday and returned on Saturday. About a month after sunset, the first week it dropped below minus 80 F on the high plateau, they didn't return as scheduled.

Jiang, the winter manager, tried to raise them by radio to no avail. On Sunday, he sent his deputy Xi Lin to check on them. Xi found blood all over the small ice core lab, and only one of the glaciologists inside.

The man was dead, and looked like he had tried to claw his skin off with his fingernails.

Xi found one of the other two behind the site, face down in the snow, completely naked.

Jiang Cheng looks shocked just saying it, and Tim knows exactly how he feels.

He continues in Mandarin, pausing periodically, and Khaled translates on the radio.

Xi found one other strange thing in the glaciology hut. A transparent sphere just slightly larger than a soccer ball, fractured along built-in fault lines. The sphere was empty, had no markings on it, and was beeping loudly.

Xi brought the sphere back to the main Station for everyone to look at. They speculated on what might have been inside, if anything.

It stayed on their dining table.

Xi Lin was married to the only woman on site, Lingling Mei, and they were the first to fall ill. By Tuesday, Jiang had confined everyone to their quarters, but people either ran out into the freezing exterior, or flew into inexplicable rages and murdered each other. By week's end, only four crew members were left alive.

When Dr. Xiaofeng began to twitch and mutter aloud to himself, the other three unplugged the walk-in freezer and locked him inside it.

For twenty dark days and nights, they listened to Xiaofeng flare up in the freezer, then die down when his human instinct resurged. He vacillated wildly, back and forth, and when he began to lose his grip on reality, Jiang made the decision to abandon their Station, and the environmental poison he thought had to be in the air or the walls. Zhongshan Station was too far, the ice too unstable. They would flee nearly seven hundred miles to South Pole, the nearest human settlement, and hope to survive the journey. Trading one Antarctic endurance game for another.

They couldn't leave their crewmember behind, no matter his crazed state. So they lured Xiaofeng into the back of the truck. He ran after Qu Tanzhou eagerly, his mouth grinning, tongue lolling out of his mouth. They locked him inside and packed up their Sno-Cat and the cab of the truck.

On the grueling drive across the continent, they moved across uncharted terrain at five miles an hour, never succumbing to the urge to hurry. Luck favored them; by the first time they had to tow the lead vehicle out of a deep crevasse field, they were off the high plateau.

"What was the temperature?" Wei asks, and Khaled translates the question. "When you stepped outside on your journey to us."

Jiang speaks. "Approximately fifty below," Khaled replies.

"So they didn't face the wrath of the cold-activated microbes."

"Not yet," Tim says heavily.

Jiang nods, slowly. "We did not know we were not really escaping," he says in Mandarin.

Only heading to a new prison, bringing their problem to a fresh group of people who would soon suffer the same fate.

There is one thing Jiang Cheng leaves out of his story – how Xiaofeng went from a prisoner in the truck to smeared across half of it. Looking at Jiang's grey face, Tim recalls TC's superhuman strength, his own fear at what he saw inside the arches, and knows he doesn't have to ask.

The Chinese traverse to South Pole had been a fight for survival, and all fights for survival were fights to the death.

Chapter Thirty-One

Jiang Cheng and his crewmates are indeed crawling with dormant microbes. After analyzing their slides, Tim scrutinizes himself with the microscope for almost an hour, just in case he has inadvertently touched anything they've touched. A quiet voice mocks him as he goes over his arms and neck for the third time. *Doesn't seem like you want to die a martyr anymore.*

He wonders if Summer's thinking that she misjudged him.

Tim raises his ski mask and steps outside ARO, pulling the door closed behind him. It's brutally cold, but he can hear the comforting rumble of the Sno-Cat. He fumbles for the microscope, then a gasp tears at his throat like a thorn.

"Doc, this is crazy."

"What happened?"

"Uh. Well."

"Exponential growth?"

"More like explosive."

The microbes on Kathryn's sample have grown so aggressively that the glass slide is cracked. A transparent river of microbes has leaked onto the metal landing like spilled glue. Tim feels a chill crawl down his spine. They have grown with purpose… reaching out toward the slide that holds Doc Wei's clean cells.

He bends to his knees, squinting at the gel-like finger stretching from the broken slide. "Ugh, it's *moving*. Pulsing–"

That's when Tim realizes the long transparent finger is writhing in a different direction now. Toward him.

He jerks back, heels knocking into the closed door of ARO. Small ghostly tendrils of microbes weave off the main finger, climbing into the air, a mat of snarled threads swirling and glinting in the breeze.

Trying to locate him.

Tim leaps over the metal landing, and takes the stairs two at a time toward the Sno-Cat.

11:00 PM

Tim is both mentally and physically drained but sleep eludes him like a mocking lover.

(*ohhhh*)

He'd come out of the sauna to tumultuous applause. The hallway had been packed with Polies clapping for him. For the first time in days, Tim had felt comfortable being around his crewmates. People had come up to him while he ate in the galley, slapping him on the shoulder, telling him how they admired his courage. How getting food to starving Polies had been absolutely the right thing to do. No one looked at him like he was an injured dog about to be taken to the vet.

For the first time, it was okay that people were talking about him.

But then it happens.

Headed back to his room, Tim isn't aware of concretely realizing it. The poisoned apple is just there, in his head, for the taking. He finds himself walking by Summer's door, like a magnet drawn toward its pole.

He hears a soft, whispered giggle from behind her door.

The rumble of a male voice, indistinguishable.

And then, an *oh*, as if murmured in pleasure.

He'd somehow known all along what he'd find if he walked by at *exactly* the right moment, and now he can't sleep, because that *oh* is looping in his head like a maddening ad jingle. Oh. *Ohhhh.*

The bitter flood of mental images is a brisk slap waking Tim from the dream his act of heroism had briefly lulled him into. He has seen Rajan naked in the sauna, and his brain renders Rajan in bed with Summer in anatomically accurate high-definition. Rajan's veined hands, knotted on her shoulders. Her hips, etched with a tattoo of the ballerina she had once been, arching against his. Summer saying you can take the ass, too. Tim was always too chicken to ask. Not Rajan. Rajan would ask. *Oh,* she would murmur as he pushed into her. *Ohhhh.*

Tim springs up from the bed, fists knotted at his skull. A viper's poison sac is surging through his brain, and his room is suddenly too small. He wanders into the hallway, pacing with no destination in mind, but the hallway is too small. The whole fucking Station is too small. He wants *out,* to be anywhere else, just walking in no direction at all, away from the thoughts corroding his last and only hold on his will to live.

He drifts into the game room, and Siri starts awake from a doze on the sofa.

Her bloodshot eyes are circled with bruised-looking dark rings, burrowing deep lines into her heart-shaped face. Her limp wrist still holds a plastic cup with a dark ring of boxed wine at the bottom.

"Can't sleep?" he says to her.

She shakes her head tiredly. "Can't turn off the pictures in my head."

Tim sinks down in front of her. "God, I know. My brain feels like it's on cocaine."

"It's in the air or something." Her large green eyes are serious, too serious. "I look at people and I swear I *hear* things that can't be real. Feels... like I'm slowly going insane."

A slow *ohhh* begins building up in Tim's ear, and the words want to spill out like a monsoon flood from behind a dam. *Like Summer and Rajan in the galley at dinner today. They weren't even sitting near each other but somehow I knew they'd been physically intimate. My rational brain didn't even try to deny it. I just* knew *it.*

Siri leans forward and touches his leg. "You look haggard, boss. You look like I feel."

Tim lets out a long breath. He's tired of living like a roach under the lights, just trying to scuttle back to his hidey-hole before anything can smash him into the linoleum. He starts to respond with something trite and face-saving, but the truth tumbles out before he can catch it.

"It's getting bad for me, Siri. I really don't think I can bear it."

"It's just cabin fever. Things are on their way back to normal. Thanks to *you*. Once we don't have the shadow of death hanging over our heads, and something to *do*, it'll get better for all of us."

Tim gives her a watery smile. One thing is undeniable: there's no evacuation possible until summer, and it takes work to keep the lights on at the bottom of the world. Which means soon he'll have to deal with people regularly.

Deal with Summer and her Benji. And he doesn't feel even remotely ready to do that.

The next morning, Tim wakes up with his head in his hands. He doesn't remember falling asleep. But when he stands up, he feels an extraordinary sense of relief.

He knows what he's going to do.

Today, I'm starting my journey home.

Tim pulls his almirah open. At the bottom lies an orange US Antarctic Program deployment bag. He'd been issued all his cold-weather gear in that bag, and it will be returned in that bag when he's done. He reaches up.

Sweeps all his neatly folded T-shirts into it.

His pants are next.

Then his postcard collection. His pajamas.

He opens the almirah, frantic now.

Socks, sweatshirts and gym clothes get pulled out. He yanks his other duffel and suitcase out from under the bed.

He dresses in his cold weather gear. Thermals, two layers of thick woolen socks, blue boots. Windpants and overalls, fleece jacket, Big Red. Goggles on his head, ski mask around his neck. He stands his black, beat-up suitcase upright, stamped with the USAP logo. *United States Antarctic Program, National Science Foundation*. He slings the orange deployment bag across his body, then hoists the other duffel onto his shoulder.

Tim walks out of his room for the last time.

It's the breakfast hour and the hallways are bristling with people, but he sets his eyes straight ahead. Ignores all attempts anyone makes to talk to him. One or two people drift behind him as if they're lost, but he knows right where he's going.

He drags his suitcase and tired body up the stairs.

He's packed. He's done. He's leaving, never to return.

He pushes through the swinging doors into the upper gym.

He places his suitcase up against the floor-to-ceiling glass pane looking down into the basketball court, then heaves his black duffel atop the suitcase. These are his checked bags for the long flight to Mac Station and the Antarctic coastline, but there's no Hercules airplane waiting for him yet.

He tosses the orange bag over his shoulder, then steps onto the treadmill. His gloved hands punch the button, and the treadmill begins to move at a walking pace.

Can't leave on a jet plane, but I'll be damned if I stay here.

Mac Station is a thousand miles away. Tim can walk forty miles a day. A month of walking is ahead of him, to leave all the soul-crushing isolation and heartbreak of the Pole behind. And if it doesn't, he'll keep walking until the Herc is waiting to pick him up.

Then, maybe, the end. But not here. The ice doesn't get to take his soul *and* his life.

He keeps his eyes fixed ahead.

Walks, and keeps walking.

Chapter Thirty-Two

SOUTH POLE STATION POPULATION: 28 (PRISONERS: 3; DECEASED: 13)

June 25 bangs into Wei like a truck into a deer. The first shock comes after breakfast. He's eyeing microbe slides taken from the crew when he becomes aware that Jamie has been trying to get his attention for a while now.

His head comes up, wearily. "Yeah."

Jamie fixes him with an intense stare. "You good?"

There is only one thing that will make him *good,* and it's in the pharma cabinet shrieking his name like a banshee. "I'm fine."

"You sure?"

"Why?" he snaps irritably.

"Because you're a drug addict," she replies.

He stares at her, frozen. Jamie doesn't reply. Waiting.

At last, he just says, "I'm fine."

Jamie doesn't say anything more, but he knows she's seen it all. Docs abusing prescriptions, hitting on nurses inappropriately, writing down the wrong thing on a chart because they're hazy with sleep deprivation. If she's saying something to him, it's because she thinks he's losing control.

And is she wrong?

No, he thinks. *No, she's not wrong.*

He forces himself to meet her eyes. His voice is quiet,

humbled. "I'm sorry," he says. "I'm trying to cut back. Watch my back, will you? Make sure I don't do anything stupid?"

She gives him a warm smile. "Like it's my job, doctor. But you need to do one thing for me."

June 25 is the gift that keeps on giving, because he is now without his keys to the drug cabinet. He *can't* get the yum-yums, even if he wants to, and his body goes into a full-on tantrum just after lunch, cramps and shivers playing him like an accordion. Wei barely makes it through the day, and just as he's about to pack it in, an alarm buzzes in the clinic.

It's the emergency medical page number.

His eyes snap to the display. Room 113. *Gaudin.*

"Come on, come on!" he shouts, already breaking into a run.

Chapter Thirty-Three

None of the doors lock at South Pole, which allows Wei to burst right into Bill Gaudin's room.

The stink inside knocks him back into Jamie. The sour smell of throw-up and acidic urine coats Wei's throat, almost closing it up.

Gaudin is spilled onto his side on the floor, vomit dribbled down his cheek and chin, pooled underneath his face. The vomit is black; it smells like something has died inside it. Gaudin must have been standing-up, falling-down drunk. Enough to worry even a seasoned alcoholic like him, because the room phone lies beside him. He'd called in his own emergency medical page. Not a moment too soon, because he's unconscious, lying in the middle of the ooze he probably almost choked on.

Wei checks his pulse. "Weak, but he's alive," he says.

"He's a big guy," Jamie says, doubtfully.

"Go down the hall and get Jonah," Wei says. "He knows how to keep his mouth shut."

The dry scratching in the back of Wei's throat is his thirty-minute warning of his body's next impending tantrum. Highlights will include a flop sweat, stomach writhing, a clamoring headache and sixty-nine walk-bys of the medicine cabinet. But, at that moment, he's more afraid of Jamie's glare than his withdrawal symptoms.

He goes back to feeding the nasogastric tube through the unconscious Gaudin's nostrils. Over the next six hours, it will flush his stomach out, clearing toxins from his body. They had barely gotten to him in time.

"Dammit," Wei growls at her. "I know, okay?"

To his surprise the nurse laughs. "Long as you know who the boss is." She jangles the keys to the medicine cabinet in her coat. "You'll get your one for the day before bed, like you said."

"In the future, don't listen to me."

A dimple appears in her cheek. "I should make you beg for it? A girl could get ideas."

Wei is about to let out a growly response when the door to the clinic swings open. Both their eyes flick to the curtain, behind which lies the rest of the clinic. It's drawn, so at least the Station Manager's near-death experience won't be gossip-fodder yet.

Go, Wei mouths, and Jamie disappears around the edge of the curtain, careful to draw it fully behind her. The doctor listens from the other side.

"Uh, I'm a little worried about Tim?" Summer Kerce's voice.

"What about, specifically?" Jamie says.

"I think he might be taking things a little hard. He's packed his bags and, uh, he's walking."

Wei's head snaps up so fast his neck pops. Jamie's tone mirrors his alarm. *"Outside?"*

"No, just on the treadmill. With his bags. He's packed up everything and he's walking on the treadmill."

"Why would he do that?" Jamie's voice is oozing with

mordant New Yorker as Wei steps around the curtain to join them. "Did something happen?"

Summer glares at her. "You know what happened."

"I'm sure I have no idea," Jamie says sweetly.

"I broke up with him," she snaps.

"Aw come on now, Summer," the nurse drawls. Wei watches with amusement as she ambles closer. Like a hyena circling its prey. "Tim's a big boy. A breakup wouldn't upset him *that* much, right?"

Summer looks at Wei, as if for support, but it's all the doctor can do to hold in a sardonic chuckle. The drama beats thinking about the Netflix he can't watch and the drugs he can't have.

Jamie cocks an eyebrow at her, and she's forced to say it.

"I broke up with Tim and I'm… kind of… with Rajan now."

"And he has to *see* that every day?" Jamie exclaims. "Damn, I'd be worried about Tim too."

Summer bites off a *bitch* under her breath.

"Did you just call me a name?"

"Could you just do your job and check on him? Is that asking too much?"

"Sure, Summer, I'll check on him," she says. "Sounds like he caught a hard kick to the groin. That's definitely worth checking on."

"Actually," Wei calls out as she spins on her heel. "Summer, I'd like to have your biologist opinion one more time. Hang out for a moment?"

"Uh… sure," she says stiffly.

"Jamie?"

They step around the curtain together. "Was that really necessary?" he whispers, mock-sternly.

"Heck yeah," Jamie snorts. She isn't trying to be quiet. "She acts like she's the prettiest piece of ass out there, in this small fucking pond. Excuse me if I can't stand that."

Wei suppresses another chuckle, trying not to encourage her too much. "I'm done here, I think." He gestures at Gaudin. "Can you button this up and go find Tim? Unless you want me to talk to him."

"Nah, you take care of the important stuff."

"Just... let me know if we need to put Tim on a suicide watch."

Jamie winces. "Maybe I'm flattering myself by thinking I know him, but if he's walking to McMurdo in his head, that's his catharsis. If I can get him to promise to radio me before leaving that treadmill, I say let him walk."

Chapter Thirty-Four

Bill Gaudin's eyes open drowsily. His pupils swim around his eyeballs independently of each other. The animation flows slowly back into them like water dripping into a bucket.

Wei walks around the bed, dragging a chair behind him. The more serious the conversation, the longer he waits before speaking. It sharpens the patient's attention. Primes them to listen carefully for bad news. The conversations about the microbes with Summer –

(*and no drugs doc don't forget that*)

– has whetted his focus to a point. He needs to get this conversation right.

He waits. Lets Gaudin watch him. Lets the manager get nervous.

"You nearly killed yourself, Bill," he says at last.

Gaudin's dry lips crack. "It was an accident." His words are slurred.

(*very bad crazy when very bad cold*)

Wei reaches up and places a small black notebook on top of his belly.

Gaudin looks suddenly afraid in the way of a lone deer, alone in a darkness that smells like wolf.

"You were writing in that when you passed out," Wei says.

Gaudin's mouth moves, but not much dribbles out.

"Let me read you the last passage." Wei picks up the book. The scrawls on the page are vicious, wild, cutting through the page in places; the ravings of a man barely hanging onto reality.

> *Weeks is soft - know it like its tattooed on his pasty forehead. Last century glasses - round chin - squashed nose - that fuckin chuckle when he don't know what to say - it all screams take me out back and pound the blood out of me. That bitch of a bitch didn't pick LUIS fuckin WEEKS because he's charming or has a footlong for a schlong. No way, Andrea picked him because out of anyone on Station she could fuck, Weeks would drive me the absolute. Craziest. Bitch saved it like a knife riding up her pantyhose. Last resort, but deadly if used correctly. I OUGHT TO KILL HER FOR THAT. SHE WOULD DESERVE IT.*

Wei closes his eyes like a pastor praying over the words he has just read. "These are the ravings of a very angry man, Bill," he says softly. "This is the kind of bottomless, starving, sinewy anger that would make you medically unfit to lead this Station."

"You hate me," Gaudin mumbles through parched lips that are starting to peel. "Everyone hates me."

"It doesn't matter what we think of each other, because *thirteen people are dead.*" Wei's tone is that of a parent reading a nursery rhyme, but every word rings clearly. "I don't know how the world will react when it finds out about the deaths, but we are central players to them. Just like Rodney Marks, our roles – the doc and the manager – will be analyzed in papers around the world." Wei's eyes meet his. "For all of our sakes… I need to know if you're able to stop yourself from doing the most destructive thing you possibly can."

Wei watches realization trickle in. Gaudin isn't restrained to his bed on an involuntary psychiatric hold for a reason.

"A military man being here, right as a mysterious extremophile ravages the Station, is a coincidence I just can't get out of my head. But when lives are on the line, Rajan is making good decisions, while you're pickling yourself in Jack Daniels, and your deputy isn't qualified to lead herself out of a paper bag."

(*and I can't go two seconds without thinking about a pill I can't have*)

Gaudin nods. Neck creaking. "Yeah," he whispers. "I hear you."

Wei's eyes are sad. This winter has been educational for him, too. "No, you don't. You've got a monkey on your back, and it won't *let* you hear me. But you will."

He steps back from the bed. "I've written you a prescription for the withdrawal symptoms. You're cut off, Gaudin. You're going cold turkey." His voice is fiery, and not just because he's had Jamie prescribe the same medication to him. "You need to live up to your job title, whether you want to or not. Do you hear me?" He fixes Gaudin with his eyes. "If something like this happens again, I will confine you to quarters and it will be *public*. Don't make me turn you into a cautionary tale."

Gaudin doesn't reply.

He steps back. "The ice tunnels are safe, and the SATCOM

has been repaired. The satellite comes overhead in three hours, so it's time to get ready. You've got quite the story to tell Washington."

Gaudin reaches for the black book, and Wei plucks it out of his limp fingers. "I'll hold onto this," he says. "Just to make sure you don't trip over a bottle again."

Chapter Thirty-Five

SOUTH POLE STATION POPULATION: 28 (PRISONERS: 3; DECEASED: 13)

June 25th, 1:25 PM

...a powder keg waiting to blow. We've got the immediate emergency under control, but everyone just seems on edge.

A strangled sigh escapes Rajan as he types the last paragraph of this email. He tries to email his sister in Chicago every week, half to keep in touch and half to keep an unclassified diary of his time on the ice. Behind the email, his laptop is open to the black command prompt.

```
ping disa.smil.mil -a -encryptkey=yes
> ping: cannot resolve smil.mil: Unknown host
```

Refreshing itself every second.

This far south, SATCOM transmit windows range between forty-five minutes and two hours of reliable signal per day. In truth, however, the access windows are a little longer. The signal is clipped, the first and last five minutes restricted to select users with a special encrypted connection. In a few minutes, he will be the first person to connect to the outside world since the first death at South Pole four days ago.

Rajan resumes typing. *But maybe that's just me feeling out of sorts in the dark down–*

The screen changes.

```
ping disa.smil.mil -a -encryptkey=yes
```

```
> PING disa.smil.mil (172.217.89.02): 56 data bytes
> 2 packets transmitted, 2 packets held, enter token
```

Rajan is on the clock now. Five minutes. He inserts a token card into a USB reader and types quickly. The front of the card is blank except for a bald eagle with a red and blue shield, clutching a silver key in its talons.

Persons in some circles might have recognized the logo of a three-letter intelligence agency.

```
ssh keygen -t rsa -C "rajan.chariya@cia.ic.gov" -sha512
> 12 packets transmitted, 12 packets held, RSA key
```

He types a sixteen letter-and-digit password, followed by numbers from an RSA fob small enough to fit on a keychain. The numbers on the fob, generated by a cryptographic scheme, change regularly.

```
> Connection successful.
restorecon -R -v /root/.ssh dirops.cia.ic.gov/cobra
request encryptlevel=TS -SI -TK -HCS -SAP:HAVE-VIKING
> Access granted.
```

Rajan is now connected to a Top Secret-level server, protected at both the Special Compartmented Intelligence and Special Access Program levels. A green dot appears next to his only contact on the encrypted messaging service. Just one terminal in one room at Langley is cleared to the HAVE VIKING level, and someone there is online.

```
uploadpath /users/Rajan/documents/(TS-SI-TK-SAP-HV)
```

```
upload report-day-*
> Report transmitted. Urgent priority. 13 dead at Pole.
```

He doesn't expect a speedy response to his forty-page report on the events of the last five days. The deaths of thirteen Americans on international territory will require coordination between senior types at both CIA and State Department.

To his surprise, a reply comes in almost immediately.

```
> Report status of Dome Argus visitors.
```

Rajan frowns, then types.

```
> 3 alive, 1 dead en route. Isolated ARO pending legal direction.
```

The cursor blinks for a long time.

```
> Establish comm, this level, in 26:30:00 from now. Acknowledge.
> Acknowledged.
```

The green dot turns grey, and Rajan returns to his email.

...feeling out of sorts in the dark down here. I'm looking forward to sunrise. Give my love to Abe and the kids.

He'd planned to end there, but when he stops typing, the cursor blinks at the end of:

I killed someone again, at the last place on Earth I thought I'd ever take a life.

He stares at the screen.

Keeps typing.

After Syria, what brought me out of a very dark place was realizing I'd gone to a war zone with a gun. Could it really be surprising I ended up taking a life? I justified what I did by labeling myself a victim of my circumstance. You can't enter a boxing ring and be surprised when you walk out with a black eye, right? But that excuse doesn't work this time. I didn't hesitate. He was going to kill me, I killed him first, and in the moment it was just that black and white. I didn't even consider showing him mercy. It haunts me to think about what that means.

Rajan's hands freeze above the keyboard.

(*I think it means I'm not a good person*)

He gazes at his words. His eyes feel like he's weeping sharp glass.

He deletes it.

Word by word, all the way to *give my love to Abe and the kids.* Before he can think about it further –

(*when I think about what I've done I wish myself dead*)

– he clicks send.

His email pops up an error message.

`Temporary error (502). Unable to send – no connection.`

Huh?

Rajan checks his Ethernet cable, but it's still connected. The satellite will be above the horizon for another hour, so he should have a signal.

He logs back into his Terminal window.

```
ping disa.smil.mil -a -encryptkey=yes
> ping: cannot resolve smil.mil: Unknown host
```

He scrolls up until he finds the last time stamp where he had a positive data connection.

Five minutes ago.

Four minutes after he signed off with the CIA.

They killed the signal. They don't want this getting out.

Rajan rejects the thought as ridiculous. His report is forty pages long. There's no way anyone could have read it in just four minutes. Hell, it would take that long just to block the connection.

But without the signal, the CIA is the only organization that knows what went wrong at the Pole. And they'd asked him about only one thing: the Chinese visitors from Dome-A.

Chapter Thirty-Six

3:30 PM

The greenhouse is Rajan's go-to place to clear his head, but the rows of hydroponic plants have no answers to the questions swirling around his cottony skull. A feeling of worry, tinged with fright, has settled on him like a heavy cape. Ever since the satellite signal blinked out, he has been thinking hard and not liking what he's coming up with.

Suddenly he wants a breath of thick salty ocean air more than he has wanted anything in his entire life.

A knock on the window behind him.

He looks up to see Siri, and waves her in. "Hey girl," he says, with real pleasure. "Come to share my rock?"

"I don't mean to intrude," she says. "I just wanted to say one thing. Between us."

She perches on the edge of the futon. She looks peaky close up, the bags under her eyes deep as tunnels under a railway overpass.

"Uh-oh," he says, trying to sound light and casual.

"I'm not saying this because Tim's my boss, or my friend. I'm saying this because I think you should know. I know you've liked Summer for a while. She's smart, she's beautiful, you're both scientists... it's natural, probably... but Tim's a good guy."

Rajan straightens on the futon. "I know he is. I thought

about talking to him, especially once he got on the treadmill, but I thought it might make things worse."

"Well, he… he's been through a lot in the last three years." She looks down at the floor. "Tim's kid died of cancer."

"*What?*"

She takes a deep breath. "He lost the kid, and a year later he lost his wife over it too. It's hard to make a marriage work when all you remind each other of is the kid you lost. That was Tim's mental space when he came to Pole and met Summer." Rajan's face feels like it's swelling, the horror in his thoughts pumping into it like silicone through a needle. "So you can maybe see that, in a lot of ways, she became his shield during a shitty time in his life. A way to rebuild himself while something good was happening. I'm not saying it's fair of him to raise her up on a pedestal like that. I'm only saying it so you can understand his state of mind."

"I had no idea," Rajan says, and it is all he can say.

Her eyes come up to meet his. He doesn't see any judgment on her face, and finds himself almost pathetically thankful. "I can't imagine this wouldn't have come up with Summer," Siri says. "She must know. She must."

He flashes back to the conversation they'd had earlier, right here in the greenhouse. *Every year I learn something new and shitty about myself.*

"Thanks, Siri," he says, with an uneasy smile. "I appreciate you trying to help."

"I'm glad it came across that way." Her voice betrays her worry, which makes his smile touch his eyes. He slides over on the couch and hugs her, and she hugs him back.

He pulls away, cheek sliding against hers, and finds himself looking right into her eyes, as clear and dark as emeralds now. Her eyes on his face, frankly and openly, make the sharp loneliness in every pore of his skin swell. Make him feel weedy; even a little desperate.

She blinks, then clears her throat. "I should get back."

"Yeah," Rajan says thickly. "Yeah, okay."

She stands, then turns back to him. "Hey, maybe I'll come by your little Dark Sector hut one of these nights," she says. "It saved my life, after all."

"I want to believe you."

"How is it going out there? I'm sorry I've been so caught up in my own… things… I haven't asked in a while."

"The eau de cologne of my frustration is baked into the walls at this point. But…"

"But?"

"Being down here really is something else," he says softly.

"That's why I keep coming back." She has a smile in her voice. "The first time I came to Antarctica was for the thrill of the unique. Tell everyone back home I'd been somewhere, you know? Prove I was more than just a farmer's daughter. All the wrong reasons." She laughs a little. "The second time, I came for the money. The food is free, the rooms are free, and the soap opera entertainment of forty people trapped in a tiny building for half a year of darkness comes for free whether you subscribe to that channel or not. But now?" Her voice is tender. "I keep coming back because now I feel like I don't belong anywhere else."

She slips out of the room, and Rajan nods to himself. Despite himself, he can understand the feeling intimately. There are two types of people who come to Pole. Those who come once and will never be seen again.

And those who never stop trying to make it back.

Abruptly, he springs up and sticks his head out into the hallway. "Hey, Siri!"

"Not your iPhone!" she yells back.

"What's going on with you and Khaled?"

She turns in her tracks then. She smiles at him with the eyes of a woman in a Victorian painting. Still and dark and knowing the answer to every secret thing.

"Don't you think you waited too long to ask?" she says.

June 26th, 9:00 AM

The next day dawns dark and flat. By nine AM the whole crew is gathered in the galley for the all-hands meeting, waiting for Gaudin to arrive. Even Ben, who hasn't been seen much, is standing against the back wall, grinning widely at everyone and no one, looking so flushed he seems almost sunburned. Everyone is there except Tim. He'd stopped walking to sleep on a gym mat beside the treadmill, and to grab a leftover can of spam from the kitchen, but then he'd picked up his bag and started on his self-inflicted trek again.

Wei sees gaunt and worried faces across the galley. Ben and Tim aren't the only ones behaving oddly. It has been four down days since the sauna treatment; two days since Tim braved the cold at ARO. With little to distract them from the friends they've lost, and the oppressive omnipresence of the microbial threat on everything they touch, including each other, the Station is restless.

If nothing changes, there will be trouble soon.

With the ramp-down in Percocet that Jamie is imposing, Wei's head feels clearer than it has in months. He has already filled half a notebook with his observations on the microbe samples. Summer's thoughts on Antarctic extremophiles have caused his newly sharp brain to reexamine Tim's report of the microbes building a bridge between samples in the cold at ARO. Without a host for a food source, an individual microbe couldn't survive for more than a handful of minutes in an active state. Building a bridge was an effort that would span multiple generations, something that didn't quite map to a base evolutionary instinct. The microbe bridge nagged at him, like a painful tooth he couldn't stop feeling out with his tongue. A question that needed an answer.

The alternate solution was an unfathomable, generational intelligence; a hypothesis that seemed too crazy to consider, even for an audience of one.

Gaudin enters the galley. The dominant and overbearing cruise ship of a Station manager looks gaunt, ruddy cheeks sunken into his face. Withdrawal is hitting him hard. The galley begins to shush itself, but before he can speak, Wei rises to his feet.

Withdrawal is wilting him in unexpected ways too, but he feels more like himself with every passing day. Which means he's now just as concerned with how the story is told as with the story itself. Real life, it turns out, isn't much different from his Stanford admission essay.

"A couple of medical announcements to kick things off." Eyes turn to him and he stands up on his bench-seat. "Firstly, I can confirm that the sauna treatment has beaten the microbial infection back. In the follow-ups Jamie and I have done with people previously infected, we haven't found a single regrowth!"

Thunderous applause breaks out across the galley. There are loud whoops, catcalls, and it goes on for a long time. They clap for themselves. For their survival. It's something worth celebrating. It's a while before Wei can speak again.

"Secondly, we should all acknowledge the huge contribution of Tim Fulton. Thanks to his guts, we now know that the ice tunnels are a safe temperature. This is a really extreme environment bacteria. Even at minus fifty, it's barely above a dormant state, and that's good news for getting our season back on track."

"Where *does* it go active?" Dave Atkins yells over another outgrowth of clapping.

"Somewhere between minus 70 and minus 85. It's a shelf, so they're dormant until that point, then it's like a switch flipped to on. That's a good segue to Katie for the weather."

Katie Caberto stands up in the center of the galley. "The wind is shifting after the storm. It's minus 64 out now; temperatures will rise above minus 60 and stay there for twenty-four hours. A short drop down to the low seventies after that, then sixties again for at least a week."

Claps and *huzzahs* ricochet around the room. A charged atmosphere of can-do excitement has taken over the lassitude with which the all-call had begun.

"Between the sauna and the temperature coming up, we can get back to something like a normal life," Wei says. "Everyone will hit the sauna if you're going outdoors. Call comms for a weather check. If it's above minus 65, you're clear to head out. However, I'd like to leave MAPO and ARO quarantined. My apologies to those staff members, but the microbes transfer by touch, so I'm worried about re-contamination from Philip's body or our Chinese visitors. I'll work with Jonah and Rob on a sanitation plan, but I want to be cautious so we don't reintroduce the microbes to the Station. Questions so far?"

No one responds, so Wei continues. "Let's hear from IT about SATCOM."

Marty Horn, the system admin and IT lead, lets out a noisy belch. Marty's an odd duck. He's been heard to describe his unabashedly public farts and burps as *I beep and squeak before I fix your beeps and squeaks*. Beside him are Kevin Eastburg and José Ager, both rookies, both growing out their neck beards.

Kevin stands. "Everything seems to be working on our end," he says in a reedy, nervous voice. "The servers are green, satellite visibility is there, but the connection is being refused. Same thing with the Iridium sat-phones. We'll keep troubleshooting."

Ben boos in the back. Bethany Hamidani reaches up and pokes him, and a wave of wry chuckles sweeps the galley.

Wei stands back up. "One last announcement before I hand it over to management." He raises his voice to a boom. "I would like everyone to *please*, put your hands together for Bill Gaudin… who is celebrating one day sober today!"

Surprised applause picks up across the crowd. Gaudin sits still as a statue, looking stunned. His face turns pink, then red, then a snotty purple.

"There are many hard things about being down south, and addiction is one of the hardest," Wei says. "If he comes to you for alcohol, remember we're all human. We all have moments of weakness. But please, do *your* part to help keep our fellow Polie sober!"

Gaudin stares at Wei from eyeballs full of a nearly inhuman rage. The doctor beams right back at him. It's time to retire the risk of Gaudin relapsing into a drunken wild card. It'll be a long road between now and the first summer plane, and he can't run this Station himself in that time.

And he can't shake the feeling that he doesn't want Rajan running it, either. His instinct has been trending in that direction for a while, and he's decided to stop fighting it.

Jamie catches his eye as the galley claps for Gaudin. She winks and touches the side of her nose.

Right. Then again, he has his own battles to fight between now and summer, too. Addiction would wait for no man, manager or doctor.

We need more. We need more. We need more.

As Wei talks, we nudge Ben forward.

This time we sidle him close to Daniel, Clint and Siri.

We brick a smile onto Ben's limpid face and let his mind relax.

We need more people with us. We need more. That churning thought is like a heartbeat, calming us, letting us slip lower and lower. Below the verbal, into another range that isn't open to human ears.

We wait, breathing deeply, then the tap turns on.

(*can't wait till that arch is open I'm so tired of peaches and spam*)

(*show the world no fear boy and it gonna bend like a twizzler*)

(*I'm so glad we have Doc and Rajan I don't know WHO IS THAT*)

Ben's eyes bounce from side to side like a Ping-Pong ball slapped between a wall and a paddle. A headache suddenly *whangs* in behind his temples. We snap his head around to see Siri's green eyes burning holes through us.

Sticky static fills our head, like an AM radio needle between stations. We can feel it *moving,* scanning up and down, hearing blips of noise and trying to home in on them. Panic rises inside us like a wayward tide.

(*hidden hidden must stay hidden*)

"...the connection is being refused. Same thing with the Iridium sat-phones. We'll keep troubleshooting," Kevin is saying –

We boo, loudly.

Siri blinks, surprised.

"Hey, shut the fuck up," Bethany hisses behind us and pokes Ben.

"Sorry," we whisper back, but we aren't sorry, not one bit, because that staticky feeling is gone now. Only a few confused thoughts –

(*who is that what was what*)

– bounce around, scattered like leaves in a strong wind.

Siri rubs her forehead and we step forward quickly, before she can refocus her attention on us. We watch her out of the corner of Ben's eye as we stand just behind Weeks and Sheryl, and there isn't a smile on Ben's face anymore.

Chapter Thirty-Seven

Siri's headache is growing and she feels almost limp with relief when the all-hands concludes. The vice around her head relaxes, reluctantly, but then she remembers, like déjà vu from a dream –

(*hidden hidden*)

(*who is that*)

– and turns, looking for Ben, but he has disappeared.

Her eye catches someone else, though, and this time she doesn't hesitate.

"Keyon!"

He keeps walking. "Hey, Keyon!"

(*Keyon I know you can hear me don't walk away*)

Keyon's eyes snap right to her. He pauses, an island in the ebbing flow of people streaming out of the galley.

I knew it, she thinks. *I knew I heard him the other day.*

It had been the day after the big fire; the day it had seemed like the whole Station was moving in slow motion. She'd ended up next to him in line at the breakfast buffet, just a choose-your-own-adventure of canned goods without TC or Lisa. She'd been thinking something –

Still seems odd to be calling it breakfast when it's dark as night out.

– and then his voice, clear as a bell:

(*Amen sister*)

Her head snapped up. His lips hadn't moved.

A weird tickle ran through her skull. She was watching his closed mouth, staring right at it like a dumbfounded alien seeing a human for the first time, but she was *hearing his voice nonetheless.* She recognized the tone of his stilted drawl –

(*the hard stripe voice ain't exactly normal but this sounds like siri and that's not*)

(*but it's not even the first time*)

(*clint remember clint*)

Across the galley, Keyon is leaning in to Katie. Siri can hear them as clearly as if she's standing between them.

Katie, I'll catch up with you later–

I thought we were going back to my room–

I'll be there soon. I just have to chat with–

Katie's eyes turn toward Siri. If she focuses, she knows she can catch what Katie's thinking, but she snags something else instead, full of longing and fury.

(*yuh fuckin PRICK fuckin CUNT just WAIT*)

(*twizzler twizzler twizz*)

Keyon's head whips around, hearing it too. Hearing it through her, maybe. Clint scurries by, suddenly walking faster, casting a fearful look over his shoulder at Keyon. Siri can sense Keyon's reluctance to let Clint leave, like there's a hand in the small of his back urging him on. At last, he turns back to Katie and puts a smile on his face.

This won't take long, baby–

I'll wait for you. Hey, tell me something–

(*are you fucking her*)

(*do you want to fuck her*)

Siri walks toward them. Keyon's face is tight, and she puts her hands up in a peaceful gesture. "I'll make this super quick. Just want to ask you something, Keyon."

"Shoot."

Siri says it, even though Katie's listening. "Does Ben give you the creeps?"

Keyon shrugs. "Haven't run into him in a while."

"Go run into him," she urges him. "I want to know what you… think."

(*I want to know what you hear*)

Keyon's eyes sharpen a little. "Yeah? Yeah, okay."

Siri's headache is back, a large Cadillac-sized pain rocking her head. Maybe it's just her concussion acting up, but maybe it's more than that.

"Come find me when you do," she says.

Clint walks away from the galley, neck hunched down into his sweatshirt, and though we don't see him yet, we can tell he's trying not to cast nervous looks over his shoulder. He's scared.

He's thinking that–

(*maybe gotta start carryin my utility knife around just in case that monkey carpenter*)

Clint opens the door to the ham-radio room, nestled behind the game room, and we stand there. We grin widely.

"Ben? What–"

The breath shoots out of him with a pained *whoomph* as we run Ben right into him with all the force of a moving train. Clint's shoulders hit the back of the sofa out in the game room, then Ben yanks him around and we *shove* him.

Clint shoots back through the door into the radio room. He smacks hard into the metal shelves and sags to the floor, reeling, clutching his back with pain.

We fill the doorway. We look leaner and more fit than

Clint remembers, we can tell. There are sharp edges to our features. Ben's weedy chin and baby-fat cheeks have faded into angled, cruel lines. We drive a jolly grin deep into Ben's new face and gently close the door behind us.

"Clint. Clint, where is it?"

"What…" His mind is slow, wrapped around his aching head. "Huh?"

"We *heard* you, Clint. You bought a stash from TC. We want that stash."

(*we need it we need more*)

(*more of us*)

A hot flare of anger stabs across Clint's face like a gout of flame from an oil-well fire, shooting its way into the night. "Screw yuh, beaker. That shit is valuable."

We move so fast Clint doesn't even see us lunge, and suddenly Ben's arm is a bar across his throat. Clint's indignation is cut down into a pained gasp. "The hell yuh doing, man?"

We puff our breath on his ear, hot and moldy, and widen Ben's grin, stretching it like rubber, wrapping it around his whole face. We leer at Clint from behind the empty caverns between Ben's teeth.

"Tell us what we want to know or we'll hurt you, Clint," we sing to him in a whisper. So quiet it's almost intimate. We can feel Clint's heart, pounding, so hard. Dark spots dance and pulse across Ben's eyes in rhythm with that heartbeat. "We'll hurt you worse than your daddy did the night before he went to prison."

"Okay, man! It ain't that serious, lemme go!" Clint wheezes.

Ben relaxes his arm and we stand. We blink expectantly.

Clint clears his throat – then bolts for the door.

He almost makes it. His fingers brush the door handle. Then we yank him off his feet, back into the shelves, and this time the vice on his throat is unrelenting.

Clint's lips move but no words come out. He can't breathe at all.

"Try harder," we murmur. The humidity of our breath in Ben's mouth bursts all over Clint, like rotting leaves in a rainforest. "*Squeeeeeeeze* those words out. Your life depends on it."

Real fear enters his eyes. At last. "In… cryo… lab," he manages with a terrified hiss of breath. "With… spare weather balloons. Please…"

His fingers scratch weakly at Ben's arm, begging us to let go.

Our manic clown grin is spot-welded onto Ben's face, and the vice remains unrelenting.

Clint's eyes bulge. His hands scrabble against the tile frantically.

(*because yer weak, boy, this world is all about weakness*)

Abruptly, we let go. Clint doesn't move a muscle. Doesn't even dare suck in a breath. He understands we *want* to kill him, and we are struggling to convince ourselves why we shouldn't.

"It has been a frustrating few days, Clint," Ben's face twitches. "You made the right choice."

And with that, we're gone, like a quick waft of spoil on spring air.

But just because we're out of sight, doesn't mean we're out of *mind*. Oh, no.

The first generation is an exterior phenomenon. A mindless mosquito feasting on exposed skin. We are no mosquitoes. We are the grey generation… we are *inside*. We can be partners, but without the catalyst to build our new nest, there is just one nest, in one host.

We are Ben, but we are also Adam. First of our people, and the harbinger of many.

Chapter Thirty-Eight

Bethany – she prefers Dr. Hamidani until she tells you otherwise, thank you very much – knows these old codgers frown upon her. Frown on her *choices*. Would they feel quite the same way if it's one of the *men* carrying on with two women at a time? They'd probably congratulate him. So fuck them and all their whispers.

It doesn't help that tensions have been rising ever since the stars did. She's instituted a fair system – Mondays, Wednesdays, Fridays for loving with Dave Atkins; Tuesdays, Thursdays, and Saturdays for loving with Yanis Pohano, and Sundays for self-love – and yet it has still turned into a pissing contest. Snide remarks had escalated into Yanis smashing a plate over Dave's head. A week later Yanis's iPad shocked him when he touched it, burning two of his fingertips. The day after the great shaving, as she thinks of it, had brought the most recent round.

Yanis had been with her in the far corner of the galley. He'd made them matching beanies to cover their stubbling heads, and while they were *not* the right color for her caramel complexion, it was still a sweet thought–

Dave slammed his fist into the table. His red eyes stared holes into Yanis. "Did you fuck with my–" He lowered his voice. "– my tattoo supplies? My ink is gone."

"Are you missing something?" Yanis crossed his hands

neatly on the table. "That sounds like an issue for station management."

Dave's face darkened. "You know perfectly well that shit is contraband. I'm gonna feed you your fuckin' teeth, you mother–"

"You're interrupting my Bethany time," Yanis said perfunctorily. "Unless you want yours interrupted tomorrow, I suggest you cry about it somewhere else."

Bethany could see Dave wanted nothing more than to cold-cock him, it was all over his face. But perhaps there was one thing he *did* want more, and that was to continue to have sex with her, so he settled for a threat. "Hope you got eyes in the back of your head, buddy," he'd snarled.

Male mating rituals are extremely strange to the evolved female, she'd thought then, and she thinks it again now as she looks up in time to see Dave's face contort as he finishes inside her.

He sags to the bed next to her, all angles in the dull lighting of her small room, a sheen of sweat on his skin. His craggy face knots with concentration as he leans over and pulls open a plastic bag. It holds two small brownies.

Two small, special brownies.

No more than a B-minus on that fuck, Bethany thinks, but this bonus assignment might just get him to an A.

Dave wolfs his brownie down immediately, grinning from ear to ear. Bethany nibbles at hers delicately, then leans her head against the cork wall, waiting for the high. The sweat on her naked body dries. Her eyes slip closed in a sleepy rapture, and when she wakes up, she's high. She lets out a warbling giggle, and stuffs her fist into her mouth.

"I can't believe fucking Yanis," Dave is saying. "I know we

pride ourselves on not being like Mac Station and needing locks on the doors, but–"

Bethany cuts in sharply. "Dave. You know my rule. Do I want to hear what you think about Yanis?"

"No," he says sulkily. His eyes grow a hard mirthless shine. "So maybe I take care of this problem myself."

"What a tough *man* you are," she says mockingly. "Taking on Yanis the particle physicist. They'll talk about that in the prison yard for *years*."

His face flushes. "You know, sometimes there's just no talking to you."

Bethany can feel her lips tightening. She had an acid tongue, her father used to say. Wielded it like careless nunchucks, slicing anyone in her blast range–

(*she looks so disapproving even when she's having a good time*)

(*good thing I like a bit of a bitch in a woman*)

Her long narrow nostrils flare, head snapping toward him.

(*what the*)

"I told you when the season started, I'm not a sympathetic ear for that shit." She knows her lips have disappeared into a tight line her mother had always called unattractive. *Careful, Beth, or the wind will change and your face will freeze that way.*

"Fine," Dave says ominously.

"Damn right it's fine. You have another edible?"

"That was the end of TC's latest batch."

"Oh, TC," she sighs, slumping back to her pillow. "A good cook but a *great* entrepreneur."

"Some dealers break laws. TC breaks motherfucking treaties," Dave says, and they laugh.

(*You know, you're beautiful when you smile*)

(*Too bad I don't smile more, you mean?*)

The laughs dry up quickly. Bethany frowns, unsure –

(*pig*)

– if she's mad at him, and if she is, for what exactly. She makes a conscious effort to push her lips back out. Puffer fish, puffer fish. That's what she thinks to herself whenever her face draws up into a scowl her mom would have disapproved of. *Young ladies don't make those faces, Beth.*

Dave begins playing idly with his cock. Not yet, she thinks, but maybe in fifteen minutes. She isn't feeling it anymore. Isn't feeling *him*... though she'll be damned if she can put her finger on exactly why. They lie enjoying the buzz of the weed brownie, and her thoughts wander. "I'll miss the hydroponic weed," she murmurs.

"I know, total bummer. TC had a source somewhere, and it's going to go to waste now."

"A source?"

"He was growing it somewhere."

Bethany turns to him, her eyes wide and full of suggestion. "Yeah?"

"Hey, maybe we should go peek in his room," he says. Like it's his idea. The male ego was the bedrock of the patriarchy, but a girl could throw a saddle on that stallion and ride it to her own benefit, given the right circumstances. "There's some advantages to no locked doors at Pole."

"I guess," she shrugs. "If you want to."

When they're both dressed, Bethany opens her door –

– only to recoil in surprise.

Ben Jacobs is standing right there, smiling widely at her.

"Ahhh *gawd*, you run into a wall teeth first?" The words slip out before Bethany can catch them.

"Can I come in?" Ben says, blithely ignoring her comment.

"Uh..."

He slips lightly past her. Dave turns. Ben puts both hands in his pockets and takes an exaggerated, deep breath.

"Guess it's a party in here!" He takes turns smiling at them, jaw opening wide. Bethany looks away quickly. "Can I join you in a friendly toke?"

"Sorry, bro." Dave shrugs. The look of puzzlement on his face quickly settles into a sullen stare. "Just ate the last of it."

"That's too bad," Ben says. "Too bad, too bad. But y'all were looking for TC's source, right?"

Bethany feels shocked and uncomfortable with this conversation. She fixes her gaze on Dave, lips tightening into a slash in her face, and Dave says nothing.

"So was I!" Ben exclaims, so abruptly they both jump a little. He slaps his leg as if swatting a fly. "And I know the first place we should look!"

His lips pull back in a wide grin, baring his canines. "It's not where, but *who*."

Bethany finds out the Station has lost its slender connection to the world in the most uncomfortable way possible – from Marty Horn. An uncomfortable man if there ever was one.

Marty looks up at Ben, Dave, and her. He takes a deliberate sip from his large Coke, rips off a jangling fart and turns back to his computer, adjusting the thick glasses perched on the edge of his nose. "I'd love to stand around all day and chat about what fun it is to be a junkie, but I have to work now," he says. "Our satellite internet isn't responding, and dear leader Gaudin apparently needs to report to his Washington overlords."

"Just tell us where TC was growing, Marty." Ben's wide

smile is still fixed on his face. "I know you two were tight."

"Exactly why I wouldn't tell you even if I knew." Marty looks up long enough to cast a contemptuous look at all of them. "A man is dead, and all you junkies can think of is how to get a hold of his source."

"Hey!" Bethany yells. "Stop calling us junkies."

When Bethany raises her voice and puts some bite in it, attitudes usually do a quick one-eighty. It's something of an unspoken rule: never piss off an attractive woman at Pole. Even if you don't stand a chance with her, she probably has a staggered-out train of backbenchers hoping to be called up to the big leagues by doing her a favor. But her snap rolls right off Marty's back. He doesn't even bother looking in her direction as he speaks.

"Then have some respect for TC, instead of sniffing up my ass." Marty heaves himself up long enough to let out another ripping fart. His glasses jump down his nose, and he laughs in his irritating way. "Now I gotta figure out why we lost SATCOM in the middle of a perfectly good pass, so go on and fuck yourselves off out of here."

"It's okay," Ben says as they walk down from the IT office toward the galley. Bethany notices the somehow tropical smell emanating from him. Like damp-rot in hay, sour and cloying.

"Yeah? How the fuck you figure?" Dave says.

Ben beams a huge Sylvester grin at them. She wonders if she's the only one who finds his tombstone teeth unsettling. "I wanted the source, but I know of another stash. Better than nothing, am I right?"

Dave cocks an eyebrow, but Bethany's lips have retreated

into her face, clamped tightly in disapproval. Oddly, though she has no reason to think this, she has the strong feeling that *it's Clint's weed*.

"It's out in the cryo lab. Y'all up for a little session?"

Dave shifts in his stride. "Uh, I'm not too keen on going outside, man."

"You heard Doc at the all-hands. Bugs are dormant until minus 70."

"I ain't gonna be the first lab rat to test out his little theory."

"Same here," Bethany says immediately. Dave's odds of getting laid again are increasing by the minute. "Penny and his IceCube masters need their 99% up time. South Pole Telescope is doing just fine, so fuck that."

Ben keeps grinning, but clock-springs of veins bulge at his temples. "We can't smoke in the Station, guys."

"Just bake it." Dave shrugs. "Saves the smoke detectors, too."

Ben shakes his head so hard it might vibrate off his spine. "Can't, can't eat it." His grin stretches around his face, the vacant gaps leering and exposed. "It's a better high when you get it in the lungs, you know? That sweet, sweet vapor."

"I'm good, man," Dave says. "If you decide to go get it and bake it up, I'm in like Flynn, but otherwise I'll wait until someone else comes back sane and bug-free."

Bethany takes the opportunity to loop her arm through Dave's and stop walking. "Yeah, thanks but no thanks. I think it's fucking insane to even consider going outside after what just happened." She gestures toward the berthing door to the bedrooms. "Dave, you're about to get lucky. Hustle up."

A shit-eating grin springs onto Dave's face. "Later, Ben!"

Men, Bethany thinks. *Maybe there's hope for them as a species after all.*

We look after Bethany and Dave, smile coming unpinned and disappearing. Then Ben's head turns and we see Yanis stopped on his way into the galley, also watching the disappearing couple. The look on his face is unmistakable.

Ben's grin reappears.

Chapter Thirty-Nine

"It sucks, doesn't it."

Yanis turns to see us sitting across the table from him.

"Oh, it's fine," Yanis says quickly. He looks uncomfortable, as if he's been caught snooping. His eyes flick over Ben's red skin, and our stretched smile winking from between dark gums and missing teeth, and he starts to get up. "Well, I've got to head over to–"

Ben's fist slams into the table and our grin vanishes as if flipped off by a switch. "Sit down, Pohano," we tell the weasel. Our tone is unmistakable.

Yanis sinks back into his chair. When he looks up, our smile is nailed back onto Ben's face. One sharp shard of a broken tooth gleams.

"Let's not mince words," we say. "Dave has the inside track with Bethany."

Yanis's hand goes reflexively to his beard, which is growing back in awkward patches. "I don't – you know, I don't think – dude, what happened to your teeth, anyway?"

"Any day now she'll chop you loose, like Summer chopped Tim. You want to be walking on the treadmill next week?"

Yanis puts his hands out. A pacifying gesture. "Look, Ben. I don't want to talk about–"

(*dude I don't even know you*)

"Of course you don't want to talk about it." Our grin widens, exposing our canines. "You'd rather pretend like everything's okay, right? Sure, cool. That's what Tim did. Saw the signs and did nothing."

Yanis tries not to flinch.

"Do you really want that?"

"I mean, of course not, but what can I do?"

"Finally!" we exclaim, as if Yanis has just solved a riddle. "The right question." Our jolly smile stretches like a rubber band about to break. "Dave has all the loggies on his side. Shouldn't us scientists get together and spitball, on behalf of each other?"

We know Yanis has been called beaker enough to know the resentment the support crew harbors for the scientists. He's seen enough different crews to know he can't change where the battle lines are drawn. We're not lying. The loggies *are* on the same sheet of music when it comes to the scientists.

"That sounds fine, I guess," Yanis says cautiously.

"Can we suggest something, buddy? A thought exercise."

He nods.

We lower our voice and lean in. We ignore his nostrils wrinkling, and his nasty flitty thoughts (*dear lord his breath it's like opening a storm gutter and raking the dark muck at the back into the open*). "Ask yourself why Dave and Bethany are so close. Dave's a dirty hands and dirty nails type. What does she see in him? What do they have in common that you don't have?"

We pause, then draw Ben's fingers up to his lips in an unmistakable gesture.

Yanis's eyes grow large.

"That's right." We nod Ben's head. "They get high together.

They smoke up and that's when Dave brings out the daggers and puts them in your back. She likes you, Yanis, that's why she slept with you in the first place. She wants to like you more. But as long as there's that barrier…"

Our voice is kind and regretful, but our eyes glitter with black amusement, because we can immediately tell Yanis is floored. Eight seasons at South Pole, and he's never had a *clue* that there was marijuana here.

(*the madrid protocol annex two conservation of antarctic fauna and flora what the fuck*)

The idea that somebody would violate an international treaty to get high is incomprehensible to him, which is probably why he has never been inducted into the need-to-know club. He looks at us and we see simple, almost absurd gratitude in his eyes.

It feels like coming home.

(*no wonder that crass hirsute son-of-a-bitch machinist always has the inside track*)

There will be more of us, very soon.

Two then three then four then all.

(*oh my God I AM LIKE TIM oh I've been so fucking oblivious what can*)

"What can I do, Ben?"

"Simple, friend," we say. Gently, so gently, trying not to let our excitement show. Two then three then four then all. "Bring her what she likes and throw some daggers of your own. Do you know who the dealer was?"

"You mean who smuggled the marijuana in?"

"Not smuggled. Grew, hydroponically. It was TC, the breakfast cook. He's gone now, so Dave has nothing to share with Bethany. But you?" We grin. "You know friends in the right places."

"How much will it cost?"

Our eyes gleam like sunshine on the water of a deep lake. The water looks summery and pleasant, but it goes down to black depths where the sun never reaches. "Does it matter?"

(*Tim's just the walking man now walking nowhere oh God please not me I guess*)

"I guess not."

"Have you ever smoked before?"

Yanis shakes his head. Not even in high school, we know it as he thinks of it, when Deanna, the girl he'd had a crush on since fourth grade, furtively showed him a spliff at the bottom of her flute bag and asked him if he wanted to share it with her. He'd said no, and thought himself a righteous hero for it. But now he's thinking all it did was help Deanna decide she'd rather hang out with two-Coachella Steve. Two-Coachella fucking Steve, who'd gleefully told everyone that even though Deanna had braces it had still felt pretty damn good when she'd given him a blowie.

"You don't want your first time to be in front of her," we say. "Come on. We'll head out to the Cryo lab and we'll show you a couple of things."

"Um…" Yanis hesitates. *Outside?*

We sigh. "It's your day with her tomorrow, right?"

"Yeah."

"There's no time to lose, then."

Yanis hesitates, then stands, and our smile practically wraps around Ben's head.

Chapter Forty

June 26th, 10:45 AM

"Hey, Ben, hold up."

We're dressed in Ben's suffocating cold-weather gear, clumping along the hallway with Yanis, almost to the Destination Tango doors. A heavy trunk of dread lands with a leaden weight.

Dread, because the voice has an echo –

(*hey Ben*)

– that causes us to bristle.

We look over Ben's shoulder and Keyon's eyes are fixed on us.

Behind him, every light in the long hallway seems to wink out, one by one, until Keyon is walking at us out of the winter darkness. Eyes boring right into Ben's head.

Right into *our* head.

"Come on," we mutter to Yanis. "Come, come–"

"Hey, BEN."

(*HEYYYYY BENNNNNN*)

(*go run into him what do you hear*)

Yanis drifts to a stop. "Yo dude, Keyon's calling you."

We want to kill both of them right then. Just *punch* Yanis's head through the plaster of the wall and *wrap* Keyon's skull around an I-beam. We summon the last tattered shreds of our cunning and draw them around Ben.

"This damn loggie has been hounding us for the last of the weed," we hiss through gritted teeth. "Come with us now or miss your chance with Bethany."

We turn away and push through the door, into the cold. No time for niceties.

Keyon is like Siri. Somehow, they can *tune themselves* to the frequency of the *us* that lies inside Ben.

And we can't let our plans be heard yet.

(*more more we need more one then two then*)

(*shut up SHUT UP SHHHHHhhh*)

We look back to see Keyon's face framed in the porthole window. Watching us… but not daring to follow us into the cold.

The door to the Station opens and Yanis scurries out past him.

We turn and begin walking toward the Cryo lab.

It's a nice day, by winter standards. Minus 59 F, comfortably outside the microbe zone of activity.

But that's the first generation.

They don't know about us yet.

We lead Yanis over to the cryo lab, where Clint's stash is carefully hidden right where he said it would be. Then we take him back to Ben's home turf; up the outside stairs of ARO, to the Dobson room on the second floor. Half-in, half-out of the doorway. We show Yanis how to stuff the pipe; take the opportunity to hammer home that Dave machined it using NSF resources meant for fashioning telescope instrumentation.

"Now, one little toke for you, so you know what it feels like."

Yanis hesitates, and we push gently. Just a little push.

"So Bethany will think you're a pro at this. Then Dave won't know what hit him." We place Ben's lighter against the bowl of the pipe. "Ready? Deep breath in and hold."

Yanis takes a tentative puff on the pipe. He coughs almost immediately. We laugh good-naturedly. We feel good-natured, and why not? Everything is about to be all right.

"Don't worry about it. Even world-class athletes need reps, right? Hold it in your lungs this time. We'll light you up."

He bends his head, clutching the pipe between his teeth. We flick the lighter, and he takes a deep breath in. Clint's weed flares up sullenly.

Yanis looks up and Ben's eyeballs are caves of black.

"What the–"

Ben's mouth yawns open. A thick swarm of something grey swims out (*we we us more*), and into Yanis's mouth and nostrils.

Yanis coughs, stumbling back.

He rubs his chest.

We catch him as he sags. He looks up at us, eyes large and confused.

"I'm on fire inside," he says, in the humble whisper of a very sick man.

"Don't worry," we say. "We'll make everything better."

Ben's jaw opens. He vomits another stream of *us* into Yanis's gasping mouth.

Yanis collapses to the metal landing, arms stiffly at his sides. We reach Ben's hand out for the fallen pipe, then lift him up against the cold railing. "Now you'll die if you don't smoke," we whisper, brushing snow off his lips almost tenderly. "The grey generation won't hurt you if you can bond with them. That's what the THC in marijuana does. Come on."

We put the pipe between Yanis's lips and light it.

"As deep as you can. Give us a home in your lungs."

Yanis coughs, spit dribbling out of his mouth. The lighter flares.

"More," we whisper.

Smoke drifts out of Yanis's mouth with plumes of vapor, and his eyes flicker black.

"That's better," we purr. Our smile feels like the sun breaking through an ominous cloud deck. "That's much better."

Chapter Forty-One

From inside ARO, through the window of the couch room, Qu Tanzhou and Jiang Cheng watch in silent horror as Ben vomits another tight cluster of microbes into Yanis's mouth.

Chapter Forty-Two

At first we burn Yanis from the inside out, like swallowed lava crawling its way into his abdomen. Then we boil up into his lungs, where the smoke soothes us down to a steady warm throb. The throb spreads to his fingers, legs, and finally, his brain, and he *wakes up*.

He is no longer *him*.

He is *us*.

The invader is powerful, strong, compelling. It feels like Yanis is being boxed up and pushed aside, successively folded up inside his own mind like macramé, smaller and smaller until he doesn't matter. He sits in the darkness for a very long time.

But the darkness isn't suffocating. There's something else in it with him.

A dot. A small dot of white light.

He concentrates on it.

What are you?

The dot doesn't move.

What do you want?

The dot doesn't move, but the answer to his question drops into his mind. Cleanly, like it's been there all along.

We want to be partners.

He feels himself *agree,* and a force he didn't know he'd been exerting releases. The white light draws closer to him. He asks it things and the answers ping into his consciousness. The white light feels no emotions; those are Yanis's to bring to the partnership. But it does have an intelligence. Something that reaches for him as he reaches for it.

Yanis can see into the light now and it isn't white at all, it's a transparent window. Dozens of memories shuffle brightly through it like a pack of cards, faster and faster until they become a movie. A movie of his humiliations. As far back as grade school, when he peed his pants while Mean Mohit was beating him up and no one sat next to him for the rest of the year. As recently as Bethany the nympho needing to be convinced to say yes by the complete obsequiousness of his gratitude, and even then he could only get half of her.

The white light doesn't feel, but it knows Yanis wants to feel good. It shines through the reel, speaking to him through the movie of his life, and this time he sees it not as it had been with *him,* but how it *could* have been with *us*. As individuals, Yanis and the light are both prisoners to the weaknesses of their genes. But *together*…

Yanis opens our eyes.

We are alone. We stumble inside the Dobson room, feeling heat in Yanis's abdomen. This isn't a burning bush of pain but a slim warm knife of purpose. We heat his body up; the fat burns, hotter and hotter. Ridges carve into Yanis's firm stomach, abs popping out like fruits from a bush. Yanis balls up his fists and feels our strength surging through them. We step back outside and reach down to his feet and effortlessly pull a seventy-five-pound cargo sled up with one hand. With little more than a grunt, we toss it over the edge. It soars out of sight, into the darkness like a stone from King David's sling. We don't hear it fall to the ground.

(*fuckin' A*)

We walk back to the Station.

Chapter Forty-Three

June 26th, 11:30 AM

Siri climbs down from her bunk bed. She opens her door just as Keyon is lifting his hand to knock.

"You saw Ben," she says. It's a statement.

"Sort of..." Keyon looks doubtful. All he has are impressions, like faded photographs on an old Polaroid. Hatred. Fear. An image of a radio-tuning needle. A nonsensical chant: *one then two then three then all.* Then Ben had hurried off into the cold.

Siri nods as if she understands perfectly.

(*something is about to happen*)

"Definitely a nasty vibe from Ben, but yes... something more."

Siri's tone is low, worried. "People are on edge across the Station and I don't know–"

(*things are about to get out of control*)

"Yes," Keyon nods. "Out of control."

"Not yet, but soon."

They look at each other. "This is going to sound crazy, but we–"

(*should build a nest*)

(*where*)

"Rajan's hut in the Dark Sector." She pictures LANDIT in her mind. Half a mile from the Station, windows on all sides, with its own power generator and emergency radio.

(*we'd see anyone coming*)

Keyon stops short. "Hold on a minute. Do we really think that–"

But they already know. Talking about it is only an acknowledgement of that.

Except, they haven't done much talking, and isn't that something worth talking about?

Like how this is *happening*, how it *works*, how they have become like two wind-chimes exactly in sync?

(*we were infected and it left us with something when it died*)

(*how much time do you think*)

(*not much*)

Siri nods. "We'll need lots of things to make fire with. It's the only thing that will kill this microbe."

Chapter Forty-Four

SOUTH POLE STATION POPULATION: 28 (PRISONERS: 3; DECEASED: 13)

June 26th, 12:00 PM

The white light doesn't understand why the human wants to instigate a confrontation, but it knows a partnership relies on Yanis being shown what *we* are capable of.

Together.

We walk into the Station as the clock on the wall strikes the dark of noon.

We find Bethany and Dave together in the game room, playing foosball against Mike McCafferty and Jamie. The room breaks off into Clint's ham radio closet, stairs to the weather station on the roof, and a larger darkened movie room with comfortable sofas and old VHS tapes. Music drifts in from the movie room. People trying to get back to normal. We watch Dave spin the handle and pump his arms in the air as his plastic men score.

A voracious grin stretches Yanis's lips over aching teeth. We start walking, purposefully.

Dave looks up just as our fist loops into his face like a runaway asteroid.

He recoils, hands flying up to his nose, which is suddenly a squashed, dripping tomato. He sees blood streaking his fingers, and his eyes flash with rage.

We see his punch coming like it's in slow motion. It's almost childishly easy to duck under it. We are already moving Yanis's fist, crunching it right into Dave's pouchy middle.

Dave's breath forces itself up from his stomach, into his broken nose, then back down in a painful snuffle. He doubles over, gasping.

"Time to settle this, Davie Dave." Even our voice sounds stronger together. "All accounts payable starting now."

Dave puts up his arm like a cringing child, and we shove him back against Bethany. "Yanis, stop!" she screams.

"He talks so tough," we say, mockingly. "So tough he must be able to take us, right?"

Dave stumbles backward, clutching his belly. His eyes are full, too full.

"Look at the big man on campus," we sneer. We stick Yanis's jaw out at him. "Not afraid to fight a *beaker*, are you? Could it be?"

The whole room is staring, but no one dares to move toward us. Fucking tourists. They've come to the zoo to see the animals, but the tiger is no longer in the cage.

Dave backs up, out of the game room into the hallway. "You're crazy," he wheezes. "He's crazy."

Bethany runs out after us, fists knotted in her hair, tugging so hard her fingers fill with dark strands. "Stop this, Yanis! Have you lost your mind?"

We point. "Look, Bethany. Look at who he is when you strip away the tough guy act. Just a bag of pus and hot air. Now that you see it, you can pick." We raise Yanis's chin confidently. Feel muscles bunch up under his shirt. "Pick one. This shitbag or us."

"Him!" Bethany screams.

We stop short. "What?"

Her piercing voice has reached a pitch that would have shattered crystal. "You're lucky to be in this mix, Yanis! The only good thing about you was what a nice guy you were… and now even that's gone!"

Yanis's face goes dead pale except for two hectic spots of color, like rouge on a doll.

Dave stumbles over to Bethany, a grin growing, but she shoves him back strongly. "And screw you too, dickhead! Always taunting him, baiting him… just couldn't leave it alone, could you? Always had to be such a *man* about it."

There is nothing but contempt in her eyes as she looks at us, then at Dave.

Her voice drops, dry and dead as a rice paddy after an ice storm.

"You know what? I don't need any more *men* in my life."

Yanis's feet stumble backward, confused and crushed. Our throat closes to a raw slit of humiliation.

The *us* from Ben slides into our thoughts, like a sly radio announcer on a sports show. *Wait until she's us. Then she'll see.*

"Yeah," we mumble. We look around at the crowd the screaming has attracted. "Yeah, then."

Come find us. It's time to make it happen.

"Yeah," we mumble. "Yeah, okay."

12:30 PM

We wait in the hallway.

We (Ben) are good at waiting. We understand its importance. We (Yanis) are more impatient. We want to lunge with our newfound strength, enough of this hunt-and-peck bullshit.

We raise Ben's hand, and gently blow into it. A few

thousand grey microbes drift out like fine pollen, and we guide them under the door of Marty Horn's room.

They'll die soon, but you can't make an omelet without breaking a few eggs.

On the other side of the door, Marty grunts as he settles his naked body into the pillow fortress on his bed. He sets his laptop on top of his round belly and pulls up his directory of porn.

(*today's a 32, 33, 44 and 45 kind of day*)

(*when you just need to feel appreciated*)

After a long day bashing his head against a SATCOM wall that shouldn't have existed, the corny stuff will do the job.

We watch him –

(*dying death hurt*)

– meticulously size four windows down to exactly a quarter-screen. He clicks play on all of them. Slathers his left hand from a half-empty bottle of baby oil, then reaches under his large stomach. On video number 33, a woman is suggestively eyeballing the IT guy's bulge. Video number 45, a woman is already naked and taking the thong off her mother-in-law.

We put both Ben and Yanis's shoulders into the hinge, and Marty's door splinters free.

He doesn't have time to react. His laptop falls to the floor, and we drag him out of bed on top of it. Oil spills across his hairy back and drips onto the carpet. We grab him by the rolls of fat on the back of his neck and yank him face-up.

We sit on top of him, Yanis's feet crunching the plastic of his glasses, Ben's arm leaning down on Marty's throat.

"We're here for the location of TC's source, Marty, and this time fuck-off is not on the menu." Atop our rubber-band grin, Ben's eyes are still. Clint's tiny stash was enough to get us Yanis, maybe one more of us, but isn't enough for the rest of the Station. "Tell us where TC was growing."

(*more more we need more*)

(*we are two then three then four then all*)

Marty's thoughts are confusing, a blurry checkerboard of fears and squeals darting this way and that, but two bright neon lights pierce through the haze. One says, BULLY. And the other says NEVER AGAIN.

Marty manages to get the words out clearly, despite the bar on his throat. "I will not."

We lean Yanis over Marty, close enough to kiss him.

Yanis's mouth yawns open, releasing an odor like dead vegetables in a wet cellar, then a stream of grey microbes rushes out in a dark deluge.

Marty's eyes bulge. He clamps his mouth shut, but *we* are already burning our way down his throat. Heat rushes against the back of his face in bloated warm waves. His nose quivers and he sneezes violently.

We use Ben's arms to pull Marty to his feet. His head thrashes from side to side, lost in the burning pain, as we force him into his windpants. We are the heat crawling up behind his pharynx, popping his ears; the voice whispering to him until his eyes widen to dinner plates in his puffy reddish face–

(*quickly*)

(*tell us where TC's grow source is*)

We manhandle his arms roughly into his sweatshirt.

(*tell us or die*)

(*tell us or we die*)

Marty whimpers, then makes an effort to shout. He draws in a breath, and nothing comes out. His lungs flare up in fire and all that peters out is a pitiful mewling sound.

(*you'll tell us when it starts to hurt*)

Chapter Forty-Five

It has been a series of incomprehensible days of late, but today, Rajan feels like he's a bit player in a particularly dramatic Greek tragedy.

First there was Summer, staring at him from across the galley, trying to meet his eyes. Then Gaudin, spilling out of the South Pole store like an old laundry sack, wearing only briefs, socks, and a backpack over one shoulder. The Station Manager had caught sight of Rajan in the hallway and literally frozen, like a thief caught in the spotlight, keys clutched in his hand. Rajan stood still and Gaudin had hurried away, muttering under his breath, backpack clanking like anchor chains knocking together. It only occurred to Rajan in hindsight that he'd probably been pilfering alcohol from the store; their manager turning into a thief to jump off the wagon didn't bode well for the future.

Later, playing foosball and drinking wine, only to hear about Yanis picking a brawl an hour ago in that very room, like a sophomore wrestler high on steroids.

And now–

Rajan stares after Ben and Yanis as they march by, Marty bobbing up and down like a kid's balloon between them, beads of sweat popping out across his upper lip. Marty's glasses are missing. Spit leaks between his clenched teeth. He looks like he's had a seizure.

Ben tosses a bright smile over his shoulder. "Just a little afternoon drunkie!"

Rajan has heard stories about strange behavior at the Pole, once the darkness sets in and the isolation becomes more than a state of mind, but seeing it first-hand is surreal. It's all too loud, like a daytime soap opera, complete with exaggerated expressions and bad acting. His thoughts start to scatter like roaches under a light and he draws in a deep breath, trying not to feel overwhelmed. *Not my problem.*

He has enough problems.

Rajan's nightmares about Allen McKenzie have been getting worse. He keeps banging awake *convinced* that Allen is hunched in the dark rectangle between his door and the almirah, drowned eyes staring at him. That Allen has been hissing at him while he sleeps (*die die die die*), the sound like water between his teeth.

Rajan knows he's in a free-fall toward depression, the dreams first in a horribly familiar list of PTSD symptoms. He has taken to leaving the bright fluorescent light on as he crawls into bed. He hasn't slept in so long it feels like he's been punched in both eyes.

And the air feels thick with brewing psychosis.

It's time to check out for a few days. Get out before he becomes just as crazy as everyone else. LANDIT is connected to the Station by buried Ethernet cable. Rajan can be alone in his shack during the contact window the CIA had assigned when he'd uploaded his report nearly twenty-four hours ago. Katie is predicting a drop back toward the seventies starting that evening; he doesn't want to be trapped in the zoo of the Station when that locks people in.

Rajan's feet are already moving. To his room, his supply of dried food, and then the gear room. "Comms, this is

Rajan," he says into his radio as he laces up his bunny boots. "Temperature check?"

"Minus sixty-one and dropping, scheduled to break minus seventy in six hours," McCafferty replies.

"I'm heading to LANDIT. Anyone else out now?"

"Two in the tunnels, and Penny's at IceCube trying to get their servers up and running, but you'll be the only one outside. You sure, man?"

"I'm sure, thanks."

He turns toward his backpack and sees Summer standing in the doorway.

"Summer!"

"Hey there." Her hands wring quietly by her stomach. "Kinda feels like you've been avoiding me."

Words fail Rajan. Tim is still on the treadmill... and she's not wrong.

Her eyes fall to his bulging backpack. "You're... not going out there, are you?"

"Yeah, I am. I'll be back in a day or two."

Her eyes are wide and sad. "Rajan. Surely Jupiter can wait."

"It's not that, I just..." He runs his hands over his face. "There are weird vibes all over the place, and I need to get away to clear my head." He tries to smile. "I guess Pole really does turn extroverts into introverts."

Summer takes a small step forward. "What if I came with you?"

He winces. "I don't want to create any drama."

"Neither do I. But if you leave now, and we don't talk, things will get weird between us. I don't want that."

Silence falls with an almost audible thump. With her standing in front of him, blue eyes limpid and large, all he wants to do is crush her mouth against his. Lie to her, and himself, that they'll work it out somehow.

Rajan turns away, not able to face the mute need in her eyes. His desire for her is now irrevocably colored with Tim's fragile mental state, and the emotional cost the whole Station will pay for them being together. When it comes right down to the nuts and bolts of it, though, he's not doing it for Tim or the crew.

(*water. drowning*)

Rajan simply doesn't think he can bear yet another reason to feel like a bad person.

"Summer, if we go out together… I think something might happen that maybe shouldn't happen."

Her eyes flash. "You think a lot of yourself if you think I'm just going to suck your dick the second we walk into LANDIT."

"I promise we'll talk when I get back," he says, trying to be gentle. "I just need a chance to breathe. Alone. Can you understand that?"

An appalled, slapped expression sets into her face. She opens her mouth, then she turns on her heel and walks away wordlessly.

Rajan's face sags as he watches her go, as if the small screws that hold his skull together have come loose a turn. "I guess not," he says gloomily to himself.

We march Marty up the narrow stairs to the Station roof. He's barely moving, eyes blinking gray, pulsing with a sizzling pain that keeps climbing. The pain's not all his, though. Not anymore.

(*death dying hurt*)

Yanis wrestles the hatch open and Ben shoves the IT man up into the cold.

Marty screams with agonized horror as the heat inside him magnifies. We *feel* the microbes pouring out of his ears, billowing over his body like a sandstorm, multiplying viciously and gleefully. They pinch and burn and writhe and his bowels let go.

Ben straddles him as his flabby legs thrash, pumping snow out in every direction. "These microbes are a second generation, Marty," we say. "They can be active even at this temperature, but they won't survive long. *Listen to us*. The only way you can save each other is to bond to each other. With a catalyst. *We need the catalyst.*"

Marty gives out a mewling sigh, the heat implacably pressing the breath out of him from the inside. He's fighting us. Refusing the white light. He blinks, eyelids drooping ...

We shake him, frantic now. "Come on, you fat fuck, tell us! Tell us where the weed is, and we can save your life!"

(*if you don't tell us where the weed is, they'll die*)

(*they'll kill you as they die*)

Marty holds out for as long as he can, until his stomach turns liquid from the inside. He screams out what we want to know, but it's already too late for him.

Chapter Forty-Six

Siri stacks cans, and Keyon pushes them into their bulging packs in silence. The I-beams in the food arch above are exposed, snow hissing in a gentle waterfall to the floor. Abruptly, both of them freeze. Their heads move in unison.

Looking up at the roof, back in the direction of the Station.

They look at each other, then begin packing faster.

Chapter Forty-Seven

It is just past one in the afternoon and Marty Horn is dead on the roof.

We walk down the stairs toward Dave Atkins's room. Deep inside *us* is *him*, the Yanis-in-the-box behind the white light. The rest of him is slipping away, squeezed into a tighter and tighter box farther from the light, leaving only *hungry* Yanis behind; the piece of *him* that can feel the power of *us*, and wants to harness it for vengeance.

But there is also *it*, the white light. It wants only one thing: to spread and increase its numbers. Ben is mostly *it* now, quietly slipping out of the Station, following its call to chase down Marty's information and recover TC's source. *It* speaks to Yanis gently, a cool hand on a feverish cheek. *Marty fought to the end, which means there are fewer of us. Join Ben. Bring them all over to us. Bethany will come too.*

But hungry Yanis is in the driver's seat; keeping us amped and our rage bright.

Jonesing for round two.

We stamp through the berthing door and down the hallway to Dave's room, almost knocking over José Ager. The slender IT man blinks owlishly at us. His fingers pull at Yanis's sleeve as we push past.

"Yanis. Hey, man, listen."

Ager's voice is kind. "I know what it's like to have

someone leave you. If you want to talk, we're all here for you."

A muscle in Yanis's cheek twitches, hot and angry and humiliated. We push forward, but Ager doesn't let go. "This isn't the way, man."

"Says who?" The hungry voice bursts out in a frayed yell, clear and tinged with hysteria. "Who fucking cares?"

(*you can show ager the way we need more he could be more*)

(*shut up SHUT UP*)

We clench Yanis's fists into a claw. We shove Ager into the wall, then lift him effortlessly out of his loose slippers. Hungry Yanis is angry, *fucking furious,* no time for this *more of us* bullshit. We snarl up at Ager and his eyes grow large in his head.

Two doors down, Dave Atkins pokes his head out of his room.

We drop Ager to the floor in a heap. A low growling noise comes from our chest. We step forward, but Ager reaches up and grabs us.

We stumble.

Dave lunges forward. His hip swings fully behind his punch and Yanis's nose shatters in two places.

"He's crazy," Ager gasps, scrambling to his feet as we sprawl, ass over kettle.

(*when very bad cold*)

"Get moving, José," Dave grates. "Come on. Quickly, quickly!"

Ager runs toward the end of the dorm wing. Dave casts a look over his shoulder in time to see us peel off the floor, rising vertically upward with sinuous fluidity.

Our head swivels.

Then Yanis's body swivels.

We run right at them.

"Move!" Dave pushes Ager through the berthing door that separates the rows of small sleeping rooms from the Station's main hallway. We race at him, Yanis's arms pumping, face peeling in a rictus grin. Dave fumbles behind him as we reach Yanis's hand through the jamb –

– and whips the door shut on it.

We put the pain away, quickly and efficiently, but Yanis's hand doesn't work right anymore. We push through the swinging berthing door with the other hand.

Enough of this hunt-and-peck bullshit. It's time to *maul.*

Dave bounds down the mid-hallway steps, four at a time. He tumbles, feet tripping –

(*yes fall DIE*)

– but catches himself on the banister and manages to heave himself upright. Down the hallway, then into the empty lower gym after Ager. He ducks out of sight as we run right at the door.

The volleyball net is wrapped around a long bar, lying just inside the door. Dave hefts it up like a javelin and rams it through the door handles, a second before the door shudders.

We thrust Yanis's face against the porthole. We back up, keeping our eyes on Dave's gasping face through the glass. Yanis's shoulder blades touch the opposite wall, our manic grin widens, and we *spring* forward.

The door quavers on its hinges. Dust drifts down gently.

Behind the door, the spindly bar warps between the handles, bent like an umbrella handle.

On the other side, Ager looks panicked. He's screaming something at Dave. His voice flakes like rusty iron.

We back up again.

Dave braces his body against the door and the bent metal bar.

"Eat shit," we bellow. "Eat shit and keep eating TILL YOU GET IT ALL DOWN!"

We *run* forward.

The door shakes violently. The bar bends toward Dave with a loud squeal, bulging against the handles. A gigantic dent appears in the metal door.

"Go for the phone!" we hear Dave scream. "Call comms, call for help!"

Not this time, Dave, we think. *No help for you this time.*

Yanis's eyes flare wide. We drop his jaw down all the way to his chest.

A thick cloud of microbes floods under the door, through the gap between the floor and the carpet, between Dave's legs. He whips around to face a grey cloud of *us* about the size of a soccer ball, dense except for a slim root reaching down to the floor. Coiled and tight, a swaying snake ready to spring.

Like a silent explosion, the cloud diffuses outward. Streamers of thick grey microbes expand, arcing down on him like dark rain. We're dying already, forced out by our host into the heat, but we can live just long enough to reach–

Dave screams, letting go of the door.

On the other side of the door, Yanis stands quietly, puzzled. Unsure. He blinks. His nose and left hand pulse like pumpkins lit from within.

Yanis's clothes hang on his body. He can feel his ribs under them. His face is gaunt and stripped, eyes too small for their yawning sockets. He is a corpse encased in a skin suit. Suddenly *him*, and not *us*.

Fantasies of the white light buzz in and out of his mind like blowflies. He looks up, and Dave bursts through the lower gym door, hands clawing at his nose and mouth.

His face is strangely dark.

Dave streaks past him and out through Destination Alpha into the snow.

The second the cold air hits Dave Atkins, the grey microbes swarming all over him strengthen, rousing themselves to an active state.

He screams, and keeps screaming.

A small crowd gathers just inside Destination Alpha, including a limp and empty Yanis. They watch through the window, horrified, as Dave rolls in the snow, clawing at his back. The cloud on his face swells into a grey mass, cancerous and hungry. Crawling down his neck. Growing transparent, like thick glue.

Dave wrestles his sweater off. He screams again.

It takes almost three minutes for him to fight his way out of his clothes, by which time the grey-white mask has covered his neck and shoulders. It slides down his bare chest now, greedily multiplying.

Then Dave's whole body goes rigid.

Every last sinew of muscle on his neck and chest stands out…

He keels over into the snow, face-first.

Not a sound from anyone watching. The night stands still.

The snow eddies gently around him.

Dave's fists clench.

He planks straight up to his feet, arms pinned to his sides. A ghoulish naked Pharaoh rising from his tomb. His eyes are a grey cavern. Ice gleams between his teeth, which reveal themselves one by one as his lips peel aside, all the way back to his canines.

His head turns toward the Station.

He grins, and the grin freezes on his face.

He breaks into a run, right at them.

Screams, as people scatter away from the window. Dave smashes through the door, neck snapping like a hungry rooster. The skinny corpse of Yanis stares at him with horror, rooted to the spot, belly turned to water. Yanis knows the voice that is screaming into Dave's head. Inside the body it's a quiet partner, capable of strategic thought in partnership with the human brain. Capable of *us*. But outside, multiplying in the cold as fast as its single-minded metabolism will allow, it's a bellow of famine. An unending tunnel of senseless rage.

Dave's eyes fix on Yanis.

He turns to run but it's too late.

Dave seizes him by the collar. Yanks him, like a limp bag of potatoes, out through the doors, and Yanis's face smacks dully into the snow. He gets to his elbows; gets a chance to look up at the naked madman that was once Dave, clown-wide grin and grey eyes glinting savagely, like icepicks in the starlight.

Dave's fist smashes into the side of his skull. Yanis's neck makes a popping sound and he sees nothing more.

Then Gaudin shoulders his way out of Destination Alpha.

His fleece jacket is unzipped, and he wears an earpiece connected to the radio clipped at his waist. Dave's head turns to look at him, rictus grin nailed on, and Gaudin's hand emerges from behind his back. Clutching a Beretta 92 pistol.

Dave screams, jaw hinging open, microbes bunching up in the back of his throat like a pitcher winding up at the mound–

Gaudin pulls the trigger.

The shot hangs in the cold air, and Dave tips slowly backward.

His bloody fists tumble to the snow.

The Station Manager lowers the gun and fires. Once, twice more. Bloody holes appear in Dave's exposed chest, the blood quickly turning viscous.

The grey-white shroud continues to grow, slowly seeping over and into the bullet holes.

Gaudin backs away, warily watching the microbes with red-tinged eyes. He stumbles and weaves a little. Then he turns toward the horror-stricken faces framed in the higher windows of the Station. "Everyone into the gym," he roars. The gun waves in an unsteady arc. "NOW!"

Chapter Forty-Eight

SOUTH POLE STATION POPULATION: 25 (PRISONERS: 3; DECEASED: 16)

June 26th, 1:30 PM

Bill Gaudin herds the onlookers into the lower gym, onto the volleyball court. His eyes feel glassy and dead, like a cod's eye in an icebox. His kidneys are a worn boxing bag. He grabs the bent metal bar Dave had used, pulls it out behind him; wrenches the double doors to the gym closed.

Slams the bar through the outer handles on the door.

He is still the manager. Still the fucking boss. Still has keys to the store and the booze, so fuck Wei and his cold turkey therapy. And he still has the only gun, so fuck everyone else, too. They want to act like animals, by God, they can all get in one damn cage. Free will revoked for the season. Eat that, animals.

He stomps upstairs to the galley first, then the game room, drunken rage pounding through his skull. "Everyone out!" he yells, brandishing the gun. "Curfew! Curfew right fucking now."

The Polies move quickly, scurrying like rats, afraid either because they've just witnessed one man beat another to a pulp with his fists, or because a man who has just killed someone is waving a gun while telling them where to go.

Gaudin doesn't particularly care which. He pulls the bar out of the door handles, waves them in, then slams it back into place.

Gaudin marches up the stairs, panting a little, then throws open the door to the upper gym. The only light comes from the dim glow of mileage on the treadmill, already approaching a hundred miles. Tim walks determinedly, orange bag over his shoulder. An empty can of peaches sits on the windowsill by his packed bags. If he registers the group of people locked in the gym below, through the floor-to-ceiling windows, he gives no sign of it.

The Station Manager waves the gun. "Fulton," he says in his boss voice.

Tim keeps walking.

"Hey, FULTON." Gaudin steps forward.

Still no response.

Gaudin's lips peel off his teeth. He steps up next to Tim and points the gun at his temple.

"Get off that treadmill or get your head blown off," he growls.

Tim keeps striding. His eyes stay fixed ahead.

"Do what you gotta do," Tim says tonelessly. "I'm doing what I gotta do."

Gaudin almost pulls the trigger right then. He imagines Tim's body falling to the side. The treadmill would keep on moving until summer, nothing but a brisk *slap-slap-slap* against Tim's dead face to mark his insolence. A suitable end for anyone who casually ignored his orders.

He looks down. From the floor of the court, Weeks and Greg Penny look right up at him.

Watching.

A speck of sanity flares in the darkness of his cornered

mind. Gaudin gnashes his teeth and lowers the pistol. "You step out of here, Fulton, and I'll fucking kill you. I mean it."

He leaves the room and returns with a lock and chain. Tim still walks in the dark, eyes caged into the gloom.

He snaps the lock onto the chain, locking Tim in.

He steps back, and catches sight of Ben's head poking out of the Science Lab.

"Hey!" he yells, and Ben takes off running down the hall toward Destination Zulu.

Fuck it, Gaudin thinks. *Gotta draw the line somewhere.*

He pulls the trigger.

The blast of the gun inside the Station is deafening. Ben weaves in his run like an ostrich, his head seeming to move one way and his legs another.

"Back soon, Billy!" he sings over his shoulder, then barrels through the door into the beer can.

He's gone, but the sound of the gunshot brings a few more heads into the halls.

"Curfew!" Gaudin shouts at the onlookers. "Get over here RIGHT NOW or I WILL BLOW YOUR FUCKING HEAD OFF."

Keyon and Siri climb the stairs from the ice tunnels, each wearing a heavy bag crammed with food and gasoline. Abruptly, a door above slams open.

An unmistakable sound reverberates. A gunshot.

Footsteps clatter on the landing.

Siri crouches fearfully. A second later Ben rockets down the stairs, four at a time.

"Ben, what just–"

"What's going on?"

He runs right by them.

(*BEN!*)

"Good luck with Gaudin!" he calls gaily, then he's gone, the darkness of the stairwell swallowing him up.

(*this is it*)

(*yes it's happening*)

Keyon looks at her with dread. "The survival gear is upstairs. In the janitor's closet."

They leave their bulky packs on the steps and creep upward, trying to muffle their boots on the metal landing.

Keyon raises his head through the porthole.

"Gaudin's got a gun!" he gasps.

"What the hell?"

"He's leading people into the lower gym, I think. He's at the far end of the hallway. Janitor's closet is ten yards away, by the first berthing door."

(*I can make it*)

"Keyon, wait–"

He pulls the Destination Zulu door open and bolts in.

(*shit he sees you*)

At the other end of the hallway, Gaudin's neck snaps toward them.

"Hurry up!" he bellows to Wei, Jamie, and Kevin.

"Gaudin, think about what you're doing," Wei says in a low voice. "You're not well."

"Say it again." He touches the tip of the gun right to Wei's sweaty forehead. "Maybe you want to bring up that diary? Go on, I dare you."

Jamie tugs at Wei's sleeve. "Come on," she says urgently. Gaudin's fish-eyes are staring in an intense haggard way. "Come on, Wei, please."

The doctor steps backward. Gaudin keeps the pistol pointed as he closes one door, then the other. His bloodshot eyes linger malignantly on Wei, then he rams the bar through the door handles, locking them in with the others. He turns.

Gaudin charges toward the other end of the hallway. Breath coming in great heaving puffs.

Siri holds the door to the beer can open–

(*come on COME ON*)

Keyon runs toward her, dragging the heavy pack on the floor behind him. Gaudin skitters to a stop and points the gun, grasping it with both hands. "KEYON!" he yells.

The carpenter freezes.

"You're not going anywhere. No one is going–"

Siri jabs her radio and screams, full-throated, into it. A loud electronic squeal erupts into Gaudin's ear. He claws at his earpiece, roaring in pain. His finger tightens on the trigger and a bullet punches up into the ceiling tile, raining dust down on him.

"Move!" Siri yells.

Keyon yanks the bag through the beer can door and it slams behind them. With one smooth motion, he hefts it up and tosses it over the banister. It plummets into the darkness below.

They bound down the stairs. One flight, two flights, then the door crashes open above them. Siri throws herself against the wall, arm out to stop Keyon. Her heart beats wildly in her throat.

Her neck turns up into the dark stairwell.

She can hear Gaudin, breathing raggedly. For perhaps the only time, she's happy the station manager isn't one of the Polies who finds release in exercise.

The door above opens again, closes. There is a long bout of silence, a few minutes, and then they hear the unmistakable sound of chains.

"He's locking us out," Keyon breathes incredulously. "At the freaking South Pole."

"We're not coming back," Siri says.

"He's got Katie," he says plaintively.

"He's one man guarding eleven exits. He can't hold them prisoner forever."

(*we both know what you're going to decide just hurry up and do it*)

Keyon hesitates –

(*hard stripe in you like biting into a dinner plate*)

– then nods. "Let's get gone before he decides to come after us."

Chapter Forty-Nine

Jonah looks up sharply as the knock sounds again. He considers letting it go unanswered but the problem with doors that don't lock is that people can just decide to poke their heads in anyway. Jonah puts his book down, stands, and opens his door just a crack.

"Well," he says. "Of all the gin joints in all the world."

"I know we don't really talk–" Bethany Hamidani looks red and flustered –"but I… I need some place to be that's – that's –"

Jonah sighs, and waves her in. "Please, just the cliff-notes version."

"Men being men, vomiting macho bullshit over each other," she says. "I want to be somewhere they won't find me. Since you hate everyone, I figure no one will think to look here."

Jonah hesitates, then beckons her over to the wall. "I don't know if you knew this, but our dorms were originally built to be twice as big. But when they were building IceCube they needed more room for the construction crew. They put these panels up to double the occupancy overnight, and they never came down."

He reaches up and pulls a detachable wall panel loose. The tall square of cork and plaster comes away, leaving a neat gap in the wall between Jonah's room and the next.

Bethany steps through and sees a reading nook by the

uncovered window, with a small rug and deep armchair. There's also a fridge, a tall cupboard filled with bags of Skittles and shelves of vacuum dried food. Surprise spreads across her face.

"This puts introvert on a whole new level, Jonah."

"As you're figuring out," he replies coldly, "it can be more trouble than it's worth to be out there with the drama queens."

"Oh, I'm in total awe of the ingenuity," she says. "I assume you know someone who makes sure no one's assigned the room next to yours?"

Jonah has learned a few things about self-care after two decades in Antarctica. "I may know a person who keeps the winter residents at an odd number," he says, a rare twinkle in his eye. "I usually take down the wall, just to give myself more space but, if we have it up, this is a room no one uses. There's food and water. Even bottles to piss in if you really feel like withdrawing. You can use this space as long as you follow my one rule."

She turns to him and wrinkles her nose. "Is this where I find out you're an old lecher?"

"I'm no more lecherous for you than you are virginal for me."

"What's the rule?"

"This room, and the fact that I use it, stays with you. No one else."

"Sounds fair."

Jonah turns, stepping through the wall to his room, and Bethany says, quietly, "Thank you."

"Just remember that one rule," he says, then replaces the cork panel.

* * *

Hours later, Jonah is awoken from his nap when the door to the berthing area smashes open.

"If anyone's in here, come out NOW!" Gaudin roars down the dorm hallway.

Jonah knows that tone.

Knows it is perhaps his only warning of an anvil about to drop.

He moves quickly to the wall and through the partition. On the other side, Bethany is bolt upright in the reading chair, face paper-white except for the dark circles under her eyes.

"Be very quiet," he whispers, and puts the panel back into place. She reaches up and turns off the light, and the room plunges into darkness.

Outside, Gaudin bangs open a door. Then another. Jonah's small eyes stare into Bethany's in the gloom.

"Jonah!" Gaudin yells dimly, then the door on the other side of the wall swings open with a crash.

"Damn hermit," they hear him mutter. Withdrawing footsteps.

Jonah waits a beat, then gives one big nod.

They pull the panel out of the wall together. Bethany dives through to the other side. Jonah ducks in after her and her fingers grasp for the panel. Right as they pull it flush, light flares on the other side as Gaudin bangs open that door.

They crouch, hearts beating hard. Jonah looks tensely over his shoulder. His door stands open against a cracked wall, light from the hallway illuminating them like burglars in the spotlight.

Then the next door, two doors down, bangs open.

Jonah edges to his door. Softly, he pushes it. It starts to swing closed, then creaks.

Loudly.

He freezes.

Then a voice sounds out in the hallway. Cheery, almost casual.

"Hey, Billy," Ben chirps, and Jonah slips his door the rest of the way closed. "Did I miss the party?"

"Ben." Gaudin sounds surprised. "You must be stupid or crazy to come back, but now you're coming with me."

"When you say jump, I ask how high, Billy," Ben replies. "Lead the way to the gym."

Eighteen people are bundled into the basketball court. At first they cluster together, scared and worried, sharing what little information they have. Some have seen Dave beat Yanis to a pulp, and Gaudin shoot Dave in the head. Andrea and Khaled both swear Dave had been naked in the snow, and everyone knows what that means.

Doc Wei worries himself sick over how Dave could have been re-infected despite the sauna treatment and *two* post-sauna skin examinations, and whether the microbes being active at minus 62 degrees instead of minus 70 means a forced mutation has already occurred, faster than he would ever have anticipated. Ager breathlessly recounts his story of Yanis lifting him out of his shoes. Katie asks everyone if they've seen Keyon, then lapses into worried silence. Rob Booth wonders where Jonah is and hopes he's hiding somewhere Gaudin won't find him. Daniel suggests that the Station Manager might have been right to lock the hallways down for safety – after all, they'd given him a secret gun for a reason. Jamie disagrees violently. People begin to pick sides, bicker and argue, even while worrying about crewmates who aren't locked in with them. The group spreads out across the lower gym, re-organizing into familiar clumps. Even at the hands of a gun-waving Station manager, cliques at the South Pole remain.

Except for one person, who sits alone.

Ben's gap-toothed grin is like a red sun raying through a dark cloud.

By his side, he holds a large bag of weed, a metal pipe, and a lighter.

Chapter Fifty

June 26th, 3:45 PM

In 1912, after Robert Scott found himself second to Roald Amundsen in the race to the South Pole, only the misery of the journey back was left. And he didn't survive it. *This is an awful place,* Scott wrote, *and terrible enough for us to have labored to without the reward of priority*. Rajan huddles down into his sleeping bag on the floor of LANDIT, legs curled up as far into his stomach as the bag will let him. Once, he'd been excited to come here; to make new friends and do field-leading research in one of the world's most unique environments. But now, lying atop two miles of deep ice at the bottom of the world, the misery of the thing is all that's left. The winds tugging at the stilts, trying to peel up the side of the container; snow particles rasping on the impact-resistant glass.

(*Allen's eyes going blank and empty*)

His breath an icy cloud, condensing on his face inside the sleeping bag.

He falls asleep thinking about Mummy running away from a snowball.

Repeated exposure to the fluorescence of recollection has faded the memory down to just a few flashes – fine flakes of snow peeling off as the snowball tumbles its way toward his mother. Her maroon scarf, double-wrapped around her face.

The laugh of a child who is still a child; a boy who can still grow up to be the good guy. A terrible sorrow sweeps over him like a wave, carrying him limply down into darkness and dreams, where the Dome-A truck is waiting for him. The burning arches. Syria. Allen. All mashed together, one goulash of guilt.

He is startled awake, going straight from dream to reality –

(*die die die die*)

– when Siri and Keyon barge into the LANDIT container. Both are puffing from the exertion of lugging bags –

Bags?

– up the untamed snowdrift. Dread comes to roost in his heart, a malicious bird returning to an old nest.

Siri and Keyon reach out and grab his arms, one each. They wind their fingers through his. Close their eyes.

Adrenalin spikes through him. "Guys?" he says tightly. "The hell are you doing here?"

Siri looks at Keyon. "Anything?"

He shakes his head. "I don't get the Ben vibe off of him."

"I don't either."

They release him and step back, visibly relieved. He kicks himself out of his sleeping bag. "Is this some kind of Pole ritual I'm not aware of?"

Siri lets out a high scream of laughter that sounds a little crazy. "Told you I'd visit."

Keyon's eyes are grave. "The station has officially gone nuts."

"Okay," Rajan says. "Okay, I'm listening."

Chapter Fifty-One

LANGLEY, VA.

June 25th, 10:15 PM

(June 26th, 4:15 PM New Zealand Standard Time)

It's night in Langley, but Dr. Richard Mason is not at home.

Despite his most savage glare, the messenger dot for `CHARIYA, RAJAN H MAJ USAF` remains stubbornly grey.

"Ping him," he snaps.

"I'm sorry, sir," the technician says. "Satellite's over the horizon. He never came online."

"When's the next satellite pass?"

The tech looks up the access table. "One in twelve and another in thirty-six hours, sir."

"Fuck!" Mason kicks the chair in front of him. "Keep the blockade up. No one from that Station connects to the SATCOM."

Chapter Fifty-Two

5:30 PM

Bill Gaudin awakens on the floor of his room. The barrel of the Beretta is loosely clamped in his sweaty fingers and pointing right at his own nose.

He scrambles back, pushing the gun away, and his head pounds with the after-effects of a severe drinking binge. Several of the bottles he'd pilfered from the South Pole Store are scattered across the floor like empty glittery grenades.

Gaudin rises, shakily, and almost falls over. He moans raggedly. *Really tossed it around the curve of the universe falling off the wagon,* he thinks.

He takes a tentative sip from a half-empty bottle of Jack. Then a bolder one. The spinning of the world slows down. Memory trickles in, like a leaky faucet.

Showed 'em good, didn't we?

Yeah. Yeah we did. Showed 'em all what happens when you poke the fucking Billy bear.

The shroud of inebriation descends back onto his shoulders, warm and cozy. His eyes focus on the gun on the floor and a bleary little smirk comes to his face.

Come to think of it, maybe the boss bear has one more fuck-you errand to run.

He staggers out of his room, humming tunelessly, rolling in his stride like a rubber boat in the tub. He pulls the gun out of his waistband as he yanks the bent metal bar from the lower gym's door handles.

Inside, the Polies sit neatly clustered together, backs to the walls. Except for a group in the corner, their heads turn as one to look at him. A premonitory chill crawls up his spine.

Above them, hidden in the shadows of the upper gym, Tim is on his treadmill. Still walking to nowhere.

"Andrea," he says loudly.

She stands from the shadows under the basketball net. She walks across the court to him.

There are dark bags under her eyes. Painfully short spikes of hair poke out of her bare skull. Her grey fleece matches her grey eyes.

He grins liplessly. "Let's have a talk at my place."

It's a little disconcerting how almost no one in the gym reacts. As if they don't care what happens to her.

Or as if they want him to take her away.

He secures the door to the lower gym and walks behind her. Watching her lithe body move. No whisky dick here, no sir, nothing but whisky firm.

He's already breathing hard.

She turns around to face him inside his room. Her face is blank, arms dropped to her sides, ignoring the empty bottles and the lingering smell of unwashed drunk. He'd had a whole speech drawn up to reason with her, to charm her back, but now all he wants is to feel the mocking curve of his gun against her bare flesh.

"Take it off," he says thickly. "Take it all off."

"If you insist, Billy." She smiles, and her face splits open.

The inside of her throat is crawling with microbes, pulsing like a deadly heartbeat.

(*this one's from Weeks*)

Her cheeks puff up and a cloud of grey leaps at him.

They flood over his face, turning it spotted black. He lets out a startled shout, and the cloud swarms down his throat. Gaudin drops the gun, blind. His insides are burning. His breath shortens into mewling ragged gasps.

It feels like dying.

Then she inhales deeply. A massive sucking sensation hits him, like a torch of fire in his belly being dragged up through his throat. He lets out a whimpering cry –

– it's over.

He opens his eyes. A swarm of microbes hang between Andrea and Gaudin in a fully formed column. An onyx tide, rising and falling. It touches the floor in faint roots of blackening dots. The tree oozes over to Andrea's legs. It climbs up her body, over her fleece, and swims into her mouth, up her nostrils, squeezes into the sides of her eyes. She blinks black, then grey. Her cheeks sharpen in the low light.

All the fight collapses out of Gaudin. All he can do is stare at her, taxed heart thundering crazily in his shivering chest. His high drunk color is gone. His face feels like a window made of very clear glass.

She walks up to him.

She smiles into his face, so close he can smell old fish and spoiled oranges and the sweet tinge of dust baking in radiant heat.

"Pick up the gun and give it to us, Billy," she says. "We'll let you have it back once you have a little smoke with us."

BOOK FOUR
Mutation

JUNE 27TH

Then I saw an angel standing in the sun,
and with a loud voice he called to the birds that fly in mid-heaven,
"Come, gather for the great supper of God,
to eat the flesh of kings, the flesh of captains,
the flesh of the mighty, the flesh of horses and their riders."

Revelations 19:17-18

EXCERPT from:

In the Wake of War: A First-hand Account of Humanity's Deadliest Struggle,

Assembled from the diaries of Mariana Egan

[Excerpt begins]

While embedded at PACOM headquarters, first in Honolulu and then forward-deployed to Kunsan, I had the chance to chat with General Rason frequently. Mostly late at night, when he would come down to the bar and have a drink with his young staff officers. He had spent time in Suzhou as a young Army Captain on an Olmsted Fellowship. He spoke Mandarin, understood the history of China, and respected the competence of his PLA counterparts. Rason knew, from the very beginning, that a swift decapitation was the only way to swing the war his way. So he went about trying to assure it.

But when Russia began offering military aid to China, the pace of the war ground to an abrupt halt. Suddenly it was a standoff, because Rason could not fall into the same trap he had lured his enemy into: an unwinnable two-front war. There was nothing to do but dig in as winter came to the Korean peninsula. Fortify his position at the Tripoint border, keep the nuclear B-21s in the sky, keep sinking Chinese ships whenever they left port, and let the ground war in Taiwan fight itself out. There would be no more bombs over Beijing. No Molotov cocktails lobbed into the fire. Russia had to be kept on the sidelines, which meant drawing back hostilities against a limping China.

Which, of course, gave them time and space to rebuild.

One of our late-night conversations changed my life. It was the week before Christmas, 2027. Rason hadn't seen his family in a year and he had just gotten a call from the President of the United States - a man who held no love for the Chinese, but also many hazy ties to Russia.

"What did the President want?" I asked the General, wishing this was on the record because I knew, even then, what he might say. The next year was an election year, after all. Perhaps it was inevitable.

Rason stared into his whisky glass. Rotated it slightly, casting the light of the lamp behind him against it. "What men in power always want," he said. "A way to keep it."

"What are you worried about, General?"

I could see him weigh his words. Decide if they might drag him down if he cast them into the air between us.

"I'm worried that Russia will win this war from Washington DC, because they have a man in the White House," he said. And then, much softer: "I'm wondering what I'm willing to do about that."

But he was wrong, of course. The war was lost in a place far away, a place so far south Rason hadn't even thought about it.

Chapter Fifty-Three

June 27th, 1:00 AM

Missing from the gym are nine people.

Greg Penny, at IceCube.

The three Dome-A scientists, at ARO.

Jonah and Bethany, location unknown.

Rajan, Siri, and Keyon. Location unknown.

The others are clustered around the Station, but accounted for.

Lurking near the sauna in case anyone tries to use it, silent as ghosts, Luis Weeks and Joe Haskins, facilities. Eyes blinking gray. Communicating without words.

In the upper gym, still walking on the treadmill, Tim Fulton.

In the lower gym, sixteen people. Bill and Andrea, management. Rob and Khaled, MAPO. Ben from ARO; Summer from SPICE. Mike McCafferty and Sheryl Whitney, research assistants. Wei and Jamie, medical. Daniel Baia and Michele Reinert, sole survivors of the dining and materials teams. Kevin and Ager, IT. Katie and Clint, weather.

The heat in the Station has been turned off for hours. The temperature, both inside and outside, is dropping.

The gym has reformed into two groups, one forming a ring that encloses the other.

Katie, Summer, Jamie, Wei, and Rob Booth sit with their

backs to one another. They are pallid and shivering, eyes anxious. Ten people surround them, lips peeled back to reveal unsettling rubber-band grins that haven't flickered for hours.

The eleventh, Clint, stares the other way, up through the glass window set high in the wall, at Tim Fulton on the treadmill. His gaze doesn't vary. His eyes don't blink.

Then the outer circle dissolves as one, and Ben steps forward.

Behind him is a pile of food cans.

He looks nothing like the portly unobtrusive scientist Philip Cunningham had once known. Ben's skin is stretched so tightly across his face that it's translucent, the skull seeming to extrude through it. His gap-toothed smile is wide and glittering. It's a hatefully happy face, radiating an angled, horrible warmth from behind the coldest grey eyes.

Ben sits on a chair that Khaled pulls up for him. He stretches out his hand, and Michele places an open can of beans in it. Not a word is spoken. Ager and Kevin set up a camping stove. When it's hot, they take the can out of Ben's hand and place it on the stovetop. Almost unconsciously, the small group leans in toward the heat of the stove, and the sizzling smell of baking beans.

"It's been over twelve hours," Ben breaks the silence at last. "*Someone* must be hungry."

No one moves.

Ben picks up the can of beans. It sizzles against his palm, but if it hurts, he gives no sign. The circle parts, as if by silent command, and he hurls the can at the wall.

It smashes and flattens. The five watch it slide toward the floor, leaving a wide streak of cooked beans plastered to the wall.

Ben dangles a half-empty Ziploc bag of weed in front of Katie. "Just a little toke and you can eat. I'm sure it won't be your first time. Nor yours, Summer."

Katie turns her head, clutching her knees and shivering.

"Fuck what you're peddling," Jamie says clearly. "And fuck your mother for good measure."

Ben's face turns dark. "We can make you."

"You can fucking try." Jamie's breath plumes around her reddened nose. "I'd enjoy biting your ear off."

Ben lunges forward and screams into her face. "You won't eat a damn thing else!"

The nurse doesn't flinch.

His face rearranges itself back into a blank grin. "It's not dangerous," he says. "It protects you against them."

"Are you the doctor now?" Jamie says loudly.

"Tell them, Doc. Tell them how the microbes don't know any better than to eat you." Ben looks around. "No matter how many sauna baths you take, the grey generation is going to get you. They've already mutated to be active in ice tunnel temperatures. They'll mutate again. A few more generations, and they'll be at summer temperatures. And if you won't let them bond with you, they'll eat you. It's just a matter of if you want to die..." He dangles the bag of marijuana again. "Or surrender to the white light and be inoculated. Survival of the fittest."

Rob shakes his head and stares at the floor. Jamie and Wei are holding hands, and Jamie looks defiant enough for both. "I'm not going to do it," Katie says quietly.

Ben looks up –

(*Summer*)

– and Khaled and McCafferty leap forward, grabbing Summer.

Jamie lunges, wrapping her arms around Summer's legs. "Help me!"

Rob spins around, reaching for her –

Gaudin and Andrea step forward. Their jaws open, and they vomit a grey-white flood of microbes over Jamie and Rob.

The two of them immediately scream with pain. The transparent microbes begin blackening. Summer slips through Jamie's itching fingers and the circle closes to block her off.

The microbes scurry back, as if summoned by an invisible vacuum. They slope across the floor to Gaudin and Andrea. Two conga lines of microbes crawl up their sides and into their throats, disappearing up their nostrils. They open black eyes that slowly turn grey.

Wei blanches. "It's a host mechanism," he whispers, horrified.

"What do you mean?" Katie says.

The circle of four tightens, frightened zebras outnumbered by lurking predators. "I think," Wei mutters, "the grey microbes are not parasitic but symbiotic. They form a partnership with the human body. Based on how Ben is pushing it, I'd bet the THC in marijuana somehow catalyzes the partnership. Maybe–" Wei's eyes grow in horror. "Maybe THC helps the microbes bind to our endocannabinoid system."

"Which is?"

"It's been described as a bridge between body and mind. A six-lane highway into our central nervous system, which is what makes us... *us*." Katie's face now mirrors Wei's dread. "And once the grey microbes are inside... then *they* become hosts for the old-school microbes. The transparent ones, the ones that turn black in the heat. Like branches on which leaves can grow. A symbiotic relationship that can last for generations, ultimately feeding on us. And then… who knows what evolves when they don't have to worry about species survival?"

Behind the circle, Ben gives Summer his most winning smile. He crouches in front of the chair they've pushed her into. "You're cold, you're hungry, and for what?" he says gently. "I'm offering you the vaccine to the South Pole pandemic. Seems silly to fight it, don't you think?"

She stares at him.

(*he smells*)

(*they all smell*)

(*like the depths of New York subway tunnels in the heat of summer*)

"It's just hydroponic weed," Ben shrugs. "What's the worst that can happen?"

Her eyes flicker up to the windows above the gym, to the treadmill. When she looks back, her eyes tell him she's decided.

"Finally!" Ben exclaims. "Someone sees sense."

"Don't do it, Summer!" Jamie cries, getting to her knees stiffly.

"Summer, no!"

"Guys, relax. No one ever died from smoking pot," Summer says. She laughs, a lonely sound. "Gather round, boys and girls, don't be shy. A girl can do with an audience."

The circle turns outward and drifts over, surrounding them. Ben gets on one knee before her, as if proposing marriage. Summer hesitates, looking around. Looking at Clint.

"Clint," Ben says.

Clint turns away from his unrelenting upward stare and joins the circle, in time to watch Ben light the metal pipe.

Summer takes a deep drag. Holds the smoke in her lungs, then expels it in three neat rings.

"One more," Ben says. His grin widening. "But first..."

Michele steps forward from the circle. She kneels beside Summer, then leans forward and kisses her.

A thick helix of black and grey and white connects their mouths as she draws back.

"Oh my God." Jamie's voice is all strangled horror as she watches from across the gym.

A moan escapes Summer as the microbes swarm down her throat. "One more," Ben whispers.

She fumbles for the pipe and takes a deep drag. Michele unhinges her jaw and vomits more microbes all over her. They swarm into her nose and ears eagerly. Ben can feel her stinging pinpricks already, blistering and scorching their way to her stomach.

Summer spasms in her chair. She groans.

Her eyes open. They blink grey, but only for a moment. Then her body heaves, throat locking up.

"Relax, Summer," Ben says. "It doesn't hurt if you just let it happen."

But her whole body is vibrating now, hands clawed in her hair as if trying to rip it out. A small rivulet of blood drips out of her nose, joy and fury at war on her face, then her grey pupil-less eyes shoot open and she screams, "Up there! *Look up there!*"

As one, eleven heads swivel up to the windows of the weight room above them.

The treadmill is empty. In the corner of the window, Bethany's ponytail and Tim's orange bag whisk through the open door.

"NO!" Ben screams.

(*get them they're ESCAPING get them GET THEM*)

Gaudin, Daniel, and Khaled take off running. Ben whips around to see Summer smiling at him from under heavy eyelids that are bleeding grey.

"Guess I did have something to lose after all," she says.

Her body snaps rigid as Ben shrieks his rage into her mind. She lets out a gasping laugh, and keeps laughing even as Ben roars at the others in the circle to tighten around her. Their minds link up in sync with his. She begins thrashing in her chair, but still she laughs and laughs and laughs. The merriment of a slave who knows she will die for it but has set the plantation on fire nonetheless.

She hasn't done much right by Tim, but at least she did this.

A worthy trade.

The sounds of screaming in her head blur into a sweet hum, and she lets herself fall away on it. Her eyes fill up with blood. One last perverse wheeze of joy fades into a bubbling gasp, then Summer is still.

The ghost of a smile disappears from her once-beautiful face. A small tear of blood slips down her cheek.

Summer sags slowly out of the chair and onto the floor.

Chapter Fifty-Four

SOUTH POLE STATION POPULATION: 24 (PRISONERS: 3; DECEASED: 17)

June 27th, 1:30 AM

Bethany Hamidani races down the mid-hallway stairs and breaks left at the bottom. Heavy boots start down the stairs above. She throws open the door to the greenhouse.

"Quick!" she hisses.

The heat and humidity in the hydroponics room hit Jonah and Tim in the face immediately. Jonah opens one of the three doors separating the observation area from the growing area. They run in, bodies brushing between leaves and plants, then Bethany throws herself to the floor, pushing the long-handled bolt cutters she'd used to chop Tim out of the upper gym ahead of her. She rolls underneath a bench that holds small pots of strawberry shrubs. Jonah dives left; Tim rolls under a bench immediately behind her.

They freeze. Eyes wide, mouths dry.

Footsteps cross back and forth in the hallway.

The door to the greenhouse creaks open.

Almost immediately, gagging. A cough, then another cough. The door closes.

They wait for several long minutes. Jonah slowly raises himself onto his elbows and looks out, past the potted plants and through the thick leaves.

"They're gone," he whispers. "They never even came in."

"They don't like the heat in here," Bethany says. "This is the only room in the Station not on the central heating system."

Jonah looks back at Tim. "You were watching it all. What the *fuck* is this nightmare?"

Tim grimaces. "The microbes are living inside them, somehow. They're all infested, with a few possible exceptions." He looks up, eyes haunted. "Summer wasn't. She saw me. She saw us all up there. And I think..." His face twists into a rictus of pain and horror. "I think she distracted them so we could get away."

"Let's make sure it's not wasted, then," Bethany says grimly. "Are the three of us the only ones left?"

"I didn't see Penny in the lower gym."

"Probably at IceCube."

"Rajan wasn't there. Let's see, uh, neither was Siri. I don't think I saw Keyon, either."

Bethany turns to Jonah. "You're practically a South Pole native," she says. "Anything that might improve our odds of surviving this?"

Jonah's lips tighten. "I need some time to think."

"Think about what?"

"How to burn this fucking place down." He looks up toward the solar lamps. "In the meantime, I know a place we can hide."

2:20 AM

The temperature has been winding down.

Minus 72, then minus 73...

Then it rolls over to minus 75 degrees Fahrenheit.

In the lower gym and the cold sauna, the thirteen microbe hosts swivel in unison. Shadows stripe their faces in expectant masks of light and murk. To them, there is suddenly a smell in the air. Something delicious.

They drag the four resisters out of the gym, ignoring their fighting and screaming.

Andrea opens the door to Destination Alpha and the cold wind ducks inside.

"It's your choice!" Ben shouts. "Out there, the first-generation will kill you. You'll strip off what little clothing you have and run into the wilderness, never to be seen again. Or! You can become part of the hive mind."

He draws in closer to Katie, Rob, Wei, and Jamie. "It's horrible when they take over your skin," he hisses. "The inside is so much nicer. Let us in."

"Please, Ben," Rob begs. "Don't do this."

Ben steps back, tongue probing the gaps between his missing teeth.

(*let them see it*)

He grins at Jamie. "Start with her."

Jamie screams shrilly as Gaudin and Khaled grab her on either side, levering her up into the air. She twists to look back at Daniel Baia, sneakers kicking at the tile. "Danny, please!" she cries. "Help me!"

Exquisite clusters of sweat form on the young cook's cheeks and across his forehead, but he stares at the floor and doesn't move.

"Look at me, you chickenshit!" She begins to struggle and writhe. "*You chickenshit motherfucker LOOK AT ME*!"

Gaudin and Khaled carry her forward implacably, through the two sets of doors into the sharp night. The stars above are a billion holes jabbed in black velvet, bathing them in cold witch-light. Almost immediately, both men let out groans of pleasure. Their eyes dance black.

They toss Jamie at their feet. "Told you it wasn't over," Gaudin says, and his voice sounds quite human.

Jamie leaps to her feet and scrambles up the snowbank. Cold rushes through her sneakers, numbing her toes instantly. She claws her way to the top, then runs into the cruel wind, down the side of the Station, full of moaning, grinning panic.

Ben turns to Clint.

(*do it*)

Clint takes a deep breath and exhales a gigantic plume of microbes into the ground.

The microbes grow upward, dizzyingly rapidly, a long gluey pole shivering in the wind. The pole hits an apex, creating a bow, then grows downward, creating a surface for others to multiply on. It touches the ground, then telescopes forward and upward again.

It lands right in front of Jamie.

The pole collapses into a shapeless transparent pool. Her arms flail like she has stepped on marbles, and she falls right into it.

"Get up!" Wei screams feverishly. "Get up, Jamie, get up!"

Jamie's legs spasm, like she wants to run, but her body doesn't move. Her shrieks are carried into the Station by the wind.

They last a long time.

Daniel Baia shakes. His knees quiver, but he doesn't take a step toward her.

Clint shivers. He takes a deep breath, closing his eyes –

(*come back come back*)

– and the pole gallops down the snowbank toward him. It's thicker now. It winds around his leg like a sinuous snake, and disappears into his ear.

Ben looks over his shoulder at Wei, Rob, and Katie. His words pierce the silence like icy daggers.

"Fight us and you die now," he says. "Choose."

A partnership is only as strong as its weakest partner. The microbes were strong and numerous but they had no leader. Focused on survival, they couldn't plan past the most basic needs.

The human hosts, on the other hand, were excellent at scheming. Their minds were built for it.

Together, they could do more than survive.

They could colonize.

In Ben, the microbes found a leader. The white light lived through his repressed childhood. *It* wrapped around his self-loathing as he went through pray-the-gay-away camp. Endured his humiliation at the hands of a homophobic mother and abusive father. Palmed through the private corners of his mind and found his most deep-rooted fear of *not belonging*. In yielding *him* to *us*, Ben discovered an opportunity, for the first time in his life, to no longer be on the outside looking in.

He could hope for more than just to be accepted; *we* could build a *following*.

The microbes' need for survival, coupled with Ben's darkest desires to be at the top of the pyramid, created a symbiotic *us* that could recruit, charm, lead, and be ruthless when disobeyed. Someone to bring the other microbe-human partners into line. No one would soon forget the price Summer paid for her betrayal; for Jamie's rejection of the white light.

But while the microbes found their leader in Ben, Clint found his strength in the microbes. Like Yanis, the white light showed him the power of *us*. But when Clint exhales the microbes at Jamie, he is suddenly, sharply, painfully himself. The power and strength are gone, and he is shocked at how little is left behind. For the first time, Clint sees himself as his father must have seen him. Weak. Content to take the scraps from the big dog's table, to lull himself to sleep with a bullshit song of consolation.

The runt of the pack, too afraid to do more than rot away with self-hatred.

When he sucks the microbes back into his body, the white light roars toward him at once, crammed tightly and screaming like a freight train whipping through a narrow tunnel. Only this time, he's ready for it. This time Clint isn't plastered by the snow-white high-balling train like a fly between the pages of a book. He makes himself into the glaring headlight piercing the darkness of the tunnel, ready to impale anything with *his* light. Even the train itself, if need be.

We have an agenda now. Clint will be his father's son. He will be weak no more. The microbes can enjoy their Clint snack but, by God, there will be a cost to the meal.

And no slight will go unavenged.

The microbe-humans gather in the dark lower gym. Gaudin and Andrea. Weeks and Joe Haskins. Khaled and Clint. Kevin and Ager. Daniel and Michele. McCafferty and Sheryl. And the new arrivals to the hive: Rob, Doc Wei, and Katie.

Still negotiating with their hosts, trying to find where their (*our*) balance would settle out.

And *us*. The pliable pudding formerly known as Ben Jacobs, reborn as the Adam of a new generation.

No words are spoken. None are needed. Our Ben-voice is louder than anyone else's, setting the priorities for our shared mission. We need to increase our numbers, then trench into our nest and guarantee survival until the planes start landing again. The Hercs won't be just full of new people to bring into our hive. They are a gateway to a much larger world.

Regret flows from Doc Wei.

(*shouldn't have killed Jamie she could have been one of us*)

We clamp down on that at once. The loss of one gained three. This will be an important lesson to remember for the outside world. Sacrifices will need to be made to increase our numbers.

The microbe-partners murmur approval. We understand the need to lose a few thousand spores to chase a host who can create millions.

(*until we are unstoppable*)

(*unstoppable yes more of us more we need more*)

We nod Ben's neck stiffly. Yes, it's time to find more.

We turn our mind outward. Across the empty snow dunes and through the sweet wind, reaching out for our brethren. Searching for the dead but not dead.

Our minds fly over Philip and Akinori and Spencer and TC and Lisa and the others, already buried by the blowing snow. Our first-generation cousins are awake now, eating through their hosts. They won't survive, long-term, but long-term is a new concept to the hive. The human hosts seem to have an excellent grasp on the *future*. On more than a nest but a *kingdom*. Walls and weapons and protections that can spawn *thousands* of generations.

The hive-mind reaches out beyond them. Smaller, quieter. A presence so quiet its very physical instantiation has been erased by the hated heat.

Two presences, together.

We look up.

(*Keyon and Siri*)

The hive pushes aside sadness from the Katie unit. We could trace our way closer to that signal, using each microbe-infested body in the snow like a homing beacon, but we already know where they are.

They're at LANDIT. Rajan is probably there too.

There are more. The Chinese scientists, at ARO.

There are more. Greg Penny, likely at IceCube.

There are more. Jonah, Bethany, Tim. We do not know exactly where they are, but they will not dare to leave the warmth of the Station.

Our (Ben's) mind flares brightly, overriding their conversations. The threat. Where is the threat? The stragglers will be easy after that.

Rajan, most of the hive agrees.

We shake Ben's head. No. *Siri and Keyon were scarred by the first-generation. They can hear us. Not all the time, but enough to make them a danger to our survival.*

(*rajan is still dangerous military here no accident I'm telling you*)

The threats are all at LANDIT.

And ARO?

The Chinese scientists are no threat.

I will go.

I will go.

Sheryl, Michele, Kevin, and Ager peel away from the

group silently, heading for ARO. The other twelve make a different stop: the Comms room, upstairs in the management wing, to grab radios. We will need to stay off the hive mind so Siri and Keyon don't hear us closing in.

Rajan-Siri-Keyon. Jiang-Tanzhou-Liu.

Six targets.

Six more bodies for the hive.

Chapter Fifty-Five

The sight below makes Jonah's skin break out in goosebumps.

From the crawl space above the second floor of the Station, Jonah, Bethany, and Tim peer down into the gym. The group beneath them is clustered in darkness, silent. They bounce up and down on their heels, leaning in and out from the center where Ben stands. Like they are listening to a hymn no one else can hear.

Abruptly, a group of four peels away. Jonah points at Tim, who backs up on his hands and knees. His back brushes against the dusty ceiling as he crawls away. Jonah hears Tim muffle a sneeze. His eyes widen –

– but the larger group is already on the move, a herd behind Ben.

Bethany taps her radio and Jonah puts his earpiece in, changing to Channel 49. They nod at each other, and Bethany crawls in one direction, Jonah in the other. The rooms are marked off in the crawl space, metal rivulets corresponding to the walls they are crossing on top of. In each room, Jonah carefully lifts the edge of a ceiling tile and ducks his head through.

Checking if there is anyone in the room below.

Bethany's whisper comes into his earpiece. "Big group in the Comms room getting radios," she whispers. "I think they're leaving."

Tim's voice sounds in their ears, tight. "Group of four headed to ARO. I think they're going for the Dome-A scientists."

"Are they still locked in the liquid nitrogen room?" Jonah whispers into the radio.

"No." The relief in his voice is distinct.

There is a radio in ARO, tuned to the emergency channel. Jonah has always left the volume all the way up, so he can be untethered from his handheld radio but still hear anything critical.

Jonah presses his transmit button.

Hears his voice squeal, painfully loudly, from the Comms room below.

"To the Chinese scientists at ARO. If you can hear me, you have unfriendly visitors coming to you. I repeat, these visitors are not friendly. There are four of them, and they will be there within ten minutes."

He releases the button. Holds his breath. If any of the infected have their radios tuned to the emergency channel…

Nothing.

In fact, it would be surprising if they have the radios turned on yet. They certainly don't seem to need words to communicate.

He repeats his message, then looks up to see Bethany crawling toward him. "A big group just left the Station. They're headed grid-west."

"The Dark Sector. How many?"

"Ten."

His head comes up sharply. He lifts two fingers, eyebrows raised, and she nods. Still two people in the Station with them.

"No sign of them," she whispers. "Must be on the ground floor."

"Time to arm up," he says. "We're going to war."

Chapter Fifty-Six

Jiang Cheng sits on the sofa, on the second floor of ARO, feet folded under him. The Dome-A manager's breathing is even, mind fading into the darkness behind his eyelids. Whether facing the Antarctic wilderness on the traverse, or locked up in ARO, meditation has helped him stay calm.

And staying calm has kept him alive long past his expiry date.

The emergency radio breaks into life, and English.

"To the Chinese scientists at ARO..."

He looks up to see Qu Tanzhou standing at the edge of the room, a fearful look on his face. Qu's eyes ping-pong between him and the radio he doesn't fully understand.

Jiang Cheng stands slowly. He has had a feeling, ever since seeing that peeled containment sphere on their dining table, that his time is at an end. Driving the cargo truck and hearing the frenzied screaming behind him, he'd felt sure the traverse would be his last act.

But it seems he has one more fight left in him.

He looks out of the window at the stars, dim specks struck on the dark of the galaxy that he has spent his life studying. When he speaks, his voice is calm and resigned.

"Let's get ready to welcome guests," he says in Mandarin.

Chapter Fifty-Seven

Quietly, Rajan places the ladder that was lying against the wall up to the hatch in the ceiling. Through that hatch he climbs into the base of the telescope dome on top of LANDIT. Hot air pours from powerful heaters that keep the dome de-iced and the telescope slewing freely. He enters his password into the telescope control computer, then opens a command window and enables the ping script.

The Internet is still down with no connection. If his guess is right, the CIA will allow his signal to go through around 4 AM, right before the satellite access window closes.

Back down in the container, Rajan's shuffling has awakened Siri and Keyon. It's too cold to sleep more than fitfully inside the small container. Even with the heater turned up to full blast, puffs of icy breath flicker in the low light. They wrap their sleeping bags around them and eat a cold cheerless breakfast just after 3 AM.

Siri stands and stretches. The wind has shifted, clearing a crescent at the top of the drift-packed windows. "They look clearer from down south, don't they?"

Rajan steps up beside her. "The stars? They actually *are* clearer." He allows himself a moment to enjoy the furtive light of the aurora australis dancing above them. "There's no light or air pollution, and at this altitude the atmosphere is one-third its thickness at sea level." He smiles at her. "South Pole is a great place for astronomy."

She changes the subject. "I still think we should head for End-of-the-World. Get lost in the berms. LANDIT is the very first place Gaudin would come looking for you."

"You should go. I have to be here at 0400."

She shakes her head. "This telescope isn't worth your life."

Except it's not that. With Siri and Keyon surprising him, and with the jaw-dropping story of Gaudin's power trip, Rajan had missed his designated contact window with the CIA. He needs to make this one.

The crew needs answers, and he has a nasty feeling that Langley has them.

The emergency radio lights up in the bottom drawer. Keyon yanks it open in time to hear Jonah re-transmit his warning message to ARO.

"Gaudin didn't get Jonah!" Rajan exclaims.

Siri and Keyon look at each other in an almost intimate way. It makes him feel a little envious, except that he has the feeling they are somehow arguing, silently.

Siri looks at him. "I don't think it's a good idea to reply."

"I disagree," he says, and Keyon nods mutely. "We need ears inside the Station. If Gaudin's heading to ARO, it means everyone else is locked up in the lower gym without a guard. If we let them out, it'll be all of us against him, and this craziness ends."

"Then Jonah can do it. He's right there."

"At least let's get some intel," he pleads.

"We risk exposing ourselves," Siri says. "Right now we're lying low–"

She bites her own words off.

Rajan starts to speak but she throws up her hand urgently.

(*shhhh just shhhh*)

Keyon's eyes are squeezed shut as well. Rajan frowns, trying to listen for whatever they are hearing.

Siri looks at Keyon and her pixie-like face looks terrified. "Did you get that?"

"*Get off the net.* They know we can hear them."

"They felt... closer."

"Yes. Too close to still be at the Station."

"What's going on?" Rajan demands.

"Something has changed." Siri gestures to the radio. "You're right. Reach out to Jonah."

Rajan doesn't question the win. He draws the hand mike up, thinks for a second, then transmits across the common frequency. "Jonah to my channel, five seconds. Jonah."

He doesn't identify himself. He dials back to Channel 51 and Jonah's voice comes through the radio. "Here."

"Do you know Siri's channel?"

"Yes," the reply comes back almost immediately.

"There."

"Unlucky channel thirteen," she flashes him a grin. He realizes, with a little shock, that he hasn't seen her smile in a *long* time. Siri is the type of person who always manages to find a smile for everyone, even people she dislikes. This brutal season has changed them all.

"Are you safe?" Jonah says.

"I'm safe, me plus two. You?"

"Also safe, also plus two."

"Is Gaudin headed to ARO? If so, are you able to let the others out of the gym?"

There's a long pause, then Jonah says, "Uh, well. A lot has happened since you left."

* * *

The hive knits together as we hear Rajan's initial transmission on the common channel. Our radios are on now, and as soon as we link up across the mind-net, we know –

(*Gaudin*)

– that it's Rajan's voice, and –

(*Wei*)

– his channel number. We hear him ask for a switch to Siri's channel, and –

(*Khaled*)

– we come to a stop in the snow, spread out in a bedraggled formation.

Listening to Jonah bring Rajan up to date.

Ben looks up to the dark sky, eyelids flickering. Reaching out to Weeks and McCafferty back at the Station.

(*Jonah plus two in there somewhere find them find them*)

Abruptly Siri cuts in. "Jonah, radio silence. Leave the Comms room, right now."

Jonah cuts off in mid-sentence. The channel falls silent.

(*no need to be silent now*)

(*the comms room find him find them*)

(*everyone let's go move hurry HURRY*)

As we break into a shuffling run, kicking up clouds of snow around us, a piercing scream rips through our heads –

(*NOOOOOOOO*)

– then cuts out just as quickly, leaving our ears ringing in the emptiness.

The hive breaks into a more urgent run.

Chapter Fifty-Eight

Sheryl, Michele, Kevin, and Ager ease the first-floor door to ARO open quietly. The thermostat is cranked up and we quickly rid ourselves of our jackets. Taking the clothes off feels good. Sheryl is the first to take off her pants. Her windpants rustle gently as they slide over her bottom. The others follow suit wordlessly. Layer after layer comes off until there's a heap of clothes between us and the door, and we are naked. A sheen of sweat covers our bodies. As symbiotes we are better adapted, but this is still too warm.

The males look down at our erections. The microbe halves don't understand the reaction, but the human halves are interested in what they see of their female counterparts.

We turn as one and creep up the steps, Sheryl leading the way.

Suddenly, a man appears at the top of the landing.

His hair glints grey in the semi-darkness. He wears tall green rubber gloves, and holds a metal thermos in one hand.

Sheryl comes to an abrupt halt. We are suddenly afraid, in the instinctive way of an animal on the front lawn when the porch light flicks on.

(*send them send them*)

"Do not come more," the man says. "You go now."

A transparent curtain seeps between Sheryl's legs, funneling upward. It blackens as it spills quickly up the steps toward him. Another dark tree slides onto the wall, branching over the winter-over plaques.

We bare Sheryl's teeth in a grin. "Just have a little smoke with us."

The man spins the lid of the thermos, tightening it –

(*careful careful*)

– and he throws it at the wall.

Sheryl ducks as the thermos smacks the wall and bounces past us. It tumbles harmlessly down the stairs, but we are already vomiting out of Sheryl, pushing up in a heavy flood. We curl around the man like a whip, snaking up and over his leg –

Sheryl's back lights up with pain as we hear the flat *whoomph* of an explosion behind us.

We turn Sheryl's shoulder to see a cluster of rusty nails poking out of the back of her knee. The back of her thighs. The nails are everywhere.

Down the stairs, wisps of volatile smoke clear. Ager and Kevin both lie dead, dozens of long nails driven into their nude bodies like nauseating pincushions. Thick blood drips down the stairs. Michele stirs weakly, hunched against the wall on her knees. Her side is studded with nails.

We lift Sheryl's head, confused and terrified. We reach for our tendril wrapped around the old man, but as soon as we start to move up his body, instead of fighting us, he runs down toward us. We reach out instinctively, but his legs have already left the ground. He drives flatly into us. Sheryl loses her footing and falls backwards, her body wrapped up in his. Her head spins with stars as we knock into Michele's knees, sweeping her down too. We greedily multiply up the man's back, then Sheryl's head smacks into the wall at the base of the stairs.

She breathes in deeply, flooding us back toward her. She

needs our strength to get out from under the heap of arms and legs.

"Please, catch."

We move Sheryl's head up in time to see another thermos spinning over the banister and down the stairs. Michele turns. We reach out and catch it instinctively, holding it above the Chinese man's head like a trophy –

(*NOOOOOOOO*)

– then the thermos, filled with stirred liquid nitrogen, warms up to its flash point and explodes in Michele's hand.

In the crawl space, Bethany's face lights up like a lamp.

"Siri said the Comms room! That's where they'll go," she hisses.

Jonah's head snaps up. "Get moving! I'll join you as soon as I can."

She turns, springing down the crawl space like a mad rabbit. Snarls of wires tug out of their sockets in her wake. Jonah pokes his head down through the ceiling tile.

"Hurry, Tim!"

Below him, in the kitchen, Tim drags over a large cloth shopping bag. He reaches in and hefts a five-gallon bottle of cooking oil up. Jonah catches it; his face disappears from the gap, then reappears.

Tim tosses up three more bottles. The bag is empty now, except for cloth napkins and lighters lining the bottom. Jonah's long arm snatches it out of his hand.

At LANDIT, Keyon's head snaps up, like a dog hearing footsteps at the gate.

"They're coming."

Rajan: "How much time?"

"Minutes. Maybe less. They're moving fast."

Just then, a calm and thickly accented voice speaks from the radio in Rajan's splintered desk drawer, each word deliberately enunciated, like it's being read from a piece of paper. "Hello," the voice says. "We kill monster four. We still alive two. There are bacteria many. These are on fire."

A long pause, then, "Thank you."

"That was ARO," Keyon breathes.

"They killed four of our friends." Siri's eyes swim with sudden tears. "And we… we have to do the same if we want to survive this."

Rajan sees Keyon's eyes skitter; notices Siri's hands shaking. Fear coils lazily in his belly like cold oil. If they really are about to be fighting for their lives, they can't hesitate in the heat of battle. Or they'll all die down here.

He knows what he must do.

It's now or never, but it's still painful to scrape the words up his throat and into the world.

"Nine years ago, I killed a man in a shootout in Syria," he says hoarsely. "I watched him bleed to death."

Their heads snap around.

Rajan forces himself to push through what he sees on their faces. "I haven't stopped seeing the face of the man I murdered when I close my eyes at night." His voice is full. "But the men who were next to me put their children to bed every night because I pulled that trigger, and that's what lets me fall asleep."

A solitary tear spills over and traces down Rajan's face.

"Summer told me that every year she comes back to Pole, she learns something new and shitty about herself. I have too. As much as I loathe myself for it, I've learned that I'm a killer." He swallows painfully. "There's nothing I can say that will change the way you'll feel about it. All I can tell you is what I've learned... that I'd rather live with my nightmares than with the regret that I didn't save your lives."

He looks at both of them. Siri has been his friend since his first day on the ice; Keyon is an unlikely ally, but impending death makes for strange bedfellows. "Those aren't my friends out there anymore," he says. "My friends are the people in this room. So I'm going to do what's necessary to make sure that we all make it through this, *and I know you will too.*"

Keyon makes a strangled sound.

"Let's kill our monsters," he says hoarsely.

Siri's lips tremble, her eyes wide but now tearless. She nods.

Rajan wipes his face. "There's a hatch in the back of the dome that's just big enough to squeeze through if we move a few things around." He jerks his thumb up to the roof. "Let's get to work."

Siri hurries up the ladder into the base of the telescope. Keyon pulls the survival bag open and, in no time at all, creates an impressive pile of empty lighter fluid cans. Siri sits at the edge of the roof hatch, catching the cans Keyon tosses up to her. Then he comes up with the food. There's barely enough room for three people in the dome. The bulky instruments mounted to the telescope backboard dig into the back of Siri's head. Keyon folds himself up at the back of the dome, and begins peeling away insulation, layers and layers of it, to reveal the small hatch where an air conditioning unit would have exited if the dome had been deployed in more temperate weather conditions. Siri pulls up the ladder and scoots it under her butt; he pulls it through the hatch and tosses it down to the snow behind the container. She pulls the hatch up, sealing them into the dome. All of this happens without a word.

"What the fuck is this frequency you two are on, and how do I get on it?" Rajan exclaims. All he has managed to do in this time is unbolt the heater from the wall and drag it over by the door.

"Both Keyon and I had the microbe measles pretty bad before we burned them off. They dug in somehow." Siri taps her blackened cheek. "Microbe telepathy."

"Are you serious? Because–"

Siri plants her knees and lithely maneuvers under Rajan's arm. Her face comes up against his and she kisses him, hard, her teeth knocking into his.

"Aren't you glad you didn't see that coming?" she says.

He grins.

He kisses her again, and this kiss is soft and tender. There's no guilt in the touch of her lips. No sensation of a boulder rolling downhill that he must stay ahead of. His mouth parts from hers reluctantly.

Her eyes twinkle for a moment, then they go still.

"They're here," she says, voice flat.

Behind her, the telescope computer pings.

```
> PING nsa.smil.mil (172.217.89.02): 56 data bytes
> 1 packet transmitted, 1 packet held, token detected
> Connection successful.
Please identify.
```

Siri looks over her shoulder at the screen, and the eagle on the token poking out of his card reader. "What the fuck," she says clearly.

"Siri, I..." Rajan begins, then his jaw snaps shut as they hear the freezer handle on the front door to LANDIT creak.

The door pulls open, slowly. "Keyon?" a soft voice beneath them says.

In the dome, Keyon's fists clench on his legs.

Katie Caberto's head edges around the door. "Keyon, I know you're here." Her lips curl away from her teeth in a steady grin. "I can hear you thinking."

CHAPTER 59

Katie is sweating profusely, face actively roiling. She springs forward, over the heater, and rips the electrical cord out of the wall. Her feet lash out, kicking the heater backward, down the snow-covered stairs with a loud sizzle.

She straightens. Khaled Zaidi and Joe Haskins step into the container behind her. The door slips closed. Her eyes dance around, then catch sight of the trapdoor in the roof.

In the darkness outside, the other seven hive members loosely surround the stilted building. Watching through the eyes of the three inside.

Katie raises her hand but can't reach the trapdoor.

Khaled looks around, then pushes the desk chair over.

"I always wondered whether you loved me. Whether you even liked me." Her voice is gentle. She climbs up onto the chair.

"You like your games. You like to stir the pot. Were you stirring me too?"

The chair slides, wheels slick on the sodden carpet, and she jumps off.

"I have a voice in my head too, Keyon. It talks to the hard-stripe voice." Katie looks up. "And you *do* love me."

Khaled pushes the chair back under the trapdoor.

He holds it in place, and she climbs onto it.

"You've never loved anyone before, but you love me."

She reaches her hand up. Pulls on the handle. The hatch falls down into the room and she stares up into Keyon's haunted eyes. The blood drains from his face.

"I love you too," Katie whispers. The microbes spill out of her ears, climbing up toward him in a wavy tendril. He sees a black gleam in her eyes, dancing like legs dangled over the edge of a well. "I love you too."

"Every year..."

"What's that?"

The microbes lick up onto the hatch, eagerly reaching toward his knees.

He looks up, and the words taste like death in his mouth.

"Every year at Pole I learn something new and shitty about myself, but this might be the worst year yet."

A flat click, like a door slotting into place.

He tosses a butane grill lighter through the trapdoor.

Katie's eyes flash black. Her head snaps down to follow the tongue of flame at the end of the lighter. It bounces off the handle of the chair, and the licking red of the flame throbs, about to go out.

She looks back at him. Her wide eyes bleed black like the Red Sea collapsing on itself, her blue pupils peeping out to meet his, then the spark catches the lighter fluid soaking the carpet. A bright hot fire roars across LANDIT in a vicious wave. The heat is instant, incredible, like being trapped inside a microwave. Khaled screams as his feet catch fire, releasing the chair.

"I'm sorry," Keyon says, and pulls up sharply on the chain connecting the dome to the hatch door. It hits her as it swings up. The chair bucks, rolls, and spills her onto the burning floor.

For the first time in his life, the hard-stripe voice is utterly silent.

"Go!" Rajan stops typing, slams his computer closed and rips the token out of the reader. "Go, go, go!"

Thick pungent smoke is already seeping up around the ill-fitting trapdoor. Siri throws the small hatch in the back of the dome open, pushing the nearly empty survival bag out in front of her. She perches on the lip of the dome, the wind almost tipping her over, then edges around the rounded dome of the telescope.

She looks out and sees (*hears*) Ben –

(*no what the fuck what the FAAAAACKKKK*)

– screaming. Below her, a sharp tongue of flame stabs through a porthole window. Daggers of glass whip through the air, and the ring surrounding the container shrinks back a few steps. Except for Ben, who is rooted to the spot, his body a freezing floe of icy shock.

Siri screws up her fists by her side and *thinks out* as hard as she can.

WE KILL MONSTERS THREE!

Every eye surrounding the container swivels to her, instantly. The hatred of the hive gushes at her and it feels like getting broadsided in the face with the force and fury of an ocean. She screams back into the noise with everything she has.

WE ARE STILL ALIVE! THERE ARE BACTERIA MANY! THESE ARE ON FIRE!

The hive mind *surges* and she feels suddenly weak-kneed. Blood seeps from her nose in a thick river. Then Keyon's voice joins, echoing with hers, clearing the noise like a snowplow.

WE KILLED THREE MORE OF YOU!

Three of you!

WE ARE STILL ALIVE!

Still ALIVE! STILL ALIVE!

Into the commotion, somehow, Siri hears Jonah on the radio. "Two of the monsters here at the Station are burning–"

Below them, the microbe-humans clutch their skulls as screams of agony from Luis Weeks and Mike McCafferty rip through their minds.

TWO MORE! TWO MORE!

"The Station has been deloused," Bethany Hamidani says across the all-channel. "And we're ready for the rest of you motherfuckers."

Ben's plan wasn't a bad one. Sending most of us to tackle the group who could see us coming made sense. Two of us to comb the hallways of the Station for scared stowaways, also common sense. Four of us to tackle three defenseless scientists at ARO, borderline overkill.

And yet somehow, brutally suddenly, sixteen microbe-humans have become only the seven standing in the snow around LANDIT. *Just seven of us*. Our hive-mind *lives* through the agonizing last moments of those lost, leaving us feeling dazed and half-alive ourselves. We mourn the holes in our collective consciousness where Sheryl-Michele-Ager-Kevin and Weeks-McCafferty should be. Our minds are split with the *hated heat,* feeling Katie-Khaled-Joe burning inside LANDIT.

We burst into that restless quicksand.

The thoughts are already churning amid the hive, too quick to even be heard individually–

(*Summer lost for no reason*)

(*Jamie lost for no reason*)

Ben turns, buzzing with disbelief at how quickly the situation has slipped through our fingers –

– and Clint forces us to leap on him, knocking Ben to the snow. Our Clint-face is a snarl, eyes shot deep grey. Clint's arm slams down onto Ben's throat like an anvil.

Ben looks up into our eyes, and –

(*get those words out like yer life depends on it boy*)

(*every slight avenged you goddamn beaker*)

– Clint's frozen claw of a fist punches down into his throat, ripping out his Adam's apple. Blood bursts from Ben's shredded neck in a gaudy arterial pump.

The roof of LANDIT crackles and snaps. Keyon looks over his shoulder to see Clint on the ground, crouching over Ben and screaming in hoarse victory. The rest of the hive stares at the two of them in total confusion. Keyon pulls the last full bottle of lighter fluid from the survival bag. His eyes glitter maniacally as he stuffs a glove into the opening and flicks a cigarette lighter into life.

He sets his eyes on his target. There's a queer flat light in his eyes.

"Hey Gaudin!" he roars.

(*HEY GAUDIN*)

"This drink's on me!"

He hurls the blazing can down at the Station Manager, hitting him squarely in the chest, then he leaps into the snowbank below like he's cannon-balling off a diving springboard.

Chapter Sixty

CLASSIFIED
HANDLE VIA SAP CHANNELS ONLY

TOP-SECRET//SPECIAL ACCESS PROGRAM HAVE-VIKING/SIGNALS INTELLIGENCE-GAMMA/TALENT KEYHOLE/HUMINT CONTROL SYSTEM/NO-FOREIGN (TS//SAP-HV//SI-G/TK/HCS/NF)

(SECRET/NOFORN) Standard declassification procedures do not apply.

TRANSCRIPT OF ENCRYPTED COMMUNICATION

LOCATION: AMUNDSEN-SCOTT SOUTH POLE STATION, *JUNE 27th, 2028*

(TS/HCS/SAP-HV) Identity of Subject: Major Rajan Chariya. Subject is a US Air Force officer (career field specialty code 61A, Physicist) assigned to the Air Force Research Laboratory. Subject was recruited by Case Officer [CENSORED/HUMINT SENSITIVE]. Subject was presented with funding, selection as US Antarctic Program Principal Investigator, in return for limited support to HAVE VIKING Phase II operations.

(*ops-desk*) Please identify.
(*Subject*) rajan chariya / not much time / summary follows.
(*ops-desk*) Report status of visitors?
(*Subject*) 13 crew dead from initial contact with extremophile microbe of unknown origin / microbe since mutated into new form able to co-exist inside human hosts. 7 add'l dead since initial contact / station mgr compromised / request evac asap
(*ops-desk*) Say nature of mutation?
(*ops-desk*) Symptoms?
(*Subject*) Confirm medical evac as soon as wx permits.
(*ops-desk*) More information needed. Do you have a report with details?
(*Subject*) You're not fucking listening.
(*ops-desk*) Evac confirmed asap wx.
(*ops-desk*) Say nature of microbe mutation, upload report?
(*Subject*) Fuck you. Details available on evac so better hope we make it. Persons touching down must have Level A Hazmat gear. Aircraft must have USAF Transport Isolation System or equiv.
(*ops-desk*) Can you say symptoms, possible mitigation?
(*Subject*) Consider all survivors infected until tested negative.
(*Subject*) See you at Pole.
(*ops-desk*) Is sauna treatment still an option as with initial contact?

(*ops-desk*) Major Chariya, are you there?

(*ops-desk*) Rajan?

CONNECTION TERMINATED: SUBJECT END.

Chapter Sixty-One

SOUTH POLE STATION POPULATION: 13 (PRISONERS: 2; DECEASED: 32)

The run to Pole is the hardest thing Rajan has ever done.

The air around him feels packed with ice-cube molasses. Keyon and Siri run determinedly, able to sense exactly what their fate will be if they slow down, and he battles to keep them from becoming vague humps on the horizon. A quarter-mile behind them, the five remaining microbe-humans have re-centered on their goal.

Gotten their fucking shit together, you might say.

The Station looms like an oasis illusion at the end of a deep white quilt, never seeming to get closer. Siri and Keyon follow the flag line along a wind-ridge that bisects ARO to their left and the Station ahead. Rajan's flashlight bobs unsteadily in the snowy dark. The wind strikes them over and over, cold as the flat blade of a well-honed sword, blowing snow in errant sheets.

At last they half-tumble down the snowbank, too tired to step, toward the metal rungs of the beer can.

Siri pauses, like a dog sniffing the wind. "They're on the move." Her eyes are heavy with fear. "They're thinking about whether to come here or head to ARO first."

"Let's get the fuck inside before they figure it out." Keyon pushes past them.

They climb the steps to Destination Zulu, thankful to be out of the wind. Keyon reaches for the door, and stops short.

Chains rattle unceremoniously on the other side.

"Gaudin, you motherfuck!" Keyon shouts.

Rajan reaches into his jacket and fumbles for his radio. "Jonah, this is Rajan, come back," he says, trying to catch his breath.

The radio squawks. "Rajan, where are you?"

"Thank God. We're at the Station! Zulu, first floor. We got five of them, but there's five more coming in hot behind us. Is there another door that's open?"

"Let me come to you."

Rajan lets out a weak laugh and bends over, clutching his knees. "We made it," he pants. "We're gonna make it."

Siri and Keyon just nod tightly. They are on the enemy's wavelength. It won't be over for them anytime soon.

Jonah appears on the other side of the door. Rajan sees Bethany and Tim Fulton on either side of him. "Hey! You guys made it!"

"I have the key." Jonah's voice is muffled through the door.

"Great!"

"But I can't let you in."

"Excuse me?"

"I can't let you in. We can't let you in."

Keyon shoves his nose against the porthole glass. "WHY THE FUCK NOT?" he bellows.

"Because you could be one of them," Jonah says flatly.

"One of the creatures we just killed five of? *One of the creatures hunting us right now?*" His voice picks up a shrill mania.

"Jonah, I see where you're coming from–" Rajan starts.

On the other side of the door, he sees Tim's lips moving, whispering, while Tim stares right at him.

His gaze is unflinchingly cool.

"I'm sure you'd do the same thing."

"But there's an easy way to solve this. Just put us in the sauna. We'll sit in it for however long it takes."

Jonah shakes his head. "Not good enough."

"How is that not good enough?" Siri says. Now her voice also carries a little hysteria.

"You didn't see what we fucking saw!" Bethany shouts back. "You didn't see Michele vomiting microbes right into Summer's mouth like she was baby-birding her a freaking meal! Millions of the fuckers, just chilling in her stomach at *room temperature*."

"Summer's dead?"

"Boss, come on!" Siri pounds the door, staring at Tim, but he looks at Rajan with a glass-like glower, rooted to the spot.

"I saw Ben get examined when he came back from ARO," Jonah says heavily. "There wasn't a single microbe on his skin. Nothing the sauna could kill. And just like that–" he snaps his fingers –"he got everyone else. It was all inside him somehow."

Bethany's voice takes on a peculiar flat emphasis that beats its way into the cold air like a hammer on metal. "We let you in, then we wake up and we're one of them, no fucking way." She shakes her head again. "I can vouch for these two. I can't vouch for you."

Rajan turns his head away from the door. "Go check Destination Alpha," he mutters.

Siri starts to sink back toward the stairs.

"We've locked all entrances to the elevated Station," Jonah says loudly. "Even the roof hatch. You're not getting in."

"Yeah?" Keyon yells. "Well, we'll just fucking see about that."

Jonah parts his jacket. So do Bethany and Tim Fulton. They are armed; an axe and a heat gun each. Sharp-looking kitchen knives hang from their belts.

Jonah's eyes are shiny. The look of a man who has peered into the darkness and seen something terrible glimmer back. "I've known Luis Weeks the better part of a decade. Today I poured cooking oil on his head and lit him on fire. You don't want to test me."

"You're giving us no way to prove to you that we're not one of them," Rajan pleads. "You're dooming us."

"And I'm sorry to do it," he says. "But I don't know a foolproof way to make sure your insides aren't crawling with bugs – and, dammit, *I've spent too much time here to want to die here.*"

Rajan swallows anger. "At least lock us up somewhere inside."

Jonah just shakes his head. "I saw what happened when Doc Wei let Ben in, Rajan. I won't make his mistake."

He takes a step back, toward the inside set of doors.

"I'm sorry," he says, then he's gone.

"That FUCKING WEASEL!" Keyon's face crumples and he sags to the ground. His head hangs between his knees. "I can't come this far and not make it," his voice is a whisper. "Not after what I did to Katie. Not after that."

"Can we make ARO? Combine forces with the Chinese scientists?" Rajan says urgently. He can't imagine running any more, but if it's that or die here, then he'll have to find the strength.

Siri's emerald-green eyes grow dreamy for a moment, then she shakes her head. "The five monsters are headed there. Smaller building, and they won't be caught off-guard this time."

"So we've got a little time, but we'll face eight instead of five."

"Seven." Keyon taps the side of his head. "There's only two Dome-A folks left alive."

"And we might have a little more time than you think. From what we felt, those Chinese scientists put up a hell of a fight. They took out four for only one of theirs lost. I don't think they'll go easily." Siri's voice is strained; it's clearly taking every ounce of her self-control to keep from throwing herself at the locked doors. "Regardless, we need a plan that doesn't involve the Station and these assholes."

"Get up, Keyon," Rajan says. "Get up, come on. I've got a really fucking dumb idea."

Chapter Sixty-Two

Rajan leads them down into the ice tunnels, grid-east toward the arches.

They walk quickly as he talks. "Guys, we're fucked."

"I thought you had an idea!" Keyon howls.

"Just listen. In military tactics, this is textbook last stand. Which means that if we don't hole up somewhere that we can defend, we're going to die. Jonah is sitting cozy in the only defendable real estate for two thousand miles, and we can't make a run for it in a Sno-Cat because of you two."

"What do you mean?"

"You've got them in your heads." He looks over his shoulder. "That's how they found us at LANDIT and it's how they'll find us again. If we flee, we die."

"You think we should split up." Keyon's voice is flat.

"No," he says firmly. "We survive this the same way we survive a bear attack."

"You're living up to the dumb fucking idea you promised," Siri says.

(*how do you survive a bear attack*)

(*you run faster than someone else*)

Rajan's voice grows serious. "We run faster than Jonah, because he's sitting still at zero miles an hour. What do the monsters want?"

"Numbers."

"So if we give them a juicier target, they'll go for it. We need to time it right to push them in the direction we want, and that turns your monster radar into our ace in the hole."

His thoughts are dark and full of wrath. "We're going to need fire extinguishers and gasoline. A lot of gasoline."

Chapter Sixty-Three

In the fuel arch, Siri starts up the van and cranks the heater as high as it will go. The modified Ford E350 is emblazoned with the NSF logo and four massive articulating snow-tracks in place of tires. It's a summer vehicle, because the battery tends to seize up at low temperatures. She steps on the gas while it sits in Park, trying to build up heat in the battery case. If the battery dies, so will their plan.

She looks over her shoulder into the gloom of the van.

(*I killed her I killed her I killed her*)

Her eyes find Keyon's, and abruptly she hears nothing but silence.

"Keyon?"

(*Keyon is ready*)

Siri adjusts her radio earpiece. "We're ready."

Static, the sound of wind and panting breath, then Rajan, wheezing: "I need five minutes."

She closes her eyes. She understands how this works by now. She visualizes a radio, like the one she saw in Ben's mind. She knew something was wrong back then but she didn't understand her new sixth sense. Didn't trust it.

She pictures herself tuning the radio. Listening.

Abruptly her eyes fly open. "The fight at ARO is over. There's seven of them in the hive mind now, and they're all on the move."

"Then you have to go," Rajan gasps into the radio. "I'll make it. Go!"

Siri slams the van into drive and guns it up the ramp of the fuel arch, keeping the engine revving. Headlights splash through pitch-black sky and white snow. She spins the wheel expertly, treads skidding toward the Station. No different than an icy winter night in Minnesota.

She grips the wheel, teeth rattling in her head, and *shouts* in her mind as loudly as she knows how.

WE'RE GOING TO THE STATION! WE'RE OPENING A DOOR INTO THE STATION!

Keyon's voice syncs to hers, growing to a booming shout. *THE STATION IS OPEN THIS WAY. FOLLOW THE VAN.*

Follow the van!

She drives, recklessly fast now. Straight for Destination Alpha.

FOLLOW THE VAN!

They bang over and down the incline of the massive snowdrift piled up in the shadow of the elevated Station. She swings to a halt under the broad snow-covered steps leading up to the second floor. Keyon jumps out, a full gasoline can in each hand and a fire extinguisher under one arm. Siri slams the gas pedal down. Leaps forward and up the drift.

The treads spin in the loose snow. The van begins to slip, rearing up like a wary horse–

– then the front treads catch and she bounces up to the snow level. She turns the corner, now racing along the side of Station, headed for Destination Tango.

She presses the all-channel.

DESTINATION TANGO! FOLLOW THE VAN!

"Hope you're ready, Jonah!" she screams into the radio. *You motherfucker.* "Because here comes the big finale!"

Keyon flicks the lighter.

The sleeve of his torn thermal shirt flares with flame despite the breeze. He shoves the gas can against the outer door of Destination Alpha and, as he does, he catches sight of Bethany Hamidani behind the inner door, face contorted into tight severe lines, screaming into her radio.

He turns and runs down the stairs.

The gasoline can explodes with a flat boom.

He races back up to the landing.

The outer doorway of Destination Alpha is off its hinges, collapsed into the Station. The inner doors are caved inward, sagging, porthole glass cracked. He raises his ski mask over his nose and peers through the oily smoke. The volatile gas flames lick at the carpet between the doors. It's hot, very hot.

He clutches the second gas can and turns, away from the Station, facing outward. Flames flicker behind him. He furrows his brow, thinking outward, eyes dark and far away.

Follow the van! We're opening a door into the Station!

On the other side of the door, Bethany Hamidani hefts her fire axe.

The van fishtails to a stop at the base of the stairs to Destination Tango. Siri grabs a gas can with one hand, an extinguisher with the other, and hurries up the metal stairs.

She stoops on the landing, at the railing, five steps away from the door to the Station. Bends over the gas can, unscrews the cap, and stuffs her balaclava into the opening.

A noise.

Boots crunching on snow.

Siri's head jerks up just in time to see Tim running silently at her. His axe is high above him, bald head gleaming in the spooky aurora light.

One step away from burying the axe into her skull, he trips against something, arms windmilling for balance. The axe drops to the landing and he catches himself on it like a cane, sinking to one knee. Tim looks down and sees the gleam of a metal wire, almost invisible, running across the landing just in front of where Siri crouches.

He looks up, eyes growing wide with awful comprehension.

Rajan slips up over his shoulder. His clothes and face are black, covered with soot. He blends into the darkness with everything except his eyes, which flicker dangerously.

With one clean motion he circles Tim's neck with a strand of metal wire double-wrapped between his gloved hands.

Then he leaps off the ground and plants both his knees in Tim's back.

Tim falls backward on top of him, fingers clawing at the wire buried in the flesh of his neck. His legs pump frantically like a mad bicyclist. "Stop it, Tim," Rajan grunts. He turns his head away from Tim's grasping hands, which are feeling for his eyes. "Stop it, for fuck's sake!"

Siri steps over her former boss and brings the extinguisher down onto his head. Tim slumps, hands flopping down to his sides. Rajan relaxes his grip.

Siri looks down at him. "He really was going to kill me," she whispers.

Rajan looks back, grimly. Whether they like it or not, the battle lines have been drawn.

Together, they roll Tim over, then off the landing, down to the soft snow below. Siri walks through the unguarded and unlocked outer door of Destination Tango, carrying the extinguisher and gas can, and disappears into the warmth of the Station.

Clint and the other microbe-humans see the van's headlights in the distance. Without one strong leader, we are uncertain about whether to follow it. Two of the minds don't speak English, and it has taken us a while to rebalance the hive mind. To reinforce the old goal with new minds involved. But then, like bees to honey, the hive-mind hones in on Siri's horror and revulsion. Through her eyes, we watch Tim try to kill Siri, and Rajan roll an unconscious Tim off the landing. We see Siri walk into the Station.

Tim is one more for the hive

Follow the van.

Another flat boom. A tongue of flame shoots out from Destination Alpha.

Yes that way there is safety and numbers yes

Not the fire way

No but the other way

(*we should leave*)

The van way

(*it could be a trap*)

Follow the van

Follow the van follow the van follow the van –

Keyon's dry eyes roll in their stinging sockets as he stares through the flames and thick black smoke at Bethany

Hamidani. The fire from his second gas can leaps across the walls inside the Station, flickering eagerly up to the roof. She hefts her fire axe again, but the pulsing noisome waves of her fright lap against his mind, and he lets out a feverish roar.

He steps forward through the flames, fearless, and she drops her axe and runs.

Jonah Mitchell stands in the darkness of the galley, looking out of the windows. The reflection of the distant fire at Destination Alpha is mirrored in the dark snow. Seven – no, eight – shadowy figures slip into the light of the Station, moving in lockstep toward Destination Tango. Tim is one of them now. He has lost Tim to the hive.

"You shouldn't have kept us out," Rajan says from behind him.

Jonah turns. His hand rests on his fire axe. "So what now, my friend?"

"Friends again, are we? I'm going to give you a choice, *my friend*. Even though you didn't give me one."

"I'm listening."

Rajan looks down at the fire extinguisher at his feet. "This is filled with gasoline. Destination Tango's outer door is open, but by now Siri will have chained the inner door shut. Option one is you pick up that extinguisher, leave through Alpha, run around the Station and light those microbe creatures up from behind as they try to come through Tango. We'll push at them from inside and pincer them."

"Sounds like a suicide mission."

Rajan's mouth is a line burning into his face. "You sentenced me to death earlier."

"And what's option two?"

Rajan just stares at him. His fingers twitch by his side.

"Okay," Jonah said. "Okay, I'll do it."

He steps forward. The axe stays, rested against the window. He keeps his eyes on Rajan, then bends down and hefts the fire extinguisher.

"How do I light the fire?"

"There's a flare strapped to the side."

Jonah nods. "I see it. I'll get–"

He pumps the plunger of the extinguisher, blasting Rajan with foul-smelling gasoline. His hand swipes at the flare, pulling it loose. He drops the extinguisher, steps back, and pulls the cap of the flare off, exposing the striker.

"Don't, Jonah," Rajan splutters, frantically wiping the gasoline away.

Jonah's eyes harden to blue chips of ice. He strikes the cap against the end of the flare.

Nothing happens.

He strikes it again, eyes widening, then looks down at the flare.

The match end is gone. There's nothing to light it with.

Rajan seizes the fallen extinguisher; swings it at him like a club.

It catches Jonah in the shoulder and neck, knocking him flat. He scrambles backward, hands slipping in the gasoline, blood running into his nose and mouth. The expression of cold steel has been replaced with a muddy look of fear.

"At least I know you're human, too," Rajan's voice shakes with anger. He hefts the fire extinguisher and brings it down on Jonah's head.

* * *

Keyon races up the stairs and down the long hallway, carrying Bethany's axe. He knows the way to the top hatch; Katie had used it to make her daily weather measurements. The thought of Katie, and her burning body spasming on the floor of LANDIT, makes him feel like a hamster trying to escape a powered-up microwave. His heart is just one wrench away from exploding wetly over the walls.

He swings the axe against the chains looped through the hatch handle and they rush to the floor in a metallic pool.

Keyon climbs up through the hatch and almost immediately recoils, axe jumping up.

Marty Horn lies on the ground. His fleece gapes open, exposing his large belly and the heaving black-tinged mass gently throbbing on it.

Flexing toward him.

Keyon gives the body a wide berth, then runs toward the north point of the Station. The snow muffles his footsteps. He gets down on his hands and knees and gently pokes his head forward, trying not to spill snow over the flat edge. It takes a moment for his eyes to adjust, then he sees four shapes, strung out across the stairs and the metal landing outside Destination Tango. Someone stands in the outer doorway, directly under him.

"I'm ready," he whispers into his radio.

Down below, in the mid-hallway, Siri strikes her flare. The sparks light her face in a deathly red glow. With her other hand, she turns the key in the lock clasping the inner door of Tango closed. She steps back, depresses the plunger on the gasoline-filled fire extinguisher next to her, then kicks open the door.

* * *

Clint is first into the Station and catches a high-pressure blast of gasoline right in the face. It doesn't slow him down. The flare flicked at his chest, however, does.

He erupts in flames, going from charging man to funeral pyre in under a second. Siri steps around him with the extinguisher, sweeping the stream of gasoline behind him. The fire follows it like a faithful hungry puppy, splashing up the legs of Andrea Rivey, the deputy manager out of her depth all season. Andrea screams as she lights up like kindling, and Siri hears it with both her ears and her head. Behind her, Daniel backs outside, the microbes turning him away from the growing heat. He doesn't see Siri heft the fire extinguisher and hurl it like a bowling ball through the outer door.

Above Siri, on the roof of the Station, Keyon sees the cylinder fly out of the door past Daniel. He leans over the side and uses the nozzle of his fire extinguisher to douse the two dark figures on the landing below him. A crazed laugh bubbles from his lips –

(*very bad crazy when very bad cold*)

– then he strikes his flare.

Daniel's head jerks up toward him like a fish on a line.

"Jamie sends her regards!" he yells and tosses the flare over the side.

Siri's extinguisher explodes in Rob Booth's face, twisting it into a new and senseless shape. The shock wave sweeps Daniel, already on fire, over the side of the stairs. Qu Tanzhou and Tim Fulton, the newest member of the hive, are knocked back. Keyon stands tall on the roof and aims his extinguisher squarely down at them. The fire races after his streaming arc of gasoline like a hungry predator, eager and willing, ensnaring them.

From the galley window, Rajan sees two shadowy figures running down the stairs. Doc Wei and the last Dome-A Chinese scientist trip over themselves to pile into the snow, away from the fiery Destination Tango landing.

He turns his face away as the van parked at the base of the stairs erupts in a huge toneless explosion. A bright orange ball ruptures the Antarctic darkness. Waves of flame spill across the last two microbe-humans, and keeps burning, long after their screams have faded into the cold night.

Greg "Lucky" Penny listens to his workout playlist three times over the course of the night at IceCube Laboratory. The emergency radio squawks, but it's turned way down so he can hear the music. It has been a productive day of repair and he needs to rock to keep on rolling.

He makes decaf coffee an hour before bedtime, does a set of fifty pushups, rubs out a quick one thinking about Summer and Bethany tag-teaming him in the greenhouse, then rolls himself a pinched blunt with the last of the weed Clint had sold him. Way overpriced, but it's the South Pole, after all.

Penny curls up on the hard cot in the corner of his lab space, earbuds in, head gently nodding. His eyes blink black, then slip closed.

Chapter Sixty-Four

SOUTH POLE STATION POPULATION: 5 (DECEASED: 39)

September 23rd, 2028. 88 days later.

The sun is just a stab on the horizon, scattering the cirrus clouds into pink and red and orange wisps. Siri and Rajan stand on the roof of South Pole Station, wrapped in their jackets and ski masks. It has been getting lighter at Pole for two weeks now, but this morning it is definitely morning.

"What do you think, Raj?" she asks.

"You mean you haven't read my mind to find out?"

She nudges him and grins.

He looks at the sun, barely peeking above the shiny ice. It's still cold, in the low negative fifties. "I honestly didn't think I'd see it again."

She looks up at him, eyes cloudy, and he answers her unspoken question. "I told you, I wasn't read into the full program. Special Access levels are need-to-know, and they decided I didn't need to know."

"All the CIA told you was that they might need you." Her face is full of a familiar skepticism. They've had this argument many times.

"They might need me *after* this season. They said I might head elsewhere on the ice before I went home, to offer an expert opinion. They said I'd be briefed only if they ended up using me. The Agency equivalent of the backup quarterback, I suppose."

Without much to do after burning down his own telescope –

(*with three people inside*)

– Rajan has spent most of the last three months thinking and building theories. He suspects the CIA introduced the microbes to Dome-A, and he can hazard a guess why. The war between China and America is at a stalemate. Russia is providing back-door help to China, like the US did for Britain in the early days of World War II, but they are weak from their war with Ukraine and haven't jumped directly into the conflict yet. Most military strategists believe it's only a matter of time, and when they do…

A microbe that could pass by touch and grow in the cold would be a very useful weapon to contain an icy country so large it couldn't feasibly be occupied by a foreign invading force.

In theory, the extremophile nature of the microbes would present a natural safety catch for allies in warmer climates.

But to really test how the microbes would respond, you would need to release them back into their native environment.

Dome-A was Chinese, making it a convenient target, but it was also the coldest place in the world. The microbes would be closest to their indigenous ecosystem, sequestered from other humans by a thousand miles of ice.

The CIA had turned Dome-A into an open-air laboratory.

They were reading Rajan in to the HAVE VIKING Special Access Program for his expert opinion, they'd said. But what expertise? The answer came to him at the end of the first month, when it had been his turn to cook and take the prisoners their food; Bethany in the upper gym and Jonah in the lower gym, both of which had been converted into makeshift prison cells, doors chained closed from the outside.

As with so many things on the ice, it came down to geopolitics of the Antarctic Treaty.

Ironically, introducing the microbes to the ice wouldn't be a treaty violation, since they were native to Antarctica. And the treaty would allow the CIA a level of visibility they were rarely afforded during black ops. Any country could "inspect" another country's Station in the name of treaty compliance. The Chinese couldn't shut the Americans out. The Agency could go into Dome-A, observe the Chinese investigation and even take samples away for analysis, all under the auspices of the Treaty.

But they couldn't send someone from Langley. That would raise the specter of underhand involvement. Someone who had just spent a winter at the South Pole doing legitimate civilian science, on the other hand, would be an unsuspicious candidate.

Which led to other uncomfortable questions. Would they have briefed him enough to know how to protect himself from the microbes at Dome-A, or kept him in the dark for plausible deniability? Would they have shipped him off to a black site to delouse him, or let him waltz onto a commercial flight back to Honolulu?

Rajan doesn't care to dwell on that too much, but Dr. Richard Mason better pray not to meet him in a dark alley.

Siri interrupts his thoughts. "And you still think they didn't mean for this to happen at Pole."

He nods. "An operation like Dome-A would have oversight all the way to the top. In a time of war with China, I can see the Senate Intelligence Committee agreeing to let the microbes loose on an all-Chinese station. There's no way I see them authorizing a deliberate release of lethal microbes at an American station."

"So what happened?"

"I think the Agency underestimated the will of those three Chinese scientists to live. They survived a first-ever winter traverse between Dome-A and South Pole against the odds. And they brought the Agency's curse with them."

"But the CIA saw the traverse coming toward us. They could have warned us."

Rajan nods. His first inkling of this had been when the CIA had cut off South Pole's SATCOM access. "Someone did the math and decided that their experiment was more important than our lives. Our deaths could even, maybe, be *useful*."

They are silent for a long moment. "I still dream about it," he says, very softly. "What I saw in that Dome-A truck. All the deaths. They're all burned onto the backs of my eyelids."

"I know. You cry in your sleep."

He looks away. "So do you."

"Fucking CIA," she says. "Fucking assholes."

"That's why we can't let them find the bodies," he says heavily. "Especially anyone that hosted the microbes inside them. That's a legitimate bioweapon. They might intend for it to be used only in Russia or northern China, but like Summer used to say… life finds a way."

"The microbes have already mutated once."

"Exactly. That poison has to stay on this continent."

Siri looks behind her. The scorch marks of cremated

bodies on the roof – Marty Horn and others – have almost been swallowed up by new snow. Over the last two months of darkness, they have found and burned all the others, with two exceptions. "We'll find TC and Ben's bodies. There's a whisper every time it gets cold."

Rajan nods gravely. "How's Keyon doing?"

She looks away. "It's... going to be a while before he feels like himself again, and even that might not be good enough." She chuckles a little. "Penny, on the other hand."

He rolls his eyes. "He's still trying to convince me to stop keeping Bethany locked up. Apparently, it was all Jonah's idea, and she didn't *mean* to try and kill us. She *definitely* wouldn't murder us in our sleep if we let her out, promise."

"You really think–"

"They didn't trust us, Siri. We shouldn't trust them. I'd just rather not take the chance."

"That girl could fuck her way out of the Lubyanka."

Rajan blinks at Siri. "Speaking of which..."

She puts her hand out and smiles at him. "Let's go see what the sunrise looks like from your bedroom, Dr. Chariya. While we still have the South Pole to ourselves."

They didn't have the South Pole quite to themselves.

Invisible to the facility on the horizon, Dr. Richard Mason scans South Pole Station with his binoculars from the Basler, callsign Borak 12, flying just below the clouds. It's still too cold for an airdrop but a brief warm spell is forecast in a week. At the controls, in the left seat, is a young pilot from Ken Borak Air. He has been promised three years' salary for one flight that ends with them parachuted down five miles from South Pole Station. In the right seat is the same Air

Force SOLL pilot who had been at the controls for the initial drop of the microbe payload into Dome A, back in February.

If successful, Dr. Mason, Dr. Jon Kim, and the six Arctic-trained Special Operators crowded into the back of Borak 12 will get the Station to themselves for two weeks before the NSF even attempts a landing.

Mason has been to the South Pole once before, twenty years ago, as a young military aide to the Air Force Scientific Advisory Board. The strangeness of the place had left an impression on him. But nothing he's seen can ever compare to the ARO footage they've tapped into. To NOAA Lieutenant Benjamin Jacobs leaping off the second floor into the snow and chasing down a member of the dining staff dressed in nothing but a shirt.

There is much more strangeness waiting to be discovered at the South Pole.

Dr. Jon Kim, Jonny to his friends and Professor Kim to his Harvard students, leans across the aisle. "Quite something, right? Two summers of misery at Lake Byrd and I still miss the ice."

Mason ignores him. Rajan's last transmission about the microbes evolving validated Kim's theories, so DARPA is now along for the ride, but how he feels about that doesn't matter. The ARO video proves that his experiment had been successful. The microbes can be weaponized.

He just needs to get on the ground and find out how they mutated.

"Hey, Mason?" he hears the SOLL pilot's voice in his headset. "Get up here and take a listen to this."

Mason crouches and hop-walks up to the cockpit. He holds his headset in his hands; the co-pilot shows him where to plug in. "What am I listening to?" he asks.

"Short-range HF radio," the pilot replies. "Probably good only to fifty miles out. It's an old military frequency; hasn't been used since they got satellite internet down there. I picked it up with the spectrum analyzer. Some kind of recording, it just loops over and over."

Mason listens. A scratch, a hiss, and then a voice.

"Our internet is being blocked here at South Pole Station. Turn on the internet and we will plow the runway and allow you to land. Pass this on to whoever is running the HAVE VIKING program at Langley."

Mason listens to the message three times. By the third time, he's fairly certain he's listening to Major Rajan Chariya's voice. The man he'd recruited to be a stooge for his operation, until the microbe infection had found him. Now he was a survivor; a bitter one.

He'll have to be one of the first to go when they clean this op up.

Mason heads back to his seat. The Basler banks into the sun, headed back toward Mac Station. Mason touches his glove to the little dark speck on the ice, so small it could have been dirt on the window.

"See you soon," he whispers.

Epilogue

The Antarctic plain stretches in every direction, unending, starting to shine more with every passing day. Nothing but white in the snow ahead and the white of the Trans-Antarctic Mountains behind. The sky is still tinged with the winter dark, but is retreating by the day.

The cold wind surges into our raw throat and peeling face, but we don't feel it anymore. We heal faster now; we feel nothing anymore. There is nothing left, except the journey to *more*.

Ben walks. We walk. We keep walking, a speck on a vast untamed desert. Into the sun, now, heading east to warmer climes.

Acknowledgments

A few years ago, I had the opportunity of a lifetime: to deploy to Amundsen-Scott South Pole Station, for the summer season, as a National Science Foundation (NSF) and Air Force Office of Scientific Research (AFOSR) Principal Investigator.

Yup, I was a Polie beaker. And it was a life-changing experience.

It's hard to describe how it makes you feel to stare out into a sea of white and know that the whole world, everything you've ever known, is north of you. That except for the small, impossibly self-sufficient building you're living in, the next stop for civilization is a thousand miles away, at McMurdo Station. And you'd never survive the journey there on your own.

There are two types of people who go to Antarctica. Those who step foot on the ice once and will never be seen again, and those who want nothing more than to go back. I'm definitely, whole-heartedly, that second type. Both the South Pole itself and the incredible people I met there inspired this book, and I hope life gives me the opportunity to go back one day.

Yes, I really did write this book in Antarctica! Twenty-five thousand words of scribbled longhand made it off the ice with me, together with a lifetime of memories that would later be expanded, cut, shaped and shined to become the book you hold in your hands today.

But, of course, it's never as simple as that.

I wrote four books before this one. Across all of them, in searching for an agent, I sent out a total of 380 queries, and received 210 heartbreaking rejections, a response rate of 55%. 16 partial and full manuscript requests were ultimately declined, a response rate of 4%. I learned something from every rejection, even if it was discovering, from the tone of an agent's rejection, that I'd never want to put my career in their hands. For this book, I sent out 97 queries, got 73 form rejections, and 16 rejections with a useful tidbit I could use to improve the book. I had 4 partial requests, 12 full manuscript requests and 3 offers of representation that ultimately ended in signing with a wonderful agent. So, for all you #amwriting and #amquerying authors: *Don't quit on yourself!*

Speaking of that wonderful agent: Lindsay Guzzardo of Martin Literary Management has been the wind in my sails to get this book into your hands. I owe her a huge thanks: for her vision, patience and enthusiasm. Because there were more rejections to come! But now there were two of us in the trenches. Even as we went through some agonizing near-misses, she refused to be anything except firmly positive it would only be a matter of time until we broke through.

A huge thanks to all-round power editor Gemma Creffield at Angry Robot Books – she saw what this book could become, and tag-teamed with publisher Eleanor Teasdale and lead publicist Caroline Lambe. I'm so happy with where their vision has taken it. My thanks to Andrew

Hook, Robin Triggs, Desola Coker, Amy Portsmouth, Dan Hanks, Karen Smith, and the rest of the Angry Robot crew: their energy and hard work made *Symbiote* a reality!

Back to story-telling for a quick moment. I wrote my first story when I was seven years old and it was… *awful*. Truly the worst thing you've ever read. When I showed it to my mother, common sense tells me she probably thought the same. But instead, Kannama Nayak (now Kannama Lord) talked me through improving my sentence structure, and "showing, not telling". She made me write something else to show myself I could do better next time.

Fast forward a few years to being a young egotistical thin-skinned teen: I'd gotten a few short stories published but a whole lot of things rejected, and decided to hell with it all. I said it loudly and I said it proudly. My mother considered this, and responded by saying that she wanted us to write a novel together. I would write a chapter and she would write a chapter. I said *the hell with it all* again, with the grim-jawed certainty that only a young egotistical thin-skinned teen can summon. My mother nodded, sat down at the typewriter that night, and banged out a first chapter so enticing I had to know what happened next.

What did happen next? She said I'd have to write it to find out.

Those pages have since been lost, but the passion they kindled were not. Mom, you were my first editor, my first beta reader and my first cheerleader. I would have never have been able to keep writing if it weren't for you. This book, and every book I have the fortune to write after, is for you.

Grace Persico weathered my writing anxiety, querying anxiety and publishing anxiety with her unique poise. Grace enjoyed a backstage pass she didn't apply for, to the hot mess that frothed behind these pages. She somehow managed to handle it with just the right amount of eye-rolling; one that said: *haven't we been here before,* but didn't add *you daft prick* to the end of it. Thanks, Gracie.

Without the people who got me to Antarctica, this book wouldn't exist. A special thanks to Dr. Stacie Williams (formerly Air Force Office of Scientific Research), and Stan Straight (formerly Air Force Research Laboratory), for seeing the potential in my mad-scientist idea, and giving me the funding to make it a reality. Paul Kervin was a terrific mentor willing to take a chance on the new guy. Dr. Thomas Swindle, Dr. Cody Shaw and Chris Shurilla helped design, test and assemble the telescope I took to the South Pole – called LANDIT. Yes, LANDIT was real! I chose the name, then and now, to denote the herculean coordination effort it took to get military researchers down to the South Pole, even though there's a treaty that says you can do pretty much exactly that. I was disappointed, but not entirely surprised, when the LANDIT 2.0 team was unable to repeat the feat after I'd left. Sometimes it takes a village; sometimes it just takes one stubborn-as-a-mule mother*fucker* too dumb to quit.

A special thanks to Dr. Anne Cheever, who was literally the very first person to spend money on buying this book; she pre-ordered it before it even had an ISBN number assigned to it. Thanks for being an early adopter, friend, and my first fan, Anne!

Thanks to glaciologist, fellow PhD cohort member, and Antarctic explorer Dr. Sarah Neuhaus, and to veteran Polie beaker Professor Stuart Jefferies, who both shared their tips with me on how to make it on the ice.

At the NSF Office of Polar Programs, thanks to Dr.

Vladimir Papitashvili, Program Director for Astrophysics and Geospace Sciences, and Jessie Crain, Antarctic Research Support Manager. At the Antarctic Support Contract (ASC) headquarters in Denver, thanks to Timothy Ager (who was also on the ice with me) and Leah Street. Without you, the logistics of deploying a telescope to the South Pole would have been too daunting to overcome.

My thanks to the rest of the ASC crew that helped support my deployment: Elaine Hood (travel support), Neal Scheibe (McMurdo support), Paul Sullivan, Jack Corbin, Kevin Schriner, Joe Rottman, Scott Morland, Pat Daley, Bill Coughran, and William Turnbull.

I want to share a special acknowledgment of Johan (John) Booth, a fellow Polie crewmember who is no longer with us, but always remembered. Johan lived a life worth remembering.

And at South Pole Station: I'd like to thank the entire summer crew of 2018. Thank you for helping me find my ice legs, and for showing me what it really means to be a Polie. Please forgive the many dramatic liberties I've taken with the stories you shared with me, and know that I respect and admire you all. Katie Koster, Siri Gossman, Mike Legatt, and Jaime Hensel: there's nowhere else in the world I would have met unique people like you, because you're off doing incredible things like wintering at the bottom of the world.

Now, another quick story. Every day, I "commuted" to work: from my home at South Pole Station to a small building just under half a mile away called SuperDARN. Under good conditions, it was a 15-minute walk; but with blowing snow and wind-chill, all while body-dragging a two-hundred-pound sled with generator equipment on it... it was frequently longer. Sometimes I made that trudge in feel-like temperatures as low as -78 degrees Fahrenheit (and yes, that's "summer" weather). South Pole Station sits at 11,000 feet barometric pressure, so I was also short of breath and a little hypoxic. I'm not complaining about the walk: it took me around and past the Geographic South Pole, which means I commuted around the world every day on my way to work. But I'd be lying if I said I wasn't on the struggle bus when I first got there.

And the Pole can get lonely. Especially when you're a team of one.

But then, packages from my friends back home started to arrive. More chocolate than I thought I could possibly eat (but I found a way). Snacks of all kinds. Things to mix into hot water like coconut and hot chocolate and so much good coffee. Music on a CD, so I could jam out while working and not be bored without Spotify and the internet. Air Force stickers I could zap in out-of-the-way-places, as the only active-duty member resident at the Pole. Sleep balm to help me fall asleep while it's light outside 24-7. The warmest felt-lined socks for my daily walk to work. And, most importantly, notes and letters that put so many smiles on my face. So I'd like to thank the people who turned my struggle bus at the Pole away from something I'd want to forget, into something I cherish to this day. Your mailed morale kept me going, and you are another reason why this book exists today: Andrea Luethi, Gisela Muñoz, Andrew Emery, Angela Phillips, Bethany Nagid, Jeannette van den Bosch, Sarah Kerce and Liz Hyde. Thank you for being part of the journey with me. A special shout out to Liz for giving me her Pelican case to use as a telescope control unit! It traveled around the world with me every day.

Shoutout to *The Antarctican Society,* "by and for all Antarcticans", and USAF Test Pilot School Class 19A, "Capax

Infiniti". I'm proud to be a card-carrying member of both.

I'd also like to thank some of my other friends: Ashley Gonzales, who for some reason I'll never understand, thinks I'm as smart as she is. Bogdan Udrea, my enabler since undergrad days. Christina Doolittle-Straight, for listening to more than her fair share of rants over the years with an unending sense of humor. Julian McCafferty, who shared an office with me as I struggled through understanding South Pole logistics, and listened to different (but just as long) rants. And, in no particular order, for mentorship, friendship or support too varied to even begin to describe: Joe Nance, Mark and Teri Persico, Kevin Amsden, Brian Bracy, Erik Stockham, Rachael Bradshaw, Randy Warren, Brian Young, Alissa Vigil, S. Pete Worden, Sneha Thomas, Shubha Kesavan, and S. K. Shamala. I'm grateful for each one of you. Thanks to Robin Amber Despins, who asked me to write her a book as a present over ten years ago, and continued, over the years, to ask me when I would be writing another one.

I'd like to thank you, dear reader. Thank you for picking up this book and making my dream of being a writer come true. Thank you to the supportive and humorous #WritingCommunity on that website that was once known as Twitter. Join me there @mikeynayak.

On the long road to being both an Antarctic scientist and author, there were many who told me "no". No, I was too young to be a Principal Investigator. No, I didn't have enough (ahem, any) ice experience. No, I had to wait my turn behind senior scientists who'd been proposing to AFOSR longer than I had. No, going to the Pole was just a public-relations stunt. I'm not unique in that. There are "no-people" around each of us. But they only make another type of person all the more important, and I'd like to acknowledge *them* with a quote from *The Last Black Unicorn,* by Tiffany Haddish: "I want to thank EVERYONE who ever said anything positive to me, or taught me something. I heard it all, and it meant something."

Finally, I'd like to thank and praise God for seeing fit to give me a mission and purpose. Everything I've done, and everything I have, is thanks to His unfailing mercy. I don't know what I've done to deserve it, but I hope I can keep being worthy.

Rajan's story will continue. Stay tuned for the next chapter from Angry Robot Books – I can't wait to tell you all about what becomes of Rajan's intrepid crew of survivors, who have seen and been through so much together.

Mikey Nayak
Yokohama, Japan (June 2024)

Rajan and the survivors will return in

PARASITE

February 2026…